PRAISE FOR *THE CRESCENT STONE*

Matt Mikalatos has built a compelling fantasy world with humor and heart.

GENE LUEN YANG, creator of *American Born Chinese* and *Boxers & Saints*

Matt Mikalatos has penned a tale straight out of today's headlines that will tug at your heartstrings. *The Crescent Stone* is a compelling story that will get under your skin and worm its way into your heart.

TOSCA LEE, *New York Times* bestselling author of *Iscariot* and *The Legend of Sheba*

The Crescent Stone hooked me from the first page! With the rich characterization of John Green and the magical escapism of Narnia, this book is a must read for all fantasy fans!

LORIE LANGDON, author of *Olivia Twist* and the Doon series

This is what sets Mikalatos's epic world apart from so many other fantasy realms: the characters feel real, their lives are genuine and complicated, and their choices are far from binary. Mikalatos's creativity and originality are on full display in this epic tale for adults and young readers alike.

SHAWN SMUCKER, author of *The Day the Angels Fell*

The Crescent Stone blends . . . glitter unicorns, powerful healing tattoos, and an engaging cast of characters into a funny and thoughtful story that examines the true costs of magic and privilege.

TINA CONNOLLY, author of *Seriously Wicked*

The twists keep coming in *The Crescent Stone*, a fabulous young adult fantasy with a great cast of characters. I particularly loved Jason, whose humor, logic, and honesty will make readers eager to follow him into a sequel. I found the Sunlit Lands a fantastically engaging place to visit and grew ever more delighted as I discovered more about each culture, their knotted histories, and how the magic worked. Fantasy fans will devour it and ask for seconds.

JILL WILLIAMSON, Christy Award–winning author of *By Darkness Hid* and *Captives*

From C. S. Lewis to J. K. Rowling, the secret magical place that lives alongside our own mundane world has a rich history in fantasy literature, and *The Crescent Stone* is a delightful tale that is a more-than-worthy continuation of that tradition. Matt Mikalatos weaves a rich tapestry that is equal parts wonder, thoughtfulness, and excitement, while being that most wonderful of things—a joyful and fun story. From the first page, you can't help but root for Madeline as she stumbles about trying to navigate a future that is uncertain and fraught with pain. The beauty of Madeline as a character is that her journey is both all too familiar and yet entirely contemporary—the magical land that is her salvation is so much more. I don't know where this series will go. All I know is that I don't ever want it to end.

JAKE KERR, author of the Tommy Black series and a nominee for the Nebula Award, the Theodore Sturgeon Memorial Award, and the storySouth Million Writers Award

The Crescent Stone inspires thought on matters of compassion and privilege in a breathtaking and fun fantasy setting. This is a book that will leave readers empowered—not by magic, but by the potential within their own hearts.

BETH CATO, author of *The Clockwork Dagger*

PRAISE FROM READERS

Jason's personality throughout the whole book brought a smile to my face the entire time.

✦

[The book is about] injustice. The rich taking advantage of the poor. The powerful taking advantage of the weak. How desperate people will do desperate things for their loved ones. That all of our actions affect others around us. Change starts within.

✦

I thought the story itself was very compelling and left me with the excitement of wanting to get to and through the next chapter so I could see what would happen next. . . . I thoroughly enjoyed reading the story and the cultural commentary that was throughout the book.

✦

I love the parallel world aspect of this book. It was unexpected and kept the discussion of privilege and race a fresh perspective.

✦

Overall, I loved the book. I thought the characters and the alternate universe were interesting. I loved the struggles of each character and the surprises within the Sunlit Lands.

Lewis wrote Narnia as a fun story that provided thinly veiled allegory and life lessons. Mikalatos does the same thing here for today's generation. Tackling issues that divide the most rational of adults, Mikalatos shows all these issues with honesty, a story that keeps you engaged, and characters that keep you smiling.

✛

The Crescent Stone is a rare book that shows incredible depth that is matched only by its fun and whimsy.

✛

One of the most engaging stories I have ever read. Nonstop fun meets a conversation-starting masterpiece.

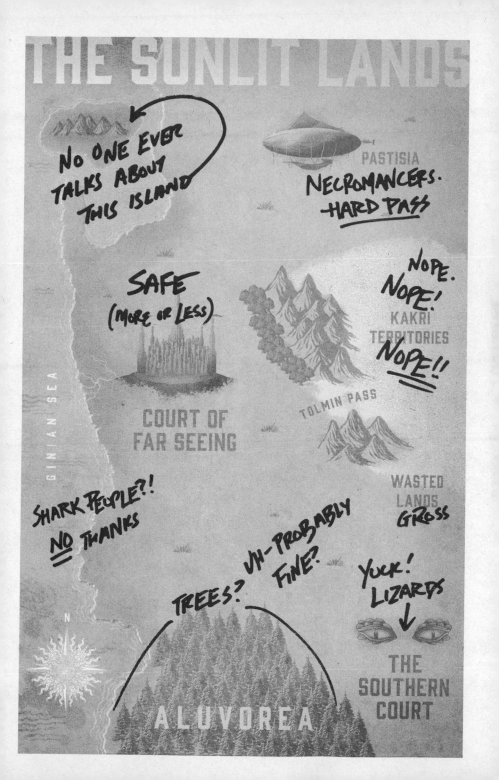

THE SUNLIT LANDS

BOOK ONE

THE
CRESCENT
STONE

MATT MIKALATOS

wander
An imprint of
Tyndale House
Publishers, Inc.

Visit Tyndale online at www.tyndale.com.

Visit the author's website at www.thesunlitlands.com.

TYNDALE and Tyndale's quill logo are registered trademarks of Tyndale House Publishers, Inc. *Wander* and the Wander logo are trademarks of Tyndale House Publishers, Inc. Wander is an imprint of Tyndale House Publishers, Inc., Carol Stream, Illinois.

Designed by Dean H. Renninger

Edited by Sarah Rubio

The author is represented by Ambassador Literary Agency, Nashville, TN.

For information about special discounts for bulk purchases, please contact Tyndale House Publishers at csresponse@tyndale.com, or call 1-800-323-9400.

Library of Congress Cataloging-in-Publication Data
Names: Mikalatos, Matt, author.
Title: The Crescent Stone / Matt Mikalatos.
Description: Carol Stream, Illinois : Tyndale House Publishers, Inc., [2018]
| Series: The sunlit lands ; book 1 | Summary: When Madeline, a teen with terminal lung disease, accepts healing in exchange for a year of service in the Sunlit Lands, she and her friend Jason enjoy being privileged members of Elenil society, until they learn that magic carries a high price.
Identifiers: LCCN 2018007553 | ISBN 9781496431707 (hc) | ISBN 9781496431714 (sc)
Subjects: | CYAC: Fantasy. | Sick—Fiction. | Friendship—Fiction. | Magic—Fiction.
Classification: LCC PZ7.1.M5535 Cre 2018 | DDC [Fic]—dc23 LC record available at https://lccn.loc.gov/2018007553

Printed in the United States of America

24	23	22	21	20	19	18
7	6	5	4	3	2	1

To Shasta

CAST OF CHARACTERS

ARCHON THENODY—the chief magistrate; supreme ruler of the Elenil

BAILEYA—Kakri warrior who has come to Far Seeing to make her fortune; daughter of Willow, granddaughter of Abronia

BASILEUS PRINEL—one of the Elenil magistrates; in charge of celebrations, rituals, and communal events

BLACK SKULLS—elite fighting force of the Scim; there are three known members

BREAK BONES—a Scim warrior imprisoned by the Elenil

BRIGHT PRISM—a "civilized" Scim man who works in the archon's palace

CROOKED BACK—spokesperson of the Scim army

DARIUS WALKER—American human; Madeline's ex-boyfriend

DAVID GLENN—American human in service to the Elenil

DAY SONG—a "civilized" Scim man who serves Gilenyia

DELIGHTFUL GLITTER LADY [DEE, DGL]—a unicorn

DIEGO FERNÁNDEZ—Colombian human in service to the Elenil; has the power of flight

EVERNU—gallant white stag who works alongside Rondelo

FERA—Scim woman; wife of Inrif and mother of Yenil

FERNANDA ISABELA FLORES DE CASTILLA—Lady of Westwind; human woman; older than most humans in the Sunlit Lands

GARDEN LADY—mysterious old woman who has taken an interest in Madeline

GILENYIA—an influential Elenil lady; Hanali's cousin; has the power of healing

HANALI—Elenil recruiter who invites Madeline to the Sunlit Lands

INRIF—Scim man; husband of Fera and father of Yenil

JASON WU (WU SONG)—American human who follows Madeline into the Sunlit Lands

JASPER—American human in the service of the Elenil; in charge of the armory

JENNY WU—Jason's sister

KEKOA KAHANANUI—American human in service to the Elenil

KNIGHT OF THE MIRROR—human in his mid-forties; fights the Scim without magic

MADELINE OLIVER—American human in the service of the Elenil

MAGISTRATES—the rulers of the Elenil. There are nine of them, including the archon.

MAJESTIC ONE—the Elenil name for the magician who founded the Sunlit Lands

MALGWIN—half fish, half woman; harbinger of chaos and suffering; lives in the dark waterways surrounding the Sunlit Lands

MALIK—Darius's cousin

MOTHER CROW—a Kakri matriarch

MR. GARCÍA—the gardener at Madeline's home on Earth

MRS. RAYMOND—English human woman who runs the Transition House for humans in the Sunlit Lands; fifty years old

MUD—Scim child who lives on the streets of the Court of Far Seeing

NEW DAWN—a "civilized" Scim woman who works for Gilenyia

NIGHT'S BREATH—a Scim warrior

POLEMARCH TIRIUS—one of the Elenil magistrates; the commander of the Elenil army

PEASANT KING—the figure from Scim legend who founded the Sunlit Lands

RAYO—the Knight of the Mirror's silver stallion

RESCA—Hanali's mother

RICARDO SÁNCHEZ—American human in service to the Elenil; healed by Gilenyia

RONDELO—Elenil "captain of the guard" in the Court of Far Seeing

RUTH MBEWE—Zambian eight-year-old who lives in the Knight of the Mirror's household

SHULA BISHARA—Syrian human in the service of the Elenil; has the power to burst into flame

SOCHAR—a member of the city guard; Elenil

SOFÍA—the housekeeper in Madeline's home on Earth

SUN'S DANCE—a "civilized" Scim man; advisor to the Elenil magistrates

THUY NGUYEN—Vietnamese human guard in Westwind

VIVI—father of Hanali, son of Gelintel

YENIL—a young Scim girl; daughter of Inrif and Fera

PART 1

There must be something better,
I know it in my heart.

FROM *THE GRYPHON UNDER THE STAIRS*
BY MARY PATRICIA WALL

1

THE GARDEN LADY

The king's gardener spoke the secret language of all growing things.
She knew the songs of the morning flowers and spoke the poems
of the weeds. She spent long afternoons in conversation with the trees.

FROM "THE TRIUMPH OF THE PEASANT KING," A SCIM LEGEND

✛

The bench stood twenty feet away. Such a short distance. Such an impossible one. Madeline clung to the trellis of ivy that bordered her mother's garden path as she tried to force air into her ruined lungs. Every gasp felt like pushing sludge through broken glass.

It was late morning on a Sunday, and she'd taken her inhaler an hour before—a quick, sharp breath of cold that disappeared much too quickly. She should have been in bed, flat on her back—not sitting, not standing, much less walking. But if the doctors were to be believed, it was one of the last spring Sundays she would ever see. Her chest and back hurt from the coughing.

The sunlight caressed her face. She couldn't stand at the trellis forever, and the return path to the house was longer. A few steps set off the coughing again. She pushed her fist hard into her ribs. She had dislocated them cough-ing three days ago, and they still didn't feel right. Three steps brought her to the maple tree which crowded the path. Her vision dimmed, and her knees softened. She slid down the trunk, and when the coughing fit passed she dropped her head against the rough bark.

A hummingbird spun into the air beside her, its shining green body hang-ing to the right of her face. It chirped three times, then zipped to her left, its small, dark eyes studying her before disappearing toward the pineapple sage. The citrusy fragrance of the roses hung heavy across this part of the path. She took little half breaths, and it felt close to natural. The bees hummed as they visited the flowers. A squirrel hung off a sunflower by its hind legs, plucking seeds out of the wide circle of the flower's face with its forepaws. This garden never quite seemed to follow the seasons . . . sunflowers bloom-ing in spring instead of summer, roses year-round, frogs singing in the eve-nings no matter the weather. It was an oasis of near-magic in their suburban lot. Madeline used to build fairy houses along the "shore" of the fountain when she was a kid, using bark, leaves, and flowers to make tiny homes for make-believe friends.

Her mother had never cared for those little homes. She had planned the garden, a full acre of wandering paths, stone bridges, and small fountains. It was eclectic and a bit overgrown in places. Mr. García had done the plant-ing and did the upkeep, too. Mom liked it a bit unkempt, and he worked to give it the impression of slight wildness. It didn't look manicured, but there weren't weeds, either. The fairy houses, Mom had said, looked like someone had forgotten to clean up after doing yard work.

Everything in its place, Mom always said.

Then again, Mom also wanted her house to "look lived in." That meant strange habits like telling their housekeeper, Sofía, that she couldn't imme-diately put an abandoned glass in the dishwasher. Once Madeline had come home and smelled fresh cookies, only to discover it was an air freshener her mother had bought from a Realtor. "To make it smell like home," Mom had said, seemingly oblivious to the reality that she was, indeed, home, and that actually baking cookies would have been simpler.

A few more steps, Madeline decided, but halfway to the bench a rack-ing army of coughs marched across her chest. She touched her lips, then wiped the blood in the grass. With her eyes closed and the little half breaths coming again, she counted to twelve. When the jagged feeling in her chest passed, she lay flat and watched the clouds drifting in some high, distant wind. Air moved so easily for everyone but her.

It may have been a mistake, sneaking into the garden without telling anyone, with no way to call for help. She had chosen the perfect moment. Mom and Sofía had gone upstairs, something about washing the curtains. Dad was at the golf course, or work, or both. Her phone sat inside, turned off. The constant texts from Darius were making her feel guilty, but she had made a decision, and it was final. He couldn't waste his life waiting for her. There wasn't a cure. He needed to live his life. She needed to live what remained of hers.

Birds chirped in the maple. The warmer air made it easier to breathe. Going outside in the winter had been nearly impossible. And the sun felt nice. She closed her eyes. The tree shaded her face, but her hands and feet baked in the sunshine. Last week the doctor had said, "If there are things you want to do, you should do them." He was trying to be encouraging, she knew that, but it sounded too much like "enjoy your last spring." Her mom didn't think she should sit out in the backyard because "she might catch cold," as if that would change anything now.

And here Madeline was on her back, stranded and straining to breathe. So much for doing whatever she wanted.

The hummingbird wheeled overhead. It zipped back and forth over her, then shot off again, chirping incessantly.

"I see her, I see her."

Madeline struggled to prop herself onto her elbow, looking for the source of the unfamiliar voice. It sounded like the voice of an old woman, but there was no wavering in it, no sense of weakness. It sounded, in fact, almost musical . . . as if the woman had been a professional singer once upon a time and the music had never left her. Still, she was trespassing in their backyard. A small thrill of adrenaline coursed through Madeline.

A woman made her way toward Madeline, hunched low, as if carrying a heavy load on her back. She wore a broad hat with pale violet flowers along the brim, and her grey hair stuck out like the straws of an overworked broom. Her patched and dirty skirt trailed the ground, and she carried a canvas sack. Madeline couldn't imagine how she'd gotten in through the hedge that ran around the garden.

Another coughing fit overcame Madeline. Her vision blurred at the edges, and she pressed hard against her chest.

"Don't get up, dear, rest yourself. It's the hummingbird who's in such a hurry, but I saw you, don't worry, I already saw."

"Does my mom know you're . . ." Madeline couldn't finish the question.

"Of course not," the old woman said. She settled next to Madeline with a great deal of groaning. She looked at the house, her eyes sparkling, a smile tugging at the edges of her lips. Her face was weathered and wrinkled, but her eyes shone like black stones in a clear river.

"You shouldn't be here," Madeline said. "My mom won't . . ." She stopped to catch her breath. "She won't like it."

The old woman nodded thoughtfully, then smoothed her skirt. "Mothers rarely do, dear. Now, to business." She reached into her sack and pulled out a small white button, crusted in dirt, then a recently unearthed bottle cap and a small roll of twine. "I would like to borrow these."

"Borrow them?" Madeline pushed her hand against her chest again, trying to get a deeper breath. "I don't understand."

"They are yours," the woman said. She raised her hand. "Don't deny it. I found them in your garden. The birds brought me the twine, and the squirrel mentioned the button, but I dug it out with my own hands. The bottle cap—well, I've had my eye on that for several seasons."

Madeline tried to call her mother, but she couldn't shout loud enough. She coughed and coughed, and the old woman put a fleshy arm around her shoulders. "My mom," Madeline managed between coughs.

"I won't cheat you," the woman said. "I only want to borrow them. In exchange, I'll give you three favors and one piece of advice." The hummingbird zipped in front of them again and chirped twice. The old woman made a shooing motion. "I know what time it is, go on with you."

Maybe the old woman would go if Madeline gave her what she wanted, and it was only a few pieces of trash from the backyard. "Take them," Madeline said.

The woman beamed at her and collected the bits of junk, scooping them into her bag. "Thank you, dear. Thank you, thank you—and that's three thanks for three items, so all has been done proper."

Madeline wheezed a you're welcome. She took a shallow breath. "Could you . . . Do you think you could ask someone to come out for me?"

The old woman looked to the house again, and her face crumpled. "Not for the wide world, dear."

"For one of my favors?" She took the woman's hand. "I can't breathe."

"The flowers sent word of that, they did. That's why I came. But have they come to you? Have they offered you a bargain?"

Madeline gasped for breath. What was wrong with this woman—couldn't she see that Madeline couldn't breathe? The old woman stared at her with a steady gaze, waiting for an answer. Hoping the woman might help after she answered, Madeline shook her head. "Who? The flowers?"

"No, of course they haven't. Not yet. I can't get involved until then. Not much."

Madeline lay back, coughing. The bright green leaves were waving in the branches. Clouds scudded in from the west, much too fast, covering the sun. She shivered and thought she could see the cloud of her breath when she exhaled. But it was too warm for that on this spring day. "Call my mother," she said. "Or Sofia."

The old woman's face appeared over her. "No favors yet, my sweet seedling. But I can give you the advice now."

Madeline closed her eyes. "Okay."

The old woman squeezed her hand and whispered in her ear. But Madeline could scarcely hear her over her own racking cough, and when she could breathe enough to roll on her side, the sun was shining brightly again, and the old woman was stepping into the hedge, like a rabbit running into a thicket of thorns. She was gone.

Her mother's cry of horror came from the direction of the house, and feet pounded along the garden path toward the shady space beneath the maple.

2

DARIUS

Love comes hand in hand with Joy.

FROM "RENALDO THE WISE," A SCIM LEGEND

adeline used to sing. In fact, she was lead soprano in the school choir last year, her junior year. She used to dance—ballet, contemporary, hip-hop, swing. She used to drive down the road with her friends, all of them shouting over one another, laughing at each other. She used to run track, her specialty being the marathon runs, where she could pace herself and feel her legs moving like pistons, her arms like pendulums, her whole body like the gears of a clock, ticking off the seconds to the finish line with precision. She had gone to State last year. She used to drive herself to school. She used to walk upstairs to her bedroom without stopping to catch her breath, clinging to the banister like a sea star suction cupped to a black rock.

She used to be able to breathe.

"I arranged your ride to school today," Mom said, her voice making it clear this was a final decision. Madeline had used a similar tone of voice when her parents tried to get her to stop going to class. Stay home, they said. You're too sick, they said. But when she did stay home, her parents didn't. Dad had work, Mom had activities, and Madeline ended up in bed, hacking her lungs out, sweating through her sheets, lonely and miserable.

Her mom took a cup of steaming coffee from Sofía and leaned against the kitchen counter, brushing an invisible speck of lint from her ice-blue athletic top.

"I thought you would take me," Madeline said. She had taken her inhaler fifteen minutes before, and for the next thirty minutes or so she should be able to breathe with relative ease. It was like pushing water in and out of her lungs, but at least the air moved. Sofía had made pancakes this morning, Madeline's favorite. Madeline had barely touched them. Like it or not, she wasn't well, and the thought of trying to rally the energy to pretend she was while her friends drove her to school, blaring music and trying to cheer her up . . . She didn't want that today. A silent, uncomfortable ride with her mom would be better.

"I have badminton this morning." Of course. Mom wore her pleated white badminton skirt, her platinum hair pushed back just so with a white headband.

"I can set up my own rides, then. It's not far for Ruby."

Her mother raised her eyebrows. "It's fifteen minutes out of her way. I texted Darius."

"Mom!"

"It's not right, the way you've been avoiding him."

"Why the sudden concern for Darius?"

Mom tapped her nails against her mug, taking another sip before saying, "You dated the boy for over a year and then dropped him without an explanation. He deserves better than that."

"Without an explanation? Who told you that?"

"People talk, Madeline. Your friends were worried, and they mentioned it to me. Poor boy. He was always good for you. You should spend more time with him."

"You don't even *like* him."

Mom shook her head. "Not true."

"Oh yeah, then why the big sit-down in the living room before prom?"

Mom's lips pressed together, making fine lines branch along her mouth. She always did that when she was done with a conversation. "He'll be here in ten minutes." She blew on her coffee and shook her head. "I'll see you after school."

As her mother walked from the room, Madeline shouted, "Dad's exact words were, 'He won't provide for you the way you're accustomed to.' If that was meant to convey approval, I missed it." She hadn't raised her voice like that in a while, and it cracked, followed by a deep-chested cough. She put her hands flat on the counter and tried to relax.

Sofía put a hot mug in front of Madeline. Steam infused with lemon and honey wafted to her. Sofía's gentle hand brushed her shoulder. "For your breathing," she said, and then she was off, cleaning the breakfast dishes.

"Thank you," Madeline muttered. Sofía had a way of smoothing everything over in this house. The drink was warm and soothing, and Madeline told herself it worked, but reflecting on the conversation with her mom made her angry. There was no way one of her friends had told her mom anything about the breakup. Most of her friends barely checked on her now. It was hard to be friends with the dying girl. Oh, they responded to texts. Most of them did, anyway. But she couldn't imagine any of them sitting down with her mom to talk about Madeline's dating life. Or lack thereof. What did her mom know about Darius, anyway? Next to nothing. Madeline had dated him for over a year, and her mom hadn't shown a moment's interest. Now she was setting up a car pool with him? Whatever she was up to, it was infuriating.

Madeline's backpack was by the door. Probably also Sofía's doing. Everyone treated her like an invalid, which she basically was, but it still made her angry. Her mom made her angry. Embracing reality made her angry. She should stay home—that was reality. She shouldn't wander in the garden alone—that was reality. She shouldn't have a boyfriend—that was reality. It wasn't fair to Darius to ask him to walk this road with her, wasn't fair to keep him tied to her, like an anchor. Breaking up with him had been an act of love, a way to set him free from her illness, and now her mom was trying to undo that.

She waited by the door so Darius wouldn't have an excuse to come in. His beat-up black Mustang pulled into the driveway, and he jumped out to come get her at the door. He moved like an ice skater, the ground roll-ing away beneath him like a moving walkway. Today he wore jeans and a button-down shirt, with his letterman's jacket tossed over it. She knew the buttoned shirt was for her. She had told him on their first date that wearing something other than a T-shirt might show he was at least a little bit excited.

She had met Darius in track. He was beautiful, with dark skin and an angular face. He kept his hair short—she could tell he had probably shaved it the night before—and when he smiled it was like the sun rising. That wasn't the reason she had started dating him, though. It was because of the day she'd turned her ankle during track and he had noticed and turned back for her. She'd told him to keep running, it was no big deal, she was alright. He'd told her they were a team and he needed a breather anyway. He'd walked beside her, gotten her back to the coach, stayed there while they put on the ice, made sure she was okay, and checked in with her the next day. After that, he was checking in on her every day. It started with the ankle, but from there he wanted to know how she was doing in class, with her parents, her friends, with life in general, and pretty soon they were texting, calling, laughing, deep into each other's lives. She asked him about his cousin Malik, who was away at college. Darius helped her think through how to respond to her parents when they were being difficult.

And when her breathing trouble started, and her mom took her to the doctor, Darius offered to come. Madeline's mom said no, that it wasn't right for "a stranger" to come to a doctor's appointment, and anyway, it was probably just a little infection. But when she and her mom came out into the hospital parking lot after the appointment, Darius was leaning against his car, reading a book, his cell phone in hand. He grinned and put the phone to his ear. *Call me.*

Saying good-bye had been hard. It was the right thing to do, but it was impossible, and now here he was, on her front porch, beaming. He reached for her backpack.

Madeline flinched away. "I'm not broken." She winced. She hadn't meant to come across like that, but seeing him here . . . There was a gravity there, a desire to come back together, and she couldn't allow that. It would be too hard on him, too painful for her.

"I know," he said, and bowed with a flourish. "But I . . . am a gentleman."

She smiled despite herself. She debated for a moment, then unslung her bag and let him carry it. "How's your breathing?" he asked, once they were settled in the Mustang and he was backing toward the road.

"Terrible. How did Mom get your number?"

He shrugged. "How does your mom always get whatever she wants? Called the principal maybe." He tapped his hands against the driver's wheel. "Listen, has your mom told you she's been calling me the last month or so?"

"What?! No!"

He raised a hand. "Don't be mad, she's just worried. Ever since you . . . uh . . . Since *we* broke up." He glanced at her, then back to the road. "Worried that you've given up."

Madeline watched the neighborhood spin past. Her parents had made it clear they didn't like Darius. What they hadn't made clear was why. Dad said he wouldn't make enough money, but that was years away, and what did he know? She and Darius were getting the same education, after all. He had grades nearly as good as hers, and if she wasn't in honors classes, his GPA might even be higher than hers. She didn't know if it was because they were both seventeen, or because Darius was black, or because he was at her private high school on a scholarship, but something about him didn't meet Mom and Dad's approval. And now Mom was texting him to check up on her? She gritted her teeth. Mom would hear about this when she got home.

And "*worried that she had given up*"? She hadn't given up—she was embracing reality. That was part of the stages of terminal disease, right? She had gone through denial. Through anger (well, maybe not all the way through). Now she was approaching acceptance. There was nothing more to be done. No more treatments, no miracle cures. She was walking a path her parents couldn't go down, not really. She was alone, and no one else needed to suffer this with her: not her parents, not her friends, and certainly not Darius.

She turned his radio up and kept it loud until they got to school. Darius, without even asking, pulled up alongside her classroom instead of parking in the lot. So she wouldn't have to walk so far, of course. She didn't know how to explain to him how infuriating she found his thoughtfulness. Especially when she was already mad at him. She knew it wasn't his fault—everything made her angry—and she knew he wouldn't understand if she tried to explain.

The car chugged to a stop, and the radio fell silent. Darius stared out the windshield. She knew that look. He was gathering his thoughts, trying to find words. She put her hand on the door handle, but despite herself, she paused. She missed hearing his voice. Missed talking about life, about things that mattered. "Maddie," he said. She melted a little at that. She had missed hearing the way he said her name. "I got you something."

He held a package wrapped in brown paper. He'd never been great at wrapping gifts, and this one was no exception: too much paper crookedly cut, with tape all over it and an attempt at a bow made with twine. It was obviously a book. She couldn't take a gift, though. It wasn't fair to him. Or to her, really. "Darius—"

"I bought it before we broke up, but it just got here. Shipped from England." She didn't say anything. "I know you're going to love this, and I want you to have it." He held it out. When she took it, their fingers brushed against each other.

Madeline pulled the tape loose and slid the book out. "Darius. I can't believe this."

It was a copy of her favorite book, *The Gryphon under the Stairs* by Mary Patricia Wall. It was the first of the Tales of Meselia, a series of children's fantasy novels. The final novel had never come out, so it wasn't as popular as other series, and not as easy to find, but Madeline loved it best. Darius had never read the Meselia books until she got sick. He had come to her house, sat on the floor while she curled on the couch, and read aloud the whole series, a couple chapters at a time. It had taken months to get to the end. She had loved seeing the books through his eyes, listening to him talk about them, hearing his thoughts and questions and insights.

"First edition," Darius said proudly. "Hardback, too."

She ran her hand over the cover. It had been released in 1974, and the picture on the front was of a gryphon crouched under a stairway, two children standing to the sides, stepping back in surprise. Ivy grew up around the outside of the picture, and the whole illustration had the look of a wood-block print.

Her anger drained away. She couldn't believe it. She had always wanted a first edition, though she had never mentioned it to anyone, not even Darius. Holding it in her hand now, feeling the texture of the cover, the weight of the book, seemed almost miraculous . . . like maybe things that were impossible could happen. She didn't know what to say. She settled for "Darius, thank you so much." Then, before the emotion choked off her words, she asked, "Where did you find this?"

He grinned. "I started calling bookshops in the UK. Little places that didn't put their books online."

She flipped open the book, shocked by the crispness of the pages. "It looks like no one has ever read this copy," she said. "Like it's untouched by human hands."

"Nah," Darius said. "Look at the title page."

She looked from him to the book, then back at him. It couldn't be. She turned the first page, a blank one, and there it was. The name Mary Patricia Wall was written in a neat, curved script in black ink, just beneath her typeset name. Mary Patricia Wall had held this book in her hands, had put her fingers on these pages to keep them open.

Tears cascaded down her face, and she couldn't keep away from Darius anymore, couldn't pretend, even for his own good, that she didn't want to be with him. She let his gravity pull her in, leaning into his embrace, and he didn't say anything, didn't ask for anything, just wrapped his arms around her and let her cry. She cried for his thoughtfulness, for thankfulness to have someone who knew her so well, for fear of what was to come. She cried because she was angry and sad and afraid and loved and so, so tired. There was no way out, no solution to her illness, but at least there was this, a moment of loving human touch, a gift from someone who knew her well.

The warning bell for first period rang.

The crying set off a minor coughing fit. She sat up, bracing herself on the dashboard. Darius put a comforting hand on her shoulder. When it passed, she wiped her eyes with her sleeve and slipped the book into her backpack.

"'There must be something better, I know it in my heart,'" Darius said, quoting a line from the book. The main characters, siblings Lily and Samuel, are standing at the space beneath the stairs, and the wall has fallen away, and there is a swirling of color in the space. The gryphon has disappeared into it, and beckons Lily and Samuel to follow. "'And the only impossible thing is that I would leave you.'"

Madeline wiped her eyes again, then replied with Samuel's words, "'If we're together, I won't be afraid.'"

Lily's next line was, "Then take my hand, Samuel, and let us see what beautiful things await," but before Darius could say it, Madeline took his hand and squeezed, and before she could stop herself or think about what it meant or what the consequences might be, she leaned toward him and kissed his cheek.

She pulled away, the heat from Darius's hand familiar and comfortable. She looked into those dark-brown eyes, so deep they were nearly black. It was like looking into the night sky if all the stars blinked at once. It had been weeks since she had looked at him like this, and she wanted him to reach out, to touch her cheek.

Instead, he opened his door and came to get her. He walked her to class, her backpack on his shoulder, his hand on the small of her back, ready to catch her if she fell. Did she look as weak as that?

"If you need to go home early, text me," he said. His words were so gently delivered that she didn't get angry at the suggestion she couldn't make it through the day.

"You're going to be late for class," she said.

He grinned. "Impossible." Then he ran toward his classroom in that loping, long-legged stride of his, leaping like a deer over a planter, so full of life and joy and breath.

"Your car," she gasp-shouted.

He changed directions immediately, sprinting, a sheepish look on his face. "I might be late to class!" he yelled back, just as the bell rang again.

3
PARTNERS

Humans! Ye shall live upon another earth,
a people of science and dust.

FROM "THE ORDERING OF THE WORLD," AN ELENIL STORY

✛

After what had happened to his sister, Jason Wu had made a decision. He would never keep quiet about what he saw again, and he would never lie. No matter the cost, he would speak up and speak truth.

Sure, he'd gotten detention over the whole Principal Krugel fiasco, but his toupee *was* on backward. Maybe Jason shouldn't have mentioned it in front of the football team. He almost certainly should not have repeated it over the school intercom. He could still hear the principal's shrill voice shouting, "JASON WU!" from his office. That could have been the end of it, but when Jason refused to apologize or retract his statement, the principal had taken to the intercom to explain he did not wear a toupee.

That didn't excuse what Jason had done next. He saw that now.

Seeing Principal Krugel in front of the whole school at the football rally

16

the next day, his ridiculous fake hair sitting on top of his head like a shag carpet, had driven Jason right to the edge of madness. Then Darius Walker had shouted to Jason, "Krugel's hair looks real to me! What are you going to do?"

Jason had said, "Pull his toupee off," meaning it as a joke.

But then he thought, *I promised never to tell a lie.*

Taking off the man's toupee wouldn't be good.

But if he didn't, he was a liar. Again.

It was a moral conundrum.

Anyway, it had earned Jason detention and earned Principal Krugel the nickname Principal Cue Ball.

He had received a second detention when the principal called his parents, put them on speakerphone, and made Jason explain what he had done. When the principal said there had been a mini riot at the assembly, Jason's mom asked if it was true. Of course Dad didn't say anything. He hadn't spoken—well, hadn't spoken to Jason—since things had happened with Jenny. Before he could stop himself, Jason said, "Yes, everyone was wigging out." Even that didn't get Dad to speak up. It had, on the other hand, turned Principal Krugel's face a shade of red Jason had never seen before, so it wasn't a complete loss.

So he wasn't trying to be insensitive when his chemistry partner, Madeline Oliver, came in to class looking like someone had given her a swirly. "You look terrible," he said. "Your mascara is running everywhere. Your eyes are red." All true.

Madeline choked out a sarcastic thanks, then started coughing. She coughed a lot. He knew she was sick. She didn't talk about it, ever. Everyone at school acted like it was a big secret, but he noticed that meant they couldn't take care of her, either. Couldn't ask how she was doing, couldn't make sure she was taking care of herself. That's why he'd asked to be her chem partner. She didn't know that—she had been at the doctor the day they picked partners. Besides, she was better at chemistry than he was. So they were watching out for each other, in a way. That's what partners do.

"You sound terrible too. Should you even be in class?" Jason spun a pencil in one hand, twirling it like a baton.

"I can't skip school all the time." She slammed her bag down and slid onto a stool, leaning against the counter.

"You already skip half the time," Jason said. "You're the worst lab partner I've had. Besides, it's a sub today. We're probably doing some idiotic worksheet."

"You just described half of high school," Madeline said. "Who are you to say I look terrible, anyway? Your clothes look like they're on day three of being picked up from your floor."

"Day four," Jason said. He hadn't combed his hair, either, and he knew it went five directions at once. Only one of his shoes was tied. The other one he had overknotted yesterday and couldn't get it undone. He had actually worn his left shoe to bed last night. He watched Madeline coughing and digging through her backpack for her textbook. She really shouldn't be here. She didn't even notice the substitute call her name. "Here," he said.

The substitute looked at Jason over the top of his glasses. "Your name is Madeline Oliver?"

"Nah, it's my partner, but she's busy coughing up a lung. She needs to go to the office."

The sub regarded Madeline skeptically. He had a big nose and a wreath of brown hair that stuck up on the sides. He looked like an angry koala bear. "It's not my first time as a substitute," he said.

"I'm fine," Madeline said, still coughing.

"Try not to distract the class," he said, and continued calling roll.

Jason spun on his stool. He knew what was coming. He leaned over and whispered to Madeline, "He's going to read my Chinese name, I can feel it. And he's gonna say it wrong. I hate this guy already. Maybe you should take your inhaler."

"Already took it," she said, gasping for air between words.

He opened her purse—she tried to stop him, and yes, he knew you shouldn't dig in a girl's purse—and pulled out her inhaler. He shook it three times and handed it to her. She took a deep puff, her eyes shut. She leaned on the counter, panting.

"Song Wuh," the substitute said.

"Jason," he called. "It's Jason."

"Says Song Wuh here."

Jason sighed. Should he correct the guy? He got so tired of correcting people when they said his name wrong. "With Jason in parentheses, right? And it's pronounced *woo*, and the *o* in Song is long, like in *hope*. Wu Song, that's how you say it—family name first. It's not that hard. Seriously."

The substitute wrote something on his paper. "Ah. Jason. Yes, the principal mentioned you."

The principal *mentioned* him? It made him sound like some sort of troublemaker. One little incident with a man's fake hair and you're branded for life. Was it in his personal record? Would it follow him to college? *Make sure this boy never gets near a toupee—he will take it and run around the gym, waving it like a hairy flag.* Oh yeah. He had done that, too. He hadn't run it up the flagpole, though. That had been someone else.

"Is my name so hard?" Jason asked Madeline. "Wu Song is famous, too. Killed a man-eating tiger with his bare hands. Doesn't seem like it's asking too much to get my name right, especially when I'm named after a famous guy."

"Your life is hard," Madeline gasped. She had her phone out and was texting someone.

"It's like mispronouncing Robin Hood."

"Jason." Her body listed to one side, like a sinking ship. She grasped at the counter, trying to keep herself upright. Jason grabbed her sleeve, pulling her toward him, pulling her upright, and then she was slipping, falling. Her arm slid out of her jacket, and she half rolled, half fell onto the floor, her head knocking against the polished cement.

Jason jumped off his stool, knocking it over with a clang. He threw Madeline's stool out of the way and knelt over her. He asked if she was okay, but she didn't answer.

"Mr. Substitute," Jason shouted. "Call an ambulance."

"You two stop messing around."

"She's actually sick," Jason shouted, and other kids in the class chimed in, telling the sub it was true, that she had some lung sickness or something.

"I'll call the office," he said, but he was still standing there, staring.

Madeline's eyes rolled back into her head, and her skin went pale. Jason put his hand on her face. Cold and clammy. She wasn't breathing. A knot of panic sat in his chest, small and cold as her skin. For a second he was looking at Jenny's face, still and pale, but he shoved the image out of his mind, hard. He needed to think about right now. He tilted Madeline's head back and got ready to do chest compressions.

One of the other kids said, "Dude, you're not going to—"

"Shut up," Jason said, and started chest compressions.

He pinched her nose shut, sealed his mouth over hers, and breathed two quick breaths into her mouth. Her chest rose, she coughed, and she started to breathe again.

"Her color is coming back," one of the kids said.

The substitute stood there at the end of the row, the stack of worksheets in his hand. His mouth was open, and his glasses had slid down his nose. He cleared his throat. "Calm down, class. We'll—"

Jason interrupted him. "Mr. Koala Bear. Snap out of it. Call the office. Right. Now."

This was taking too long. The sub was in shock or something. Jason pointed at a kid in the row in front of him. "You. Kid with the braces. Call 911. Tell them we're headed to the hospital."

He leaned over Madeline. "It's gonna be okay. Keep breathing." He slipped one hand under her neck, grabbed the belt loop on her jeans with the other, and lifted.

The classroom door slammed open, and Darius stood on the other side, panting. "What happened? She just texted me."

"Help me get her to the car," Jason said.

The security guard in the parking lot said something to them, but Jason rushed past. Darius shouted an explanation, and then he helped sling Madeline into Jason's sports car and put her seat belt on.

"Where are you taking her?"

"She can't breathe, Darius, where do you think? The hospital. Get in the car or step back." Why were people such idiots during times of pressure?

The car settled under Darius's weight as he got in the back. "Drive," he said.

Jason peeled out of the parking lot and screeched onto the road.

"Red light!" Darius yelled.

Jason punched it through the intersection.

"An accident won't get us there faster," Darius said.

"This isn't driver's ed," Jason said. "I know what I'm doing." He glanced at Madeline. She was coughing up blood now. There's no way he was going to stay quiet, no way he was going to wait for an ambulance. No way. "Hang in there, partner."

She coughed until she fainted. Jason laid on the horn and sped toward the hospital.

4

THE STRANGER

And he placed a tower in the center
of the Sunlit Lands and called it Far Seeing.

FROM "THE ORDERING OF THE WORLD," AN ELENIL STORY

✛

I t felt like someone had put cinder blocks on her chest. Transparent tubes snaked into her nostrils. A red plastic band clung to her wrist. Sensors were stuck to her chest, an IV line dripped into her left arm, and a clip on the finger of her right hand monitored oxygen levels. Her lips were dried and cracked.

The hospital again. More and more of her life found its way here. Appointments, tests, paperwork, treatments. Meetings to talk about tests and treatments. The harsh lights, the antiseptic smell that came even through her oxygen tube, the incessant beeping and nurses checking in and noise. She hated finding herself here. Hated that she couldn't make it through one day of school, hated the reminder yet again that she should just stay home like a good girl, hidden away and waiting, alone, for the end to come.

Darius was in a chair beside the bed. Jason was sitting in a windowsill to Darius's left, half an arm's length away. Even with only two visitors, the room felt crowded.

Darius touched her hand gently. "You're awake."

Madeline looked at her hospital gown. "How—?"

"They cut off your clothes," Jason said. "Don't worry, they kicked us out until you were dressed."

"Are my parents here?"

"Not yet," Jason said. "The hospital called."

"I texted your mom," Darius said.

Jason was chomping on an apple. "When I said you looked terrible, I didn't realize how low the scale goes, you know? You looked pretty good earlier, all things considered."

Darius punched him in the arm.

"What was that for?"

Madeline asked, "What did the doctor say?"

Darius's brow furrowed. "You don't remember?"

"Was I awake?"

"You told them we could stay," Jason said. "And that it was okay for us to hear, um, your diagnosis."

Madeline blushed. She hadn't really told the other kids at school what was going on. Darius knew the basics. Jason, weirdly, seemed to have figured it out, but they never talked about it. She didn't want to talk about it at school, didn't want to answer the endless questions. What's interstitial lung disease? Is it common in teens? Will it kill you?

Scarring in the lungs. Not really. Probably, yes.

Madeline's scarring was advancing. Every hour, every minute, it progressed through her lungs, like an army gaining a few yards each day. Where the lungs scarred, they didn't process oxygen. Eventually she'd run out of usable lung tissue, and she'd asphyxiate. It was only a question of how long. All the doctors' appointments and medications and oxygen tanks were to prolong her life, not save it. She was on the list for a lung transplant, high on the list, actually—no previous illness, a fatal disease that wasn't responding to treatment, she was young. But every time a donation came up, something got in the way. The tissue went bad. Another donor somehow jumped in line. Her application was mysteriously deleted. It was like an unseen hand kept intervening, frustrating any chance of her getting better. And now she was getting so weak, the doctor wasn't sure she'd survive the surgery. She cleared her throat, which felt raspy and raw.

"Could I get a drink?" Madeline asked. "Maybe some ice chips."

"I'm on it," Jason said, stepping away from the window.

Darius said, "Could you bring her something soft to eat, too, like some applesauce?" Jason nodded and scooted out of the room.

The oxygen tubes in her nose rubbed, and her arm felt stiff and uncomfortable where the IV entered. Darius leaned in close and squeezed her hand.

A blinding light hit her full in the face. Her first thought was that it was the kind of light they put in an operating room, the bright white light surgeons use, but it wasn't in one place, it seemed to come from all over. Her second thought was that she was passing out or something, but she knew what that felt like, had experienced the light-headed, rolling blackness more than once, and this wasn't that.

Then the light started to burn, and she could feel it searing her skin. It seemed to be coming from the end of the bed, so she turned away, but even with her eyes shut, that white light pierced her eyes, as if her eyelids weren't even there.

The light disappeared as quickly as it had come, leaving the room dim and Madeline shivering in the sudden cold. Darius's hand still held hers, but it was rigid, though still warm. He was leaning toward Madeline but not moving or blinking. She slipped her hand away from his, and he didn't move, didn't so much as breathe.

"Darius?" What was happening? Was this a hallucination brought on by lack of oxygen? She felt coherent, but her brain couldn't process what she was seeing. Her own heart ratcheted up, beating faster. She took a deep breath, ready to call for help, and instead gave an involuntary shout when she looked toward the door.

At the foot of her bed stood a tall, slender man. He had the palest skin she had ever seen, almost the color of platinum, with a bluish undertone. His silver-white hair was fine and long, falling to his shoulders. He wore a brocade jacket with pale-pink roses worked into the silk and veins of gold shooting through the design. Stiff lace blossomed from his sleeves, nearly covering his gloved hands, and more lace covered his neck, where a white cravat was tied with perfect grace. He inclined his head to her.

"It is customary you should bow," the man said. "But there will be time to learn such pleasantries. I am called Hanali, and I have come as a representative of the Sunlit Lands."

Madeline tried to speak but found herself choking instead. It was like a dream, but in a dream she wouldn't be in so much pain, would she? Darius still hadn't moved. She managed to get a breath and said, "What did you do to him?"

The slim man looked at Darius as if seeing him for the first time. "Ah. Your friend is unaware of our conversation. After our business concludes, he will continue about his day."

Something about the strange man reminded her of the lady in the garden. Madeline didn't know if these were hallucinations or fever dreams or real, but the woman had gone away when Madeline gave her what she wanted. Maybe the same would be true for this strange man. "What do you want?" she asked.

"More importantly, child, what do *you* want?"

Annoyance flared up in Madeline. She gestured to the tubes coming out of her body. "Nothing you can give me."

Hanali reached into Darius's jacket pocket, slid out his cell phone, and dangled it in front of Darius's face. With a flourish he released the phone, and it stayed there, unmoving, floating in the air. "Which is easier? To stop time or heal lungs?" Hanali asked.

Jason walked through the door. "Stop time? Huh. Is that what happened?" He had a cup of ice in one hand, and his arms were full of pudding cups. "The nurses stopped talking all at once. I thought it was performance art."

"Starless night," Hanali said. The way he said it, it sounded like a curse. "How are you unaffected by my spell?"

Jason dumped all the pudding cups on Madeline's bed and handed her the cup of ice. He shrugged. "The world is full of mysteries. Why are you cosplaying at a hospital?"

Hanali gaped at him. "You can see and hear me and move about."

Jason tore open a pudding. "I forgot spoons."

"This has never happened in my lifetime."

"Wait!" Jason dug around in his pockets. "Here they are!" He held one out to Madeline. She shook her head, popping an ice chip in her mouth and sucking it.

Hanali's eyes narrowed. "Did an old woman speak to you? Did a stranger approach you in a garden?"

Madeline's ears perked up. He knew her, then, the Garden Lady. Had she spoken to Jason, too?

Jason shoveled some pudding into his mouth. "I don't know what you're talking about, dude."

"Remarkable." Hanali turned reluctantly away from Jason. He tugged on the frilled cuffs of his sleeves, straightening them. "I am here, Madeline Oliver, to offer a bargain. In exchange for one human year of service to the Elenil, lords of the Sunlit Lands, we will cast a magic spell that will heal your lungs. You will be able to dance and run and sing again."

Madeline's chest ached. She didn't understand everything the strange man was saying, but she had caught the basics. A year of work in exchange for healing. "I won't last a year," she said. She glanced at Jason. He had paused, another spoonful halfway to his mouth. "The doctor said three months. Maybe a little more."

"We would, of course, give you the magic as soon as our terms were agreed upon. You can have your breath returned to you this very day. You will come to the Sunlit Lands, and in one human year we will return you to this place, permanently healed."

Jason said, "Wait, why are you going to school if you only have three months to live?"

"My friends are there," Madeline said. And then, to Hanali, "Explain this again. You want me to serve . . . the Alelni?"

"Elenil. They are the lords of the Sunlit Lands."

"Hawai'i, I'm guessing," Jason said.

The strange man scowled. "The Sunlit Lands are not part of Earth—they are another world. Smaller than Earth, but full of magic. No doubt you've read of such places. Faerie lands."

Faerie lands. Something about the way he said it set off all the associations in her mind, all the places she knew and loved: Meselia in the books of Mary Patricia Wall. Narnia. Hogwarts. Earthsea. How many times had she pushed her hand against the back wall of a wardrobe or stood in front of a painting wishing she could jump into it? How often had she wished for a magic ring or button, a hidden passageway, a garden gate grown over in ivy that would transport her to some magical land? She thought of the hobbit Samwise Gamgee and his aching desire to meet the Elves, and she, too, felt a piercing longing to walk among a strange and beautiful people. She thought of Lily and Samuel standing at the portal beneath their stairs, watching the color-swirled space where the gryphon had gone. They had been afraid and just scarcely believing. She remembered Lily's words in *The Gryphon under the Stairs.* "There must be something better, I know it in my heart," Madeline whispered, and for the first time in many months she felt a flutter of hope. Every book she had read in her entire childhood, every book she still cherished, had prepared her to believe in a moment like this.

Jason spoke up, his mouth still full of pudding. "Sounds like Harry Potter–land. Which means more school. If you want to learn magic, it apparently involves a lot of school."

"It is more like Mount Penglai," Hanali said. "Or Tír na nÓg."

Madeline tried to mask her excitement. She wanted to leap up and take Hanali's hand and do whatever was necessary to go to these Sunlit Lands, but she needed more information. "Why do the Elenil need people like me?"

Hanali smiled, and his teeth were white as seashells. "The Elenil scour the world for people in need—people without food, or in the midst of a crisis, or dying. If the magic of the Elenil can help, we make an exchange. Some small token of their lives in exchange for a bit of magic. Your world has precious little magic, so our help is keenly felt."

"Sounds too good to be true," Jason said, opening a second pudding cup.

Madeline shushed him. "What is it like? The Sunlit Lands?"

A smile spread over Hanali's face. "In the heart of the Sunlit Lands lies the capital city of the Elenil. The Court of Far Seeing is bright and beautiful. All things fair and wonderful are there. There is music in the city squares and art upon the streets. No one is hungry, and the white towers fly crimson flags in the warm breeze from the Ginian Sea. Above the city stands the Crescent Stone, bright beacon of our magic, a reminder of the good things available to those who inhabit the blessed city."

"If this place is so great," Jason said, "why do you need us? You need janitors or something?"

Hanali glared at Jason. He yanked on the lace at his cuffs, pulling them down over his hands. "A corrupted people called the Scim live to our south. They call themselves servants of darkness, of shadow, and they wish to tear down the Court of Far Seeing. We are in need of your help in this conflict."

Madeline coughed for a minute, holding up a finger to pause the conversation. "So . . . what exactly is the agreement? What do I have to do?"

"You agree to serve the Elenil in our war against the Scim for one human year. In exchange we will heal you. You must leave your friends and family behind. You will not be able to say good-bye or explain your absence."

Another coughing fit overcame her. When a coughing attack came, she couldn't think about her mother or father, her friends, Darius, school, the way she liked to wake in the morning and lean her head on her windowsill, listening to the birds in the garden. She could only think about the way her chest constricted and squeezed every molecule of oxygen out of her body, of the blackness that pressed in against her eyes, and the burning pain that burst through her every cell. She knew how her life would end . . . like this, a million minuscule knives in her chest. One day, she would inhale, pull as hard as she could with her ruined lungs, and there would be nothing. Just thrashing and panic and death. There would be no peaceful final smile, no gentle bedside farewells. Wouldn't this deal be better than that? No good-byes, but she wasn't going to get good-byes when she coughed herself to death, either, not really. And she'd be back in a year. Panting after the coughing fit, she tried to wheeze out an answer, but Jason spoke up first.

"No offense," he said, "but this is one of those candy-and-strangers situations."

"Not having candy and not being able to breathe are quite different," Hanali said.

Jason said, "You're recruiting desperate people who won't ask questions. What's your angle?"

Hanali's smile remained on his face, but his eyes bored into Jason. His words came out clipped and perfectly enunciated. "A human year of assisting in the war against the Scim in exchange for healthy lungs for the rest of her life. The conditions are plain."

Jason sat at the foot of Madeline's bed, putting himself between her and Hanali. "It's a bad idea, Madeline. You could die in the war. You won't be able to say good-bye to your friends and family. Also, I don't trust this guy."

Madeline shook her head. Jason didn't understand. She didn't expect him to. How could he know what it was like to stand on the precipice of death, never knowing if this was the last time you'd pull a breath? Sometimes she was terrified she'd go faster than the doctor said, but if she was being honest, there were also days when she was afraid she'd last longer than the doctor said. She couldn't take this pain, this slow descent. If there was a way out of this sickness, what price would be too much? "What's the worst that could happen, Jason?"

"You could be eaten by a dragon." He looked at Hanali. "Are there dragons?"

Hanali raised an eyebrow. "Dragons?"

"Giant lizards that breathe fire? They have wings. Hoard gold. Eat people."

"No, we do not have 'dragons' in the Sunlit Lands."

Jason shrugged and looked back at Madeline. "You could get gored to death by a unicorn."

She almost laughed at that. "Better than suffocating."

"It's a high price," Jason said, and for a moment she saw his genuine concern. No bravado, no jokes, just a sweet, almost brotherly desire to protect her. He seemed to think that she didn't understand the cost, but it was Jason who didn't understand. She knew the cost. She had been paying it every day since her diagnosis. She was on a journey of saying good-bye, of leaving everything behind. Jason didn't understand that Hanali wasn't asking for anything that wouldn't be taken from her anyway. But he was offering a chance—maybe it was a gamble, maybe it was a bad deal in some way she couldn't see, but it was a chance at least, which was more than she had now—a chance at life. No one else was offering her that.

"I'll be able to breathe the entire year?"

Hanali nodded gravely. "So long as you follow the agreement, yes. With the exception of the Festival of the Turning—an Elenil festival day without magic. Other than that, you will breathe freely."

"So long as I follow the agreement," Madeline repeated. "How does it work? What do I have to sign?"

Hanali pulled a thin bracelet from his jacket. It had a tiny, clouded jewel set in it and intricate patterns etched into the silver. "No signature. Only slip this onto your left wrist, and we shall be on our way. The power of the Crescent Stone will seal our bargain."

She turned the bracelet over in her hands. It was lighter than she expected, and delicate. Was she hallucinating? The whole thing was so surreal. But if it was real—and it did *seem* real—she could be healed. She'd have to leave her life behind for a year, but that was worth it, right? She imagined Darius waking from this strange moment of frozen time to find her gone. Her parents. Her father would sue the hospital into the Stone Age. Her mom would weep and scream and yell and never be the same.

She wished Darius could move. He still sat beside her, frozen and unseeing. She wanted to talk it through with him, ask his opinion. In these last couple years, even before they were dating, he had been there for her so many times, had talked about everything with her. She had been trying to say good-bye, trying to make some distance, but now she wanted to hear his steady, reasoned voice weigh the pros and cons. He would understand, she thought, the excitement of this magical land. He had often said, "If only there was magic, if only there was some way out of this . . ."

So maybe Jason was right. She should think about it. Consider it. For a few minutes at least. She shouldn't just take this deal and jump headfirst into some world, some war, she didn't understand.

"I want to think about it," she said, choking it out before another bout of painful coughing.

Hanali shook his head. "Do not contemplate too long," he said. "There are others who are suffering, and we can take our offer to them should you reject it."

"If I decide to . . . to come to the Sunlit Lands, how do I let you know?"

Hanali looked at her carefully. "The Sunlit Lands exist alongside your

Earth. Not below or above, but beside. Parallel. You have but to leave this life behind and follow the narrow road that opens before you."

"Second star to the right," Madeline said, her coughing growing worse. "And straight on till . . . till morning."

The stranger crossed his arms, plucking at the lace at his wrists. He reached out and took the bracelet, tucking it into some concealed pocket in his sleeve. "Send your strange friend to find me should you change your mind."

"Yeah, yeah, we got it," Jason said. "Now you heard the lady, get out of here. I'm allergic to all that lace."

"Beware," Hanali said. "When time crashes in on you again, you will be reminded of your weakness. The shock of reentering normal time can cause great stress on the human body."

Hanali spun and walked from the room, and the world came to life again. Darius's phone clattered to the floor and he shouted in surprise, looking down in confusion to find Madeline's hand no longer entwined with his.

Madeline's breath left her completely, and her heart rate spiked. She fought to stay conscious. The machines attached to her blared shrill alarms.

"Maddie?"

It's okay, she tried to say. It's going to be okay. But she couldn't speak, couldn't draw a breath. Her eyes met Jason's.

"She's turning blue," Darius said, pushing Jason back. "Give her room."

A doctor hurried in, close behind the nurse. "You kids get out," the doctor said. "Right now."

"We don't have time to argue," the nurse said, speaking over their objections. "If you want us to save your friend, get out now."

"Jason," she managed to wheeze. "Bracelet." She didn't have any choice, did she? She didn't have time to think this out, to weigh the consequences. She was drowning. Hanali hadn't offered her a choice, he had offered her a life vest.

She *needed* the bracelet. There was no guarantee the doctors could do anything for her in this moment. Tears squeezed out of her eyes, her hands clutched the bedsheets, her back arched up as her body cast about desperately, trying to find breath. Jason paused in the doorway and looked back at her. Had he heard her? Why wasn't he running to get Hanali? Did he understand how serious this was? She tried to lift her hand, tried to show him her wrist, but then a nurse shut the door, and there was only the shriek of the alarms and the struggle to breathe.

5
HAMBURGER

Bereft of magic, short lived and passionate,
there shall still be beauty and wonder among you.

FROM "THE ORDERING OF THE WORLD," AN ELENIL STORY

✛

The door shut, and Jason put his hand against the hallway wall. Madeline was dying. He didn't have any question. So he needed to find that magic man, and there wasn't much time. He started down the hall, but a viselike hand grabbed his arm.

Darius said, "What was Madeline talking about when she said 'bracelet'?"

Jason debated whether to explain. Darius didn't seem like the kind of guy to go in with dragons and unicorns, but Jason didn't know him well. But then again, he had promised to tell the truth. How much of the truth was the question. "This Renaissance faire reject came in the room and offered her a magic bracelet to help her breathe. She's telling me to go find him and get it."

Dairus's face clouded over. "What are you talking about? Nobody came into the room. I was there the whole time."

"You were frozen," Jason said.

Darius's gaze sharpened, and he looked at Jason critically. "But you weren't frozen?" His grip on Jason's arm tightened.

Jason peeled Darius's fingers off. "Listen, man, I don't have time to explain. You saw Madeline in there."

Darius's hands relaxed a fraction. "Okay. Right. How do I help?"

Jason's mouth fell open. "You believe me?"

Darius shrugged. "I don't know. But if Maddie wants this bracelet, let's go get it. Whatever's going on, Madeline gets what she wants. Got it?"

"Okay," Jason said. "I have to figure out where this magic guy went. You want to help look for him?"

Darius looked back at the closed hospital room door. Jason could practically see the relational connection between the two of them, like a glowing string. "I'll wait here," he said. "If the guy comes, I'll grab him. What does he look like?"

Jason was already trotting down the hallway. "You'll recognize him, believe me."

Now. Where would a magic person go in a hospital?

Not the waiting room. Everyone hates waiting rooms. The other direction was just more rooms, another hallway. Jason ran full speed through the maze of hospital hallways, keeping an eye out for the long, whitish hair of the stranger. He collided full force with a priest, sending them both sprawling to the floor.

The priest picked up his fallen glasses and put them on. Jason helped him to his feet. "Sorry."

"What's the rush, young man?"

"I'm looking for this magic guy. Looks like he fell in a closet full of lace. Long white hair. You know him?"

"A magic guy," the priest said, his eyes widening. He looked more carefully into Jason's eyes. Jason knew that look, too. It was the are-you-on-drugs look. "No. Not in recent years, anyway."

Of course not. Jason tossed a half wave at the priest and started down the hallway. Then he stopped, turned around, and trotted back. "Hey, uh, Mr. Priest. In past years or whatever . . . Do you know how to find a magic guy?"

The priest shook his head slowly. "It's dangerous, my lad, to invoke powers you don't understand."

Invoke. He knew that word. *Invocation.* It meant, like, to speak an invitation to someone. "He's a person, don't worry. He's not a demon or anything."

The priest grabbed his forearm. "Son, I'm not talking about demons. There are such creatures, and they are dangerous. But I am talking about the people of the Sunlit Lands."

Wait. "You know them? Creepy guys who want to trade a year of your life in exchange for letting someone breathe again?"

The priest nodded. "When I was a boy, I was orphaned in a fire. I lived on the streets, and a man came to me and said that in exchange for a few years in the Sunlit Lands fighting the accursed Scim, I could have wealth and a family."

Whoa. So the bargain . . . it was real. This guy had taken a deal, and here he was, alive and back in the real world. But the old man didn't seem exactly happy about it, either. And he said he had made the deal when he was a boy. How long had this war been going on, anyway?

Everything in Jason told him there was more to the story than the lacy stranger was saying, that somehow—and he couldn't see how—the deal was rigged. But then again, here was this priest, alive and well, as far as Jason could see. His bargain had been different, though . . . "wealth and a family." There was a big difference between wealth and a miraculous healing. And also, so far as Jason knew, priests weren't known for being wealthy. Or for having family. At least, not a wife and kids.

"They're trying to make a deal with my friend. She's dying, and they said they can make her well."

The priest's eyes softened. "Perhaps they can. But enter into agreements with them carefully, and—" He looked into Jason's eyes, as if studying his soul. "Don't send her alone, young man. It's a hard road to walk, but without a friend . . ."

"It won't matter if I can't find the guy. My friend's not going to last long."

The old man's lips began to tremble. "What was his name? This magic man?"

"I can't remember. Starts with an *h.* Hamburger? Something like that."

The old man echoed the name. "Hamburger?"

"Hamburglar? Hambutcher? Hamolee? I don't know."

"Hanali?" the old man asked, tears welling up in his eyes. "Listen to me very closely—"

And then Hanali stood in the hallway, leaning against the wall, plucking at the lace around his sleeves. "You only had to say my name," he said nonchalantly. "I was listening for it." Hanali looked at the priest, whose tears had frozen on his cheeks. Time had stopped again. Hanali studied the old man's face, and his eyes darted to Jason, then back to the priest. "You are fortunate this old man said my name," he said slowly.

"I said Hamburger like five times."

"But my name is Hanali," the thin man said, standing up straight. "Though I suspect you knew that already."

How long had it been now? Three minutes? Five? Was it too late already? Jason knew about bargaining, knew that you can't show how badly you need something. Everything in him wanted to grab the guy by his oversized lapels and shake the bracelet loose, run down the hallway, and slide it onto Madeline's wrist. Instead, Jason shrugged. "Madeline is thinking about taking the bracelet."

Hanali produced it from his sleeve. "And the bargain which accompanies it?"

"Yeah. Except I'm going to go with her."

Hanali hesitated. "I did not come to bargain with you."

"On the other hand," Jason said, "your weird magic doesn't affect me, which must mean something."

"Indeed." Hanali's expression clouded just for a moment, and then his face smoothed, as if he had put on a mask. He pulled out a second silver bracelet and showed it to Jason. "If you are to join her, you must agree to a year of service to the Elenil in exchange for your heart's desire."

"No. I'd make a terrible servant and a worse soldier. How about I agree to come to the Sunlit Lands, but no guarantees on any service or allegiance or anything like that. In exchange I get a unicorn."

The stranger shook his head. "Of what use is that pledge? We give you entrance to utopia in exchange for a unicorn? They are war beasts, in any case, and not given to civilians."

"Aha! So you admit you have unicorns! Okay. New deal. I get to ride a unicorn. And in exchange I live among you for a year."

"It won't do. You asked to own a unicorn, so clearly to ride one is less than your heart's desire. The archon and the magistrates would punish me for such a bargain. Though I must admit many would find you entertaining, and perhaps you are meant to join us. Still, it is a frivolous vow to make. Especially when sealed with the power of the Crescent Stone."

It hadn't occurred to Jason that Hanali might not take him. The thought of Madeline going alone made him feel sick. He thought of his sister, Jenny. He thought of his failure. He needed to go with Madeline. To make sure there was someone with her, whatever happened. "Final offer. I pledge allegiance to Madeline. Whatever she tells me to do, I do. In exchange, I get my non-unicorn-related heart's desire."

Hanali touched his fingers to his mouth. "It might suffice. For if Madeline is pledged to the Elenil, and you to her, then are you not in some sense pledged to them?" Hanali stepped closer, peering into Jason's face. "And I sense in you a deep sorrow. Perhaps it is sufficient to meet the conditions necessary to come to the Sunlit Lands. So be it. What shall your payment be?"

Jason paused. It felt dangerous to share anything real. And the things he wanted most, well, honestly, even if it was in this weirdo's power, he didn't think it would end well. "I really like those hospital pudding cups."

Hanali's eyes widened. "A pudding cup?"

"One pudding cup a day," Jason said. "In the morning, at breakfast, when God intended pudding to be eaten."

Hanali looked at Jason warily, as if sensing a trap. "One pudding cup a day, in the morning, for the duration of your human year in the Sunlit Lands."

Jason looked at Hanali as if he had said something insane. "For the rest of my life," he said.

Confusion flitted across Hanali's face. He didn't understand the request, didn't know if he was being played in some way. Good. Let him wonder.

Hanali weighed the bracelets in his gloved hand.

"Now or never," Jason said. "I know it's a lot of pudding—"

Hanali grimaced and held out the bracelets. "The deal is struck," he said.

Jason reached for the bracelets, then paused.

Hanali raised an eyebrow.

"*Chocolate* pudding," Jason said. "Don't try to pull a fast one with that fake vanilla stuff."

"Yes, yes, infuriating child, chocolate pudding. The deal is struck. Will you make me say it thrice?"

Jason shook the bracelets together. They were cold, like they had been in a freezer. "Deal."

Hanali scowled and lightly touched Jason's arm. He leaned close to the priest. "What is this man's name?" Hanali examined his face. "He has a familiar look." He sniffed experimentally. "There's a whiff of smoke to his life, don't you think?"

"I don't know. I randomly bumped into him."

Hanali studied Jason's face, looking for a lie. "Randomly. Hmm. What a strange creature you are." He straightened and put his arms behind his back. "Once your friend has her bracelet, you must follow the way to the Sunlit Lands. She won't be permanently healed right away. The magic responds to intention. So long as she is moving toward fulfilling her promise, her breathing will improve."

"How will we know the way? Is it over on Fifth Street? There's weird stuff over there."

"The way will open if you follow," Hanali said. "It is a narrow path. You may need to leave certain things behind." He hesitated. "Or certain people."

A jolt went through Jason. He had forgotten Darius. He would want to go too, Jason knew. He would insist on it. "Wait—"

"The deal is struck," Hanali said. "The bargain final." Then the Elenil man disappeared, and time flowed in around Jason like water in a tide pool.

"—you must not make a deal with Hanali under any circumstances," the priest finished.

Jason pulled away and flashed the two bracelets at the priest. "Too late."

The priest's mouth gaped open. "He was here? Hanali?"

"Yeah," Jason said, and he slid one of the cold bracelets over his left hand. It constricted like a snake around his wrist, digging in deep until it felt like it would break his bones. Jason gasped and leaned on the old priest for support. Then there was a sound, a pop, and it disappeared into his skin, leaving only a silver-looking tattoo with a glowing circle where the clouded gem had been.

"Oh no. My child. What have you done?" Tears slid down the old man's cheeks. He helped Jason straighten, and the left sleeve of his black jacket pulled up, revealing a shiny mess of old scars. The scars crisscrossed and spun around his wrist in a pattern similar to the silver tattoo on Jason's own wrist.

"She can't *breathe*," Jason said. "There wasn't another choice."

The priest looked at him sadly. "There is always a choice."

But Jason was already running toward her room. "She'll die without this!"

The priest shouted something, but Jason couldn't hear. The words kept ringing in his ears: *There is always a choice.* But if it ends in death, is that really a choice? Can that even be on the table as a possibility?

No.

Blood rushed to Jason's face.

Definitely not. Not if he was making the call.

Darius was leaning against the wall outside the room. He straightened when he saw Jason. "They won't let me back in," Darius said.

"She needs this," Jason said, panting. He couldn't breathe now, either.

Darius looked skeptical. "This is the bracelet?"

Jason didn't have time to keep explaining everything to Darius, and in the end, did it matter? Darius wasn't going with them. Jason's stomach clenched with guilt. He hadn't meant to make that decision for them, but he had. "Yes, Darius, this is it," he snapped, much more curtly than he had intended. "This is magic jewelry from Hamburger, and it's gonna make Madeline better as soon as we stick it on her left wrist. Then we're going on an adventure to Narnia or whatever, and when she gets back you can figure out if you're going to date. But in the meantime, she can't breathe, so first things first, yeah?"

Darius searched Jason's face. "Narnia?" he asked, with a sort of quiet reverence. He looked at the bracelet, turning it over in his hands. "It's cold."

"Magic," Jason said and showed Darius his wrist.

Darius nodded. "Okay. You open the door. I'll do the rest." Jason yanked the door open, and a nurse came flying over to close it, but Darius dodged the nurse, and then he was soaring toward Madeline like a rocket, the bracelet stretched out in front of him, the silver designs shining in the artificial light.

6

TO THE ENDS
OF THE EARTH

How can I be loyal to the king and disloyal to my beloved friends?
I will never leave you. I will follow you to the ends of the earth.

PRINCE IAN, IN *THE GOLD FIRETHORNS* BY MARY PATRICIA WALL

✛

arius saved her. Whatever came later, that was something to remember. It was Darius who saved her life.

The room was crowded with people in scrubs and the blaring screams of the machines, the clipped orders from the doctor, the quick replies of the nurses. Darius burst in, spinning past the nurse who stepped in front of him. He danced through the crowd of medical people until he arrived on the left side of her bed and slipped the bracelet onto her wrist.

The bracelet did nothing for a terrifying three seconds.

Then it tightened.

It kept tightening until it was cutting into her skin. She gasped, and then the burning started. The bracelet seared her like it had been in an oven. It glowed furnace bright. Just when she thought she couldn't bear it, the bracelet cooled. On her left wrist was the latticework of a silver tattoo, and the clouded jewel had grown to the size of a watch's face, glowing beneath her skin.

And she could breathe.

The sudden burst of oxygen rushed to her head, and a dizzy wave of giddiness washed over her. She was breathing again, gulping in the sterile, cool hospital air. She wrapped her arms around Darius and felt his strong arms encircle her, almost lifting her from the bed.

The doctors pulled him away. Someone called for security, and Madeline tried to object, but she was so shocked she couldn't speak. She just kept breathing, and for the first time in a long time it felt like she could keep breathing forever, like a normal person, breathe for ten, twenty, seventy years without thinking about it.

A security guard had Darius by the arm and was pulling him out of the room. "Can you breathe?" Darius shouted.

"Yes! Thank you," she said, but it was more whisper than words, and she wasn't sure he heard. She wanted to tell the guard to let him stay, she wanted to explain to the doctors that she was okay now, but she was overwhelmed, confused, and *breathing*. There was scarcely room in her head for anything but that.

A smile like sunlight spread across his face. "I'll wait for you downstairs," he called. "I won't leave."

Tears welled up in her eyes. Darius always said that. *I won't leave.* She knew it was true. He had already stuck with her through some terrible things, and there was no evidence he would stop. It was what Prince Ian said to Lily in *The Gold Firethorns*, the third Meselia book: "I will never leave you. I will follow you to the ends of the earth." That's what Darius always said to her. When she first started to get sick. When the diagnosis came. When she couldn't stand the thought of seeing another doctor's face. *To the ends of the earth.*

She heard Darius scuffling with the security guard until the door closed, muffling the sound. She laid her head on the stiff hospital pillow.

Madeline's head throbbed where it had hit the classroom floor, but her lungs felt brand new. She could run a marathon. She could do jumping jacks or swim or dance or sing at the top of her lungs or yell at someone and still she could breathe!

The doctors ran tests. Tested her oxygen levels. Listened to her lungs. They didn't have much to say. They weren't sure what had happened, but in the past her lung capacity had seemed to come and go. They wanted to keep her for observation. Given what had happened with Darius barging in, they said no one else could come in until her parents arrived. No one mentioned the bracelet. They didn't comment on the tattoo. It's like they hadn't seen that part, had only noticed a high school boy bursting into the room, hugging her, and being dragged away.

But between nurse visits, Jason slipped in. He had a pudding cup in one hand and a silver tattoo on his other wrist. "People say tattoos hurt, but I barely felt this one."

"You have one too?" Relief flooded her. She wouldn't have to go alone.

"Your friend Handy gave it to me. I figured I'd put mine on today to guarantee we'd go together to the Sunshine Place."

Madeline looked at Jason. "What did you promise to him? What are you giving up?"

Jason shrugged. "I get to go with you, and they give me snacks."

Madeline's stomach dropped. "Jason . . . you're leaving behind your life for a year. You don't . . . You don't have to do that."

The edges of Jason's lips twitched up. "I would have flunked chemistry without a partner anyway. Might as well take a gap year."

"But your parents—"

Jason didn't let her finish. "Are going to be fine, if not happy to see me gone."

Madeline couldn't imagine that was true. Picturing Jason's parents and their grief somehow made it more real. Her parents would be going through the same trauma.

"Are my parents here yet?"

Jason shook his head. "Darius texted them, though."

If her dad was in a meeting, he wouldn't look at his phone for hours at a time, and her mom often left hers in the car. "I guess we can wait to leave until they get here? Do you want to say good-bye to your parents?"

Jason shook his head. "Hanali said that unless we 'start our journey' the magic stops working. Like, if the magic thinks you're not going to follow through, it takes away your breathing. We should get going soon."

Now that he mentioned it, she did notice a hitch in her breathing. So slight, and so small compared to what she had been living with up until now, but definitely there. She took a deep breath—amazing that she could do that again—and reflected on leaving home. This was going to be hard. She couldn't imagine missing her birthday, missing Christmas and Thanksgiving and a hundred other little family traditions. But, she reminded herself, she probably wouldn't have made it to Christmas anyway. She needed to set aside the chaotic mess of excitement and fear and sadness and confusion and loss, and get ready. Maybe she could send a message to her parents, although she didn't think they'd believe it for a second. Still. It was time to go. "Close the curtain," she said to Jason.

He pulled the curtain shut around the bed.

"With you on the other side, dummy," she said. "I'm going to get dressed."

Jason blushed and disappeared through the curtain.

Her shoes and socks were in a bag hanging on the end of her bed, but the rest of her clothes were gone. Right. They had cut her out of her clothes. It had been an emergency, they had been moving fast. She put on her socks and sneakers. "You can come back in," she said.

Jason looked at her hospital gown. "Bold fashion statement," he said. "I like the shoes."

Madeline wrapped a blanket around her back. She slipped the oxygen tube out of her nose, something she had done a hundred times before. Hopefully this would be the last time. "I'll need help getting the IV out."

Jason looked at her arm, his face pale. "Maybe I should go find some clothes for you."

He disappeared, and the sound of the door clicking shut echoed in the small room.

Fine. She didn't need his help. She peeled up the edges of the tape on her inner elbow and pulled both sides toward the center. The needle bit deep. She wasn't sure how to turn off the drip or if there was some special way to pull out the needle. She grabbed the base of it, her hand shaking, and with the smoothest motion she could muster, pulled the needle away from her arm.

She gasped. It was out, still drooling liquid onto the floor. A pinprick of blood welled up. A quick rifle through the bedside drawers produced a small piece of cotton, which she put over the wound. She found a roll of colored Coban to wrap around her arm and bit the edge to tear it.

Jason ducked under the curtain with some folded green scrubs. His shirt had brown stains dripping down the front.

"What happened?" she asked.

"I spilled chocolate pudding all over my shirt and went in the waiting room and started shouting that I was covered in blood and needed a change of clothes." He looked down at his jeans, which were also covered in pudding. "I got you some pants, too. I'll wait outside."

She tugged the pants on. They tied at the waist, so although they were baggy, they would stay up. The top slid on easily. She found a rubber band in the drawers and pulled her hair back, wincing at the tender spot on the back of her head. The strange silver markings of her bracelet tattoo glimmered even under the fake light in the hospital room. The jewel glowed under her skin, but it didn't hurt.

They slipped out of her room and into the elevator. Darius was downstairs in the waiting room. Darius gave Jason a funny look when they came out of the elevator together, but then he was wrapping Madeline in his arms. She leaned into the hug, thankful for him, thankful he was here and had brought her the bracelet, and glad that, for a moment at least, this seemed uncomplicated and normal.

"Did they release you already?" he asked. "Shouldn't they do some more tests?"

Madeline squeezed his hand. "Darius. There aren't more tests. We know everything there is to know."

He lowered his head, a look she had seen too often on his face since her diagnosis. "Okay," he said. "I know that. Can I give you a ride home?"

A sharp pain came from the bracelet. "I can't go home." The whole story came pouring out. Darius held her hand loosely, his eyes on hers the entire time she spoke, but he didn't speak until she was done.

"So the magic works?"

She lifted her left hand so he could see the silver network of tattoos. "A hundred percent."

Darius's face filled with wonder. "Madeline, it's everything we dreamed about. It's just like *The Gryphon under the Stairs*."

She nodded, smiling. "Finally something is working. There really is magic."

"So we're going to fight these—what are they called again?"

"Scim."

"We're going to fight the Scim, and in a year we're coming back."

Madeline pulled her hand away when he said "we." Of course he would say that. But there was no guarantee he could come . . . He hadn't made a deal. He hadn't seen Hanali.

Jason said, "I don't think you have a ticket." He held up the silver tattoo on his wrist.

"I'm coming," Darius said, glaring at Jason.

"Darius," Madeline said. "Your parents—"

"We'll be back in a year," Darius said.

Jason was getting nervous. "Can we take this outside before someone comes looking for the kid who checked herself out of the hospital?"

Madeline led them out to the street. She walked with purpose, away from the automatic doors and toward 23rd Street. Darius paced beside her, and Jason brought up the rear, his hands in his pockets, his shirt and jeans still covered in pudding. She knew Darius wouldn't be able to go. She felt it, as deep and certain as the magic moving through her. That was how it worked. She had read all the books. Darius didn't see Hanali, Darius didn't make a deal, Darius wouldn't be able to cross into the Sunlit Lands. That didn't mean they couldn't try, but . . . She tried to think of a way to make it noble, make it helpful for him to stay.

"I need someone to explain all of this to my parents," she said.

Darius laughed. "Your parents will call the cops if I tell them this."

"I could leave a note with you. Or send them a text." But her phone was still at the school, in her backpack. Her tattoo twinged, and Jason gave a yelp at the same moment. She knew which way to go, sort of—it seemed to be almost pulling her off the main street, down a narrow alley. "You're right," Madeline said, stepping around a dank puddle. "Don't tell them anything. I don't want you to get in trouble."

"How about I just come with you? Then this won't be an issue at all."

"Okay," Madeline said, exhausted. "Come with us." Darius winced when she said "us."

The bracelet was guiding them into an old neighborhood. If she went too slow, her breath started to go ragged. She moved quickly, following it toward the end of a long cul-de-sac.

A chain-link fence surrounded a low spot where long grass grew in a slight depression. All the neighborhood's runoff water eventually came through here. No one stirred in the neighborhood. No one opened a door or looked out a window. A hummingbird sat on the fence, chirping. That was weird. She hadn't noticed a hummingbird doing that before, and it seemed larger than usual. She thought back to the bird that had been talking to the woman in her garden. Could it be the same one? Could the Garden Lady have sent it?

Madeline rubbed her chin. "I think . . . we're supposed to climb this fence."

Jason groaned. "Tell me we're not about to crawl through a drainage ditch." He wrapped his fingers through the chain-link fence and pressed his face against it. "Ugh, I can smell it from here."

"I'll go first," Darius said, but when he put his hands on the fence, a brilliant flash of light knocked him backward. He lay on the ground, smoke rising from his clothes.

Madeline's heart leapt into her throat. She ran to Darius and knelt beside him. She helped him sit up. "Are you okay?"

"Electric fence?" Darius asked, still dazed.

"I'm still holding onto it," Jason said.

The hummingbird chirped and flew to the other side of the fence, zipping back and forth in a strange, almost hypnotic pattern.

"We should come back with a ladder," Darius said.

Madeline considered this, but her breath went immediately ragged. "I can't wait."

Darius frowned. "I always told you I'd follow you to the ends of the earth."

Madeline smiled and pulled him into a warm embrace. In *The Gold Firethorns*, Lily betrays the Eagle King. Ian, Prince of the North, escorts her to the edge of Meselia after she is banished. In one of Madeline's favorite moments of the whole series, he lays his crown down at the border and steps across with her. He says, "How can I be loyal to the king and disloyal to my beloved friends? I will never leave you. I will follow you to the ends of the earth."

Madeline leaned back so she could see Darius's face. "But do you remember what happens in the story?"

Darius nodded, a frown returning to his face. "Lily sends Ian back to serve King Kartal, and she heads into the wilderness alone. He watches her disappear into the mist, and the people call him Prince Ian the Sorrowful in the years to come."

"Except I'll only be gone a year," Madeline said. "And when I come back . . . things will be normal again."

Darius squeezed her shoulder. "That's not how it works, Maddie. You don't go away for a year and come home to 'normal.' You come back and . . . you come back and everything has changed."

She didn't answer him, because she knew he was right. She stood, and he stood beside her. "So I guess this is the ends of the earth," she said.

"On the bright side," Jason said, still at the fence, "she'll be fighting evil monsters during that year. So. There's that."

Darius frowned. "How is that a bright side?"

Jason shrugged. "Monsters are bad. Somebody's gotta fight 'em."

"Ignore him," Madeline said. She pulled Darius's forehead against hers. "I'll miss you," she said. "But a year from now I'll be able to breathe. I'll be able to live life again."

Darius sighed. A deep, resigned sound. "It's only a year," he said.

"Tell my parents . . . Tell them something. Tell them I'm okay." She shook her head. "Or don't tell them anything, I don't know what's best. Do what you think is right, Darius."

"I know the right thing to do already. I'm going to find a way to come to you," Darius said, and she knew it was true that he would try.

One more hug for Darius, as long as she dared, until her breathing started to go ragged. When she stepped away from him and toward the fence, her breath returned.

Jason stood near the fence. He cupped his hands into a stirrup. "I'll boost you."

Madeline laughed and leapt onto the fence. She slung herself over and dropped to the ground on the other side. She could breathe. She'd never need help to jump or run or scale a fence again.

Jason, on the other hand, appeared to have never climbed a fence in his life. She tried to coach him, and he fell off twice. Eventually Madeline leapt back over the fence and cupped *her* hands into a stirrup. She boosted Jason to the top, and he made his way to the other side with the help of a missed rung and gravity.

"I did it!" he shouted. "King of the world!"

They grinned at each other. Madeline looked back to Darius, but the world on the other side of the fence looked grey and sluggish, like a video in slow motion, covered with a thick fog.

"Magic?" she asked.

"No turning back now, I guess," Jason said, but that had never been a real possibility. Madeline shouted good-bye to Darius and told him they were safe, but he moved so slowly she couldn't tell if he heard. She wrapped her fingers in the chain-link fence, trying to see him more clearly, but the fog only grew thicker. She could barely see him now. Madeline whispered another good-bye. The space between them had already begun to grow.

The hummingbird zipped in front of her face, and she spun to watch it, but she couldn't see where it had gone. She didn't think the bird had crossed outside the fence. The drainage area wasn't huge, but it was clear of fog, and there wasn't another way out that they could see. A cement pipe protruded from the ground, just big enough that Madeline could crawl in on her hands and knees. A sludge of accumulated mud coated the bottom. A flicker of light came from far down the pipe.

"Do you think this . . . ?"

"I absolutely do not," Jason said, but she knew this was the way. Of course it was.

They stared at it for a full five minutes, neither of them speaking. Her breathing didn't change, but she knew. "I have to," she said at last.

Jason shook his head. "There's no way Hanali crawled through there."

The hummingbird appeared between them, then darted into the pipe. A chirp echoed back. Madeline glanced at Jason. "You saw that, right?"

"I did not see that," Jason said, crossing his arms.

Madeline put her hand on the lip of the pipe. She wrinkled her nose. A dank smell of ancient, decayed leaves and old mud came from the darkness. But there was light farther down. She could see it now for sure. She took a deep breath, thankful once more that she could breathe at all, and crawled into the tunnel. The mud squished beneath her hands and knees, but she moved steadily forward. She felt a lightness, a relief to be moving in the right direction. She would miss Darius, and her family, and her friends, but she was glad to be moving, to be breathing, to be headed toward health and freedom. If only Darius could have come.

From somewhere behind her Jason said, "Seriously. Hanali would never get his costume dirty like this."

She smiled, glad for Jason's company, and crawled steadily toward the dim light ahead.

7

UNDERGROUND

In great need may ye return to the Sunlit Lands,
for ye are our cousins and neighbors.

FROM "THE ORDERING OF THE WORLD," AN ELENIL STORY

✛

J ason had never followed a hummingbird into a disgusting sewer before, and so far he did not like it. He suspected he would pass on future opportunities. It stank like something had died, then been eaten, digested, and expelled, and then died again. The stench climbed right up into your nose and just lay there.

The pipe narrowed. Crawling became difficult. "I feel like a snake," Jason said and immediately regretted it. *Please let there not be snakes in here.* His arms were folded under his chest, and he moved himself along with his fingers and toes. He felt like he was having trouble breathing, but it was just good old-fashioned panic.

"You'll be okay," Madeline said. "Pretend it's a waterslide."

"I'm afraid of waterslides," Jason said.

Madeline scooted ahead of him, also on her belly. All he could see were her sneakers as she pushed forward bit by bit with her toes. All he could hear were Madeline's muffled sounds of exertion and the sucking sound of their bodies moving through the sludge. He bumped into her now and then, or even gave her a push, a process which involved putting his forehead on her heels and wedging forward. She didn't seem to mind. His arms and legs felt like gelatin. He wished someone was shoving him from behind. He wished he wasn't in a pipe at all.

He hoped the name Sunlit Lands was not a euphemism. If they popped out of this tube into a giant sewage factory and Hanali expected them to fight giant sludge monsters or something, he would . . . Well, he didn't know what he would do. Throw a mud ball at Hanali, maybe.

The stench got worse.

"I don't know what you're doing up there," he said. "But it stinks."

Madeline didn't answer. No doubt keeping her mouth shut to prevent anything getting in there. Smart. With every hard-earned inch forward the light intensified, as did the smell of the mud.

"There's a turn in the pipe here," Madeline said. "It's a little tight. Wait—don't push yet."

Jason stopped. He lay his head down at the bottom of the pipe, trying to conserve his strength. Bad choice—now he had mud on his face. *Great. C'mon, Madeline. Keep moving.* He didn't think he could go back the way they'd come. He hoped the pipe didn't narrow any farther, or their year in the Sunlit Lands might be spent in this pipe. Stupid hummingbird.

"I can see the exit," Madeline said. "The pipe slopes down from here. I'm going to lie sideways, and when I say to push, push."

The mud slurped as she wiggled around trying to find a better angle to get herself through the kink in the pipe. "Okay," she said. "Push, but not very—"

Jason pushed with everything he could, his muddy forehead connecting with her muddy sneakers, and there was a slurping pop followed by a high-pitched scream of terror or maybe joy from Madeline. Jason reached for her, but he missed, and he stuck his head around the corner in time to see a blazing circle of light and Madeline sloshing toward it in a river of mud and water.

The pipe widened below (finally!), and Madeline managed to get her arms and legs against the sides of the pipe and stop herself from shooting out the end. "It's the exit!" she called. Her head was silhouetted against the light. "It's a big cave," she said. "Really big, with lots of pipes everywhere. They're all gushing water into a pool below. I can't tell how deep it is, but it looks like it's maybe twenty-five feet down."

Desperately worried he wouldn't be able to get himself around the corner without Madeline's help, and certain that she couldn't get back up the pipe, Jason twisted once, violently, and found himself careening down the pipe on his back, screaming and—as the pipe widened—flailing his limbs. He slid down at roughly the speed of a bowling ball covered in olive oil. He had time to shout half of Madeline's name before knocking into her and carrying them both flying out of the pipe and into the cavern in a confused tangle of limbs.

This is the end of our adventure, he thought. He was glad no one else was there to see him die by barreling down a mudslide out a sewage pipe and into a runoff pond. He felt sorry for the coroner because they both stank so bad.

The water clapped shut over them, and they sank, fast. The water was half mud and revealed little when he opened his eyes. In the thick darkness he saw a white shape nearby—Madeline? He kicked over to her.

What turned its face toward him was not Madeline.

It was a face he might have said was a woman's if not for the sickly white color and the sharp, protruding teeth. The flat, black, pupil-less eyes were another giveaway. She reached for him as he tried to swim away, kicking with all his might.

Her hands were webbed, with black claws where fingernails should be.

His head broke the surface just as the creature's hands closed around his ankle. He shouted for Madeline, who was pulling herself up onto a long metal walkway, then he descended, struggling, toward the bottom of the murky pool. He heard a distant splash, but all he could see was the mermaid thing pulling his face toward its gleaming shark's teeth.

Madeline's fists barreled into the creature with the full force of her dive behind them. It shrieked and lost its grip on him. Jason thrashed, trying to get away, then Madeline kicked off from the creature's midsection, grabbing Jason under the arms as she rocketed upward.

They broke into the air, and Jason drew an enormous, gasping breath. Madeline dragged him out of the water onto the walkway.

"Mermaids," Jason gasped. "I am now afraid of mermaids."

"We should get away from the water as quickly as we can," Madeline said and started across the narrow walkway.

"That was a scary mermaid," Jason said. "Not the nice kind who sings to sailors and then murders them. The mean kind that gets murdery without the music."

Madeline shivered. "Maybe that was a Scim."

"We should have brought some dynamite to throw in all the lakes, then," Jason said. He imagined telling his parents about this when he got home, not that they would want to talk to him. He could practically see the skepticism on his father's face. One thing Jason never understood was how often people assumed he was lying. Since he had started telling the truth about everything, he felt like people should always believe him. Which was funny, because when he'd told lies in the old days, he had always assumed he had to convince people things were true. Now he just expected them to recognize it. But whatever. People were slow to believe in scary mermaids. Fine.

"I don't think we're going to be able to get back up to that pipe," Madeline said. "So I guess we follow this walkway."

The walkway wound through a tunnel large enough for a car. It was a relief not to crawl. No obvious source of light lit the tunnel, but it wasn't dark. After a while the tunnel walls changed from concrete to brick and then from brick to very old brick: hand mortared and brown with age, half the size of a regular brick, thin and long.

Madeline walked in front, her fingers running along the bricks.

"Hey," Jason said. "Something's written on there."

They paused to look. Chinese characters were scratched into some of the bricks. "That's strange," Madeline said. "Can you read them?"

"Well, it's complex characters, not the simplified ones. But yeah, I can read a lot of them. It's people's names. Maybe the people who laid the bricks?"

Madeline ran her fingers across one of the names. "How old do you think these are?"

Jason grinned. "I'd say these come from sometime between 1850 and 1882."

Madeline's eyes widened. "How can you be so certain?"

They started to walk again, side by side now. "Chinese immigration to the US started mostly in the 1850s . . . people trying to get in on the gold rush. Then they stuck around to do whatever made money: farming, construction, stuff like that. Chinese Americans built most of the railroads, you know."

"I knew that, more or less," Madeline said. "But why 1882?"

"You never heard this before? That's the year of the Chinese Exclusion Act, when the US government made it illegal for Chinese people to immigrate to the United States."

Madeline stopped. "When they *what*?"

Jason shrugged. "Yeah. It was a mess. My great-grandpa, he got separated from his family. They couldn't come to the United States . . . They thought the ban would lift and they could get back together, but, well, it didn't."

"That doesn't make any sense," Madeline said. "So it was only the Chinese—"

"People were worried they were taking jobs away. You know, like laying steel for the railroads or laying bricks in creepy underground magical sewers. The kind of work no one else wanted anyway."

Madeline stopped, hands on her hips. "Maybe you heard the story wrong. It's just . . . it's un-American. What about the poem on the Statue of Liberty about the—how does it go? Bring the weary to me?"

Jason kicked a stone, and it went skittering ahead of them down the tunnel. "The Chinese didn't come in past the Statue of Liberty. Or not many of them. Most of them came in through Angel Island, in California. It was a different experience."

"I'm sure Ellis Island wasn't exactly fun," Madeline said. "Lots of people came through with their names misspelled, or had harsh things said to them."

"That's actually a myth about the name-change thing," Jason said. "But anyway, the average person made it through Ellis in a few hours. A quick physical exam, a couple questions, and you were on your way. People were commonly at Angel Island at least a few days. The longest recorded time someone was held there was twenty-two months. Only direct family members of US citizens were allowed in. And unlike all the English and Polish and Irish and whoever coming in through Ellis, they actually checked the answers of the Chinese and other Asian immigrants against the answers given by their family in the US. If they couldn't track them down, you had to stay until they could. If your answer looked like it might not be quite the same, they'd send you back. People were packed into small barracks with no mattresses, or kept in cells, while they waited to find out if they'd be allowed entry. I'm not saying everyone who went through Ellis had an amazing time, but on average they had it better than anyone going through Angel Island."

"I've never heard of this."

Jason shrugged. "A lot of people haven't."

Madeline started to say something, then closed her mouth. It was fine. He didn't expect her to know this sort of thing. It's not like they talked about it at school. Where would she learn about it? He wondered if he would have learned about it if it hadn't affected his own family, once upon a time. He wasn't surprised she didn't believe it at first, either. He remembered the day he had learned that it had been illegal for Chinese people to come into the United States all the way until 1943, and they changed that only because of World War II, and then it was only like a hundred Chinese people a year. That didn't change until the sixties . . . Eighty years of few or no Chinese people allowed into the States.

"Hopefully the immigration rules in the Sunlit Lands are a little nicer to Chinese Americans," Jason said, trying for a joke.

But Madeline didn't laugh. She seemed troubled.

Eventually the old bricks gave way to natural stone, as if someone had carved the tunnel through a mountain. Madeline stopped and put her hand on the last of the carved names. "I'm glad they came," she said.

Jason grinned at her. "Yeah, otherwise you'd be covered in stinky mud and walking through a tunnel alone."

She punched him in the arm, and they kept walking. *It's fine she didn't know*, he said to himself again. It was fine, but it made him sad.

The tunnel spilled out into a forest. Green light filtered through the trees, but they could still see patches of the cavern ceiling above them, a bright-grey sky illuminated by some unseen source. "Impossible," Madeline said, turning to take in all of this underground forest. A dark canopy of leaves overhead blocked most of the ceiling. Vines snaked up the trees, enormous leaves turned toward the canopy. Thick brush obscured the ground. A narrow path forced its way forward, making a round tunnel through the branches which arced over the packed dirt. Roots burst through the soil, piling over each other, wrapping each other, intertwining across the dirt path.

"They're making it hard enough to get to the Sunlit Lands," Madeline said. "I thought we'd just step into a magic painting or something."

"Instead we have to go *hiking*."

"I hope Darius is okay."

Jason snorted. "At least there aren't any evil mermaids where he is."

She stepped onto the path. "I don't think we should wander off the trail," she said.

"Me neither," Jason said. The sudden change from tunnel to underground forest creeped him out. He was standing much too close to Madeline. She gave him a look. He shrugged. "I get clingy when I'm scared, so sue me."

"Come on, you big baby," she said, holding out her hand. He took it without comment, and they stepped onto the trail.

Soon the path got too narrow for them to hold hands. They hiked in silence for an hour. At one point, something crashed through the underbrush to their left.

"That sounded big," Madeline said.

"Probably just an old refrigerator," Jason said. That was the safest big thing that jumped to mind. Yup, just an old refrigerator, wandering the underground forest, looking for someone to open it so they could have some refreshments. That's the kind of magical creature Jason could get on board with. Whatever it was, they never saw it. No birds sang in this forest, though once or twice Jason thought he saw the hummingbird ahead of them, flitting among the branches.

By the time they came to the clearing, the forest had begun to darken. A bonfire burned in the center of the open space, casting strange shadows on the enormous trees. Trails radiated out into the forest, like spokes centered around the fire, trees lining them like columns.

Madeline gasped and grabbed Jason's forearm, pointing to some people near the fire. She gestured for him to be silent. Made sense to Jason. Might be wise to check these people out, in case they were crazy land mermaids or something. They crouched behind a bush and studied the clearing.

Five people hunched around the fire, three adults and two children. Humans, as far as Jason could tell. All five of them had tan skin, with blonde hair that hung in greasy knots from their heads. The man wore only a pair of jeans. He held a long hand-cut walking stick. The women wore shorts and loose sleeveless shirts. One of the women wore shoes, a pair of muddy white sneakers, but none of the others did.

As for the children, the girl's hair was combed down over her face. The boy wore nothing but filthy shorts and a featureless wooden mask made of bark. Two small holes had been cut out for his eyes. He carried a long stick in one hand. Jason shuddered. Something about the kid was unsettling. Probably the bark mask. Definitely the bark mask.

The girl didn't look up or uncover her face, but in a dull monotone she asked, "What are your names?"

Jason winced. "Maybe they're not talking to us," he whispered.

Madeline hesitated, then said, "I'm Madeline Oliver."

"Stand here beside the fire," the girl said, still in a monotone.

Madeline stood and stepped into the clearing. Jason stayed at her elbow. His gaze flickered among the strange collection of people around the fire. "I think I'd rather fight the mermaid."

The man's attention snapped onto Jason. "You fought Malgwin?"

"*Fight* is a strong word," Jason said. "More like . . . let her try to drown me? Madeline punched her, though."

The man glanced at the boy in the mask. The boy said, "Go." The man jumped to his feet, staff in hand, and hurried back the way Madeline and Jason had come.

"Your name," the girl said again.

"Jason Wu."

The girl nodded. "Madeline is expected. The boy must stay with us."

Jason balled his hands into fists. "The boy?! I'm older than you." He took two steps toward the fire. The women pulled small, silver knives from their belts. "Uh. I mean. You can call me boy if you want."

"We go together," Madeline said. "Hanali sent for us."

One of the women spit into the fire. The girl shook her head. "Jason Wu is not a name we have been given. You must go ahead alone, or turn back together."

Jason thought back to the Chinese names on the bricks. No one ever got his name right. Never. That's the whole reason he went by Jason. So he said his real name. "I'm Wu Song."

The women watched Jason carefully. "Why did you try to pass with a false name? Are you a Scim spy? This passage is only for allies of the Elenil."

"Peace, Sister, he doesn't have the look of the Scim."

"There are magics for such things," the first woman said.

"No matter," said the girl, and they both fell silent. "Wu Song is expected. They may pass. My brother will show you the path you must take."

The boy stood, his bark mask regarding them for a long moment. Then, without a word, he turned and walked into the forest. Madeline followed, with Jason close behind. One of the women took the final position in their procession. Jason wondered if she was there to keep them from running the other way.

The masked boy led them on a winding path that ended at a ten-foot-tall round metal door, which hung in front of them with no visible means of support. A spinner, like the wheel on a bank vault, jutted from the middle. "You have agreed to the terms," the boy said. "One human year of service in exchange for what has been promised you. Do you enter into this agreement willingly and without coercion?"

"It's too late to turn back," Madeline said.

The bark mask tilted. "It is not too late. With this staff I can smash the jewel of your bracelet, undoing the agreement. If you wish to be free, only say the word."

There wasn't much choice here. Without the magic, Madeline wouldn't be able to breathe. Part of Jason wanted to go back, because of the forest and especially because of this kid with the creepy mask. Madeline was looking at him, and he thought of his sister. If he walked away, he wouldn't ever forgive himself. Again.

"I'm willing," he said.

Madeline echoed him, a profoundly grateful look on her face.

Jason tapped the kid with the mask on the shoulder. Best way to hide your fear was a joke. At least, he always thought so. "I should have mentioned that I like my pudding cups slightly chilled. Is it too late to add that to the agreement?" The boy just stared at him from behind the bark mask. "Never mind," Jason said.

The boy wedged his stick high into the wheel, jumped, and yanked it toward the ground. The wheel turned, and the metal door opened. "You have come to the Sunlit Lands," the boy said.

A series of bright, slender trees greeted them. They had yellow, almost golden, leaves and shining white bark. Jason held up his hand to shield his eyes from the dazzling sunshine. Hanali stood there in resplendent white embroidered clothes shot through with gold thread, his hands covered in lace and resting on a small walking cane. The color of the roses in his clothes had changed—they were now a deep crimson. His walking cane had roses on it too, but these appeared to be actual roses, their vines curving in on themselves to form his cane.

Jason and Madeline stepped through the doorway and into the Sunlit Lands.

At Hanali's feet was a gilded birdcage with two bright-plumed birds inside. They almost looked like parrots. Hanali motioned to the boy with the bark mask. "Two have entered, two may leave. If you wish."

The boy with the mask turned and looked at the woman. She shook her head. "Together, or not at all. We have told you this many times."

Hanali tipped open the door of the cage, and the two birds flew out joyously, through the round door and into the woods beneath the sewer. "So be it," Hanali said. "Spin the wheel well when you lock the door." The boy and the woman pulled the door, both of them leaning backward. It closed with a monstrous boom. Hanali took hold of the birdcage and shook it once, and it collapsed to the size of a matchbook. He slipped it into his coat pocket and looked them over. "You are both filthy, though you have all your limbs. All in all, a pleasant passage, it seems."

Jason's mouth fell open. "Was that mermaid going to *eat our arms*?"

Hanali cocked his head. "Mermaid?"

"Scary lady who lives underwater with green hair and shark teeth."

The Elenil raised one eyebrow. "You can't mean Malgwin, certainly."

"That's what they called her, yes," Madeline said.

Hanali tapped his cane in the dirt. He didn't look at them and spoke almost to himself, as if lost in thought. "Strange. She rarely leaves the Sea Beneath. She is not, however, a mermaid. She is half woman and half fish. It is strange indeed that she would show interest in the two of you."

"Where we come from, a half-woman, half-fish person is called a mermaid," Jason said.

Hanali pulled at the lace on his sleeves. "Is that so? An interesting bit of trivia from your world."

"Why do you play with that lace all the time? Maybe you should trim it off."

"A nervous habit," Hanali said, dropping his hands. "Perhaps it was the mention of Malgwin that set me to arranging my cuffs."

"Madeline punched her in the face and kicked her in the stomach," Jason said.

A slight smile tugged at the edges of Hanali's mouth. "I would have liked to have seen that. But no matter. You are both here now, and safe. Step over here, and I will show you something wonderful."

Hanali walked through a small grove of trees which led to the edge of a cliff. He leaned against a white-barked tree and gestured with his gloved hand. Jason and Madeline came up to the edge, and Madeline gasped. Jason looked at her, then Hanali. Both of them were staring into the distance, smiling. He looked straight down and saw stones and bush scrub and a long fall. From there a wide, flat plain stretched away from the cliff. In the distance, Jason saw what had captivated Madeline.

It was a city unlike any Jason had ever seen. Tall white towers rose from the corners, with crimson flags flying in the breeze. A low wall, smooth and white, encircled the city, and behind the wall trees grew and fountains splashed and pastel-colored houses leaned together in unstudied camaraderie. A hill rose gently in the center of the city, streets festooned it like flowers, and beautiful alabaster buildings wound alongside the streets like precious jewels. A wide river flowed from the city and toward them, and Jason could see its clear, babbling water as it passed them and watered the wood. The central tower held a massive purple stone, easily visible from this distance, which radiated energy like a lighthouse.

"I'm awake," Jason said. "I'm awake." His whole life he had been told what the limits of possibility were, and he had just discovered that everything he had been told was a lie. This city, white and glorious, made him believe that there was good in the world. If this was the home of the Elenil, he didn't need to make a deal to serve them. He wanted to protect a people who could make something so beautiful. He wanted to know about their art, their politics, their social structures, their belief systems. Because if they could make a city like this, they could do anything. He couldn't wait to walk down those streets, to see those fountains, to put his hands against the white walls.

"It's gorgeous," Madeline said. Tears were running down her face. "It's everything I ever imagined, in all the books I read, all the fantasy paintings, all the movies. It's the most beautiful city I've ever seen."

Hanali smiled. "The Court of Far Seeing. It is the capital and greatest work of the Elenil. It will be your home during your time with us. Within a fortnight it will be so deeply in your heart that you may not wish to leave. Do you see the symbol of our power atop the main tower? All that we have accomplished these several centuries has been made possible because of the Crescent Stone. Come. My carriage awaits. I will take you to your housing." He took a deep breath, enjoying the view. "Truly, it is an unparalleled place."

Jason cleared his throat. Things were getting a little too emotional. "Does it have indoor plumbing, though?" Hanali glared at him. "What? It's a legitimate question." They walked back toward the door that had brought them into the Sunlit Lands. A rounded carriage, pure white and carved with intricate patterns, arrived beside them. A human teen wearing a white wig drove the coach, and white horses pulled it, four of them, with not a spot of another color, not a single hair out of place.

The coachman opened the door and, with a flourish, invited them to climb aboard. "But the mud," Madeline said, looking at the perfect white silk on the pillowed interior, then to her own disgusting hospital scrubs.

"The smell is unfortunate," Hanali admitted, "but the mud itself is easily cleaned. Climb aboard and be at ease. I would usually have clothes and a bath waiting for you here, but we have been on an accelerated schedule. I didn't expect to invite you so soon, but with your delicate health . . . In any case, my apologies for not being properly prepared to receive you."

Jason shrugged. The worst of the mud had washed away when they fell into the water under the pipe, and their clothes were dry after the long walk through the forest.

"It's okay," Madeline said. She stepped in first, facing forward, and Hanali sat beside her. Jason flopped onto the opposite side.

"Don't you want to watch the city?" Madeline asked. She stuck her head out the window. "The trees! It's like the sunshine is coming out through their leaves. It's so beautiful!" She took a deep, deep breath.

A sudden fatigue washed over Jason. Was it only this morning he had carried her into the hospital? He looked down and saw that his hands were shaking. She could have died. She could have died right there on the floor of their chemistry room, and now here she was, her face kissed by the golden sun of another world. He shivered. If he hadn't carried her to the car, if he hadn't spoken up, if he hadn't driven like a maniac bank robber, she would be—well, he knew how a story like that ended. He knew it all too well. A heavy cold seeped into his limbs, and he closed his eyes. "Wake me when we get there," he said.

"Welcome to the Sunlit Lands," Hanali said, but Jason pretended not to hear.

8
ROOMMATES

✛

Hanali had ordered Madeline to stay in the coach, but his argument with the woman in the courtyard seemed to be about her. They had made easy time to the beautiful city of Far Seeing (properly called the Court of Far Seeing, according to Hanali). They traveled more than an hour, first down from the mountain and then through wide farmland. Farmers walked through the fields behind strange purplish beasts of burden, shaggy things with four long, curved horns. Their coach passed long citrus groves and orderly rows of some sort of berry—purple, plump, and round.

Madeline's heart felt like a helium balloon on an enormous tether. She floated above everything, taking it in, loving it all. She didn't know if it was the increase in oxygen or the fantastical world that matched every book she had ever read, but she felt almost giddy, like a kid waiting in line for a favorite roller coaster. She leaned out the window, taking deep breaths of the air and trying not to giggle uncontrollably at every wonderful thing.

At last they had come to the city walls. Everything about the place was amazing, even the traffic. Not ten minutes ago a woman in a bright-red dress and an enormous floppy hat had ridden by on a gigantic ostrich. Elephants decorated in long silks carried people in curtained rooms upon their backs. They had passed a fountain near the main gate where the falling water landed in crystal bowls that played different tones as the water struck them. The fountain sang a tune Hanali called "The Triumph of Ele and Nala." It was a beautiful, soaring thing, but he wouldn't allow the coach to stop for her to listen. She had reached out her hand, though, and when a bit of the water sprayed her fingers she had whooped so loud it woke Jason momentarily.

She knew she should miss Darius. She should be worried about her parents. She should be afraid of what was to come, of fighting the Scim and learning to live in a new world. But she didn't feel any of those things. She felt *happy*. All her life she had wanted something like this: horses and fantastical beasts and elves and mermaids and evil monsters to battle . . . and here she was, and how could she be anything but deliriously, uncontrollably happy?

In time they had come to a smaller wall surrounding a large country estate. It was on the outskirts of the city, just inside the wall. A human woman had come out to greet them, dressed as a kitchen maid, but now she was clearly giving Hanali a rough time.

Jason still snored on the opposite side of the carriage.

Madeline stepped lightly out of the carriage and walked toward Hanali and the woman, hiding behind a hedge which was covered in beautiful orange flowers. She couldn't just sit there in the carriage, not when there was an entire new world to explore. A fresh scent floated in the air, as if someone had scraped the skin of a ripe tangerine. She took a deep whiff, delighted.

"—telling you this is the girl who will bring justice for the people of the Sunlit Lands. Multiple far-seers have said so. She's going to save us, do you understand?" Hanali's voice had taken on an almost pleading tone. Surprising, coming from him.

The woman crossed her arms. When she spoke, Madeline noticed her British accent. "Oh, fine then. I suppose I'll have Scim trying to break into my place to murder her."

Hanali hesitated. "That may be."

Madeline gasped. This was not the story she had been told. This was the first she had heard about any prophecy, and definitely the first she had heard about the Scim trying to assassinate her. Her good mood deflated. Something about seeing this woman, who seemed solid and dependable and, well, ordinary . . . Something about seeing her and hearing her concerns about the Scim reminded Madeline of the seriousness of her situation. And listening to Hanali's story, a story she did not recognize, made her realize she may have come here in the company of someone who had a completely different agenda than the one he claimed.

"—ask the magistrates to provide protection, but I tell you this, Mrs. Raymond, that I won't be treated with this sort of disrespect. You didn't even wear gloves for my arrival, and now you are disparaging my deliveries."

The woman—Mrs. Raymond—scowled. "I've told you more than once, Hanali, son of Vivi, that in the Transition House we go by human rules. I can't teach the children all at once to follow the way of the Elenil. It takes time. I'll put gloves on when you invite me to visit at the palace."

"Now, Mary—"

"*Mrs. Raymond*," she said firmly.

Hanali flinched, as if slapped. "*Mrs. Raymond*, then. You know I cannot invite—"

"What's that? You're not planning to invite me to the palace? What a surprise. What a surprise."

Hanali slumped, deflated. "How do you do this to me? Here I am, five hundred years old to your fifty, and you make me feel like a child."

"You act like a child," Mrs. Raymond snapped. "Most people are just too polite to point it out. Now the girl I can see was in dire straits. You were right to bring her here. But the boy . . . What are you playing at, Hanali? The boy doesn't fit the pattern."

Hanali glanced back at the carriage. He didn't seem to notice Madeline wasn't there. Maybe he thought she had slouched down and closed her eyes.

"The boy," Hanali said, "is infuriating. But he belongs here, make no mistake."

"He's a wild card."

Hanali smirked. "A wild card can be a good thing. It depends on the game you are playing."

"What was his tragedy that allows him to come into our lands?"

Hanali fell silent.

Mrs. Raymond shook her head. "I'll not break the rules, Hanali. Not for you nor anyone else. I'll not be sent back to my lot on Earth, thank you very much. You know as much as I that only a child in dire need can enter the Sunlit Lands."

"There's a sorrow to him, Mrs. Raymond. It runs deep. Perhaps not as deep as the girl's, I will grant you that. I cannot see it clearly, but he is meant to be here."

Mrs. Raymond ran her hands over her hair, tucking away any loose strands. "A wild card is unpredictable. You of all people with your prophecies and prognosticating should be nervous about that. No matter the game, the wild card is only to your advantage if it's in your hand. You didn't even bind him to you, or to the Elenil for that matter."

Hanali inclined his head. "But he is bound to the girl, and she to the Elenil, on pain of eventual death."

"You know my feelings about this."

Hanali nodded. "I have no other choice, Mary."

She didn't correct him about the name this time, she only said, "Be careful, Hanali. Be careful."

"Any punishment that comes upon you because of these two," Hanali said, "I'll take it on myself."

"You'll bind yourself to that?"

"By sun and bone, moon and flesh, I'll bind myself."

"Humph. Well then. No special treatment, though. I don't care if she's the savior of the world and he's her servant. We split them up, and you take the girl to the storyteller tomorrow yourself. After the orientation they go to their assigned duties, just like any other human who comes to the Court."

Hanali bowed low. "Of course, Mrs. Raymond."

"Enough with your foolishness. If someone saw you bowing to a human woman . . . the trouble! The scandal, sir."

Hanali grinned. "But we're on Transition House land. Such behavior is allowed outside the Court of Far Seeing."

"No wonder you're a recruiter. No doubt your churlish behavior seems charming to the humans."

"No doubt," Hanali said. "But what's this? I see one of your new charges has hidden behind an addleberry bush."

Madeline straightened and brushed herself off. It didn't do much, given the amount of mud caked onto her scrubs. But she walked to Hanali regardless and stretched out a hand to Mrs. Raymond.

Mrs. Raymond's grip was strong. "What's your name, young lady?"

"Madeline Oliver."

The older woman's eyes dropped and rose again, taking in Madeline's filthy clothing. "You need a change of clothes and a bath. We're a good three hours from dusk, and I suppose you've had a long day."

Madeline nodded. "A bath would be wonderful. But I couldn't help but overhear that you were worried someone might try to kill me."

Hanali's eyes flickered from Mrs. Raymond to Madeline. She could tell he was worried about what she might have heard. He covered it well, though, with a bright laugh and a wave of his gloved hand. "You are a terrible eavesdropper, my dear. Actually, she was worried assassins would damage her house while trying to kill you."

"You Elenil never know when to stop talking," Mrs. Raymond said. She took Madeline's hand. "We're all at risk from the Scim here, Miss Oliver. Hanali and I have some old ongoing arguments, and one is about how much risk is acceptable." She turned to Hanali. "You take the boy to meet his roommates, and I'll take Miss Oliver here to meet hers."

Madeline didn't get to say good-bye to Jason because Mrs. Raymond took her arm and guided her toward the house. The carriage, along with Hanali and Jason, headed for the back of the house while she and Mrs. Raymond went in the front. She noticed that neither Hanali nor Mrs. Raymond had answered her question about whether someone was trying to kill her. Not really.

Mrs. Raymond ran a finger over the tattoo on Madeline's wrist. "A word of advice, Miss Oliver. The other young people will ask you for details of your agreement with the Elenil. I'd suggest keeping it to yourself. Such gossip always leads to distress, one way or another."

She guided Madeline through a wide white door. The polished wood floors smelled of lemon, and a heavy red carpet runner ascended the stairway. Something seemed strange at first, and it took Madeline a moment to realize that there were no lights in the house. No switches, no chandeliers or fixtures, no candles, nothing but windows letting in the pure sunshine.

Several flights of stairs later, they walked down a long hallway, coming at last to a simple wooden door. "Your roommate will help you find your feet," Mrs. Raymond said. "She's . . . formidable. Should there be trouble." A sharp rap on the door brought an annoyed shout from inside.

Mrs. Raymond pushed the door open. "In here," she said, "you will find a change of clothing and a hot bath."

A young woman, close to Madeline's age, lay sprawled on one of the two beds in the room. An unruly mane of black hair surrounded her like a halo. She wore a loose-fitting T-shirt and a pair of jeans. She was barefoot. Her eyes glittered with determined ferocity, and a shining scar ran from the outside of her left eye down to the corner of her lip.

"Why knock if you're only going to let yourself in?"

"I'm with your roommate," Mrs. Raymond said.

"Another one?" The girl sighed and dropped her head back on her pillow.

Madeline held her hand out and said her name. The girl stared at the ceiling.

"The bath is through there," Mrs. Raymond said. "There are clothes in the chest at the end of your bed. You'll stay in your room the rest of tonight. I'll send food up."

"What about Jason?"

"You'll see him tomorrow," Mrs. Raymond said. "After you visit the storyteller."

"I don't—"

"Take a bath. Put on clean clothes. Sleep. Answers are for tomorrow. Good night, Miss Oliver." She paused halfway out of the room. "And good night to you, Miss Bishara."

"Lock the door," the girl said, as soon as Mrs. Raymond left the room. Madeline did as she was told. "The locks don't do much," the girl admitted. "Mrs. Raymond can still get in." She sat up. "I'm Shula."

"Madeline."

Shula pushed her massive mane of hair back, then let it fall around her face again. "What deal did you make with the Elenil?"

"Mrs. Raymond said not to tell anyone."

"Ha. Of course she did. Well, I can wait. You'll tell me when you're ready." Shula jumped to her feet and opened the bathroom door. She turned the tap and steaming water fell into the tub. "There's chocolate by my bed," she said. "Take some if you want."

Some chocolate sounded wonderful. Madeline broke off a square and set it on her tongue. She sucked on it until it was gone. Shula handed her a towel and told her to come back when she was clean. A long nightgown lay on her bed when she returned, clean and relaxed, her skin glowing with heat from the bath. She put the nightgown on and crawled under her covers. Light still streamed through the window, but her eyes wouldn't stay open.

Shula said, "Good night, and may you wake to good things in the morning."

"You're being so nice," Madeline said.

Shula laughed. "We stick together, you and me. But Mrs. Raymond isn't one of us."

"So we're friends."

"In this place, our lives depend on trusting each other. So we're going to have to watch each other's back whether we like each other or not."

Madeline yawned and tried to keep her eyes open. "I like you," she said, her eyes falling shut. "And I'll watch your back." A wave of thankfulness washed over her. A bath. Chocolate. A new friend.

"You are a funny one," Shula said. "So quick to trust." She patted Madeline's hand. "Tomorrow we'll go to the storyteller."

"What kind of stories does he tell?" Madeline asked, without opening her eyes.

"Different stories at different times," Shula said. "Don't worry, I'll go with you. Then we'll fight the Scim."

9
BREAK BONES

The Scim in deep darkness accursed.
FROM "THE ORDERING OF THE WORLD," AN ELENIL STORY

✦

When you're done looking at the toilet, we can do something more interesting."

It wasn't a toilet, though, not exactly. It was a bowl with a lid, but it didn't have any pipes or a water tank or a lever to flush or even a hole in the bottom of the bowl. No water, either—it was just a dry white porcelain bowl sitting in what looked more or less like a bathroom. "Hand me that apple," Jason said, kneeling in front of the bowl.

His two roommates exchanged a glance. They were both thin and muscular. Their names were Kekoa Kahananui and David Glenn. Kekoa's short hair had bleached tips, and he had an angular, handsome face. David had dark hair swept back into a ponytail, and so far Jason hadn't seen him get worked up or excited about much. His default expression was mild but friendly.

"I was gonna eat that apple," David said.

"This is for science!" Jason snapped. "Now give!"

Kekoa slapped it into his palm. "It's not science, brah. It's magic."

Jason slammed the apple into the bowl. He peered down at it. A perfectly normal apple, with no place to go. He closed the lid slowly, keeping his head level with the rim, trying to see inside the bowl as long as he could. As soon as the lid touched the rim of the bowl, he flipped it up. The apple was gone. The bowl was pristine. "Where does it go?"

"Man, I'm hungry," David said. "I could have had a couple bites if that's all you were doing. You could have experimented on the core."

"Magic plumbing," Jason said. "Hmm."

Kekoa crossed his arms. "Jason, why don't you take a bath and get all that mud off you, and then we'll take you to see the armory."

Jason perked up. "Is the shower magic?"

David shook his head. "I don't think so. No showers, either—they only got baths."

"Hmm." Jason looked around the bathroom for something else to "flush." Besides the apple, he'd already done away with a pillow, a bowl they had served him some sort of gruel in, and a baseball cap that had apparently belonged to Kekoa. He hadn't made the strongest first impression.

"I miss showers," Kekoa said. "But I really miss toilet paper."

Jason jumped to his feet. He hadn't even noticed the lack of toilet paper. "What do we use?"

David tipped his head toward a folded pile of thin washcloths. "I like the cloths, man. They smell good."

Jason sniffed one. The scent was similar to lilies, strong and sweet. He threw one in the toilet and closed the lid. When he opened it again, the bowl was empty. "Seriously. Where do they go?"

Kekoa sighed. "Listen, brah. I know you love toilets, but you can visit this one every day. Can we go to the armory now? We need a third in our Three Musketeers, and you're our roommate, so it's gotta be you."

"War Party," David said. "I'm telling you, we should be called the War Party. Three Musketeers is, like, French dudes."

"Yeah, yeah," Kekoa said, swinging the door to their room open. "Let's go pick out weapons first, though, okay?"

"I want to check in on Madeline, too."

"You're not allowed to see her until after you hear the story of the Sunlit Lands. Them's the rules," David said. "C'mon."

They walked down the hallway. Transition House was enormous, bigger than any place Jason had been in before. It reminded him of a boarding house or military dorm from olden times, like he had seen in movies. He followed the guys down a long flight of stairs, which had a red carpet held in place by fasteners along the stairway edge. "Don't let Mrs. Raymond see you walking around all muddy," Kekoa said.

"C'mon," David said, pulling Jason along a narrow hallway that doubled around under the stairway. He opened a door, and a cool breeze washed over them. A wide stone staircase led downward, and torches lit the path.

"That shouldn't fit in this house," Jason said.

"More magic," Kekoa said. "Technically it's not in this house, it's some castle somewhere."

A wooden door with an enormous black iron lock stood at the bottom of the stairs. Kekoa unlocked it. Inside was a brightly lit white room, and much like the forest path, the illumination had no obvious source. Weapons of all kinds hung on racks and from hooks on the walls.

Kekoa threw his arms wide. "Welcome! Here is where we choose our weapons for fighting the Scim!"

"I'm not fighting anybody," Jason said. "I didn't sign up for that."

Kekoa and David exchanged glances. David said, "Yeah, but when you see the Scim you'll want to."

Kekoa ran to the far wall and came back holding a weapon that looked like a large, distended Ping-Pong paddle with a hole through the middle, sharp teeth jutting out from the edges, and a hooked handle. "This is my leiomanō," he said. "This is an old one. It's made from kauila wood. That stuff's endangered now! You're not allowed to cut it down anymore. Those teeth are shark's teeth, and the lashings that hold the teeth are handmade."

He offered it to Jason, who turned it over in his hands. It was beautifully made. "What kind of shark's teeth are they?"

"Tiger shark," Kekoa said. "My people made this. Me and David, we like to use traditional weapons when we fight. It's pretty epic when we're out there, smashing those Scim."

"What do you use?" Jason asked. "What's traditional for you?"

"I'm Apsáalooke, from southeastern Montana," David said. When Jason looked at him blankly, David said, "Crow tribe." He picked up a long hatchet. "I'll probably use this one in the next battle. Sometimes I use knives." He spun the hatchet in his hand. "I like this one because it's part hatchet and part ax."

"What's it called?"

David shrugged. "I call it a hatchet ax. I don't know. I never used one before coming here."

Kekoa slapped Jason on the shoulder. "David and I saw some stuff the other day that would be good as ancestral weapons for you, too. In fact, there's a whole outfit. It's lit. Come check it out."

Kekoa and David both seemed thrilled to show him. They took him around one of the standing racks, and there was a full set of samurai armor. The flared helmet, the breastplate, the katana, everything. It was clearly old, and the polished, dark breastplate seemed to simultaneously reflect and hoard the light. Kekoa grabbed the katana and held it out to Jason, hilt first. "What do you think?"

The katana was beautiful. He studied the sheath for a long moment before using it to whack Kekoa in the legs. "I think that it's Japanese and I'm Chinese, you idiot."

"What? So what do Chinese soldiers use?"

"Armored tanks, I hope," Jason said. "Besides, I already told you, I'm not fighting. And before you say another word, no! Ninja are a Japanese thing too."

"Chill, brah. It's not that big a deal, is it?"

"Dude," David said. "You want him to call you Samoan?"

"Nothing wrong with Samoans," Kekoa said. "But I'm kānaka maoli."

"Yeah. Hawaiian. China versus Japan, that's a big difference." David made a mock jab at Kekoa with his hatchet ax. Kekoa made a face and stepped out of the way. "So what should we be looking for? What's a Chinese dude use?"

Jason picked up a silver broadsword. It was heavier than he expected, and the tip hit the floor with a clang. "I have no idea. Weapons have never been my thing. There's a double-edged straight sword called the jian. But like I said, I'm not fighting anybody."

"It's fun, though," David said. "Seriously. I get all my war paint on to terrify the enemy. We get ourselves to look as scary as possible, and then we take those things out."

"Yeah," Kekoa said. "And so long as you don't get decapitated or something, the Elenil fix all your battle wounds, so you're good to go the next day."

So that's why it sounded "fun" to them. There wasn't much risk if there were magic cure-alls at the end of the fight. Why would they even need to fight if everyone was magically better at the end? They might as well be playing checkers for dominance. He liked his roommates, but their laid-back attitude toward war creeped him out a little. They acted like it was a video game, and granted, if they could just "respawn" after every battle, maybe it kind of was. But he was here for Madeline, not to crush skulls with a shark-toothed Ping-Pong paddle. "I'd need a crazy good reason to fight anybody. It's not my style."

Kekoa gasped like he had been punched in the stomach. "Oh," he said. "Ahhhh ha ha ha."

"Oh no," David said. "He starts making weird sounds when he has a big idea."

Jason hefted the sword back into place. "Do you hear that sound often?"

Kekoa swung his leiomanō, a whoop of joy coming out of his lips. "Let's take him to see the prisoner."

"No way, Kekoa. Humans aren't allowed to talk to him."

"Come on. There's a door right near here that goes straight into the dungeon."

"No."

"Five minutes, David! Then Jason'll fight for sure. Besides, what will the Elenil do if they catch us? Send us home?"

"I said no way, Kekoa!"

"David Glenn. We're the ones who captured him. The least they can do is let us talk to him."

"I still say no."

Kekoa's eyes flickered toward Jason. "Tiebreaker."

David folded his arms. "Fine. Jason decides."

Jason had the samurai helmet on his head and a throwing star in one

THE CRESCENT STONE

hand. He had also picked up an ancient pistol that looked like it had a harmonica sticking through the middle of it. "What kind of prisoner? Who is it?"

"It's a Scim warrior," David said.

Jason rolled back on his heels. So far he had only seen an Elenil, and he hadn't been much impressed. The toilets were way more interesting. He sort of wanted to see one of these evil Scim things. "Let's take a look," he said.

David's eyelids closed halfway. "Alright, then." He set his hatchet ax down.

Kekoa bounced from foot to foot and led the way out the door. He locked the armory, then grabbed a torch off the wall and led them through a much narrower, darker corridor. "No lock on this door," he said. "We don't know where it takes you, exactly. I think maybe the palace. David thinks outside of Elenil territory. We're not sure. So you have to come back through *this door*. Don't go up the steps in the dungeon, because we're not sure where they go. You could be on the other side of the world if you do that." He cracked the door open. "All clear."

The dungeon matched every description Jason had ever heard. Dank, dark, and smelling nearly as putrid as the dried mud on him. There was a pile of hay in a corner and massive chained manacles hanging from the walls. Attached to one wall was a heavily muscled, brutish creature. Its arms were too long, like an ape's. Its skin was the color of old concrete, though a swirl of black tattoos covered most of its chest and arms. It had totally black eyes—no whites—and a heavy brow. Its mouth jutted forward, full of crooked, yellowed teeth. A small wreath of neglected black hair encircled its grey brow. It wore a ragged cloth around its waist. Its fingernails were wide as quarters, ragged and split. Its ears were tiny and round, flat against the side of its head. Scars crossed much of its torso.

Jason's heart revved up immediately. This thing was clearly powerful, and if it got its hands on Jason he wouldn't last a second. Jason's lips curled back in disgust and terror. And yet . . . there was something intriguing about it too. It was the most alien thing he had seen in the Sunlit Lands, and there was a strange sort of grace to the monstrous form. He imagined an army of these things and shuddered.

"Not too close, brah."

Jason calculated the distance from the wall to himself, studying the length of the chains. The Scim turned its wide grey head toward him.

"This is Jason," David said. "A friend of ours from the human lands."

"I'm Wu Song," Jason said. "That's my real name."

The Scim chortled. "Truth teller, are you?" Its voice was like gravel spilled on concrete.

Jason's eyebrows rose. "Yes."

"We Scim say only three tell the truth: prophets, storytellers, and fools. Which are you?"

Jason considered this question. "Probably fool."

"Ha!" The Scim straightened, seeming suddenly interested. "I will trade you, truth for truth. I am called Break Bones."

Hmm. Interesting. "I am called Jason."

Break Bones smiled, opening his wide, frog-like mouth to display jagged and uneven teeth that were each the size of Jason's pinky. "Why do you come to the Sunlit Lands?"

"To protect my friend," Jason said. He thought about his answer for a moment. "And to lay to rest old ghosts. And you?"

The Scim stood and shook its chains. "To shatter the sun and bring a thousand years of darkness and terror to the Elenil and all who befriend them. To crush skulls and break necks. To build a temple of bleached bones that reaches to the great dome of the heavens. To humiliate every Elenil before their death, then tear down the works of their hands, stone by stone, beam by beam, brick by brick. Only then shall I rest."

"Huh," Jason said. "I guess that's why they call you Break Bones."

"The fountains will run with blood. The city walls will be shelves for their heads."

"Better make a priority list, because if you tear down all their bricks and *then* try to use the walls as shelves, you're going to have to rebuild the walls again. It's a lot of work."

"You mock me," Break Bones said, his voice low. "The Scim are not fond of mockery, Wu Song."

Jason cocked his head. "Is anyone fond of mockery?"

"I think you're ticking him off," David said.

"It's a legitimate question," Jason replied, watching the Scim.

Break Bones's chest was heaving, his breath coming in staccato pants. "Humans. Are you even allowed in this prison?"

"We should go," Kekoa said. "I think you get the point. The Scim are terrible monsters."

"No," Jason said, answering the Scim. "We snuck in."

Break Bones laughed, and the horrible sound of it filled the dungeon. "I like you, Wu Song. When I am free from this place, I will honor you with a violent death. I will not humiliate you with captivity."

"That's nice," Jason said. "Though I might prefer humiliation."

Break Bones grunted, flashing his broken yellow smile. "What is the name of your friend? The one who is under your protection?"

"Don't tell him," David said.

Kekoa grabbed Jason's arm and pulled him toward the door.

"Madeline," Jason said. "Madeline Oliver."

Break Bones wrapped his right arm into the chains holding him fast. "On the night I bring the darkness to you, I will come with her lifeless body, so you will know." He slammed his arm forward, and dust puffed out of the wall where the chain was anchored. He yanked again, and the chain rattled, starting to come free. "So you will know you failed!" Break Bones roared, pulling the chain nearly all the way out. A distant trumpet sounded, and there was the sound of feet on the stone stairway.

Kekoa pushed Jason toward the exit, David close behind. They squeezed out the door, and David slammed it shut, leaning hard against it. The three of them stood there, panting. "Should we look?" David asked.

"Nah," Kekoa said. "The Elenil will have him chained back up by now. No need to show our faces."

"You're crazy," David said to Jason.

Jason scratched his head. "I guess." He thought about Break Bones's insane violence. He hadn't even tried to disguise his desire to rain destruction on the Elenil, and he had threatened Jason—and Madeline—for little more than teasing him. The intensity of the creature's violence and his certainty that he could smash Jason to bits terrified him. "Are all the Scim like that?"

"More or less," Kekoa said.

David shrugged and nodded.

"Then I'll be beside you in the next battle," Jason said. He regretted his words the moment they came out of his mouth. He didn't know how to use a sword, and the biggest fight he had ever been in was in fifth grade when Maurice Mandrell had made fun of another kid for reading too much. Jason had gone after him with the book, determined to beat Maurice over the head with it. He had woken up in the nurse's office. His friends said it seemed like Maurice had been tired after beating Jason unconscious, so he counted that as a victory. It didn't matter, though. Now he had said he was going to fight the Scim, and that meant there was no turning back. Not if he was going to be completely honest in everything from now on. He had to keep his word.

"Welcome to the War Party," David said, smiling.

"Brah," Kekoa said. "We have not settled on that name."

They argued about it all the way back to their room. Jason tried to put Break Bones out of his mind, but he kept seeing those heavy chains shuddering under the creature's massive strength. In retrospect, he probably shouldn't have shared Madeline's name. Or his own.

10

THE STONE FLOWER

Thus the Aluvoreans left in peace to populate the woods of the world.
They are a gentle race, though some say they have come to
love their trees more than people, a great misfortune.

FROM "THE ORDERING OF THE WORLD," AN ELENIL STORY

✦

P ut these on," Shula said, handing Madeline a pair of thin white gloves. Madeline had already put on the white dress with its high neck, long sleeves, and low hemline.

She spun for Shula. "I'm not getting married, am I?"

The gloves fit perfectly, just like the dress. She hoped there wouldn't be a veil.

"Every newcomer wears white for twenty-eight days. So the citizens know to be patient when you don't know the culture."

Sunlight filtered in through their open window. A trellis of a mint-like plant grew outside, and the scent wafted to them. The temperature was perfect, and Madeline hated to cover herself completely when she could be baking in the sun.

Mrs. Raymond brought them breakfast: a warm cereal, similar to oatmeal, with tart purple berries on the side. In the future they'd be eating in the "common room," but since she hadn't had the basic orientation, Madeline wasn't supposed to be with the others. She sat on the windowsill and took a deep breath, marveling again at her return to health.

"How did you come to be here, Shula?"

Shula pulled on a pair of long leather boots. "Like everyone else. The Elenil offered me my heart's desire in exchange for fighting the Scim." She frowned. "Those monsters. I would have fought them for nothing."

"What did you get in exchange?"

Shula sighed. "I'll share when you do." She held up her left wrist, and the silver tattoo glittered on her arm. "As you can see, some of the bargain must be the same as yours."

Madeline's own tattoo shone in the morning light. "When do I start to fight?" Her heart pounded in her chest. Fighting scared her. She didn't want to hurt anyone, let alone kill them, and it seemed clear people were talking about full-out war. Then again, from what Hanali said, the Scim were trying to kill *her*. So maybe it would be self-defense.

"They won't make you fight until you want to fight," Shula said, shrugging into a light jacket. "Today we'll talk to the storyteller. The Elenil will give you a sort of history lesson to show you how unique and wonderful the Court of Far Seeing is before they ask you to defend it. When your first month is done, they'll know you well enough to give you your job for the rest of your stay here. You'll probably get some local work in the city until then . . . Maybe guard duty, or running messages, something like that."

Shula wore jeans and a T-shirt under her jacket.

"When do I get to wear normal clothes?" Madeline asked.

Shula grinned. "In twenty-eight days or so. Though plenty of humans wear local clothes even once their month is up. Easier to blend in." She slipped on a thin pair of leather gloves and pulled the door open. They made their way down the stairs and out the front door.

"Should we tell Mrs. Raymond we're leaving?"

"We're not prisoners, Madeline. We can come and go whenever we like."

Then why wasn't she allowed to see Jason?

There was no carriage waiting. Shula shrugged and said maybe Hanali was meeting them at the storyteller's. "Not a big deal. It's not far to walk."

They made their way toward the city center. Madeline couldn't get over the sights and sounds of the place. They walked through a market full of silk, strange fruits, and food cooking over coals in metal troughs. The different types of people amazed her also. She saw what she could only assume were more Elenil, dressed in elaborate clothes that covered them almost completely. They were all tall and painfully thin.

She saw guards and soldiers walking along the cobbled street. They had swords on their belts. Most of them were human. Apparently there were only a handful of Elenil soldiers.

"There are no street signs," Madeline said.

Shula nodded. "The Elenil don't have a written language."

"They're illiterate?"

"Most of them, yeah. Why would you need to write when you can just speak your message to a bird and have it delivered? Most everything we accomplish through reading, they do with magic, and without all the trouble of learning to read."

Madeline felt a small disappointment at that. She had hoped to read some Elenil fiction. She wondered what magical people would write about, and what their fantastical stories would hold. Then again, she was on her way to a storyteller, wasn't she? And no doubt she could scavenge the occasional book this year or ask Hanali for some. The humans must have some hidden away.

All colors and sizes of people moved in and out of the shops. Short, hairy men and women with dark, almost grey, skin wove through the crowd. She saw one man wrapped in a series of cloths so that only his eyes could be seen—eyes which seemed to glow from within the shade of the cloths. She even saw a woman whose skin appeared to be blue darting beneath the shadows of a rounded trellis. The blue woman stopped to talk to two human guards.

"Are all these people Elenil?"

Shula laughed. "Those shorter people, those are the Maegrom. Did you see the man wrapped in cloths?"

"With the glowing eyes?"

"Kakri. Desert people. They love stories even more than the Elenil.

For the Elenil, stories are almost sacred. For the Kakri, they are life. They use story as a form of currency. The greatest storytellers are considered the wealthiest among them."

"What about the blue woman?"

Shula stopped in her tracks. "Oh, probably an Aluvorean. Where?"

Madeline scanned the crowd. "Over by the trellis there. Talking to the two guards."

The two human guards waved to Shula, and one of them called her over.

Shula sighed. "Stay here for a second. Technically I shouldn't introduce you until you've met a storyteller. I'm sure it's just a quick bit of business." She stripped off her coat. "Hold this, please."

Shula strode into the crowd toward the guards and the blue woman. The four of them had an animated conversation. Shula clearly was unhappy with the guards. One of them gave a shrill whistle, and a small bird darted down to rest on his finger. He spoke to it. The bird tweeted twice, then zipped into the air and sped past Madeline, toward the city center.

Madeline watched the bird go, reminded of the hummingbird she and Jason had followed into the Sunlit Lands and the birds Hanali had released when they arrived. She studied the square, dazzled by the riot of colors, the sounds of the people calling out about their wares, and the sweet smells coming from the food stalls.

A hummingbird whirred by. Madeline watched it as it flew through the crowd, flitting around, hovering by a Maegrom here, an Elenil there, and then finally zipping across the crowded square to linger beside an old, bent woman in a straw hat festooned in flowers, standing in what appeared to be a tiny garden built into the side of a building. The Garden Lady. Her back was to Madeline. The hummingbird hovered by the lady for a moment, then burst off in a straight line along the main avenue.

Madeline stole a quick glance at Shula, who didn't seem any closer to ending her conversation. Shula had told her to stay put, but it wasn't that far to walk over to the Garden Lady. Madeline would keep an eye out for Shula and come back as soon as she was done with her business.

The Garden Lady, still in the small garden built along the city path, stood talking to a woman whose skin was a slightly green color, like someone who was standing under a sunlit canopy of trees. In fact, on closer inspection, her skin was multiple shades of green, as if a pattern of leaves was cast upon it, and the darker spots moved, like leaves in a breeze. Her hair was thick, short, and deep green, like a healthy moss, and she wore a nut-brown robe with silver trim.

The two women stood in front of a wall thick with ivy. Madeline came closer, feeling foolish for not knowing the Garden Lady's name. She didn't know how to call out to her. She moved closer. She came around so she could see the Garden Lady's face and gasped. It wasn't her. She had a gourd instead of a head, berries for eyes, and a mouth made of trailing ivy.

Madeline stumbled backward, trying to put distance between herself and the strange scarecrow version of the Garden Lady, but green fingers wrapped around her bicep. They felt almost sticky, like a plant with tiny barbs on it. They didn't hurt, just felt like they would cling if she pulled away.

"I am sorry," the green woman whispered. She came barely to Madeline's shoulder. "We did not know how else to get you away from them."

Madeline cast a hurried look at Shula. She still hadn't noticed that Madeline had wandered off. Which was . . . good? She wasn't sure now. She didn't want Shula to know she had immediately disobeyed her, but she also felt nervous that Shula didn't know where she was.

"Away from who? From my friends?"

"Yes. And from the Elenil," the woman said. "My sister is distracting them for a moment, but soon they will see. My people need your help."

"*My* help? I just got here."

The woman's teeth were white as birch bark. "Which is why you are wearing the white, we know. But there is trouble in Aluvorea and—it is tangled—but the Eldest believes you are the one we must grow alongside."

Madeline's head swam. "Who told you that? How can I help when I have to serve the Elenil for the next year? And what does 'grow alongside' even mean?"

The woman's grip tightened. "It is a simple question—will you help my people?"

Madeline could barely help herself. She was obligated to the Elenil for a year, and then she needed to go home. She couldn't stay here forever in this fantasyland, even though it was something she had always dreamed of. But the idea of a quest, a goal, a good deed to be done, rang in her like a bell.

Tears formed in the woman's eyes and slipped down her green cheeks. "Please."

Madeline took both the woman's hands in her own. "Of course I will," she said.

"It is a promise then," the woman said, with a desperate intensity. Her eyes widened, looking at something over Madeline's shoulder.

She turned around to see the Garden Lady—the real one—pushing her way through the crowd, still a good distance away but headed straight toward them, her face flushed, her eyebrows low, her jaw jutting out, and a monstrous frown on her face.

"I must go," the green woman said.

At the same moment the Garden Lady bellowed, "Make a dummy of me, will you, child? And a gourd for my head? Oh, you and I will have words, yes we will!" Humans and Elenil pushed to get out of her way. A Maegrom scurried from under her feet, and every eye in the square was turned toward her.

Madeline looked at Shula, whose eyes moved from the Garden Lady toward the object of the old woman's wrath. When Shula saw Madeline, her eyebrows rose as if to say, *That is not where I left you.*

"Our time is at an end," the Aluvorean woman said. She held up her hand. "For you." In her tiny palm was a flower, bright red, as red as a spot of blood on a handkerchief. It was the size of a fifty-cent piece, delicate and lovely.

"Thank you," Madeline said and reached for it, moved by the woman's generosity and kindness.

Green tendrils unfolded from beneath the flower and grasped hold of Madeline's hand, climbing onto her and settling on her right wrist. "Don't be startled," the woman said. "It's a stone flower. They grow on the stumps of dead trees, only in Aluvorea. They glow in the dark. It likes the warmth of your arm, that's why it's wrapping onto you."

"Thank you," Madeline said again. It was beautiful and like nothing she had seen before, though the crawling tendrils reminded her unpleasantly of spider's legs.

"Come to us in Aluvorea," the green woman said, then gave a yelp at the sight of the Garden Lady barreling ever closer, and turned and ran straight into the wall of ivy. There was a shaking and rattling of leaves, and the woman disappeared completely. The blue woman came sprinting from a different direction, running full speed into the wall of ivy and, like her sister, disappearing somehow into the leaves.

The Garden Lady huffed up to the wall, studied it for a moment, then paused to look at Madeline. "So you made it," she said, "and not a moment too soon."

"I don't even know your name," Madeline said, blurting out the first thing she thought.

"Well, child, that was never part of the bargain, was it? What did those two want with you?"

"She asked me to come to Aluvorea and help her people."

The Garden Lady turned her head, as if trying to see Madeline in a different light or at a different angle. "Interesting," she said. "Interesting, yes. But not any time soon, dear." She shook her head. "No, no, it will be too late by then. You have adventures and duties to perform for the Elenil first."

"But what should I—"

The lady held her palm up toward Madeline. "I gave you free advice once already, dear, and not another word until you've heeded the first." She paused. "Now what's that on your wrist, child? Did those two give you that flower?"

The flower's petals moved on their own, as if an unseen breeze ruffled them. "Yes."

"Of all the addlepated—why, those little—didn't they think for a minute—" The old woman's scowl deepened, and her face turned nearly scarlet. "I'll pull them up by the roots," she snapped, and without another word she put one arm in front of her and pushed through the ivy, grumbling as she went.

Madeline put her hands into the ivy and pushed as well, but there was a stone wall behind the vines. Nowhere to go, no way to follow.

Shula made her way over to Madeline. "Who was that green woman?"

"I don't know. An Aluvorean. She asked me to come to Aluvorea."

"That's strange," Shula said. "There aren't many Aluvoreans in the city, but one was just telling those guards she had heard a Scim plotting to sneak in."

"She said that was her sister," Madeline said. "They both ran as soon as they saw the Garden Lady."

Shula gave her a quizzical look. "The who?"

"The old lady I was talking to . . . I don't know her name. I call her the Garden Lady."

Shula gave her the sort of look you give a confused child. "I didn't see her. We sent word for one of the Elenil to come look into the supposed Scim invasion, but the woman slipped away while we were waiting. Ah! Here's Rondelo now."

An Elenil on a white stag came bounding through the crowd, the alarm bird tweeting and flitting around his head. The Elenil dismounted in an easy leap to the ground. He moved like a dancer—smooth and graceful and precise. There was never a person so beautiful in all of human memory, Madeline thought.

"This is Rondelo," Shula said. "He's a . . . well, it's hard to explain before you know how things work."

"A captain of the guard," Rondelo said, and he smiled, like a sunrise on a cold morning.

Madeline couldn't think of a single thing to say. She wanted to tell him all about the Garden Lady, the Aluvoreans, her journey to the Sunlit Lands, her friend Jason, Hanali's crazy fashion sense, Darius. She blushed, remembering that she sort of had a boyfriend. She opened her mouth, not sure what was about to come out. "I'm holding Shula's jacket," she said.

"I was going to say 'prince,'" Shula said, grinning. "I forgot what an effect you have on people when they first meet you, Rondelo."

"She asked me to hold it," Madeline said. Her face felt even hotter.

Rondelo grinned. The lopsided smile made him even more charming. He looked more human than the other Elenil. He looked like a statue breathed to life. "Miss Madeline, welcome to the Sunlit Lands. This is my companion, Evernu." The white stag inclined its head, its antlers tilting toward the ground.

"A pleasure to meet you," she said. The surreal experience of greeting a stag broke her out of Rondelo's spell.

"Where is this Aluvorean?" Rondelo asked.

"My apologies," Shula said. "She slipped away. I thought it would be best to call for you when she said she had heard some Scim plotting a way into the city, though."

"You did the right and responsible thing," Rondelo said. "I have heard rumors of the Black Skulls trying to find a shadow entrance to the city."

Shula spit on the ground. "Those three. They're not the sort to sneak around, it seems to me."

"They're after something," Rondelo said. "And their battle tactics lately are . . . different. New."

"Nothing we can't handle for a few hours each dusk," Shula said.

"Still, it troubles me that the Aluvorean would appear and then slip away so quickly. As if trying to distract us, almost. I should get back," Rondelo said, swinging onto Evernu's bare back. "Ah. What's this?"

Madeline followed his gaze. "Oh." She lifted her hand. "It's a stone flower. Another Aluvorean gave it to me."

Shula stepped back, a look of horror on her face. "Don't move, Madeline."

"It's just a flower."

The tendrils tightened on her arm. "Don't! Move!"

Madeline froze.

"It's triggered," Rondelo said.

"You're fast," Shula said to Rondelo. "You can do it."

"It's *triggered*," he repeated. "She has to do it herself. It's no longer about speed but precision."

"Okay," Shula said. "Madeline. Stone flowers are . . . they're poisonous."

Madeline relaxed. She wasn't going to eat it.

"Not poisonous," Rondelo said. "Venomous."

Shula shook her head. "They sting. Like a bee. They're carnivorous. If it stings you, you're going to be paralyzed. In Aluvorea, they swarm you and they . . . Well, there's only one, so you'll just be paralyzed. But there's no cure. They're called stone flowers because people who are stung are frozen, like statues." She snapped her fingers, and Madeline looked back up from the flower to Shula. "The stinger, it's on the bottom, between the tendrils. It extends the stinger by lifting its petals. So long as those petals stay flat, you're safe. If you put your finger slowly in the center so it can't close its petals, it can't sting. Then we can pull it off."

"Like grabbing a snake behind the head."

"Exactly. Only slow, Madeline."

Why would that green woman try to hurt her? It didn't make any sense.

Madeline realized with a distant disappointment that she had forgotten to ask for her name, too. But now she needed to focus. There was a venomous plant on her wrist.

Being careful not to move the arm with her deadly corsage, Madeline took one finger and reached slowly across. The flower tensed, like a spider getting ready to leap. She paused, waiting for it to relax, but it didn't. The petals quivered, then started to close.

No way would her finger get there in time if she stuck with the "slow and steady" plan. One sharp breath in. Here she was, day two in fantasyland, about to be stung by a flower and put out of commission. She would be able to breathe but not move . . . No more running or walking or health. She wasn't about to let that happen. She exhaled, hard, and at the same instant struck like a snake for the center of the flower.

Her finger wedged partway in, but the petals closed halfway. She pressed down until she managed to pry the petals apart. The tendrils of the flower gyrated crazily, slapping at her free hand. It snagged hold of her left hand, released her right wrist, and swung to her other arm. She shook, but it didn't come off. It tightened down hard, and before she could get her finger in, the petals snapped closed and a monstrous cracking sound echoed from her wrist.

The plant shuddered, and the tendrils loosened. The bright red flower faded and fell to the ground. Madeline examined her wrist. A pinprick of blood stood out precisely in the center of the bracelet's glowing face beneath her skin.

Rondelo's gloved hands were on Madeline's arm. He pushed her sleeve up. "Apologies," he said. "The Majestic One protect her. The stinger implanted."

Shula stabbed the flower through the center with a sword. Bending down beside it, she said, "It's spent, Rondelo. Dead."

Madeline felt the whole market fall away from her. She could only see the tiny mark where the flower had struck. "What happens now?" she asked.

Shula hugged her. "Lie down, Madeline," she said, trying to be gentle.

"I'm okay, Shula, honestly."

"It will be easier to move you when the paralysis sets in if you're lying down."

Madeline lay down, waiting for the venom to take effect, trying not to cry. Rondelo sent a bird for help.

"Why is someone trying to kill a newcomer?" he asked. "Who is she?"

Madeline felt a little annoyed that he was talking to Shula as if she wasn't lying at their feet.

Shula said, "I don't know why, but the Aluvoreans went to a lot of trouble to do this. One distracted me with the guards, the other pulled Madeline away."

Rondelo's frown deepened. "The Aluvoreans are the most peaceful people in the Sunlit Lands. What drove them to this?"

"I don't think they were trying to kill me," Madeline said, wiggling her fingers so they could see she wasn't paralyzed. After a few minutes of being ignored, she stood up and put her hands on her hips. "Obviously, whatever happened, the poison didn't take. So can we get on with our day?"

Shula and Rondelo exchanged looks.

"Should we take her back to the dorms?" Shula asked.

Rondelo scratched Evernu behind the ears, watching Madeline with careful interest. "No. But I'll join you wherever you're headed. A little extra company today can only be good."

Three times he made Madeline repeat the description of the woman who had given her the flower: once to him and Shula, once to the guards, and a third time to a bird, which he released. "They will search for her," he told Madeline. "Though since she escaped through magical means, I fear it is unlikely they will find her. Come, let us walk together."

Shula walked on one side of Madeline, with Rondelo on the other. The stag walked behind them. Shula's hand kept moving to Madeline's arm, as if to steady her. "I feel fine," Madeline said.

"Sometimes," Shula said, "when a snake bites, it doesn't release venom. Maybe it was like that." Madeline shuddered. She hated to think she had avoided paralysis by a quirk of fate. She made a mental note not to accept any more flowers. She rubbed her hand where the flower had stung her. There was an irritated red mark on her skin but nothing more.

11

LESSONS

And so the Majestic One sent away the Kakri,
and they live in the desert to the east, beyond the Tolmin Pass.
They build no houses and plant no crops.
FROM "THE ORDERING OF THE WORLD," AN ELENIL STORY

+

After the terrifying interview with Break Bones, Jason took a bath. He still couldn't get his left sneaker off, which meant he couldn't get his jeans off, so he took a bath in his jeans with one shoe on. The level of filthiness in the bathroom afterward couldn't be exaggerated, partly because Jason was fascinated with how the tub magically filled with the correct amount of perfectly hot water. He had a splash war with the tub, seeing if he could empty it before it refilled. The mud on him seemed to cloud into the water and then disappear, so he experimented with slinging the freshly remoistened muck out of the tub as well. When he was done, he was clean, but the bathroom looked as if a gigantic muddy dog had shaken itself off in the middle of the floor.

He sloshed into the room he shared with Kekoa and David. "I'm afraid to look at the bathroom," David said, "if this is you all cleaned up."

Kekoa had a book in his hands, but he dropped it onto his bed, his mouth open wide. "Did you bathe in your jeans, brah?"

"I couldn't get my shoe off," Jason said.

Kekoa reached into his waistband and pulled out a small, sharp knife. "Come here then."

Jason stepped backward, but David grabbed him and threw him onto the floor. Kekoa cut his shoelaces, then scooped up both of Jason's shoes, walked into the bathroom, threw them into the toilet basin, and closed the lid. The shoes were gone.

"Aw, man," Jason said.

"You don't have to keep messed-up stuff like that," David said. "We can order up fresh ones."

It was time for bed after that. There were three beds, one on each wall except the one with the door to the hallway. They gave Jason the bed beneath the window, so he could "smell the night rain." It wasn't night, though, not really, even though it was late. There was a sort of dimming but no true night. Out the window Jason could see the short wall around their gigantic house, and beyond that a few scattered buildings, and then the much taller city wall. It wasn't even dark enough to see any stars.

Kekoa and David had an evening ritual. They each shared a thing they were thankful for from the day. This surprised Jason. He made a joke about them being "so sensitive," and they gave him a lecture about it. "A true warrior has to be thankful for the people and places and world they are protecting," Kekoa said.

"Yeah," David said. "You have to respect the land and the people in it. If you don't take the time for gratitude, you miss your everyday blessings."

"Also if you don't participate, we will beat you up."

"It's true, dude."

"Fine," Jason said. "I'm sure I can think of something." But honestly, since what happened with Jenny, he had struggled to find things to be thankful for. Some of the rawness had begun to pass, but he still couldn't make it through a day without thinking of her. Of course he had also ditched his entire life to come to the Sunlit Lands with Madeline and had been immediately separated from her. On the other hand, he hadn't been eaten by a mermaid, which was a new category of things to be thankful for.

Kekoa said, "I'm thankful for the weather today. Clear skies, blue and deep."

David said, "Yeah, man. For me, I'm glad there's a night off from the fighting to welcome our new roomie."

Jason didn't say anything for a while, and he could tell they were waiting. "I'm glad Break Bones didn't yank his chains out of the wall and kill us," he said finally.

They laughed at that for a while. "Now one thing we hope for the new day," Kekoa said. But Jason didn't hear those, because he was sound asleep.

He woke to full, bright sunlight streaming through the window. His roommates were already up and dressed. David laughed when he saw Jason's eyes flutter open.

"Breakfast!" he said and slapped a warm bowl of porridge with purple berries into Jason's hands. The porridge was bland and the berries too sour. Then he saw the pudding cup sitting on the end of his bed.

He scooped the pudding into his porridge and mixed it in, which created a sort of chocolate-flavored chunky puddle that was somewhere between edible and delicious. Kekoa grabbed the empty pudding container and ran a finger around the inside.

"What is this? Pudding?"

"Yeah," Jason said. "My deal with Hanali was a cup of pudding every day for the rest of my life, and in exchange I'd hang out here for a year." He smacked his lips. "Magic pudding tastes exactly like hospital pudding."

Kekoa and David laughed until Jason grinned too, even though he didn't know what was so funny. "I'd love to have seen Hanali's face," David said. "Some guy who didn't ask for money or fame or anything, just a cup of pudding. Ha ha ha."

"What did you guys get in your deals? Or are we not supposed to tell each other?"

"Ah, that's poho, man. Everybody knows everybody's business around here," Kekoa said. "For me, some haole stole my family's land. I do my time here, and when I go back the Elenil give me back the land, and they said they'd take care of the haole, too."

Jason took another bite of his strange breakfast. "What does that mean, they'll take care of him?"

"I don't ask, they don't say. Maybe they'll bring him back here, I don't know."

"Me, I stay until I'm twenty-one," David said. "My parents died. Well, my mom. My dad, I can't live with him. So when I'm twenty-one, I go home, the Elenil give me a hundred grand, and I'm on my way."

Jason looked at his empty pudding cup. "A hundred grand. That's a lot of pudding."

"Yeah," David said. "But I didn't think of that 'for the rest of my life' thing. I should have just said a thousand bucks a day."

Kekoa threw Jason a pile of white clothes with a pair of white sneakers on top. "Pudding cups, that's a new one around here. There's some real interesting ones, you'll see."

Jason got dressed, though he hesitated when he got to the white gloves.

"You have to wear those," David said. "It's an Elenil thing. Hands are private—you only show them to people who are close to you."

They asked if Jason planned to fight the Scim that night, and he said he wanted to go with them, at least. See what it was all about. He wasn't sure he wanted to fight. They talked about it while David led them to a long, grassy field where they could practice. "We have to get him to a storyteller, though, yeah? They're not going to let him fight tonight if he hasn't heard the story."

A table the length of a limo had been set out, and on the table there were weapons. Bows, scimitars, maces, knives, staffs, and a variety of others, mostly hand-to-hand stuff. No guns or any sort of firearm or explosive. Kekoa sorted through them, setting aside different options he thought Jason might like. "Hmm, maybe a mace? Oh! These are cool, this is called a katar. Or what about this? What's this called again, David?"

"Tonfa."

"Yeah. Tonfa." He held it up to Jason. It looked like a night stick.

Jason picked up a bow. He didn't want to stab or smash anyone, and if he did get involved in the fight that evening he'd rather be as far away from it as possible. Kekoa pointed out a hay bale with a target draped on it. Jason grabbed an arrow and tried to put it up against the bow, but he kept fumbling and dropping it.

The fifth time it fell off the drawstring, he threw the bow on the ground. "Why do the Elenil want inexperienced teenage fighters again?"

Kekoa and David burst out laughing. David showed him a smooth oval on the bow, near the grip. "Put your bracelet tattoo right next to that," he said.

A warm sensation traveled through the lattice of Jason's tattoo. He picked up the arrow, expertly nocked it, found himself standing in the proper position, and straightened one arm, the fletching of the arrow now near his ear. He corrected slightly for the wind, loosed the string, and watched the arrow fly. It thunked comfortably into the outer edge of the target. Not a bull's-eye, but a moment before he hadn't even been able to get the arrow onto the bow.

Jason looked at his hands in wonder. A thrill of adrenaline went through him. It felt like that perfect moment when you're an expert and everything is going right and you're on top of your game. It came so naturally, so easily. "How?"

"Magic, brah. We don't learn how to fight—we learn how to channel the magic. Takes an afternoon to become the best fighter ever."

David juggled an ax and two knives, spinning them easily over his head. "The Elenil loan us their fighting skills. Most of them are hundreds of years old. So it's their skills, but we do the fighting."

Jason frowned. "Our bodies, our risk."

"Nah," Kekoa said. "You get wounded, they fix you with magic. Just don't get killed dead. They can't do anything about that. But lose an arm or get a crushed rib cage, boom! They'll fix you right up."

"That's not cool, man," David said. "Bringing up the arm thing."

Kekoa laughed and handed Jason another arrow. "One of the Black Skulls cut David's arm off a couple weeks ago. Should've seen him running for the wall with one arm, the Black Skulls chasing him. Pretty hilarious."

David gave him a fake, sarcastic laugh. "Yeah, hilarious. They would have killed me if not for Shula."

"Black Skulls?" Jason had the bow up again, the arrow nocked and ready to loose. A minor adjustment to his fingering, and the arrow sailed to the target, lodging a bit closer to the center this time. Amazing. He felt a swell of pride at his skill, at how easy it was to launch an arrow into the target from this distance.

Kekoa picked up a bow, held his tattoo against it, and started firing arrows. Three shots, three bull's-eyes. "They're like the best Scim fighters. Pretty creepy looking too. There's three of them, and they wear long white robes and black-painted animal skulls over their faces. Nothing hurts them. They're not like us, where they need to go somewhere to heal—it's like an arrow to the heart doesn't do anything other than slow them down."

"They're dead already," David said. "I'm telling you, they're dead. They don't even bleed."

"Stupid," Kekoa said. "There's no such thing as zombies."

"Man, you don't know. You're shooting magic arrows for a war between monsters and angels. How do you know there aren't zombies?"

Kekoa put a hand on Jason's bow and pushed it toward the ground. "Okay, quick tutorial. The oval on the bow, that's a magical receptor. Think of it like a permission slip. Some Elenil has given the bow permission to borrow their skill. While you have it, they don't."

"It's like your tattoo," David said. "It's the permission slip that tells the magic you're allowed to be in the Sunlit Lands and allows your pudding to be delivered in the morning."

"So," Jason said slowly, "I'm stealing someone else's skills to do this."

Kekoa shook his head emphatically. "They've given permission, remember? But when you aim, you reach out through the magic and *take* the skill. Some of it's coming through without trying, but you have to—" Kekoa struggled to find the right words, finally ending with "—you have to reach for it."

"It's like a waterway," David said. "You have to open it all the way to get the full skill. You're leaving some of the skill with the owner. You're taking enough magic that there are two mediocre archers right now, instead of one terrible one and one amazing one."

"Does it . . . does it bother them when I take their archery skills?"

"They don't even know unless they're trying to use those skills at the same moment."

Jason took a deep breath. Okay. He could do this. He concentrated on the archery skills he would need. Balance. Steady hands. Clear vision. The smooth movement of the drawstring, the careful release. A confidence came over him, the sort of confidence you feel when you've done something a million times and it's not even that it's easy, it's automatic. When he opened his eyes, his silver tattoo was shining with a white light.

"Look at how much magic is flowing through!" David said. "Good job. Shoot an arrow!"

The arrow fell effortlessly into place, and raising the bow was like taking a breath. Jason could see the precise place he wanted the arrow to go, could feel himself correcting for the slight breeze and the distance, and when he released, the arrow flew in a graceful arc, beautiful and perfect and dead into the center of the target. He raised his bow in the air and let out an enormous whoop of joy, and he and David and Kekoa danced and jumped around, shouting and cheering.

"You almost sound proud. As if you have done something worthwhile," said a voice, low and skeptical.

They stopped celebrating. Kekoa made a face. "Hey, Baileya," David said.

She was a full head taller than Jason and wore loose-fitting cream pants tied at her waist with a red sash. Her blouse was also loose, but a deep-blue color like clear water, billowing out wide at the sleeves then tapering to a tight cuff on her wrists. Her smooth skin was the tan color of sunbaked sand. Her hair was pulled back but flowed as easily as her clothing, a dark-brown wave moving around her face and past her shoulders. The color of her hair was echoed in a spray of freckles across her cheekbones. But her eyes were easily the most striking thing about her. Jason had never seen eyes that color. They seemed almost to emanate a pale silver light. He couldn't look away. If not for the eyes, he would have almost thought she was human.

He reached out to shake hands. "I'm Jason," he said.

She held his gaze, as if waiting for something, but he didn't know what. She turned to his roommates. "Have you taught him nothing?"

David shrugged. "He can shoot a bow."

"We did cut him out of his shoes," Kekoa said helpfully.

Baileya sighed. "In the Sunlit Lands, especially among the Elenil, to touch bare hands is a great intimacy. It's deeply offensive to offer such a thing when announcing one's name. It is wise to keep your hands covered and, in most cases, to keep them out of sight altogether."

"I'm not Elenil, though," Jason said. "And neither are you."

Her eyes sparkled. Or maybe it's just that they were glowing, Jason couldn't tell. "It is a compliment that you noticed," she said. "I am of the Kakri people, beyond the Tolmin Pass. My mother is called Willow, and my grandmother Abronia. I have come to make my fortune and fight the Scim."

David flopped down on the grass. "She fights the old-fashioned way. Her own skill—no magic—and she keeps her wounds."

Baileya nodded curtly. "Which is why I come here to my practice area. A practice area I assume you are finished with, as you are taking the hard-earned skills and abilities of others rather than honing your own."

"Yeah, yeah," Kekoa said. "We're done." He paused. "Hey, Baileya, we're supposed to take Jason to a storyteller to get the whole 'why we fight the Scim' story. Any chance you'd want to tell him?"

"Tell him yourself," Baileya said, studying the weapons in front of her. She picked up a medium-sized hatchet.

"It can't be a human telling the story," David said. "You know the rules. It has to be a citizen of the Sunlit Lands."

Baileya gave him a sour look. "I came to make a fortune, not spend it."

"What does that mean?" Jason asked.

Kekoa laughed. "The Kakri don't use money, they use stories. It's their only currency. So when she says she came here to make her fortune, it's like she came here to live some adventures, or learn stories their community doesn't have."

David rearranged the weapons on the table, putting everything he and his roommates had messed around with back in their places. "Please, Baileya? We'll have to hike into the city center and find a storyteller, then come all the way back before dusk, and then fight. We'll be exhausted."

Baileya shook her head, then looked at the far-off target, hefting the hatchet. With a sinewy grace, she stretched back with her entire body, then sprang forward, like an Olympian throwing a javelin. The hatchet flew in a high arc, its spinning blade catching the sunlight over and over. It descended to the target and buried itself deep into the center, shattering the arrows there and sending up a plume of hay.

Jason dropped his bow. "Whoa."

Baileya smiled at him. "You fight for the Elenil and against the Scim.

That is all the story you need to know." She looked him over carefully. "If you wish to exchange stories another time, I will consider it. You look to be from a different clan than other humans I have spoken to."

Without another word, she turned, marched toward the target, and yanked out her hatchet and what remained of the arrows. Jason just stared. David picked up Jason's bow and put it away, and Kekoa grabbed his arm and pulled him backward until he started to walk, half in a daze.

"She's amazing," Jason said.

"I don't know if that counted as you hearing the story," David said. "I hope we don't get in trouble at roll call."

Kekoa said, "Jason didn't even agree to fight in his contract with the Elenil. He can do what he wants."

"She's so amazing," Jason said.

Kekoa said, "You heard the bit about not waving bare hands at the Elenil, right?"

"Did you see that ax-throwing thing?" Jason asked.

"No handshakes," David said.

"And no high fives!" Kekoa said. "Super insulting."

"How did she even throw that far?" Jason turned back to look, but David grabbed him and pulled him toward the house.

"She'll be at the wall tonight," David said. "Let's eat lunch."

Jason's feet skimmed along the ground. *She'll be there tonight.* "She's amazing," he said.

Kekoa snickered. "First girl he sees who's good with a hatchet and he's head over heels."

David didn't laugh. "Don't tell Baileya. She'll want you to fight on the front lines with her."

Kekoa threw his arms around both of their shoulders. "Not tonight, though. Because tonight the Three Musketeers fight again!"

"Dude. The War Party," David said.

Jason had a sudden, worrisome thought that pulled him out of his reverie of Baileya. What had happened to the previous third of their Three Musketeers? Where was Kekoa's and David's previous roommate?

"Don't get beheaded" they kept saying to him. Gulp. Maybe he wouldn't be riding out to battle with them tonight after all.

12
THE STORYTELLER

O Keeper of Stories!

FROM "THE DESERTED CITY," A KAKRI LAMENT

✛

Madeline and Shula found Hanali standing outside a bakery talking to a squat grey-skinned person in a dun-brown robe. The smell of fresh bread and pastries hung in the air.

"Strange," Shula said. "I've never seen Hanali talking to a Maegrom before."

Hanali's eyes rose lazily toward them, and with a charming smile, he spoke again to the Maegrom, and it scurried off into the crowd. By the time Madeline and Shula reached him, Hanali had something that looked a great deal like an apple turnover neatly balanced on his gloved fingers.

"Someone tried to kill Madeline," Shula said.

Hanali raised an eyebrow at Shula. "You?"

Rondelo bowed. "Your Excellency. It was, in fact, an Aluvorean. She gave the child a stone flower."

Hanali sniffed. "Are those poisonous to humans?" He grinned at Madeline. "I jest. Stone flowers are quite deadly to everyone."

Trumpets blared deep in the city center. Rondelo leapt onto his stag's back and begged to be pardoned, and Evernu bounded away through the crowd.

"That was a security alarm," Shula said. "But it's full sun. The Scim couldn't possibly have broken through the walls."

Dusting the sugar from his gloved fingers, Hanali said, "Yes, and knowing it was a drill, it was rather rude of Rondelo to leap off like that."

"I should go check in with the guards too," Shula said.

"Nonsense," Hanali said. "And miss the storyteller? My dear human child, don't prattle on so."

Madeline crossed her arms. With some time to think as they walked, she had come to realize the seriousness of being offered a deadly flower. "Seems to me there should be a little more concern about the attempted murder."

"Bah. You're safe with Shula," Hanali said. "Did you die? No. Now come along."

"But—"

"*Did you die?*"

"No."

"Then *come along.*"

When Madeline didn't move, Hanali let out a great theatrical sigh. "Do you have the flower?" he asked.

Shula handed it to him. It had wilted nearly completely and lost most of its crimson color.

Hanali hemmed and hawed, then asked to see Madeline's arm. She showed him where it had stung her, and he studied it carefully. "Do you see this tiny dot?" he asked.

She hadn't noticed it until he pointed it out, but there was a black spot, oblong and half the size of a grain of rice. She licked her lips. "I see it."

"That, my dear, is a seed. Stone flowers can inject poison in their youth or, before they die, a seed." He straightened and threw the flower to the ground, crushing it beneath the heel of his boot. "Typically they inject it into a rotting log, but I suppose this one became confused."

Madeline rubbed at the spot where the seed was. "What will happen to me?"

Hanali grimaced. "Are you a rotting log?"

"No," she said, annoyed.

"Then, I suppose, nothing. Do let me know if a flower bursts from your skin. Now. May we get to the business at hand?"

Madeline frowned at him. He didn't seem to be taking the whole thing seriously. Then again, maybe that was a good sign. "Fine," she said.

The Elenil practically danced up a clay stairway that climbed the side of a two-story house. There were no railings or handholds, just simple stairs. At the top, he bent low and entered a dark room.

The woman was hard to see in the dim light. She sat against the wall, which was covered in ivy. The ivy had snaked across the woman, too, so only her face could be seen. The lines on her face branched and split like climbing vines, and her hair was tangled in the leaves. She looked almost like one of the Aluvoreans, what with all the ivy, but her skin wasn't green. Madeline couldn't tell if she was human or something else.

"I brought your fee," Hanali said and placed a small pewter spoon in front of the woman. A vine curled around it and lifted it to the woman's eyes. She nodded, and the spoon disappeared into the ivy.

"What . . . what happened to you?" Madeline asked.

The woman's dark eyes rested on her for a moment. "I'll not tell you that without a spoon, or a pair of bone dice, or a rusted knife from a knight's traveling chest."

The recitation of junk reminded Madeline of the Garden Lady. Bending closer, she tried to see the woman's eyes. The ivy shifted, and the leaves shuddered. The woman looked away. Madeline tried to put her hand into the ivy to see if the wall behind it was solid, but the ivy curled from her touch, revealing the wall.

Standing against the doorjamb, Hanali said, "Tell them of the Sunlit Lands."

The leaves spun and waved, as if in a gentle breeze. "Which story would you have, Lord Hanali?"

"Why, the story of its founding, and the seven peoples. The story of the beginning."

"As the Elenil have told it?"

"Of course!"

The storyteller nodded curtly. She glanced at Madeline and said, almost under her breath, "Listen well. The Elenil share this story, without cost, so that you may know how the world is meant to be."

Then she began the story. It was a story about a great magician whom the Elenil called the Majestic One, who saw the rebellious nature of all the people of the land and decided he would "repair the world." But most of the people refused to listen to him and continued on in their various violent ways.

The first people to agree to help the magician were named Ele and Nala, who would become the mother and father of the Elenil race. The Majestic One set out to tame the whole world, with Ele and Nala and their children at his side, and in time all the people were brought under his rule.

Much of the story was actually a long poem that Madeline had a hard time following, with all the unfamiliar names. It was about the rewards and blessings that the magician gave to the different people after the war had ended. He made the Elenil the guardians of the world, and according to the story he himself founded the Court of Far Seeing and put the Elenil in charge of the entire Sunlit Lands.

The wizard sent all the other people to different lands, giving them their places in the world. The Aluvorcans made their home among the trees in the southlands. Madeline shuddered. She wouldn't be taking any unfamiliar flowers in the future. She rubbed the small dark mark on her arm, but she couldn't see it as clearly now. Had it already faded? Maybe it would come out on its own, like a splinter. There was a parade of unfamiliar names and people: the Kakri, who lived in the desert; the Maegrom, who lived in the caves beneath the world; the Zhanin ("Shark people," Shula whispered. "We rarely see them this far from the sea."); and the Scim, who were the last people to surrender, and so were cursed to eternal darkness. The Majestic One even cursed their appearance, making them frightening monsters. The Elenil, of course, were rewarded for their loyalty and were made the guardians and caretakers of the Sunlit Lands.

There was even a stanza about human beings, a detail Madeline found surprising. She listened closely to it, interested in how the Elenil saw humans.

According to the leaf woman, the Majestic One said this to the humans:

Humans! Ye shall live upon another earth,
    a people of science and dust.
Bereft of magic, short lived and passionate.
There shall still be beauty and wonder among you.
In great need may ye return to the Sunlit Lands,
    for ye are our cousins and neighbors.

Madeline listened, fascinated. In the Elenil legends of that long-ago time, humans were considered just another magical race of beings, but magic (and apparently long life) had been taken from them, and they were sent to Earth. Interesting. They could only come to the Sunlit Lands in "great need." The story wrapped up with a poem about the rightful place for each type of person to live. Humans on Earth, Zhanin in the sea, Kakri in the desert, and so on.

The woman shuddered when the story was done, and the leaves around her trembled. Her eyes closed for a long moment, and when she opened them she said, "Now my story is done, the truth unspooled. Listen well or be a fool."

"You didn't tell her about the Kharobem," Shula said.

"They were not people made at that time. Not then."

"Or the Southern Court," Hanali said. "What of them?"

"Monsters and animals," the storyteller said. "Nor did I mention the Pastisians, for they are human. Who is the teller of tales here? Do I tell you how to fight a war, Shula Bishara? Do I tell Hanali, son of Vivi, how to choose fine clothing?"

The woman in the ivy shuddered again, and long tendrils of plant life cascaded over her face. It cleared again in a moment. Wet streaks ran down her face.

Without thinking, Madeline stepped closer. The ivy recoiled, making a path for her. Madeline bent down and kissed the storyteller's cheek. "Thank you for the story."

The look in the storyteller's eyes was one of wonder and dismay. She stared at Madeline for the longest time. "It's you," she said. "After all these years."

Madeline didn't know what to say. She whispered, "You're not . . . trapped, are you? In the ivy?"

"Not in the way you think," the storyteller said. "No more than you."

Hanali pulled Madeline back and knelt in front of the storyteller, studying her carefully. "What did you see, old woman?"

"I'm younger than you, Elenil."

Hanali's mouth snapped shut. The muscles in his face flexed. "Show some respect, storyteller. What did you see?"

A long sigh came from the woman, like air escaping a balloon. "Her blade shall bring justice at long last to the Scim."

Hanali did not move for a long time. He only stared at the woman, unblinking. He mumbled, almost to himself, "I know there's more to it than that. The Aluvoreans have taken an interest in her as well. Why would your people show interest in her?"

The woman said nothing at first, but when Hanali continued to glare at her she finally said, reluctantly, "There is trouble in Aluvorea. She may be a seed of hope. But I fear it is still a long way off, Hanali. Another time, another tale."

He studied Madeline. Then to Shula he said, "At dusk, take Madeline to the battlements to see the Scim and watch the battle."

"It's only her first full day, and she's not ready to—"

Hanali's eyes narrowed, and Shula stopped speaking. "She need not fight, but she will watch."

Shula bent her head. "Of course, Excellency."

Madeline found herself surprised by Hanali. He was kind and hospitable one moment and dismissive the next. He seemed foppish and ridiculous most of the time. But he had these moments of decisive command, and no one dared cross him then—not Shula, and not the storyteller. He was a strange person.

Hanali guided them outside, bowed deeply, and begged their leave. He wandered off into the crowd. Shula watched him go, a concerned look on her face.

"What's wrong?" Madeline touched Shula's arm.

Shula looked up, startled. "Hanali is not usually so polite to humans.

Asking permission to leave us. And *bowing* to us? It's very strange. He must think there's something to these prophecies."

They strolled along the street, arm in arm. There were so many wonderful things to see here. "Why did it seem like Hanali didn't know the story the ivy woman was telling? And why were the details different than what you both expected?"

Shula shrugged. "Storytellers tell their stories differently depending on the time of day, the audience, and their whim. That's why she asked if he wanted the story as the Elenil tell it—she likely knows the same story from different peoples, different tribes, different times. I've heard that story five or six times, and each time with different nuances."

That was interesting. Madeline wondered about that while they walked. So the woman in the ivy may very well have been tailoring that story just for her. She wanted to think about that more. She glanced at her arm. She couldn't see the seed at all now.

She didn't want to think about that anymore. She was alive. She could breathe. She had been stung by a deadly flower, and it hadn't bothered her a bit. She wanted to do something fun, to celebrate, to run and dance. She asked Shula if they could walk past the singing fountains she had seen from the coach, and Shula, delighted, agreed.

"Don't worry about those prophecies," Shula said. "The Elenil love prophecies. They use them constantly. Hanali uses them to learn what people will wear to parties so he can make sure his outfit is unique."

"You're kidding." They laughed.

"They have a low tolerance for not knowing or understanding things. They—" Shula hesitated. "They go to extremes to learn about the future. They're plotters and planners. They hold prophecies over each other's heads to get people to behave the way they want. They'll lie about a prophecy if they think it gives them an advantage."

"So the thing about me bringing justice to the Scim with my sword?"

Shula patted her hand. "Could have been invented by Hanali to advance his social standing among the other Elenil."

Madeline felt a mix of relief and disappointment wash over her. So much had changed in the last twenty-four hours. She was still getting used to the fact that she could breathe. She didn't want to be some Elenil hero.

At the same time, there was something exciting about being someone special, someone with a fate that would change the world. "Why would the storyteller say the same thing, then?"

Shula didn't respond, a troubled look crossing her face.

At the fountain, they listened to the music as the water leapt from bowl to bowl. Shula explained how the bowls represented the Sunlit Lands cosmology: a series of crystal spheres that turned like clockwork over the world. Madeline had a vague memory of learning something like it in an advanced English class when they were reading Shakespeare. It was another reminder that they were not on Earth. The people, the clothing, the architecture, even the astronomy, all looked different.

On the way home Shula bought her a snack using a few wooden coins she fished from her pocket. The fruit had a hard, purplish exterior, which the merchant (a surly Maegrom) cut deftly in two with a curved knife. She and Shula each took half, and the merchant gave them each their own wooden spoon, more like a tiny paddle. The soft, white interior of the fruit was both sweet and tangy and left her tongue tingling with pleasure. When they finished, Shula took the "bowl" of the fruit and threw it straight into the air. A large green bird sailed out of nowhere, snatched the peel from the sky, and disappeared, fighting off two smaller birds. Madeline threw hers into the air, and another bird snatched it.

By the time they were nearly home, most of the shops along the street were closing, with merchants pulling in their wares and folding up their canopies. "The market is closing for a time of rest before nightfall. We should rest also," Shula said. "Tonight you'll watch from the city wall . . . You won't get much sleep before tomorrow."

Madeline's heart began to pound. The thought of being in a battle, of being in a fight at all, made her nervous. Her palms began to sweat. Shula squeezed Madeline's shoulder. "Do not fear. You made an agreement to serve the Elenil, but there is no guarantee they will assign you to fight. They may put you on guard duty, or have you serve food in the archon's palace. You agreed to serve them, not necessarily to fight."

"But the prophecy Hanali keeps mentioning—it sure sounds like fighting."

Shula sighed. "Six months ago, Hanali was invited to a party for someone in the Elenil elite. It was a big deal. He went to sixteen prophets, four soothsayers, and three party planners. He chose his outfit and bought new gloves and obsessed about this party for more than two months. One of the prophets told him I would ruin the party. I was supposed to go as his 'bodyguard' . . . The Elenil like ridiculous shows of luxury, and that was one of his. But he was so terrified that he switched me out for someone else. The party came, and he attended, and he even spoke to some of the most influential Elenil, the magistrates. The whole city was talking about it the next day, and Hanali's name came up more than once in the gossip chains."

"So you didn't ruin it?"

"No," Shula said. "But the next time I saw him, he cornered me and said, 'You ruined the party. I spent the entire night worried about how you were going to ruin it, so I didn't enjoy it for a moment.'"

Madeline laughed.

It was definitely getting darker now, but there was still plenty of light to see. They had walked past Mrs. Raymond's house and were now at the base of the city wall. "So just because my sword will bring justice, that doesn't necessarily mean I'm fighting a war?"

Shula shook her head. In the dim light, the scar on her face stood out more clearly. "Maybe you drop a sword on someone's toe, and they get so angry they destroy the Scim once and for all. Or maybe you work in the kitchens and make a sword cake that gives all the Scim a stomachache at the signing of a peace treaty. Or—" Shula up held a finger. "—and this is the most likely one of all—Hanali is trying to get some attention and has made up a prophecy. The whole city would be looking for you if the prophets pronounced you as some sort of chosen one."

Madeline thanked Shula, then gave her a hug. Madeline's muscles unknotted, and her fists unclenched. She took a deep breath, something she would never, never get tired of doing. "I've been worried," she said, "that I would come all the way here to get away from—from the thing that was killing me back home—and that I would get killed by the Scim instead." She felt weird not telling Shula about her deal with Hanali, but Mrs. Raymond had seemed to feel so strongly about it. Maybe she would wait a few days until she better understood how everything worked.

But she already knew she could trust Shula. She felt it to the core of her being.

"The Scim can't kill you if you kill them first," Shula said. "Climb to the top of this stairway and tell them your name. I have to get ready to fight. But it's time for you to see the Scim."

13
WAR PARTY

None could stand for long against the might
of the Majestic One or his servants, the Elenil.

FROM "THE ORDERING OF THE WORLD," AN ELENIL STORY

✦

J ason debated whether to go into battle with his friends. He
debated right until the moment when another teen said to him,
"You're the guy who gets the unicorn, right?"

"I'm the—" Jason looked around, bewildered. David, Kekoa,
and Jason had just walked outside the city wall, into a sort of
staging area where the army of the Elenil was preparing for war.

The other guy, an African American kid with a military buzz cut and
green fatigues, looked him over. "Listen, kid, I know you're new here, but I
gotta get everyone outfitted. Are you the guy who gets the unicorn or not?"

David elbowed him. "Speak up, Jason. Sorry, Jasper, he's new."

Jasper rolled his eyes. "I could tell by the white clothes, Glenn."

"Yeah, I'm the one who gets a unicorn." He couldn't stop the enormous
smile from growing across his face. "Jason Wu." He held his hand out.

"Gloves, Wu. Where are your gloves?" Jasper sighed. "Come here." He led Jason to a stand that held what looked like traditional Chinese armor, but all white. "Hanali sent this over. Said you didn't like the Japanese stuff in the armory. You know how to put this on? It's a Song dynasty replica, pretty typical mountain pattern armor. Leg plates, chest plate . . . You tie this all together with the silk cords. And the helmet is there on top."

Jason had no idea how to put it on. And how did this guy Jasper know so much about ancient Chinese armor? *I guess that's how you get put in charge of the armory.* "I'll figure it out," he said. Why would he need armor anyway? He would be on a unicorn.

Jasper looked at him skeptically. "When you're fitted out, meet us outside the wall, and we'll get you mounted." Jasper moved off into the crowd.

The crowd was strange. Human teenagers, mostly. In fact, almost all of the people here looked to be about the same age. There weren't a lot of Elenil ("They watch sometimes, from the wall," David had said), and he hadn't seen Baileya, or any other Kakri for that matter. It was weird that the humans did all the fighting . . . On the other hand, they were the ones who had made deals to fight the Scim. Except him. He was fighting because . . . well, because Break Bones seemed pretty awful, and David and Kekoa had made the whole thing sound more like a sporting event than anything dangerous, and also there was a unicorn.

"We've never had a unicorn," David said. David wore an open buckskin jacket and a looping necklace of some sort that looked like a ladder of beads hanging in front. His hair was swept up in a sort of pompadour in the middle, with two thick braids on either side of his face, and he had worked a few feathers into his hair. He had two white lines on the front of his face, coming down like tears. He and Kekoa had been the ones to tell Hanali there was nothing appropriate for Jason in the armory. It wasn't mandatory to wear a traditional war outfit, it was just his roommates' preference. You could request whatever you wanted. A lot of people wore some sort of military gear from modern times or earlier. A medieval European knight's armor just seemed right to a lot of people who had grown up watching fantasy movies.

"What do you usually have instead of a unicorn?" Jason asked, trying to figure out how to put his breastplate on.

"Horses, mostly. Elephants, too. These big birds called rocs sometimes, but I think those are seasonal or something. I tried riding a giant cat once, but it went crazy and started pouncing on our own people, so we shrank it again. Lives in Mrs. Raymond's kitchen now, but I think it might have gotten a taste for human blood. I try to stay far away from it. Name is Fluffywoogins."

"Terrifying," Jason said. He had the breastplate on, he thought, more or less correctly. The other pieces tied on with silk cords that ran through holes in the armor.

"Howzit?" Kekoa called. He was barefoot and bare chested, wearing what looked like a red towel around his waist. He had his leiomanō in one hand.

"Dude got his unicorn," David said.

"What? That's epic, brah."

The leg guards fell off again. "Do unicorns talk, you think?"

Kekoa laughed. "One day I was practicing slinging stones at a bird, and it came over and asked me to stop. It's always hard to say in the Sunlit Lands."

"Help me tie these," Jason said, and the three of them set to work knotting the armor together. In the end, David and Kekoa said he looked fierce, but Jason was almost certain it wasn't on correctly. He settled the helmet on his head. The boys clapped.

"Man, you're unrecognizable," David said. "Pretty awesome."

The armor was heavy. Jason started sweating after a few steps. David slung a quiver of arrows on Jason's back and gave him a bow. "Use your magic, and you should be able to hit a Scim even while riding a giant white stallion with a horn."

They walked toward the wall, debating if the unicorn would gore people with its horn. It seemed likely, and Jason didn't think that would make for a comfortable ride. Not that war was about comfort, but still.

"Now we all line up," Kekoa said. "Not much organization to it—we sort of pick our own places."

"Some kids tried to organize us last week because they had grown up playing strategy games or something, but the Elenil don't care, so we do what we want. That's why we're the War Party," David said, and he and Kekoa tapped their weapons together like toasting someone at a party.

"Three Musketeers," Kekoa said.

"Speaking of which," Jason said. "What happened to your previous roommate, anyway? Did he, um, you know, get horribly beheaded?"

David and Kekoa burst out laughing. "No, man, he finished his service and went home. He was from Ohio, I think. Hanging out in Cincinnati right now, I bet."

"The Scim will line up over there," Kekoa said. There was a long ridge to the west of the city. "When it's dark enough—they always wait for the darkest moment—we fight. Not for long, usually. Our job is to keep them out of the city. Their job is to . . . Well, I never listen to their whole thing. You know, bring a thousand years of darkness and so on."

"I'm surprised they don't burn the farmlands and everything outside the city, or put it under siege."

"They're not the smartest," David said.

A horn sounded, and an entourage came out of the city gates. A fully armored knight led the way, his helmet under one arm. His horse was a silvery color, wide chested and powerful. The knight's armor flashed brilliantly even in the low light, and he wore an emerald-green sash across his chest, and on his flag was a stylized silver horse prancing on an emerald field. His face was weathered and scarred, and Jason realized he was the oldest human he had seen since coming to the Sunlit Lands. Ancient. Maybe in his mid-forties.

"The Knight of the Mirror," Kekoa said. A large group of warriors surrounded him, a few on horses but many of them on foot.

"He won't use magic," David said. "None of his people will, either."

"Like Baileya," Jason said, and as the words came from his mouth he saw her, taller than most of the men around her. She hadn't changed from earlier, other than to use a long white scarf to tie her loose clothing closer to her body. Probably to keep it from getting in her way during the battle. She carried something like a long spear with a pointed metal head on one side and a curved blade on the other. Red feathers hung from the base of each blade. "She's amazing," Jason said.

Kekoa rapped him, hard, on the breastplate. "Pull it together. You're going into battle, not on a date."

"Uh." Jason tried to snap out of it. "Why do they call him the Knight of the Mirror?"

"He's vain," David said, jumping from foot to foot, warming up. "Always looking in mirrors. He usually brings one out to—yup, there he goes."

The knight pulled a mirror from the inside of his sash and held it up, looking intently into it. He didn't seem to see or hear anything else going on around him, even when a monstrous cheer rose from the western ridge and a nightmare army crested the top.

David shoved Jason back toward the wall. "Go get your unicorn, dude, and meet us in the middle of the fight."

Kekoa shouted, "Some of the Scim, they target the newbies, so be careful. The white armor gives it away!"

"And stay away from the Black Skulls," David said. "Just . . . don't even go near them. Focus on the regular Scim."

Jasper stood near the wall, next to an enormous tent. Elephants came lumbering from inside, small decks built on top of them, warriors at the ready looking out the sides. Jason paused and shouted back to his friends, "How will I know which ones are the Black Skulls?" but they were already gone, pushing their way to the front of the lineup.

Jason ran to the tent—well, as close to running as he could get in his armor—and stopped in front of Jasper. He gave him a quick salute. "Jason Wu, Unicorn Captain First Class, reporting for duty."

"Unicorn Cap—" Jasper looked disgusted. "Get in here, Wu. I'll introduce you to your animal."

"Does she have a name already?" Jason asked as Jasper led him past partitioned stalls in the monstrous tent.

"You get to name your own war beast, that's tradition around here," Jasper said.

Jason stood up straight. "Then I shall name her . . . Delightful Glitter Lady!" He grinned. Now *that* was a good unicorn name. "My sister, she would have wanted Sparkling Ruby Rainbow, but I'm thinking it's too many *r*'s."

Jasper rolled his eyes. Outside there was a roaring sound, and then the muffled sounds of a gravelly voice shouting. Jasper said, "The Scim are making their declaration of battle. You have maybe three minutes. Okay, listen, kid. You ever ridden a unicorn before?"

"I've never even *seen* one. Unless you count dreams."

"Focus, Wu, I'm trying to train you. You know how to connect your magic to your weapon?"

"Sure." Connect through his tattoo, and reach out to take the skill he needed.

"Same thing, only you use the saddle. *Not* the unicorn, okay? The saddle." He glared until Jason nodded. Jasper stopped in front of a fifteen-foot-tall curtain. "If you're losing your concentration and can't focus on both your weapon and the saddle, then you should—"

"Stay focused on my weapon," Jason said, nodding.

"On the *saddle*," Jasper said, exasperated. "Better to lose control of your weapon than to fall off your mount. I'm not sure you're ready to go out." He rubbed his eyes. "Okay, look. If you get in trouble, you find one of the big magic users, okay? There's a woman named Shula Bishara, she's the one who'll be shooting fire everywhere. Or find Diego Fernández, he's the one who can fly. Or that kid—what's his name?—Alex, I think, who can make rocks move. And if you can't find them, or they're too far, you stick to the Knight of the Mirror. You know that guy, the old one?"

"I saw him, sure."

"And *stay away from the Black Skulls.*"

Jason nodded sagely. He paused for a long moment, waiting for Jasper to say more. When it was clear Jasper wasn't going to volunteer the information, Jason asked, "I'll be able to recognize the Black Skulls . . . how, exactly?"

Jasper looked at him in complete amazement. "They are wearing black skulls. Seriously, who briefed you for tonight?"

"Aaaaanyway," Jason said, "Can I see Delightful Glitter Lady now?"

Jasper waved a hand at the curtain. "Go ahead."

Jason took a deep breath and leaned his face up against the curtain. He heard a snort. He imagined her beautiful white mane and pearlescent horn. He threw the curtain aside. Delightful Glitter Lady lifted her thick neck and snorted again.

Jason cocked his head to one side. He turned to Jasper. "That's a rhinoceros," he said. "A really, really huge one."

"The Elenil are a little sketchy on zoological classifications," Jasper said. "But, yeah, I think you're right."

Not only was it a rhinoceros, it was about twice as large as a regular Earth rhino, easily as large as an elephant. It had deep-grey skin, wrinkled and tough, and a horn three times as big around as Jason's arm. "Just the one horn," Jason said. "So I guess, technically . . ." He walked carefully in front of the rhino. It turned its head sideways, watching him with a tiny black eye.

A multicolored cloth had been thrown across the rhino's swayed back, with a massive saddle on top of that. Jason kept his distance as he made his way around the rhino's side. There was a stepladder. He climbed it slowly. Jasper was nowhere to be seen. *A wise man*, Jason thought.

Before getting into the saddle, Jason looked for the spot to connect his tattoo. It was just close enough that he could touch it before climbing on. He let the magic flow through his tattoo and reached out to find the skills of some Sunlit Lands unicorn rider. A feeling of certainty came over him, and he vaulted onto the rhino's back. He leaned close and patted the thick folds of skin on the creature's neck. The rhino's ears turned back toward him.

He nocked an arrow. Then he shouted, "ONWARD TO VICTORY, DELIGHTFUL GLITTER LADY!" and jabbed the rhino hard in the sides. She made a sound that was a cross between ten untalented trumpet players and an enormous balloon shrieking as air was being forced out of it, and charged.

She went straight through the side of the tent, pulling it down around them. The tent billowed up and covered their faces, tearing away in time for Jason to see Delightful Glitter Lady trampling their own soldiers as she galloped through the front lines.

"Sorry!" he shouted back at the trampled humans. "Still getting the hang of my rhinocorn!"

He burst through the enemy front lines. Terrible beasts hacked at him with axes and fired arrows at Delightful Glitter Lady. Terror coursed through his body like electricity, and he wanted to shout at the top of his lungs. But then his leg plates came off, thrown from the side of the rhino, and Jason saw them get trampled into splinters. *That could have been me*, he thought, and all desire to shout disappeared. He frantically checked his breastplate and helmet—they, at least, seemed to be secure.

The Scim looked more frightening and terrible than Break Bones, if such a thing was possible—long limbed, with too-large heads and protruding, tusklike teeth set in wide mouths. Some of them rode enormous rats, and one streaked by flying on the wide, leathery wings of a bat. It would have seemed like a video game, except that instead of a carefully created entertainment experience, the sounds around him clashed together into one muddy roar, the smells of the creatures and the chaotic movements of the enemy spinning past him faster than he could process. He needed to focus, to try to remove the dizzy confusion of the battlefield. He chose the bat because the sight of the giant thing gave him a sick feeling in the pit of his stomach.

Jason focused on the magic of the bow in his hand, reached out, and borrowed the skill necessary to let an arrow fly. He tracked the bat as it flitted and flapped across the field until he felt the magic take hold, and then he released the bowstring. The arrow soared, straight and true, and lodged in the bat's rider. He toppled from the beast and fell into the battle below. A cheer rose from the forces of Far Seeing. Jason was cheering too. The sheer amount of adrenaline coursing through his body made him feel strong, powerful, invincible. The bat wheeled away and flew off into the dusk. A few more shots like that might make this whole experience almost enjoyable.

In the distance, Jason saw the Knight of the Mirror hacking his way through the Scim, his magic-less warriors following behind and to the sides of him. It was almost beautiful, the smoothness of their motion as they scythed through the crowd. Jason caught sight of Baileya for a moment, her strange spear spinning through the enemy.

Out of nowhere, a monstrous wolf, nearly the size of a compact car, leapt onto Jason's rhinocorn. "Gah!" he shouted, recoiling from the terrifying sight of its enormous maw and rolling backward off his mount, the wolf pouncing just behind him, missing only because Jason continued to roll when he hit the ground.

Jason scrambled to his feet, his bow and arrows scattered on the ground between him and the wolf. He tried not to hyperventilate at the sight of the mangy, drooling monster. He hadn't brought a knife. Not even a small one. The wolf advanced, and Jason stepped backward. "Is there a pause button?" Jason asked nervously as the wolf took another step forward. "Um. Time out?"

An ear-shattering war cry filled the air, followed by David Glenn's lean body leaping onto the wolf's back, hacking into its neck with his ax. Kekoa ran in from the side, slicing at the monster's legs with his leiomanō. The wolf collapsed, and the boys kicked and stabbed at it. It shook once, violently, and knocked David from its back before slinking away into the battle.

"Hi," Jason said, panting. "What was that?"

"We call those giant wolves," Kekoa said nonchalantly.

"But we liked that name you used," David said.

Then they both shouted together, looks of mock horror on their faces, "GAH!"

"Har, har," Jason said, gathering his bow and arrows, his hands shaking. "Giant wolves are scary. I do not like them."

"Nice shot with the bat," Kekoa said. "They'll be talking about that one tomorrow!"

David shouted, "Split up or stick together?"

"I wanna get that big spider they brought tonight! Did you see it?"

"Gross," David said. "Hard pass. I'm going after that wolf. Jason?"

Kekoa put his hands on Jason's. "You're shaking, brah. That's just adrenaline. It's okay. Remember, you got nothing to be afraid of. The Elenil will fix you right up if something happens, and we're keeping an eye on you. You want to go hunt a giant spider with me?"

Jason shuddered. He did not want to see a giant spider.

"Think of the positives," David said. "What are the good things happening right now?"

"I have a unicorn," Jason said reflexively.

"No one else has a unicorn," Kekoa said. "Right?"

"I gotta go find her!"

The three exchanged grins, and David shouted, "WAR PARTY, TO WAR!"

David gave Jason a thumbs-up and ran after the wolf, and Kekoa let out a whoop and dove back into the fray. Jason watched them go, his hands on his hips. He scooped up his arrows and put them back in the quiver. He had no idea how to find Delightful Glitter Lady. "Uh," he said, then cleared his throat. "Here, unicorn! Over here! Uuuuunicooorn!"

✛

Madeline watched Shula leave before climbing the stairs toward the top of the wall. The more she thought about it, the more Madeline realized she had no intention of lifting a sword against anyone, Scim or Elenil or human. War was not her thing. She couldn't imagine that a night on the wall would change that, not for an instant. She might be in service to the Elenil, but she didn't have to kill anyone. Her breath went ragged for a moment. Surprised, she pushed up her sleeve to see the bracelet tattoo pulsing in time to her breathing. Maybe it could sense her wavering in her commitment to the Elenil. Okay, okay, she was going up the stairs like she was supposed to.

It was a wide stone stairway. At the top, a shimmering golden haze prevented her from stepping onto the wall. A voice came from the haze as Madeline approached it. "Declare your race and enter."

"My *race*?" Madeline looked back down the stairway, as if for help. She wasn't sure what to say. "White?" She paused. "Caucasian?"

Nothing happened.

She waited for a minute, unsure what to do. "French? Scottish."

Hanali descended the stairs, the shimmering curtain gently making way for him. "My sweet child," he said. "Is this so difficult? It is a simple security measure—it should not be so vexing."

"I don't understand what it's asking, I guess," Madeline said.

"Observe," Hanali said, and started up the stairs.

The shimmering golden haze's voice said, "Declare your race and enter."

"Elenil," Hanali said, and the curtain parted. He walked through, glancing over his shoulder at Madeline with a look of pity.

"Declare your race and enter."

"Human," Madeline said, and the curtain parted. She stepped onto the wall. She felt a vague sense of unease at the security magic. Was being a human sufficient reason to trust someone for entry? She wondered what happened if the curtain determined you were Scim . . . or something else.

Hanali waited, impatient, one gloved hand held out to her. He wore a new emerald-green outfit and a ridiculous floppy hat. "We use the same magic at the city gates, to keep the Scim out. The only real danger on this side of the wall is that they could tear down the gate itself."

The wall was wider than she had expected. ("Wide enough for six carriages to race side by side—though who would enter such a foolish race?" Hanali said.) Below them the Elenil army gathered. Madeline noted that not many of them were Elenil, something that, again, struck her as strange. They were, in fact, nearly all humans, or at least seemed to be. She had thought maybe that was just the city guard, but it appeared to be true of their entire army.

The atmosphere at the top of the wall was not one of war. Merchants strode down the center selling snacks, and seating areas festooned with flowers and banners bedecked the outer edges, where the view would be best. Musicians gathered at the inner edge, playing jaunty tunes on stringed instruments. The musicians, the merchants, the dancers, the security guards: all humans. Elenil, taller and far more elegant, walked among them or sat on the edge chatting amiably with one another as they waited for the battle to start.

"I have someone to introduce you to," Hanali said, his face aglow with excitement beneath the ridiculous wide brim of his hat. While the other Elenil tended toward elegance, Hanali often looked like the most outrageous model at an experimental fashion show. Madeline wondered if he did this on purpose. "She's well known to the archon, and if all goes well she may bring you into the court in her service after your training. Her name is Gilenyia."

Madeline didn't know much about who the archon was, and she didn't know why it was good to be taken into the court after her training, or even how long it would be (when she got to stop wearing white?), but this seemed important to Hanali, and whatever came, she continued to be thankful to him for providing her a way to breathe.

Hanali fussed over her gloves, making sure they covered her wrists where they met the long sleeves of her dress. He told her twice not to offer to shake hands and not to curtsy and certainly not to draw attention to herself. "Be your usual charming self," Hanali said, "only more charming."

Hanali threaded the crowd, past the jugglers and actors, the poets and puppeteers, until they came to a cream-colored tent shot through with gold and silver thread. Two humans stood on guard outside, wearing a strange mishmash of medieval European armor and fantastic Elenil designs. One of them lifted a chin to Hanali, which delighted him to no end. "I brought those two into the Sunlit Lands," he whispered as they entered the tent.

The tent was lit by floating glass balls, each of which held a spark of light. "An extravagant use of magic," Hanali murmured. "Especially when the dark so rarely comes to the Court of Far Seeing."

An Elenil woman lay stretched on a divan in the center of the tent, her long dress draped carefully to cover her completely. Her laced collar crept so far up her neck that it caressed her chin. The skin of her face was pale as milk on marble, her hair like tame sunlight. Her eyes were a deep blue, almost purple, that Madeline had only seen while on an airplane, looking at the distant sky above the clouds.

"Ah," the Elenil woman said. "This must be Madeline Oliver."

Hanali had told her not to shake hands or curtsy but hadn't explained what she *should* do. Madeline allowed herself a slight smile and forced herself to look away from Gilenyia. Out of the corner of her eye she saw Hanali bow deeply.

Gilenyia laughed, and her laugh built on itself, like a handbell choir playing a particularly merry tune. "So polite, Hanali! Even your human charge did not curtsy, so why should you be so formal? Come, friends, and sit. Let us enjoy this evening together."

Two chairs waited on either side of her. Madeline hadn't seen them appear. Hanali escorted her to a chair, then sat on the other side of the divan. Why did Hanali tell her not to curtsy, and then bow himself? He was so frustrating. Her cheeks flushed with embarrassment.

Gilenyia smiled at Madeline. "He scared you, didn't he? Told you not to curtsy or shake hands?"

Madeline glanced at Hanali, who shook his head.

"Yes," Madeline said.

Gilenyia burst into laughter, and Madeline couldn't keep from smiling in return. "He's my cousin," Gilenyia said. "Or at least, that's the closest concept among your people. We grew up in the same household, like brother and sister. We are young for Elenil, born in the same year. I am not easily offended, even by the strange manners of humans."

Madeline wasn't sure if she should respond, but she said, "He acted like you were a celebrity."

"She is," Hanali said, "in her way."

Gilenyia slapped his shoulder. "You never treated me thus when we were children." She leaned toward Madeline and whispered, "He uses his youth as an excuse when he violates good manners. The Elenil at the Court talk about him incessantly. He is well known as a rogue."

"Please," Hanali said, fastidiously pulling the fingers of his gloves to fit more perfectly. "I spend so much time among the humans, I occasionally forget the ins and outs of Elenil society."

"Nonsense," Gilenyia said, laughing again, her gloved hands covering her mouth. "Ah, you have always been a rogue."

"What changed?" Madeline asked. "Why did he start treating you differently?"

Gilenyia's face darkened, and Hanali's paled. Madeline couldn't see why her question might be rude, but she hastily apologized. Gilenyia didn't respond, didn't seem to have heard her.

"In other news," Hanali said brightly, "my new haberdasher assures me this hat will be the talk of Far Seeing."

Gilenyia spoke over him. "It is a fair question, Cousin, and if she is here to fight the Scim, why not tell her all? You did not bring her to Far Seeing for her insights on hats and silk jackets."

Hanali inclined his head. "As you wish, Cousin. But I would rather she see the Scim first, and know of your work."

Gilenyia sighed. "At last fair Hanali speaks his mind. So be it then. Far be it from me to discourage you when you get the courage to speak as family and not some sycophant." She leaned her head to the side and whispered something, and three waiters appeared with drinks. Or . . . something like waiters. Again, humans, and they did not meet Madeline's eye.

The drink was sweet, like some combination of strawberry and peach, and cold, though it had no ice. It was, like many things among the Elenil, the most delightful drink Madeline could recall. She drank it faster than she intended, and a second drink appeared in her hand at the same moment the empty glass was whisked away.

"Take off your glove," Gilenyia said.

Without thinking, Madeline pulled her hand away from the Elenil woman. It was a request she wouldn't have thought twice about at home, but here it was a matter of propriety, perhaps even modesty. She knew it was the height of rudeness to show one's naked hand to the Elenil, and she assumed to ask someone to remove their glove was rude as well.

"I don't want to offend you," Madeline said.

But Gilenyia took a firm hold of Madeline's left wrist and slipped the glove from her hand. The action shocked Madeline. She looked to Hanali for guidance, but he appeared almost queasy. He gave her a look she thought was intended to seem reassuring.

"Fascinating," Gilenyia said, studying the silver loops and swirls of Madeline's tattoo. It almost pulsed in the light of the hovering glass orbs. She traced one of the leafing branches. "This is a healing spell." She turned to Hanali. "Who wrought this? Did you learn so much in the household of our childhood?"

Hanali inclined his head slightly. "Indeed. It was I who struck the deal, Cousin."

Gilenyia looked into Madeline's eyes. "So young to be at death's door. You cannot breathe?"

"I can now."

"Because—" Gilenyia traced the silver tattoo, puzzling through its knots and cords. "Because you agreed to fight the Scim. For a human year." She looked to Hanali again, "A canny bargain, Cousin."

"A canny bargain?" Madeline asked. "Isn't everyone's about the same?"

Gilenyia gave her a pitying look. A horn sounded, distracting her. Madeline pulled her glove over her hand and moved away from the woman.

"The Knight of the Mirror," Gilenyia said, sounding pleased. She made a motion, and one curtained wall opened, revealing the edge of the city wall and the battlefield beyond. Madeline bit her lip, watching the massive scale of the army preparing itself for battle. "Do not worry, child. Before this night is through I will show you the power of Elenil healing magic."

"It is a great honor," Hanali said. "So few are able to heal, even among the Elenil."

Below them, a knight and his entourage moved toward the front lines. It wasn't night yet—it would never be night here. But a sort of twilight had fallen over the field. Madeline could still see the army below with amazing clarity, and she wondered if there was some magical enhancement improving the view. Rondelo, one of only a handful of Elenil on the field, rode out on his white stag, Evernu. Madeline found it hard to imagine herself on the field of battle, wearing extravagant armor. What weapon would she use? Who would be her commander? The whole idea was odd. She wondered for a moment if she could ride Evernu behind Rondelo, her arms around his waist, then felt the heat in her face. How would she fight if her arms were full of the Elenil warrior? Madeline's heart beat faster, and she was suddenly glad Darius wasn't here to see her face. Besides, Rondelo was Elenil. She didn't think that would work, and she would be gone in a year. Darius was waiting for her.

"Rondelo has become well respected," Hanali said, as if reading Madeline's thoughts. "His insistence on joining the field of battle has drawn attention."

Gilenyia made a noncommittal noise. "I have heard his name spoken among the magistrates."

"He is young to be mentioned for polemarch," Hanali said. "And yet I, too, have heard his name among the prophets and soothsayers in the market. And he is plain for an Elenil. He could almost pass for human."

Gilenyia sipped her drink. "If he were to become commander of the Elenil army, it would give the current polemarch more time to attend to social matters. It could come to pass."

"So that Tirius can attend more parties? You have a wicked tongue, Cousin."

Gilenyia smiled slyly. "I know we are family, Hanali. You need not call me Cousin every time you speak."

Hanali said nothing.

A great cheer came up from the west, and the Scim army appeared over the ridge. A spider the size of a semi crested the hill first, followed by enormous creatures of various disgusting types: wolves, rats, bats, and even a monstrous, scabby possum.

"Now they will list their supposed grievances," Gilenyia said.

Madeline knelt at the wall's edge so she could see better. Hanali handed her a brass spyglass. Madeline held it to her eye, and the distant Scim appeared, more disgusting than she could have imagined. The Scim spokesman had massive teeth, tusks nearly, jutting from behind his bottom lip. Grey skin, ears like wads of chewed gum, and a heavy shelf of a brow over small, angry black eyes. The rags that covered his heavily muscled frame were stained and no doubt stank. His hands were too large, the wide fingernails yellowed and broken.

The Scim began to speak, his gravelly voice rolling over the field of battle and to the wall. It must have been magically amplified, because he wasn't shouting, but every word was crystal clear.

"I am Crooked Back, spokesman for the Scim. We see you tremble in fear at our approach." The Elenil forces jeered. Crooked Back continued, "We do not come seeking war but only a return of what is ours. The Elenil have stolen what rightfully belongs to the Scim. They have taken certain artifacts which are of our heritage. Five magical artifacts, made by Scim, empowered by Scim, belonging to the Scim. Stolen by the Elenil. If these five artifacts are returned to our people, we will leave in peace."

Gilenyia put her hand lightly on Madeline's shoulder. "What would they ask for tomorrow if we gave in to such demands today? Those artifacts are dangerous and were taken from the Scim for their own safety after the War of the Waste. No, we won't be returning those."

Hanali grunted. "Nor do we have them, for the magistrates turned them over to a human, did they not?"

"An excellent point," Gilenyia said.

"But . . . if they belong to the Scim?" Madeline looked at Gilenyia.

"They are weapons of unimaginable magic. The Scim cannot be trusted with such things."

The Scim spokesman had continued talking, little caring about the conversation happening on the wall. "—then we shall bring a thousand years of darkness and tear every white stone of this city down. We shall salt your fields and burn your homes, and the great darkness shall reign. Flame and darkness, death and suffering await you. What say you, Elenil army?"

In response, the Elenil army shouted jeers, and several arrows were loosed toward the Scim front lines.

"So be it," Crooked Back roared. "May darkness rain down upon you!" With that, the Scim army raced down the hill to battle. The terrible screaming and shrieks of the Scim sent shivers down Madeline's spine. The Elenil army met them, and the sounds of metal on metal resounded over the field.

It was terrible to watch, like hundreds of car accidents happening at once. The sounds of horses screaming, the shouts of humans and Scim, the bellowing of war animals . . . And yet here, upon the wall, someone was playing a stringed instrument and singing with a clear, sweet voice, and Madeline could smell the remnants of the sweet juice in her cup and someone cooking a delicious meal farther along the wall's edge.

The contrast turned her stomach. It was like a Roman coliseum, and she had a box seat with the rich and powerful. Below them, humans—kids like her who had come here because of injustice and trouble and problems in their world—risked their lives so the Elenil could sip fruit juice and discuss politics and hats. It wasn't a war, it was an entertainment. She set her glass down and waved the servant aside when he offered another.

Still, they watched.

The Knight of the Mirror and his people carved a swath through the Scim. None seemed able to stop him. Hanali pointed out an explosion of flame and explained that it was Shula, that she had the power to burn like a torch without being harmed. "It was what she asked for when I invited her to the Sunlit Lands," Hanali said.

Gilenyia smiled. "She is a fierce one."

The battle continued. An Elenil soldier in white armor rampaged through their own lines on an enormous rhinoceros.

Gilenyia winced. "Who is responsible for that soldier?"

Hanali cleared his throat. "I will make inquiries."

A gigantic spider stalked through the armies. Madeline shivered at the thought of being out there among them. The Scim moved with barbaric efficiency, tearing Elenil soldiers to bits where they were most vulnerable.

Hanali leapt to his feet and strode closer to the battle, his hands clenching the balustrade.

"What is it, Cousin?"

He stared at the field with a sudden intensity. He pointed out a strange Scim soldier in a black helmet shaped like a horned skull who was dragging a flaming woman across the field. "They're targeting the magic users."

Madeline jumped up and stood beside him. "Is that . . . is that *Shula*?"

"I am afraid so," Hanali said grimly. "And there." He pointed to their right. A monstrous bat plucked a flying man out of the sky. "They're stealing our magic."

"We have to get out there," Madeline said. "We have to do something!"

"There is nothing to be done," Hanali said. "If those upon the field cannot prevent it, we will not arrive in time to do any different."

Madeline watched in horror as the Scim in the black skull dragged her new friend away from the city walls and toward the Scim army.

14
NIGHT'S BREATH

*[The Scim] were evil things, their hearts filled
with wickedness and foul deeds.*

FROM "THE ORDERING OF THE WORLD," AN ELENIL STORY

✤

Jason couldn't find Delightful Glitter Lady, though he did occasionally hear what sounded like someone playing a bagpipe half underwater, which he assumed was her. He did, however, catch sight of the Knight of the Mirror again. The battle was so thick that if he kept an eye out for any unengaged Scim and avoided them, he didn't have to fight much to make it through the crowd. He was getting the hang of it. His fear and worry sluiced off him, his muscles relaxed, and his ability to focus came back. His hands weren't shaking anymore.

He was glad his helmet was still on, though, as one Scim warrior knocked him pretty well with a broadsword. The Sunlit Lands guy who could fly (Jason couldn't remember his name) swooped down and took the Scim away. The Scim roared the horrible things he would do to Jason when he got back on the ground. Jason knew he was getting targeted by the Scim for his white armor, but the armor also made it easier for his side to keep an eye on him. They were watching out for him.

A quick count of his arrows showed he only had nine more. He looked for a discarded weapon, but slowing down was an easy way to become a target. He ran toward the Knight of the Mirror. After a moment, he noticed Baileya running alongside him, her Kakri spear tucked beneath her right arm.

"Head back toward the city wall," she shouted. "Now!"

"What's happening?"

"The Scim are targeting the more heavily magical soldiers tonight. They are trying to not even engage with the Knight of the Mirror. There is an evil plan in motion, and I cannot see the shape of it. The Knight has ordered the less experienced to fall back to the city gates."

"But I can help—"

The flying teen dropped down beside them. "The Black Skulls! You can't see it from the ground, but they're triangulating on Shula. I think they're trying to kill her! Permanently!"

"Who's Shula?"

"The burning girl," he said. "Baileya, try to slow down one of the Skulls. I'll see if I can distract the second one. Shula should have a chance against one instead of three."

Baileya's eyes grew wide. Jason followed her gaze. She had sighted one of the Black Skulls. The Skull was riding a possum the size of a horse—its long rodent snout covered in blood, its red eyes filled with bloodlust, its bald tail whipping the air. The Skull itself wore a white robe, the hem of which was filthy with mud and ichor. It wore black gloves and boots, and on its head was an antelope skull painted a shining black, the curved horns rising several feet. In its right hand it held aloft a sickle.

"Run, Jason!"

Baileya sprinted, leaping like a deer over soldiers from both sides. Jason knew she meant for him to run for the gate. Everyone had warned him to stay away from the Black Skulls, and his own brain was screaming at him to do as he was told and run for the wall, but something else—a deeper voice—said this was the whole reason he was here. To protect people. What if Madeline was out here somewhere?

He tightened his grip on his bow and ran after Baileya.

Baileya ran full speed at the Black Skull, sliding to the ground in front of the charging possum. Jason opened his mouth to scream a warning, but she crouched calmly in the beast's path, and at the last possible moment jabbed the curved, bladed side of her spear into the mud, dropped to her knees, and tilted the blade forward.

The possum slammed into the spear. The blade sank into the possum's chest, and it let out a horrible scream as it collapsed, crushing Baileya beneath its heavy corpse before skidding to a stop.

The Black Skull stood slowly, apparently unharmed, its towering horns rising to their full height with a slow implacability, the blade of its sickle glinting in its hand. It turned, the black cavities of its eyes regarding Baileya. Distracted from its mission, it stepped toward the woman who had dared impede its path.

Baileya shoved the possum's head to one side. But to Jason's horror, she didn't stand. She scrambled backward until she found her spear, broken in half now, and used what remained of it to get to her feet. Her left leg hung limply, twisted at an angle that made Jason sick. She dropped her spear, reached behind her back with both hands, and pulled two curved daggers out of her sash.

Why am I standing here, doing nothing? A distant buzzing echoed in Jason's ears. His thoughts came thick and slow. The Black Skull had crossed nearly half the distance to Baileya. *Shake out of it!*

Jason, still a solid twenty feet behind Baileya, slipped an arrow from his quiver and onto his bow. His heart beat so hard against his chest he thought it might break through. He felt the magic, clear and strong, and opened the conduit through his tattoo as wide as he knew how. The confidence of an expert archer flooded him, and the sounds of battle fell away until he saw only one thing: his target. The heart of the Black Skull. He wouldn't allow that thing near Baileya, wouldn't let it hurt her. He breathed once, twice, then held his breath and loosed the arrow. It flew past Baileya, so close the fletching could have brushed her cheek. It sank into its mark, and the Skull stumbled backward.

It did not fall.

It righted itself, snapped the arrow from its chest, and stepped forward again, sickle raised.

"No!" Jason shouted and shot another arrow, then another and another. Five, six, seven arrows, and still the Black Skull walked, its robe an explosion of arrows but not stained with a single drop of blood. Two more arrows, and then Jason was out, and the thing still stalked toward Baileya.

Jason ran between them. "Stay away from her!"

The Skull laughed, and a chill ran down Jason's spine.

He balled his fists, ready to fight the thing to the death. He heard Baileya shouting at him to get back, but it barely registered in the face of those horrible empty eye sockets and the towering horns of the skull.

A meteor streaked between them, and its supercharged air blew Jason back. He stumbled into Baileya, and they fell to the ground. From the center of the fire, a girl's face turned toward them.

"Shula!" Baileya shouted. "It's a trap!"

"Run," the flaming woman said. "I'll take care of him."

Another bright, cascading explosion of fire came from Shula, the hot air singeing Jason and Baileya. Jason helped Baileya move farther from the flames, but the Black Skull advanced despite the heat.

The Black Skull caught on fire, its robes alight, the arrows like torches in its chest. The sickle fell from its hand, the blade red from the flames. It grabbed hold of Shula with both hands. She kicked at the Skull, but it didn't respond to the blows any more than it had responded to the arrows or the fire. The Skull's laughter came rolling over the battlefield again, and it called out in a loud voice, "Victory!"

The Scim roared and echoed the Black Skull's cry, smashing weapons against their shields and helmets as they stopped fighting and began a sudden retreat. "Victory!" they shouted. "Victory, victory, O People of the Shadow!" The Black Skull, still aflame, ran, dragging a struggling Shula. A wolf loped up alongside the Skull, and the Skull pulled itself onto the wolf's back.

Baileya grabbed Jason's arm so hard it bruised him. "Jason. If tonight's battle was only to capture Shula, then we must frustrate their plan." She pushed a curved dagger into his hand. "Slow them however you can. The Knight of the Mirror will come to your aid."

There was no time for instructions or second thoughts. Jason strengthened his grip on the dagger and ran as fast as he could, passing wounded

Scim warriors and monstrous limping creatures. A desperate need to stop the Black Skull washed over Jason. He'd been telling himself that this wasn't his battle, but now this horrible magical creature had grabbed some Earth girl and was dragging her across the field—headed to a terrible end, no doubt. And sure, the girl could light on fire, but that didn't mean she wasn't a human being, and it didn't mean Jason wasn't going to do everything in his power to help her. He tried to run faster, but he kept stumbling on the broken bits of weapons and bodies on the field. If something didn't give soon, he would lose them. He couldn't keep up with the wolf.

Then, as if in answer, the wolf caught fire. It let out a long, plaintive howl and collapsed beneath the Skull. Jason didn't lose a step, just kept running straight ahead. The Black Skull paused for a moment, getting a better grip on the nape of Shula's neck, then strode forward through the battlefield, dragging Shula behind him.

Jason was close now, close enough he thought he had a chance if Shula could slow the Skull down just a minute longer. Thirty seconds and he would be there. His skin hurt from his burns, and he could feel Shula's heat growing as he got closer. He settled his grip on Baileya's dagger and got ready to use it.

A body slammed into him from the side.

It was a Scim warrior, one grey fist holding a club nearly as tall as Jason. It growled, and its foul breath struck him like a blow just before the club did.

Knocked off his feet, Jason landed on another fallen soldier, whether human or Scim he couldn't say, but the Scim warrior was in front of him already, the club swinging toward Jason's chest. He tried to roll away, but he was too slow. He felt his rib cage go, and a cold breeze settled onto him—Shula's heat moving away. So this is how it was going to end. Jason felt a distant regret, cushioned by the thought that he could rest now. He wouldn't have to worry about his parents anymore, wouldn't have to carry his grief about Jenny. He didn't need to save Shula or Madeline or any-one . . . He could just let it all go.

A horn sounded in the distance, and the Scim's head snapped up. It gave Jason a quick sideways glance, but the horn sounded again. The Scim grunted, kicked him once, and loped after the other Scim.

Jason still had Baileya's knife. It was loose in his hand, but he couldn't tighten his grip. He had lost his . . . what was it? Unicorn? And the burning girl. But he still had other things. Like this. The knife. But someone would need to come get it, because his legs weren't working. In fact, his arm wasn't moving either. His thoughts seemed to be coming slow too. Like in a dream, or being half awake. Where was his unicorn again? He thought he heard her trumpet in the distance.

He closed his eyes, and the darkness swept him away.

✠

Madeline watched in mute horror as Shula was dragged across the battlefield by a black-skulled warrior.

"No doubt a message," Gilenyia said. "They begin the battle saying we've stolen their artifacts, and they end by stealing ours."

Hearing Gilenyia call the humans "artifacts" sent a chill down Madeline's spine. The Scim sounded retreat with a series of shouts about their victory and then a thin, shrieking blast from something like a trumpet. The battle shifted as the Elenil army targeted the Scim who carried the Elenil's magic users with them.

Gilenyia stood, and one of her attendants immediately draped a thin satin stole over her shoulders. It nearly touched the ground. "Come," she said. "We shall walk awhile among the corpses."

Madeline shivered. The thought of walking out on the battlefield among the broken dead filled her with horror, but Gilenyia said it with a complete lack of passion, like she was inviting someone to take a stroll around her neighborhood.

Madeline shot a look at Hanali, hoping for a reprieve. Instead he said, "I must speak to Rondelo. Gilenyia will return you home." So. Madeline would go and walk among the corpses with Gilenyia.

Two human attendants flanked them as they descended the stairs and followed the wide avenue through the gate. A ragtag stream of wounded soldiers headed the opposite way, entering the city. Two people held up a third person. A woman helped a man—no, not a man, he looked to be twelve or thirteen—hobble inside.

"We'll help them directly," Gilenyia said. "But first, the more heavily wounded."

She strode straight toward the center of the battlefield where the fighting had been most vicious. They passed broken spears and crushed pieces of armor, people sprawled on their backs, groaning, trampled in the mud. There was a metallic tang in the air and an underlying smell of smoke. The sound of the Scim's retreat came to them like distant waves beating on stone.

Gilenyia stopped in the center of the field, her satin stole stained where it had dragged along the ground. A teenage boy lay at her feet, the shaft of a spear jutting from his chest. His dark hair was plastered to his brown skin, his eyes closed but moving rapidly beneath the eyelids. He was breathing: a slow, irregular rasping sound. Gilenyia knelt beside him and put one gloved hand lightly on his chest. "We start here." To her attendants she said, "You know what to bring me."

Madeline's heart climbed into her throat. The entire field looked like a trash heap, only it was people and creatures strewn across it. To her left was some sort of wooden wagon, arrows stuck in the sides like porcupine quills. There were hands reaching out from beneath it, and a tall, heavily muscled beast, neither human nor Scim, collapsed beside it.

"Come here, girl," Gilenyia said.

Madeline could barely respond. Her mind felt distant and slow, but when Gilenyia snapped her name, she made her way to the Elenil woman's side. The attendants had returned, working together to drag a Scim warrior beside the broken boy at Madeline's feet. One of the Scim's jagged tusks was broken off, and black tattoos crisscrossed its skin. It was unconscious. A great gash from a sword had parted its filthy tunic and torn across its chest.

"Take hold of the spear in the boy's chest," Gilenyia said. "I have broken the blade from the other side."

Madeline goggled. "What?"

But Gilenyia did not repeat herself. She was demurely removing her gloves. The attendants looked away, and Gilenyia snapped at them to find more wounded. "There are some we can save," she said, tucking her gloves into a small pocket inside her stole, "and some who can save others. Now take hold of the spear. Good. When I say, pull it out. It will require some strength."

The wood of the spear was rough and thicker than Madeline had imagined. Something with large hands must have held this weapon. She accidentally jostled the spear, and the boy groaned. Gilenyia gave her a sharp look then put one hand on the boy's chest and one on the Scim warrior's chest.

Gilenyia's hands were not flawless white like her face. A network of golden tattoos covered each hand like spiderwebs. Her palms, fingers, and even fingernails were laced with intricate patterns and intersections and partings. A glowing pulse branched out through the tattoos, and a small wave of heat touched Madeline's face.

"Pull," Gilenyia said.

The spear did not budge.

"Harder!"

Madeline felt the spear give. The boy arched his back and screamed.

"No need to be gentle, girl—tear it out of him."

Angered by her inability to pull the spear free and the string of instructions from Gilenyia, Madeline snapped. She put one foot on the boy's chest, leaned back, and pulled with all her might, stumbling backward with a bloody spear shaft dripping in her hands.

The wound in the boy's chest closed like water over a stone. The Scim's wound simultaneously widened. The grey-skinned warrior thrashed for a moment, Gilenyia's hand still resting on its chest, and then it fell still.

The boy opened his eyes, which widened upon seeing the luxuriously dressed Elenil woman leaning over him. "Lady Gilenyia," he gasped. He leapt up and knelt before her. "Thank you, lady."

"Your name, sir?"

"Ricardo Sánchez, lady."

"You have served us well, Ricardo," she said. "Now join my attendants and gather more wounded. Start with those with the most grievous wounds."

"Yes, my lady," he said. He bounded into the junkyard of the battle.

The Scim soldier did not move, did not breathe. "Did you—" Madeline cleared her throat. "Did you kill him?"

Gilenyia gave her a curious look. "His people abandoned him. He would have died in a few hours. I sped his death and healed one of our soldiers. It was a mercy twice over. Does it displease you?"

Did it displease her? What a strange question. Of course it displeased her. It seemed unjust in every possible way to heal a human warrior by killing a Scim. But Gilenyia was right—the Scim hadn't looked like it would last long. Madeline didn't know much about punctured chests, but the boy hadn't looked like he would last long either. So maybe instead of letting two people die, she had helped one live?

"I help the Scim wounded as well," Gilenyia said. "Their people have abandoned them. We take them into the Court of Far Seeing and rehabilitate them, give them meaningful roles in the Sunlit Lands. It's more than their foul kinfolk have ever done for them."

"It seems . . . something seems wrong about it." Madeline couldn't figure out how to say it, but a sick feeling in the pit of her stomach threatened to spread to her whole body.

"I am a healer," Gilenyia said. "I had hoped you might assist me during your allotted time. To find someone with healing potential is rare among the Elenil, and I see that potential in you. But perhaps you do not have the stomach for it. No matter. Today you shall at least go among the wounded and find those I may help."

"You want me to . . . to find the wounded for you?"

Gilenyia nodded once, impatiently. "Even if I don't heal them, we must take them within the city walls, agreed? Look for the most egregiously wounded first. I cannot save them once they pass death's gate."

Okay. Okay, she could do this. She was only pointing people out, people Gilenyia would find eventually anyway. Or maybe she should run. Maybe she should look for a way home out of this crazy place. Her breathing went ragged just thinking about it. Somewhere there was a gate or portal or closet or painting that would open and land her back with her mom and dad, where Sofía would make her hot chocolate in the morning and pack her lunches, and where Mr. García would smile at her in the sunlit garden as he placed new plants in the black soil. Darius would pick her up and take her to school, and in the afternoon he would read to her.

She stumbled, her chest tightening. Her breathing was coming ragged and uneven. The tattoo on her wrist stung. She whipped off her glove. Maybe it was her imagination, but the tattoo looked wider than before. Not by much, but a tiny bit, like it had swollen.

Were these thoughts enough to invalidate her agreement? Was the magic removing her ability to breathe because she wasn't serving the Elenil with her entire heart? She tugged her glove back on. She didn't want to touch anything out here with her bare hands.

She found a wounded Scim warrior. He was pinned beneath some beast she did not recognize—like an oversize ox. She couldn't tell if the pungent stench came from the animal or the Scim's bloodied and stained rags. The warrior's eyes fluttered open, and when his eyes met hers, his lip curled up in disgust, revealing a scarcity of crooked yellow teeth.

"Can you hear me?"

The Scim licked his lips. "I . . . hear you . . . Elenil."

"I'm human. My name is Madeline."

He grunted or maybe laughed.

"We're going to heal you." She stood and called for Gilenyia.

Gilenyia arrived with five humans—her two attendants and three soldiers she had patched up. She regarded the broken Scim coolly, but she didn't critique Madeline's choice. Instead, she bent over the warrior and said, so quietly that only he and Madeline could hear, "What will you do, brave warrior, if I use Elenil magic to save you?"

"A pox . . . on your magic," he wheezed. "Darkness . . . a thousand years . . . darkness. For you and your . . ." His face contorted in pain, and his hands scratched at the hide of the ox.

"Pull him out," Gilenyia barked, and Ricardo immediately took hold of one arm, an attendant the other. The other two humans put their backs against the ox and pushed. It wasn't enough to get much movement, and the Scim roared in pain.

Madeline said, "We could dig him out," and that's what they did. The mud moved easily enough, and with a combination of hands and broken weapons they managed to get his legs loose enough to tear him away from the dead ox.

"His legs and pelvis are broken," Gilenyia said. "Some minor internal damage. Have you found someone who will balance these wounds?"

One of her attendants brushed the hair out of his eyes with a muddied hand. "I have one." They dragged another Scim warrior, much worse for wear, through the mud. Madeline couldn't believe she was still alive. She had been cut neatly from the shoulder down, and the wound already stank.

Gilenyia looked the Scim over carefully, then motioned to Madeline to join her. "This one won't last long. It is a mercy to her and to the one with broken legs. Do you approve?"

"Do you need me to . . . to approve?"

"Before we leave this battlefield I hope to see you understand the work I do. You have chosen this Scim soldier to be healed. You must have some compassion for him."

The Scim had snarled at Madeline. But still. It was right to heal him. Wasn't it? "Will it kill her? To fix him?"

"She will die regardless. My magic, remember, cannot pass the gates of death. She will die in an hour if we let her or in a few minutes if she gives her legs to her countryman."

Madeline couldn't decide. Gilenyia waited, then asked again, "Do you approve?"

She couldn't say the words. The groans and cries of the two Scim warriors were too much for her. Gilenyia grew tired of waiting and put her bare hands upon their foreheads. The male Scim arched his back and screamed, while the female exhaled once, sharply, and lay still. The black swirls of her tattoos faded then disappeared completely.

The male Scim sat up on his knees, his legs and pelvis miraculously whole, and cradled the female's body, weeping bitterly.

"Ungrateful creature," Gilenyia said, disgusted.

"May the Peasant King welcome you into his court," the Scim said soft and low into the dead Scim's ear.

"Better the Majestic One than the Peasant King," Gilenyia said.

The Scim scowled at her.

"Do not run," Gilenyia said, "unless you would have your sister's sacrifice be in vain."

The Scim stayed near them after that as they combed the field for more survivors. The sun had risen in earnest, and they had wandered far from the center of the battlefield now. The Scim soldier winced in the sunshine, which seemed to be physically hurting him. After a couple hours, Gilenyia had healed perhaps twenty human soldiers and three Scim, some with broken limbs and a few with more serious wounds. The serious wounds were the most troubling, as Madeline watched the nearly dead succumb because of Gilenyia's magic. Once Gilenyia used a badly broken human to fix a

Scim warrior, but Madeline noticed dark looks exchanged by the human soldiers when she did. Madeline wondered if this was part of a show meant for her, to try to convince her that Gilenyia gave everyone an equal chance.

Some of the soldiers were sent back into the city with the Scim warriors, but Gilenyia kept the first one she had healed, the one Madeline had chosen, there in the crowd, finding bodies. Madeline worked her way over to him. His thick, grey muscles were covered in black tattoos that whirled in loops up both arms and over his shoulders. His hair, greasy and limp, hung past his shoulders. He had the smell of someone who hadn't washed in weeks, maybe longer.

"I told you my name," Madeline said. "What's yours?"

He scowled at her. "Call me Night's Breath."

"Is that a common name among your people?"

He drew himself up to his full height and hit his chest with one massive fist. "It is my war-skin name, given in my first battle. For when the enemy feels my breath upon his neck, already night has come for him."

She helped him move a splintered battering ram off a large, hairy creature that looked almost like a goat with human arms and legs. It had wide, staring eyes. There was nothing to be done for it. "Why do you want to bring darkness to the Elenil? Why do you hate the light?"

Night's Breath spit. He mumbled something to himself, then said, "A thousand years of darkness is a mercy to the Elenil. I would crush their skulls. I would grind their bones."

"But why do you hate them? Look at the Court of Far Seeing. Isn't the Crescent Stone beautiful in the sunlight, there on the highest tower? Look at the white walls and the colored flags and the bright river winding through. Do you see the palace on the central hill? I've never seen anything so beautiful." It reminded her of the descriptions from the Tales of Meselia—the beautiful, magical cities she had longed to see her entire life. She stopped for a minute and looked at the city, reminding herself of the beauty here, of the good things, of the magic and wonder.

"Hold, little human," Night's Breath replied. "Look again at those fair walls. Do you think they would be a thing of beauty to one such as me? What awaits Night's Breath behind the walls of Far Seeing?" He snorted. "Death is a better end for one such as I."

It was a good question. What would be done with the Scim soldiers? They were prisoners, certainly, but the Elenil would be kind to them, she was sure. Thinking about it, she hadn't seen any Scim in the city proper. She hadn't been here long, though, and no doubt they were in a prison or jail cell. Or maybe they were bargained back to the Scim in exchange for Elenil prisoners? She didn't know. It was a question worth pursuing, she thought, and she promised herself she would not forget to look in on Night's Breath after they returned to the city.

The Scim grunted. "Look here. Another fallen human." It was a boy in white armor, his chest caved in. "Ground to dust beneath the wheels of war. The Elenil could return what they have stolen from the Scim, and the bones of such little fools need not be grist. But until that time comes, I will kill as many as I have opportunity."

This one looked to be too far gone. Madeline dreaded the thought of touching another dead body. Her heart beat faster. She didn't know how many nightmares she would have in the weeks to come. "Let's take off his helmet," Madeline said. She steeled herself. If she was going to walk the battlefield looking for survivors, she was going to make absolutely sure who had survived and who had not.

Night's Breath removed the boy's helmet. His black hair was plastered to his face, but she recognized Jason immediately. *Oh no. No, no!* She fell to her knees at his side. He had come here because of her, and why was he on the battlefield already? He didn't even agree to fight when he came—he shouldn't be here, broken and bleeding. Madeline put her face near Jason's. A faint stirring of breath touched her. He was alive. Barely. She leapt to her feet and screamed for Gilenyia, who made her way toward them with infuriating slowness.

Gilenyia's bright eyes flicked between Jason and Madeline, and she seemed to know immediately who he was. "Ah. Your friend. He is grievously wounded. We would need someone in full health, or near enough, to recover him."

Madeline's mind raced. Someone healthy who could take Jason's place? "Take me," she said. It would be worth it, and she didn't have long anyway.

Gilenyia shook her head. "Would that it were so simple, child. You are healthy only because of our magic. And you have a contract to fulfill to the Elenil. No, it will not work, though it is noble that such would be your first thought."

"Okay, so could we help him enough that he could heal naturally? Is there another person on the field like the last one, who is going to die either way?"

Gilenyia shook her head. "He is too far gone for that, human child. But there are ways." She turned her head slightly, enough that Madeline followed her gaze to see Night's Breath, hunched just beyond the circle of human soldiers and attendants who had followed Gilenyia. *Oh no.* Could Madeline agree to that? She licked her lips, thinking hard.

Night's Breath tightened his hands into fists. One of the soldiers, realizing what Gilenyia meant to do, turned, his ax at the ready. Night's Breath swung one massive arm in a punishing blow, and the soldier flew backward, his helmet toppling from his head. Another soldier moved toward him, but Night's Breath shattered his knee, then broke into a desperate gallop over the battlefield.

"His life for your friend's," Gilenyia said.

Jason's face was almost white. She couldn't tell if he was still breathing. "That's not fair," Madeline said. It wasn't fair at all. Who was she to make this decision? She knew Jason, knew him to be a loyal and kind person, and she barely knew this Scim soldier at all, but every indication was that he was a terrible creature, bent on destroying every good thing in this beautiful city. Look at this disgusting field, for instance. Dead bodies, ruined war machines, trampled grass and stinking mud. The Scim had done this, not the Elenil. But could she agree to kill him? Her head spun, and her stomach turned over. She couldn't make this decision. She couldn't be the judge, the executioner, even if it meant saving her only friend from home.

"It is precisely fair. What did the beast say to you? No doubt that he would kill us all. That he would rather die than join the Elenil?"

Blood rushed into her face. "He said both those things."

"They are an irredeemable race, Madeline. Violence and shadow are their meat and drink. They choose death over life, darkness over light, filth over food. And your friend—is he a good man?"

Madeline brushed the hair from Jason's face. A breath rattled out of him, as if in reply. Her hands shook. She waited for him to take another breath. *Please take another breath!* He gasped, pulling in another long drag of air. Madeline slumped against him, relieved. There wasn't time for this, wasn't time to make this decision. "He took me to the hospital when no one else would help. He came to the Sunlit Lands with me just because he is my friend." She didn't know if this was a eulogy or if she was convincing herself to do this thing. All she had to do was say yes to Gilenyia. One simple word and Jason would live.

"A noble soul," Gilenyia said. "And you would let him die so that beast can escape and kill yet more noble souls?" She clucked her tongue. "The human morality is so muddied, I cannot make sense of it."

Jason's body began to shake. "Are you going to save him?" Madeline cried.

Gilenyia smiled, but it was a sad smile that didn't touch her eyes. "With your approval, child, I will."

Jason's body trembled, and his breath seemed to be all exhalation now, a single sigh coming out for an eternity with no sign he would ever breathe in again. His hands were cold, and she tried to unbuckle his breastplate, but it was caved into his body. She couldn't tell where it ended and Jason began. "Can't you just—?"

"Quickly, child, the beast is nearly away."

Night's Breath was so far now that Madeline didn't think they could catch him if they tried, and every second that passed he moved farther away. Then Jason's body went strangely limp, and Madeline shouted, "Yes, yes, do it!"

Gilenyia whirled and grabbed a spear from a soldier. She hurled it, and it flew across the field, impossibly far and fast. Madeline didn't know if it was the angle of the light, or if the sun glinted off the shard of metal at the tip, but for a moment the spear flashed like a bolt of lightning. It struck Night's Breath in the back of the thigh. He cried out and fell.

Gilenyia's people scurried across the field toward the Scim, their weapons at the ready. Gilenyia herself scooped Jason up from the ground, paying no attention to the blood that spread across her gown. She leapt across the field with the grace of Rondelo's stag, overtaking her own people and arriving beside Night's Breath before anyone else. Madeline ran as fast as she could, choosing her footing carefully so she wouldn't fall on any of the broken remnants of the day's battle.

Gilenyia knelt between the two figures, a bridge between the too-still form of the crushed human boy and the writhing, furious Scim. "Let me live!" Night's Breath shouted. "Lady, let me live!"

Gilenyia pushed the Scim down with her left hand and placed her right palm on Jason's face. A horrible sound, half scream and half defiant shout, echoed across the field. Night's Breath's face went slack. The tattooed whorls on his arms and shoulders faded as Madeline watched, and his chest fell still. He looked even more like a beast now that he was dead, his waxy lips falling back from the jutting yellow fangs, the skin of his face sagging toward the ground.

It made it worse, almost, to see Night's Breath like that. Like he was an animal and didn't know any better. That maybe the horrible things he'd said had all been brute instinct. Madeline's stomach dropped away beneath her, and she fell on her knees beside him. She leaned down beside the Scim. She whispered in his ear, "May the Peasant King welcome you today." Isn't that what he had said to the dead Scim woman? She couldn't remember the exact words.

A stinging slap knocked her face to one side. Her own hand flew to her cheek, which burned with the imprint of Gilenyia's palm. "The Majestic One gives you back your friend, and you speak the Peasant King's name? Such small decencies should be common sense."

"I didn't know," Madeline said.

Gilenyia's gaze did not waver. "Now you do."

Jason coughed, and his eyes fluttered. Madeline rushed to him. Gilenyia removed her gloves from her cloak and meticulously pulled them on, straightening each finger.

Jason opened his eyes, and they focused in on Gilenyia, who now stood a few feet away, the sunlight catching her pale hair. She looked glamorous and perfect despite the smoke and ash of the battle, despite Jason's blood on her gown. "I knew it," he said. "I've died and gone to Hollywood."

Madeline, beside herself with joy, threw herself onto him and hugged him, long and hard. "You're not dead!"

Jason frowned. "Madeline?"

She laughed and helped him to his feet.

He leaned on her for a moment while he got his balance. "I didn't even know you were one of my groupies."

"It has been a long day," Gilenyia said. "Return to your homes, all of you."

Jason seemed slow, almost dreamy, most of the way back to the city. He kept talking about his unicorn, needing to find his unicorn. Then he stopped, agitated. "Where's Baileya?" he asked. "Did you see her?"

"I don't know who that is," Madeline said.

"Baileya. And the burning girl. I can't remember her name . . . Schoola? Something like that."

"*Shula*?"

"Yes! They took her, Mads. They took her, and we have to get her back."

"They're long gone by now, Jason. It's been hours since they retreated."

Gilenyia looked back at them. "The Knight of the Mirror has given chase," she said. "He will not fail. They will soon be returned to us."

Madeline didn't answer. She looked away, pretended not to hear, though she desperately hoped it was true that the Knight would bring Shula home.

Jason's face darkened when he saw a group of people carrying a Scim body between them, throwing it into a large pile. "Something isn't right," he said.

Madeline squeezed his arm. "Let's get home."

"Something's wrong." He stopped short. He stared out across the field, toward the ridge the Scim had appeared on hours ago. "Does the name Night's Breath mean anything to you?"

"Night's Breath?" she asked, her heart beating so hard she could feel it in her throat. "Nothing," she said. *Nothing, nothing, nothing*, she said to herself, and kept saying it all the way back to the city walls. She promised herself never to tell Jason this one thing. To spare him, at least, knowing that he owed his life to a fallen Scim warrior.

There was a strange squeaking sound from somewhere behind them, like a balloon the size of a van squealing as air forced its way out. Jason perked up, a glint of light returning to his eyes. "My unicorn," he said. "I hear my unicorn."

Madeline turned to see a rhinoceros barreling toward them over the battlefield. She thought it was farther away than it was, because it was so small. It was about the size of a golden retriever, and it leapt up onto Jason, knocking him over and leaning against him like an overly affectionate dog.

"They shrank you!" Jason shouted. "This crazy magical battle. I can't believe they shrank you. It's good to see you, girl, good to see you." He scratched her ears and patted her belly. She wouldn't leave his side, practically tripping him as they walked the rest of the way to the city.

They passed through the shimmering golden curtain that awaited them at the city's gates. Hanali met them there with a jovial shout and a promise of a ride back to their homes. He clapped Jason on the shoulder and laughed along with him as he described discovering his unicorn was actually a rhinoceros, saying, "We have always called such beasts unicorns." His carriage came, and Madeline scarcely remembered climbing into it—rhinoceros and all—or the journey to Mrs. Raymond's house. She barely said good-bye to Jason. She didn't think he noticed, because two bloodied human boys came rushing up to him, cheering and jumping around and admiring his unicorn and congratulating him on his first battle.

Her room was empty. Shula's bed was perfectly made, like in a hotel room, like no one had ever been there. Mrs. Raymond brought Madeline a steaming wooden bowl filled with stew. Madeline set it on the wooden table under the window and sat in front of it for a long time. She kept thinking of the grey-skinned corpse that had been Night's Breath. *I did the right thing. I did the right thing*, she said to herself again. He was a monster, bent on destroying the world. He wanted only darkness and pain and death.

Which is what she had given him.

Outside the birds sang, and the sun shone as bright and clear as ever.

PART 2

In the desert, there are no paths.
In the desert, the way is made by walking.

A KAKRI PROVERB

15

SCARS

*Three things we cannot live without: clear water,
deep stories, a heart that is loved.*

A KAKRI PROVERB

✛

Jason woke up with his legs pinned to the bed by Delightful Glitter Lady. The affectionate rhinoceros had gotten into the habit of sleeping at his feet. He reached over and rubbed between her huge, rabbit-like ears, and she let out a contented squeak. He had learned in the aftermath of the first battle, twenty-seven days ago, that she hadn't been shrunk by the enemy but by their own side. The Elenil didn't see much use in keeping their giant animals huge except in battle. They were easier to feed and care for if they were smaller. Jason had been given a dial—a small, round, black device with a red piece of shell set in the center—that when turned to the left shrank Delightful Glitter Lady to about the size of a full-grown golden retriever. Mini Delightful Glitter Lady weighed about seventy pounds, and she loved to climb onto his lap and get her ears scratched.

The same dial, turned to the right, made her normal rhinoceros size, and then gigantic war-rhino size. This was the reason Jason's bed had been replaced the first time Delightful Glitter Lady had fallen asleep on it. The dial was turned too easily. According to Mrs. Raymond, war beasts were not allowed in the dorm rooms. But Jason figured, what were they gonna do, kick him out? Mrs. Raymond had told him multiple times this was a possibility, but he doubted it.

David Glenn had already left the room. He got up early. He said he liked to watch the sunrise, which was ridiculous because the sun never set, not really, in the Court of Far Seeing. But David said he could feel the change as the sun came up over the horizon, if not for the Sunlit Lands, for everyone else.

Kekoa, on the other hand, would sleep until forced out of bed. Jason leaned close to Delightful Glitter Lady. "Hey, Dee," he whispered. "Dee! Where's Kekoa?"

Dee's long ears perked up, and her eyes opened.

"Where's Kekoa? Where is he?" Jason mimed looking around, like he couldn't see his roommate sleeping twelve feet away.

Dee sat up, her thick, ropelike tail thumping against the blanket. "Where's Kekoa? Go get 'im!"

Dee gave a delighted snort, scrambled from Jason's bed, and flung herself across the room, flying up to land full force on Kekoa's back. She trumpeted in triumph, and Kekoa yowled in pain. "Ay, Dee! C'mon, tita, I was sleeping!"

"I got one," Jason said. He, Kekoa, and David had been playing a game. These first twenty-eight days, Jason was supposed to be learning all about the Sunlit Lands. In this game, Jason would mention something weird about the Sunlit Lands, and his roommates had to either (a) explain it, (b) trick Jason into thinking a fake explanation was a real one, or (c) admit they didn't know the answer. Jason got a point if he stumped them, and they got a point if they tricked him.

Kekoa pulled his pillow over his head. "It's too early, brah!"

Jason ignored him. "Why aren't there any Elenil kids?"

Kekoa pulled the pillow off his head. His hair was pointing in every direction. "Man, are you serious? You just now noticed that? You've been here a whole month."

"It's weird, though," Jason said. "No babies. No pregnant ladies. No toddlers or even teenagers. They act like Rondelo is a kid, but he's—what did he tell us?—three hundred years old."

David slammed the door open and shouted, "Good morning, roomies! The sun is shining!"

"It's always shining," Kekoa grumbled, then yelped when Delightful Glitter Lady jumped off him and ran, panting, to David.

David crouched down and scratched her behind the ears. "Hey there, DGL! I brought you something. I brought you—settle down now, it's right here, behind my back. Look!" David pulled out a gigantic handful of long yellow grass that the Elenil called sweetsword. It was Dee's favorite food. She leaned against David while she chomped on it.

Kekoa sat up. "Wu Song's got one."

Jason put his hands behind his head and waited for David to look at him. He paused for dramatic effect. "Why aren't there any Elenil kids?"

David snorted. "You just notice that?"

"He's slow," Kekoa said. "I noticed that my first week."

David grinned. "That Jason's slow? Or about the kids?"

"I did see a creepy kid in a mask my first day," Jason said.

"Ugh," Kekoa said. "That kid is the worst."

"Human," David said, nodding his head. "Been in the Sunlit Lands too long. He's all twisted around with magic."

"So why no kids?" Jason asked.

Kekoa and David exchanged looks. "The Scim took them," David said. "Sixty years ago, the Scim kidnapped all the children, and they put a curse on the Elenil so they can't have any more."

Kekoa rubbed his jaw. "It's why they're such terrible enemies. Scim took all their kids, brah. No way the Elenil can forgive that. Not only did they take them away, they wouldn't let them celebrate Elenil holidays, or learn the culture at all. They made them into Scim, too."

David flopped onto his own bed. "Pretty terrible."

"So the Elenil are going to keep fighting the Scim forever, you know. There's no way out of that one. No path to forgiveness."

"Whoa," Jason said. "That makes sense. That's gotta be true."

Kekoa and David burst into laughter, jumped off their beds, and high-fived each other. "That's a point for us, Wu!"

"What do we have now, seventeen points?"

"Sixteen," Jason mumbled. "I thought for sure that was the real story. It sounded so convincing."

David picked up a ball from beside his bed and threw it against the wall. It bounced back to him, and he threw it again. "Happened often enough to the Native people. My grandpa got taken off the reservation, sent to a missionary school, and whipped if he spoke Crow. They cut his hair, wouldn't let people do the traditional dances, and wouldn't let them wear their regalia. Couldn't be any religion other than Christian, either. They even had a saying, 'Kill the Indian, save the man.'"

Jason sat up and grabbed the pudding cup by his bed. It was always within reach when he woke up. He should have put spoons in the deal too, because there wasn't ever one nearby. He saw a dirty one from yesterday on the floor, so he rubbed it clean on his blanket and started eating. "Yeah, right. You don't get points for tricking me about Earth history, only Elenil history."

David caught the ball he'd been throwing and sat still. He didn't say anything at first, and a weird silence fell in the room. Kekoa didn't move except to turn his eyes toward Jason. Even Delightful Glitter Lady stopped, as if she sensed danger, her ears perked up, her eyes still. Jason paused, a bite of chocolate pudding halfway to his mouth. A pit opened up in his stomach. He didn't know any stories like David's, but he should have realized it was in the realm of possibility. Was it really any different than what had happened to his own family not so long ago? "Uh-oh," Jason said. "I assume that actually happened."

"Man, you should know that's not a joke," Kekoa said. "Didn't they teach you anything in history class?"

Before Jason could reply, David spoke. "My grandfather," he said, "was of the Apsáalooke. The Crow people. He was whipped for speaking our language. When I was a kid, I didn't want to learn it. I heard the elders speaking it, and a lot of the other kids even, but I always liked English, you know? My cartoons were in English. School was in English. But my grandfather, even when I was little, he would point at the sun in the morning, and he would say áxxaashe. He would wake me at night and show me the bilítaachiia. He would cup his hands in the river and hold it up to me and say bilé. Some of the other elders, they didn't feel right speaking our language. Grandfather said they still 'felt the whip' when they spoke. They'd speak it sometimes, but they felt pale eyes watching them. When I was eight years old, Grandfather called me into his room, and I helped him take off his shirt. He showed me his back, and he said, 'When I was your age, I earned these scars.' That's what he said, he *earned* them. 'I earned these scars,' he said, 'so you could learn the tongue of your elders and ancestors.'" David stared out the window, and the strange atmosphere in the room slowly lifted, like a fog evaporating. "My grandfather fought to keep our language alive. After that I never complained."

"Whoa," Jason said. "That's intense."

David shrugged. He pointed to a tiny scar in his left eyebrow. "See this?"

"Yeah."

"Kid named Billy skimmed a rock at me across a pond, and it sailed up and clipped me. I always thought he did it on purpose. Point is, though, I wouldn't remember Billy skipping rocks that day without a mark on my skin. Scars help us remember. I remember the missionary schools because of my grandfather's scars. That's an important thing, Jason. That's something to ask yourself. One of your weird questions. *Why don't the Elenil have any scars?*"

The answer flew into Jason's mouth. It was so simple as to be self explanatory. "Because they heal all their wounds right away with magic."

David got up, threw his ball to Kekoa, and opened the door to their room. "Nah, man. It's because there's something they're trying to forget."

The door slammed. Delightful Glitter Lady jumped and snorted. She watched the door for a few moments, and when David didn't come back in she trotted over to Jason and leaned against his legs.

"We better get dressed," Kekoa said.

"I feel bad, man. I didn't mean to upset David." Today was Jason's last day to wear white. At the ceremony tonight, the Bidding, they called it, he would be able to wear clothes with color in them again.

Kekoa rolled out of bed, already in a pair of jeans and a T-shirt. He had a habit of going a couple days in a row in the same clothes, even though there was a magic laundry hamper. You threw your clothes into the hamper, and they returned, cleaned and folded, to your drawer within forty-eight hours. Jason had no right to judge Kekoa's clothing choices, though. It looked like someone had been using white clothes to build a nest around his bed. He scooped them up and shoved them all into the clothes hamper, forcing the lid down over the top until he heard the tiny pop that told him they had disappeared.

"He's not mad at you, brah," Kekoa said, doing a quick smell check on his T-shirt. "It's just . . . Man, you know the teachers at his grandfather's school? They didn't have any scars, either. You know what I mean?"

Scars. Jason's entire chest had been crushed. That's what they told him, anyway. He barely remembered it. There wasn't a scar or any other indication he had been hurt. There was a sort of echoing memory of something called Night's Breath. He wasn't sure what it meant. Madeline wouldn't talk about it, and Kekoa and David both said they didn't know what it was. It sounded almost like one of the Elenil names for a plant. He wondered what it was, what it looked like, and why he couldn't get those two words out of his head. Another nagging theory kept trying to make room in his head too, but he didn't want to think about it. He was curious, yeah, but he felt conflicted, too. Maybe it would be better if he didn't know exactly what had happened. Still, he lay in bed at night and turned the words over and over in his head, trying to find a new way of hearing them, some unattainable insight.

Kekoa said, "Why didn't you believe David when he told you about his grandfather?"

Jason paused, considering this. Since his vow to be completely honest, he had found questions about his own motivations difficult to answer. Sometimes he didn't understand his own decisions, and it took time to think them through. Other times the motivations were too complicated— ten different reasons, all intertwined. Some more important than others, yes, but he hated to give an incomplete answer. So why hadn't he believed David? One, he was tired of being fooled by Kekoa and David's answers about the Sunlit Lands. He felt like a fool, guessing at weird trivia about a magical and sometimes illogical place. They had just tricked him with their fiction about the Elenil's children being stolen by the Scim, and something about that rubbed him the wrong way. He was sick of the lies and exaggerations. He worked hard to be truthful, and he didn't understand why other people couldn't do the same thing. Second, he had to be honest, in some way the idea that the United States of America would systematically and purposefully destroy another culture seemed unlikely. Which was so ironic, so hilarious, because he had evidence of it in his own life, in his own family. But somehow he had bought into the lie that things must be different for everyone else, that his experience was the exception, not the norm. There was this voice in his head saying, *That can't be true, that's not the American way!* And that voice was keeping him from seeing what was true. But Jason wasn't letting lies stand in his life anymore. He was rooting them out, replacing them with the truth.

Jason finally said, "I didn't want it to be true."

Kekoa nodded. "I get that. David told me once that some Native Americans didn't get the right to vote in the US until—I can't remember—the 1950s or 60s. I told him there was no way that was true. I mean, black people had the right to vote a hundred years before that almost. But he explained that the Native people weren't even allowed to become US citizens until the 1920s."

Jason didn't know why it surprised him. He knew the history of the Chinese immigrants to the United States. It was only a month ago that he had lectured Madeline about it, and the Chinese hadn't been allowed to become citizens until the 1940s. He shouldn't be surprised by these things, but the honest truth is that he was. These sorts of facts went against his cultural narrative, the story he'd been told about the land of the free and the home of the brave. The stories had an almost fantastical quality to them, as if they had happened long ago and far away in some fantasy world, not decades ago to their great-grandparents. And, yeah, black people—or black men, anyway—got the right to vote a hundred years before Native people, but then a whole system built up around preventing that, which was part of the point in the Civil Rights movement in the 60s.

So of course David's story was true. Even a moment's reflection should have told him that. The problem was that he hadn't taken a moment to reflect before opening his big mouth. "I'll apologize," Jason said.

He stood at their window. Baileya was on the grassy field outside the dorms, running. Her leg was healing. The guys said the Kakri healed faster than humans, but still, it had only been a few weeks, and she was out there with a walking stick, practicing a strange lope that allowed her to move fast by using the stick as a crutch. He didn't know how she kept going when she had been hurt so badly, or why she refused to use the Elenil healing magic. It had completely restored him, after all, and in a matter of moments. But there she was, a month after breaking her leg, trying to stay in fighting shape and overcome the battle effects of just one night in the war. *The scars help us remember*, that's what David had said. Jason put his hand against his unmarked chest. No scars, but he still remembered. *Night's Breath.* What did that mean? He couldn't shake it. He knew, from his own bitter experience, that not every scar was visible. What happened with Jenny—that hadn't left a mark. No physical mark, anyway. But it had changed his life forever. Nothing could be the same, not ever.

Which reminded him of Madeline. He was supposed to meet her in the market to prepare for the ceremony tonight. Now that they had been here a full Sunlit Lands month, they were supposed to be inducted into Elenil society. They would get an assignment of where they would live, what their roles would be. They'd be allowed to wear whatever clothing they pleased. Jason hoped to be put back here with Kekoa and David, but that meant joining the Elenil army. He had enjoyed his one night in the war, and he loved the way some people still called him the Bat Slayer. But he had almost died. According to Madeline, almost died in the not-coming-back-even-with-magic kind of way. He wasn't sure he wanted to do that again. And Madeline had made it clear she was not planning to fight. Jason had come here to keep an eye on her. To watch over and protect her in the way he had failed to do with his sister.

"I have to meet Madeline," he said to Kekoa.

Kekoa grinned at him. "Hold up, man. David is gonna be back in a minute with a present."

"A . . . present?"

"Yeah, we planned ahead and—"

The door opened. David stood there, holding a flat white box.

"I'm sorry—" Jason started, but David interrupted him.

"You believe me now?"

"Yeah."

"We're good then. But you have to learn to listen when someone speaks their heart."

"Right," Jason said. "Sorry." Relief washed over him. He realized that he had been worried, on some level, that David would stay angry at him, that he had somehow permanently messed up their relationship. But they were better friends than that. There was room to mess things up and still be friends.

"Kekoa and I had something made for you," David said. "An outfit for the ceremony tonight."

Jason took the box, laid it on the bed, and pulled off the lid.

The first sight of the outfit assaulted Jason's eyes. It was garish. Awful. Ridiculous. "It's horrible," he said, pulling it out of the box. "I love it."

16
THE BIDDING

"Has your boon brought you happiness?"
the Peasant King asked.

FROM "RENALDO THE WISE," A SCIM LEGEND

✦

The tattoo on her wrist was growing. There were times Madeline could see it pulsing on the edges, small tendrils curling outward, moving farther along her wrist, snaking toward her palm. It was nearly two inches wide now. She kept it covered, a surprisingly easy thing to do here in the Sunlit Lands. She hadn't mentioned it to Jason. She had been about to, and then he had whipped his gloves off to share some theory of his that the designs in the tattoo reflected the magic one used it for, and she saw how thin and delicate his tattoo still was. For some reason it gave her pause. It made her nervous to share with him.

Every day, Madeline woke up alone, staring at Shula's perfectly made bed. They still hadn't found Shula or the guy who could fly, Diego. The Scim hadn't returned to battle since the night they took Shula, and although the Elenil knew where the Scim lived, knew where the army had gone, there was no sign of her. The Knight of the Mirror had ridden out two weeks ago looking for her and had returned yesterday, empty handed and grim. It made it difficult to celebrate today, which is what she was supposed to be doing.

She had chosen a sky-blue dress. The collar came just to the hollow of her neck, and the skirt fell nearly to the floor. It had half-length sleeves, but she had matching gloves to pull over her arms. It was a relief not to wear all white, but she was nervous about the day. She had been told what to expect by Mrs. Raymond. There was a sort of market, and Elenil citizens would mill around, meeting the new arrivals. People would propose to take humans like her and Jason into their households. This was called the Bidding, though no money exchanged hands. This would define what their role would be in the Elenil city and where they would live. Mrs. Raymond's dorms served as home only to new arrivals and human soldiers.

If she was taken into an Elenil house, she might be changing linens, serving food, or caring for gardens. Or helping the Elenil with their own duties, which could be a position of high status. If Gilenyia, for instance, took Madeline into her household, people would treat Madeline with enormous respect. Gilenyia had implied more than once that she was considering it, which caused Hanali to hyperventilate, imagining all the wonderful balls and parties they would be invited to attend. He would get a great deal of honor as a result of having been the one who chose Madeline and brought her to the Sunlit Lands.

However, the idea of living with Gilenyia distressed Madeline. Every time Madeline was with her, she couldn't help but remember what had happened with Night's Breath and Jason. She couldn't help but remember that she had been the one who made the decision—the Scim's life for her friend's. She hadn't told Jason, but he knew something was wrong. She didn't think he knew how the healing magic worked, or at least not when someone had been mortally wounded, but he suspected something. Because the Scim had not returned since the first battle, there hadn't been any need for more major healings.

Instead, she and Jason had been thrown headlong into a sort of training curriculum from Hanali. History, manners, and fashion. Mostly manners, with a strong running commentary on fashion. Hanali seemed particularly concerned about Jason's performance on all three topics and how that would reflect on him. They had time for other things too. She and Jason had spent some time with his roommates when their schedules matched up, which wasn't often. She had been "loaned" to Gilenyia more than once for an afternoon, to "assist" in healings of illnesses and minor injuries, which largely meant doing precisely what she was told. A few afternoons had been spent walking in the market or standing on the city walls with Jason, but mostly they had been kept busy, focused, and overwhelmed with fatigue. She fell asleep as soon as she touched her bed at night.

"Pay attention," Hanali said.

The coach had stopped. Madeline had been staring out the window, blankly ignoring the wonders of the Court of Far Seeing. A crowd of coaches lined the avenue. Some were pulled by horses, some by strange, hairless beasts with round faces. An elephant lumbered past with what looked like an entire house on its back. Some strange creature with legs longer than a lamppost walked by, carefully lifting its legs and setting them down between the coaches, wagons, and people making their way. "I'm sorry," she said earnestly. "I know this is a big day for you."

"Yes," Hanali said haughtily. "As you know, you're not the only new arrival I have brought to the Court. I need to look after my other graduates as well."

"Like Jason," Madeline said helpfully.

Hanali's face clouded, and he sniffed at a handkerchief from his sleeve. He mumbled to himself, "Where is that boy?"

"He'll show up."

"That is precisely my fear, dear girl." Hanali stepped out of the coach and handed Madeline down. "As for you, be sure to remember what I have taught you regarding manners."

This is where Jason would have said something rude and funny, Madeline thought. She wished he was here. Despite Hanali's constant assurances otherwise, Madeline was nervous something terrible was about to happen. *Only eleven months to go*, she told herself. Eleven months and she would be back in the real world. Back with her family, back with Darius, back in her own house. She would be able to breathe, and she could pick up her life where she'd left off. Yes, she'd probably have to start her senior year of high school over, but it would be worth it. It would be worth all of this.

They ascended a wide marble stairway along with a thousand other people. No one noticed her at first, but then, to Hanali's delight, a human saw her, gave a little cry of alarm, and scurried off into the crowd. "Someone has sent their people to keep watch for you," Hanali said. "An excellent sign of what is to come."

The building at the top of the stairs was set on a broad marble square. There was plenty of room for people and creatures to mill about, and that is what they did. One large creature, at least twelve feet tall, turned and looked at Madeline with yellow eyes the size of saucers. It had wide, pointed ears, and greenish-brown hair, like moss, covered its entire body. The hair was longer on its arms and legs and moved softly in the breeze. Madeline had no idea if this was another magical race of Sunlit Lands people or someone's pet. She still had a lot to learn.

Most people in the crowd were Elenil dressed for a party. Strange oversize hats, shining gowns, and canes seemed to be the prevalent style. Hanali wore a long red jacket that buttoned to the waist, then opened in an inverted V, the tails dragging on the ground. He wore black pants beneath that and tall black boots. He didn't wear a hat. ("A calculated choice to draw attention in this era of overgrown haberdashery.") Humans and colorful birds flitted among the Elenil, delivering messages and running errands.

Hanali led Madeline toward the building beyond the square, a rectangular marble edifice with Greek-style columns on the outside. The building seemed almost pedestrian compared to other things she had seen in Far Seeing. Until they passed the columns.

The ceiling disappeared, replaced by the vault of the sky. A river wended through the building, surrounded by graceful white trees with golden leaves. Living tables, made by cleverly interweaving the branches of some sort of bush, grew up from the ground. Matching chairs grew next to them. Birds darted back and forth among the people, occasionally flying off to the dark woods in the distance. There was no evidence they were inside a building. "This is the Meadow at World's End," Hanali said. "Historians tell us it was here that humans first made the choice to leave the Sunlit Lands. Between those dark trees in the distance lies a way back to your world. The humans gathered here, their belongings packed upon their backs, and made their final farewell to the world of magic, becoming the powerless,

THE CRESCENT STONE

dry people you have known. It pleases the archon and the magistrates to welcome our newest citizens here, as a reminder that you have chosen to come home to us."

All told, there were about thirty other human teenagers who were there. They all wore clothing like Madeline's, covered from head to toe in the style of the Elenil, the women wearing ball gowns and the men in formal wear of various kinds.

"Ah, a fair one," said a voice to their left. An Elenil woman stared at Madeline through a monocle held up to her face. "It would be diverting to have her in one's home. She looks nearly Elenil."

Hanali bowed deeply. "Were she not so young, lady, I daresay she might be mistaken for one of us."

"Indeed," said the woman. "Well done, Hanali, that you found such a child and brought her here."

Hanali bowed his head slightly. "It is an honor that you would consider bidding upon her, lady."

"She's a package deal, though," Jason said, strolling casually into the clearing. To say his outfit was an assault on the eyes would be generous. He wore a tuxedo with a frilled shirt, but the shirt was sunshine yellow. His pants had one bright-red leg and one bright-green leg. The jacket was baby blue on one side and pale green on the other. He had an orange top hat, and the whole ensemble was overlaid with sequins. The brim of his top hat had bells sewn into it, so when he cocked his head, it jingled.

The Elenil woman smiled politely at Hanali and moved along.

"What is this monstrosity?" Hanali hissed. He rubbed the material between his fingers. "What is this cheap cloth? I have never seen the like."

Jason twirled. The back panels of the jacket were still more colors. He looked like the place where rainbows go to die. "In my homeland we call this a tuxedo," Jason said. "They are very popular for weddings and prom dates."

Madeline laughed so hard her ribs ached. The astonishing garishness of the tuxedo went beyond anything she could have imagined. "I think you look dashing," she said, wiping tears from her eyes.

Jason swept the hat from his head and bowed low. "Thank you, my lady. And as you can see, your dress matches my jacket." He looked seriously at his jacket for a moment, as if trying to find something he had lost. "Riiiiight . . . *here*." He pointed to a pocket square on his chest. It was, indeed, the identical color of her dress.

"It does not even match itself," Hanali said. "You will change at once or suffer the consequences."

"What consequences? Our deal was that I had to come for a year and stay devoted to Madeline. If she wants me to change, I will." He turned toward her and adjusted his pink-and-green paisley bow tie with his gloved hands—one glove white, the other purple.

She took his hand, a wave of affection coming over her. "You look delightful."

Jason grinned. Hanali, unable to contain his despair, stalked off into the crowd.

Jason leaned close and said, "You know, I don't think that Elenil lady even needed a monocle. She was putting on airs."

Madeline put her arm through Jason's. "Putting on airs, huh?"

He nodded with great solemnity. "I heard that in a movie once."

A bird about the size of a parrot settled on Jason's head. Black feathers radiated out around its eyes, and emerald-green ones made a ridge down its back. "Your presence is requested," the bird said, "at the seat of the magistrates."

Madeline curtsied. "It would be our pleasure."

The bird turned its head sideways. "Only you are invited, lady."

Jason reached up with his hands, feeling the bird. "Is this a monkey or a cat or what? I can't see it past my hat."

"A bird, sir!" The bird ruffled its feathers. "A cat! How impertinent."

"More impertinent than sitting on someone's head?" Jason wondered aloud.

"Follow me," the bird said and, with a great deal of flapping and fluttering, leapt from Jason's head, knocking his top hat so aggressively Jason had to use his hands to keep it on.

Madeline gathered her skirts and did her best to follow the bird's path, but between the uneven ground, the other people in the crowd, and the trees they had to weave between, it was hard going. Jason helped as best as he was able, giving her his hand when necessary.

The bird sat on a branch and called back to Jason, "You are not invited, sir!"

Jason snorted. "I doubt a bird is in charge of the invitations."

The bird ruffled its feathers. "On your own head be it if you should anger the magistrates."

The magistrates were the rulers of the Court of Far Seeing. This had been drilled into Madeline and Jason during their lessons, so that they would not make a social faux pas in the presence of the leaders. There were nine of them, with three who were considered "first among equals." One, the chief magistrate, was known simply as the archon. The archon was named Thenody. Another magistrate was called the polemarch: Tirius, who was in charge of the army of Elenil. Then, lastly, there was the basileus, Prinel, who oversaw celebrations, rituals, and remembrances. Another six magistrates, equal but lesser, oversaw day-to-day matters, problems, and difficulties within the Court of Far Seeing.

The bird led them along a forested path that descended into a ravine. A stream ran through the center. Madeline had a dizzying moment when she tried to think about whether they were still inside a building or if they had somehow been transported outside. Ahead of them lay a tower, tall and stark white, with a stairway that grew along the outside edge like ivy. There was no railing. The bird perched on a stone at the bottom of the stairs. "They await you on the highest observation deck," it said.

The thought of climbing those stairs in this dress did not sit well with Madeline. The stairway was narrow enough that her dress would brush against the wall on one side and hang over the precipice on the other.

Madeline said, "I don't think I can climb in this dress without falling. Maybe they could come down here and talk."

The bird studied the tower. "It is not so high."

"We don't have wings," Jason said. "What we do have is a rather distressing relationship with gravity."

"Very well," the bird said. It paused and looked at Jason. "You carry a magical artifact with you?"

Jason, surprised, said, "You mean my pudding bracelet?"

"No," the bird said. "A dial. For animals."

Madeline furrowed her brow. Jason had mentioned the dial, but

Madeline had tried to convince him not to carry it around after he had accidentally enlarged Delightful Glitter Lady in the marketplace and crushed a vendor's stall. Delightful Glitter Lady had been trying to get her mouth around a pink fruit of some kind. She had eaten about forty of them before Jason had gotten her shrunk down again.

"It's for my unicorn," he said, pulling it from a multicolored pocket. "It doesn't work on birds."

"Nonsense," the bird said. "Only touch it to my beak."

Jason did so. The bird told him to turn the dial to the right, and he did. The bird was now the size of a two-person glider. "Hold my tail," it said, "but do not let go until your feet are on the ground."

"Maybe I'll take the stairs," Jason said, but he put his hand on the tail next to Madeline's.

The bird flapped three, four, times and then lifted slowly. It swept up and around the tower, and the ground fell away. They were over the trees in a moment, then making their way in lazy, looping circles toward the top. Something magical was at work—holding the bird's tail seemed to require no effort at all. Madeline's hand didn't ache, her arm didn't feel like it was holding any weight. She felt only exhilaration at flying and excitement to see the world stretched out below her.

"Your hat!" Madeline called. The horrible top hat had been swept away by the wind, its bells chiming merrily as it spun toward the ground.

"We'll get it later if we survive!" Jason shouted, but by then they had landed, the bird making a windstorm that swept over the assembled Elenil on the tower's top. The view from here was astounding. Distant mountain ranges rose out of a misty sea of evergreen trees. Madeline couldn't imagine they were still inside a building, but distant, wispy clouds, on second look, appeared to be enormous columns, larger and taller than the tower they stood upon. It was as if an entire nation had been shoehorned into a single enormous room.

Arranged before them were eight Elenil: the magistrates. Madeline hadn't met or even seen them before this moment. They wore, if it was possible, more clothing than the typical Elenil. More layers, certainly, and their collars crept up the back of their necks and furled out into giant fins behind their heads. In the center sat a ninth magistrate who was completely covered in a thin gold cloth, draped as though over a piece of furniture. Even the face was obscured. This figure stood when they let go of the bird's tail.

There was a strange Scim standing near them, his hair in a ponytail. He wore Elenil clothing: long sleeves, gloves, a waistcoat, and trousers. He didn't have tusks like many Scim, but instead had small, regular, white teeth. He stood straighter than other Scim Madeline had seen, and his small black eyes watched her with something like mirth.

On the floor in front of him was a second Scim. This one was in chains. His greasy hair fell around his face, and black swirls of tattoos covered his bare chest and arms. He grinned, and his yellow, crooked teeth and jutting tusks made Madeline shiver. His eyes fell on Jason and a low, guttural laugh came from his wide mouth. "Wu Song," the chained Scim said. "Then this must be your friend Madeline Oliver. A pleasure to make your acquaintance."

Something about the way he said it conveyed a different message. The words were polite, but Madeline could see from his face that he meant her harm.

"Uh-oh," Jason said. He grabbed Madeline's hand, then snatched hold of the bird's tail again. "Fly, fly!" he shouted.

But the bird didn't move, and the Scim's booming laugh shook Madeline to the bones.

17
THE MAGISTRATES

Elenil rule from Far Seeing,
in lands by our master bequeathed.
The Majestic One keeps all in his sight,
Elenil first in the warmth of his light.

FROM "THE ORDERING OF THE WORLD," AN ELENIL STORY

✣

ason yanked on the bird's tail feathers several times. "Stop," the bird said and knocked him backward with a well-placed wing stroke. Grumbling to himself, Jason pulled out his dial (which apparently worked on birds, too!) and shrank the bird to parrot size. He paused, then turned the dial all the way to the left and the bird shrank again, to the size of a sparrow.

"Now try to knock me over with your wings," Jason said.

Madeline's hand was on his arm. He straightened his jacket and tie.

"You were neither invited nor summoned," one of the magistrates said. He wore a blue robe and a small gold circlet on his forehead. "You may leave us now."

Jason crossed his arms. "Yeah, well, the magic bird says no. Besides, were *you* invited or summoned?"

The Elenil stiffened. "Magistrates are not summoned!"

Jason shrugged. "Invited, then?"

"Certainly not. A time was set, and I was made aware of it. I arrived at the appointed time."

"That's how I got here," Jason said. "I heard about the meeting, then I came to the meeting."

"Enough," the archon said. At least, Jason assumed he was the archon. The guy in charge. The boss of the Elenil. He was completely covered by a gold sheet. He looked like a ghost from a poorly done Halloween costume, minus the eye holes. Only fancier, because he was golden. In Jason's experience, the guy with the goofiest outfit might just be in charge.

The archon continued, "We have gathered with a specific purpose, and it is not to banter with children or our lessers."

Break Bones sneered at those words.

"Let us do this quickly, that I may return to the festivities," said another Elenil, this one in a close-fitting silver sheath, his blond hair braided, a wide hat on his head.

"We shall take the necessary time," the archon said. "Do not worry, Basileus Prinel. Your party will await you when you are finished here."

"What's the deal with the weird Scim?" Jason asked.

Prinel bristled. "You forget yourself, human. Show the proper respect. Would you care to be sent back to the human lands?"

Madeline gave him a warning look, but Jason put his hands in his pockets and said, "I've lived up to my end of the agreement. It never said I had to be respectful of the Elenil."

"You agreed to be in service to us," one of the magistrates hissed. "Respect is demanded as part of your service."

"Nope," Jason said. "I never agreed to that. I'm here in service to Madeline." He bowed his head in her direction. "All respect to you, milady."

A moment of furious whispering broke out among the magistrates. "Show us your bracelet," one of them said.

Jason pulled up his sleeve, and a magistrate studied his tattoo carefully.

"The boy speaks the truth. No pattern here suggests the Elenil are even mentioned in his terms."

Break Bones laughed heartily. "Oh, how I like you, Wu Song. It pains me that I have promised to deliver your friend's corpse and utterly destroy you."

"Promised to what?" Madeline cried.

"Long story," Jason said.

"Hanali will face brave punishments for this unorthodox recruiting," Prinel said. "Thenody, what say you?"

Jason racked his brain. He remembered the name Thenody. Hanali had specifically said to remember that one because . . . Oh yeah. Because that was the archon's name.

"Enough," Archon Thenody said from beneath his golden sheet. "I have said it once, will you make me say it again?"

All fell silent.

Thenody sat down in a high-backed chair. "Bring Hanali forward."

A door opened in the floor of the tower, and Hanali ascended to the platform, followed by the Knight of the Mirror. Jason got the idea that the knight's presence was some sort of threat. The knight's sword was buckled to his belt . . . No one else in this place carried a weapon. Hanali wore a slight, peaceful smile on his face. Beside them came a small girl, no more than eight years old, who wore a ragged dress and a long swath of cloth wrapped around her eyes.

Hanali turned his face toward Jason so the other Elenil could not see him, gave a fierce, furious scowl, and mouthed, *Say nothing.*

Hanali bowed. "Your most august Excellencies."

"You are young," Thenody said. "But surely not so young that you would bring a human into the Sunlit Lands without professions of loyalty."

Hanali's gaze flicked to Jason. "An oversight, Excellency. It shall not happen again. It must be admitted that he is, at least, entertaining?"

Thenody sighed. "Perhaps he does bring the frustrations of childhood into our presence once again, after all these centuries."

Prinel spoke up again. "We have heard rumors among the people that this girl, Madeline Oliver, has been prophesied to bring justice at last to the Scim. Is this true?"

"True that you heard it, my lord? I can only assume yes."

"Do not play games, Hanali. It is well known that you invent prophecies for your recruits."

Hanali flinched as if struck.

"Please," Prinel said. "Spare us the theater. How many girls have you brought to us saying they were messiahs or saviors, warriors or soldiers, who would bring justice to the Sunlit Lands?"

Hanali studied his gloved hands. "No more than ten." An outraged gasp came from the magistrates. "Ah, wait. I've forgotten the twins from the Congo. Twelve, then."

Jason said, "What, only girls can save the Sunlit Lands?"

Hanali's eyes bugged wide, his scowl sharp enough to slice a cement block in half. He mouthed, *Be silent.*

Prinel, sarcasm dripping from his voice, said, "Hanali. Twelve is the full number, I assume. You did not do the same thing with your male recruits?"

"In my defense, Your Grace, you did ask how many girls . . ."

"Very well, how many boys have you brought and done the same? Said they were the ones who would save the world? Or bring justice to it?"

Hanali cleared his throat. "Thirty-eight."

"That's fifty," Jason said.

Hanali gave him an exasperated glare.

Madeline said, "So there's not a prophecy about me?" She looked relieved. Almost ecstatic. But Madeline had told Jason the storyteller had prophesied the same thing.

The magistrates clumped together in a tight group, murmuring among themselves. The strange Scim stood to the side, keeping a careful eye on Break Bones. Hanali folded his hands across his stomach. The magic bird fluttered over to the girl with the blindfold and whispered in her ear. The Knight of the Mirror produced a small handheld mirror from somewhere and gazed at himself with rapt attention. Wow. He really was conceited.

"If there's no prophecy," Madeline whispered, "maybe they'll let us go home. Maybe they'll still let me breathe and send us home."

Hanali raised an eyebrow. "The Elenil follow their agreements to the letter, miss. They will not return you before the human year passes."

"Are you in trouble, Hanali?" she whispered.

Jason snorted. "These people can't get dressed for a party without talking to a prophet. Hanali will be fine."

Madeline punched him in the arm. "Show a little compassion. He could really be in danger."

The magistrates straightened and resumed their places. Archon Thenody spoke first. "Before the magistrates take further action, Hanali, son of Vivi, we shall consult with an oracle."

Jason felt smug. "Told you."

"However, we will not allow Madeline Oliver to be bid upon tonight. We have . . . certain concerns that our friend Sun's Dance has brought to us."

Hanali inclined his head. "I eagerly anticipate hearing his thoughts."

The strange Scim took hold of his lapels with two massive grey hands. "I have heard a rumbling among my people—the Scim in this city. It is said the Black Skulls seek a human girl who cannot breathe. It is said they wish to remove her from the Court of Far Seeing."

Break Bones spit at Sun's Dance. "Traitor."

Prinel sneered at Break Bones. "Traitor? Because he has walked out of the darkness and into the light? Because he has left behind a life of poverty? He rejected the foolish excuses of your kind and became something better. Do not judge him for it."

The girl with the blindfold spoke. "Did I hear Break Bones threaten Madeline Oliver? Is that sufficient evidence the Scim seek her death?"

Break Bones laughed. "That is a promise I made to Wu Song and has nothing to do with my people."

Madeline raised her eyebrows and looked to Jason. He laughed nervously. "Long story," he said again.

"A story we must needs hear," Prinel said.

Jason sighed. This whole not-telling-lies thing was getting him in a lot of trouble. "I snuck in through a magic door and talked to Break Bones. He said he would kill Madeline before he came to kill me."

"How did he know of Madeline at all?" Hanali said, his voice high and tight. His eye twitched. Jason hadn't seen that before, and he thought he had angered Hanali in every way possible.

Jason blushed. "I told him I'd come to the Sunlit Lands to protect someone. He asked her name, and I told him."

Break Bones roared with laughter. "He is a strange little beast, is he not? I shall raise a glass in his honor when he is no longer in the world."

Madeline's hands curled into fists. "Wasn't your promise that you would kill me first?"

Break Bones grinned. "Indeed. I told him I would bring your lifeless body as a warning that his own time had come."

Madeline put her arm around Jason. "Then he doesn't have much to worry about, because a miserable, sad little ogre like you won't stand a chance against me."

Break Bones roared with laughter, rattling his chains. Sun's Dance yanked on the metal collar around Break Bones's neck, choking him into silence. "You see, my lords. We cannot trust my countrymen to behave like civilized people. They do not know any better. They are uncouth and vile. They know only darkness, and is it their fault? No, for they do not know the Majestic One, having heard only the corrupted tales of our kind."

Archon Thenody raised his arms, lifting his golden sheets as if he were a kid on Halloween trying to scare his friends. "It seems clear we cannot risk the girl in the Bidding. What if the prophecy is true? No, even Gilenyia would not protect her well enough for my peace of mind. I think she must come to the Seat of High Seeing and serve in my household."

Hanali swooned with excitement, and Jason grabbed him by his jacket to hold him up. Hanali said, breathlessly, "Of course, Your Greatness, if you think it best for her to serve in your estate, we would be only too happy. She is quite fair for a human and could even pass for an Elenil. More than one Elenil has mistaken her for one of us. See how pale her skin is? And her hair, like gold. She's quite lovely for a human."

Madeline was watching Hanali as if he were a refugee from a mental hospital. "What if I prefer not to go with Archon Thenody?"

Hanali's eyes flew wide. "A joke!" He laughed uncomfortably. "A joke, Highness. Ha ha."

"I am serious. What if I prefer to enter the Bidding? I would rather go with Gilenyia and learn the art of healing."

"An art that could be learned in the house of the archon as well as in Gilenyia's," Hanali hissed.

Thenody stood. From the look of things, he was trembling beneath his robes. Jason guessed it was a big insult to reject his offer of living at his palace. Some people are so sensitive.

"You will do as you are told," Thenody said, his voice shaking nearly as badly as his robes. "Or you will face the consequences of breaking your contract!"

He made a twisting motion beneath his robes and reached out to Madeline. She gasped and took a wheezing breath. She fell to her knees, struggling to breathe.

"What is wrong with you?" Jason shouted. "Let her breathe!"

"It's her own fault," Thenody said. "Disrespecting me, the leader and head of the Elenil! Speaking back to the archon! She has forfeited her agreement! She cannot treat me thus and expect our magic to treat her well."

Jason knocked Hanali aside and advanced on the archon. The Knight of the Mirror did not move to intervene. His eyes flickered toward Jason but then returned to his mirror. Jason grabbed hold of the golden sheet with one hand and swung his other fist at the general location of the archon's head.

Thenody stepped back, pulling his sheet out of Jason's hand. He pointed at Jason, twisted his arm, and said, "I will remove your magic as well!"

Jason punched Archon Thenody in the midsection, and he flew backward, landing in a heap on the ground. "Now you're stealing my chocolate pudding?" Jason shouted, and leapt toward the pile of golden sheets.

But a stunningly fast Elenil in light armor intervened. He threw his arm in front of Jason, catching him just below the neck, and drove him onto the stone floor of the tower. With a two-handed shove he threw him back against Break Bones. "If you strike the archon again," the Elenil said, "I will run the girl through with my own sword. I swear this on my name, Tirius, and on my title as polemarch and commander of the armies of the Elenil!"

Archon Thenody rose, his golden robes disheveled, and moved toward Madeline, who was gasping, her face bright red.

Hanali fell to his knees and bowed his head. "My lord. Surely she has learned her lesson."

"Not yet," the archon said, his voice expressionless. He turned toward the knight. "What of you? You did not move to protect my person?"

The knight didn't look up from his mirror. "I am sworn to fight the Scim. I do not fight my own kind."

The archon drew a furious breath and unleashed a torrent of abuse on the impassive knight. Madeline lay on her back now. Jason had to do something. The archon was going to let her die like a fish, flopping around on the ground, breathless. He couldn't attack Archon Thenody, not directly, because Tirius claimed he would kill Madeline himself if Jason made a move.

He heard the guttural laughing of Break Bones close behind him. He turned away from the furious monologue of the archon. "What are you laughing at, Break Bones?"

"Your friend dies, and the Elenil war amongst themselves. They brought me here to show you the terrors of the evil Scim, and instead they entertain me."

A way out, or at least a chance at a way out, opened up to Jason. He would have to play it just right, though. "I took you to be a person of honor. How disappointing to be proved wrong."

Break Bones stopped laughing and leaned his wide face closer. His rotten breath, hot and foul, washed over Jason's face. "What mean you by this brave insult, Wu Song?"

"You told me you were going to kill Madeline and bring me her body. But here you sit, letting the Elenil make a liar of you."

The smile faded from Break Bones's face. He glanced at Madeline with sudden concern, then to the archon. He shook the chains on his wrists. "These chains prevent me from my oath."

Jason frowned. "I didn't realize the word of a Scim was worth so little." He pulled the dial out of his pocket. "I'm wondering if this magic dial works on people."

Break Bones grinned. "Ah, boy, I will rue the day I feast upon your bones. But do not use the magic upon my flesh, but rather these chains. I will save the girl, so that I may slay her later."

"It only works on animals, you know, not on chains," Jason said. But he touched the dial's casing against the chains and turned the dial to the right. The chains grew larger, and Break Bones slipped his hands free. Jason looked at the dial and the newly gigantic chains. "Huh. What do you know?"

Before standing, Break Bones slammed one massive fist into Sun's Dance's knee, sending him sprawling to the ground. He leapt to his feet with astonishing speed, and bounded to Thenody's side, wrapping his great, tattooed hands around the archon's neck. The sheet bunched above the archon's head, then flared out over his body, making him look a lot like a badminton shuttlecock. The archon's tirade cut off mid-word.

The Knight of the Mirror drew his sword.

"Ah, have a care, Sir Knight, lest I squeeze the archon in fright," Break Bones said. He shook the body beneath its golden sheet. "Release thou the girl, O valiant soul."

The archon, trembling, twisted his hands. Madeline gasped as air flooded her lungs again.

"Leave the magistrates unharmed, and I will allow you a five-minute lead," the Knight of the Mirror said. "Then I must follow and destroy you."

"Sporting, sir," Break Bones said. "Sporting indeed. In five minutes I could not even exit this grand building. No, I think another plan will be necessary. First, throw your sword from the tower."

The knight hesitated, then did as he was told. The sound of metal clanking against stone echoed up to them as the sword bounced against the tower, and then silence. "Nothing can be taken from my hand unless I allow it," the knight said. "It is a boon granted me some years ago."

Break Bones nodded. "I have heard tales of that magic."

"I give my word I will escort you safely to Scim territory. I will put my hand upon your arm. Your life will be in my hands, and none but I could take it. Only release Archon Thenody."

Break Bones grinned. "*Your* word I trust, sir. And Wu Song's. Perhaps the girl, should Wu Song vouch for her. The rest of these here—I would sooner trust a hungry wolf to guard my pigs. No, I have a plan in mind that will serve me better." He pulled the archon close against his chest, and there was a distressed yelp from beneath the golden sheets.

Madeline, still gasping and on her knees, looked up. "What are you going to do, Break Bones?"

Break Bones looked to the knight. "Give me your word that neither you nor any here shall leave this tower until I am safely outside the city walls."

"You have it," the knight said. "So long as you promise, on your honor, not to murder any citizen of the Elenil nor any human on your exit."

"Done," the Scim said triumphantly. "Now, Wu Song, lend me that bird you have shrunk, that I might send word when I am safe."

"It's not my bird," Jason said. Jason noticed Tirius shake his head, fast, when Break Bones wasn't watching. Tirius was meant to be the head of the Elenil army, but he hadn't done anything to help so far.

The bird said, "I will not help you, Break Bones. Indeed, as soon as you leave this place, I will fly to find the guardians of the city, and we will fight you from here to the city wall. If all goes well, you will be in chains again in an hour's time."

"I feared you would make some foolish speech," Break Bones said. "So I am forced to make a hard choice." He looked around at the gathered magistrates, the archon struggling weakly in his massive hands. "Are there no healers here on this tower top?"

The girl in the blindfold spoke. "None, save Madeline, and she has not been trained."

Break Bones turned his back to the Elenil, and with swift motions he folded Archon Thenody in unnatural directions, snapping appendages and collapsing ribs. He dropped the magistrate's still form in front of Tirius.

Jason's stomach lurched. He was thankful, suddenly, for the sheet, but even so he could tell what lay beneath was piled in a horrible shape. A keening cry came from beneath the golden covering.

"He will not die," Break Bones said, "so long as the bird goes for a healer rather than for the army. So I have kept my word." He bowed to Madeline. "You I shall see again." Then to Jason, "You have the heart of a Scim warrior. I give you humble thanks for my release."

He leapt from the side. Jason ran to the edge in time to see Break Bones grab the tower, his thick arms straining as they arrested his descent. He climbed down with unbelievable speed then loped across the plain below.

"Fly and warn the army," Tirius shouted to the bird.

"Shame," the knight said. "Shame on you and all the magistrates if the life of one Scim is worth more than the life of the archon, first among equals. The city will hear of this. They will speak of it for decades to come."

Prinel put his hand on Tirius's arm. "It is true, Tirius. The archon must come first."

Tirius shouted in rage. Break Bones was nearly to the exit now. "A healer first, and then the army. Fly with all speed, bird!"

The bird fell like lightning from the tower, then extended its wings and flew.

"Now there is nothing to do but wait," Prinel said, crouching beside the archon. He reached out a hand toward the golden cloth, then withdrew it.

Hanali cleared his throat. "If I may be so bold, it makes a great deal of sense to me that Madeline Oliver go to live with one of the nine magistrates."

Tirius barked a laugh. "Will you send the human traitor with her too? He released a Scim upon us!"

"He was killing my friend!" Jason shouted. He wasn't going to let that happen. He wasn't going to stand by and wring his hands when Madeline was in danger. If that meant folding the archon down small enough to fit in a suitcase, so be it. If that meant unleashing Break Bones on the world, that's what he would do. He didn't regret it for a moment.

"He is the lord of the Elenil and thus, your master. He can do as he pleases," Prinel snapped.

"My *master*?" Jason stalked over to the pile of golden sheets and, before anyone could stop him, grabbed hold of the fabric and prepared to yank it off. "I'm not anyone's slave! I'll throw him off this tower before I'll—"

"Jason, stop!" Madeline shouted.

Her voice stunned him. Her face was pale and creased with worry. He wouldn't really have thrown the archon off the tower. At least, he didn't think so. He had been doing the right thing, protecting Madeline. It infuriated him to have that questioned. He wouldn't have thrown him off the tower, though. They shouldn't have said the archon was his *master*. He wasn't some slave. He wasn't here to serve the Elenil. He was here for Madeline, pure and simple. But it was Madeline telling him to stop now.

He dropped the sheet. "He's not my master," Jason said. "Also, he better turn my pudding delivery back on, or I *will* drop him off a tower."

"Well," Prinel said mildly. "It seems clear the archon's estate will not be a safe home for these humans."

Tirius watched Jason closely. "He could not have harmed Thenody much. He has the anger of a warrior. Perhaps I will take him on, train him together with Rondelo."

The girl in the blindfold spoke. "The Scim will target Madeline, this much seems clear. To put her with the magistrates increases the risk to her and to them. The Knight of the Mirror should take her. Nothing can be taken from his hand unless he wills it. She will be safe in his household."

Tirius rubbed his chin. "An elegant solution, and delivered by a seer. What say you, Sir Knight?"

The knight gazed into his mirror, murmuring to himself. After a long moment he turned his attention to the Elenil. "I will take the girl under my protection. She will serve out her contract with me, in obedience to the Elenil and according to the terms of her bargain."

"And me," Jason blurted.

The knight shook his head. "You are too unpredictable and unwise. I cannot take you into my home."

The blindfolded girl tugged on his sleeve. He leaned down, and she whispered in his ear. His face, stony and impassive, did not change when he straightened. "I will take the girl," he said, "and also the fool."

Jason sputtered. "The *fool*?!"

Hanali whispered in his ear, "Bow, fool, if you wish to stay with Madeline."

So Jason bowed, and Madeline curtsied, and just then a healer came rushing up the stairs, and the bird told them the Scim warrior had left the city much faster than the city guard could be alerted. Released from the knight's agreement with Break Bones, Hanali grabbed Jason and Madeline by the arms and pulled them to the winding stairwell that led down along-side the outer wall of the tower. Hanali went first. Madeline descended holding her skirts with one hand and Hanali's shoulder with the other to keep herself from being pushed off the stairs by her voluminous dress. Jason followed.

"That could have gone worse," Hanali said when they were at the bottom, mopping his brow with a handkerchief. He gave Jason a dark glare. "It also could have gone much better."

That seemed like a fitting motto for Jason's entire time in the Sunlit Lands so far.

18
WESTWIND

Look at the walls, so bright and fair,
each stone placed by a master builder.

FROM "THE DESERTED CITY," A KAKRI LAMENT

✠

irrors stared at Madeline from every room in the knight's castle. A full-length one stood in her bedroom—a room with a flagstone floor, a fireplace large enough to stand in, and a wide, stone-framed window open to the world outside. A meticulously woven carpet covered the floor beneath her bed and spread out several feet beyond on all sides. The bed itself wore a silk canopy and stood on sturdy legs made of a dark wood unlike any she had seen at home.

To Madeline's chagrin and, for some reason, Jason's unending delight, there was no magic bathroom. Instead, they used something called a garde-robe. The garderobe, a room scarcely larger than a closet, sat perched over the moat around the castle. A wooden bench with a hole in the middle sat atop a stone floor with a hole in the middle and—well, she missed the magic toilets.

No magic was allowed in Westwind. That's what the Knight of the Mirror had named the castle, though Madeline wasn't sure why, because it stood on the eastern edge of the Court of Far Seeing. Out Madeline's window towered proud, distant mountains, the deep green of a forest at their feet. The blindfolded girl had told her that the break in the mountain range was called the Tolmin Pass. The pass led to the Kakri territories. The Kakri came through once a year to trade stories, if you dared to sit with them. They were a violent and unpredictable people, according to the girl.

The blindfolded girl was named Ruth Mbewe. She had come to the Sunlit Lands four years ago, when she was only four years old. She was the youngest human Madeline had seen in Far Seeing. She wouldn't answer questions about her eyes, but almost any other thing she would gladly talk about at length. Why wasn't there magic in Westwind? Because the Knight of the Mirror forbade it. Why? He did not like magic. It had done great harm to his family. Why was there a castle inside the walled city of Far Seeing? The knight had brought it with him. The answers to her questions, delivered so matter-of-factly, often made less sense than the thing being questioned.

No magic meant Madeline did her laundry by hand, with hot water brought up from the kitchen fires. Filling a bathtub with hot water took more work than Madeline cared to do, so she had taken to sneaking out of the castle every few days and bathing in her old room at Mrs. Raymond's house. Jason had apparently given up bathing, which was doubly unfortunate since the Knight of the Mirror would not allow Delightful Glitter Lady in the house. No magic meant no shrinking Dee, so she had to be kept in the stables at regular rhino size. Jason bunked in the straw beside her.

Their host, the knight, haunted the halls. He often rode out on his silver stallion, Rayo, in the early mornings, through the eastern gate. He never went as far as the Tolmin Pass, not that she had seen, and she had watched from her window more than once. Sometimes he rode through the heart of Far Seeing. When he rode west, he might not return for several days. He would not answer where he had been, but Ruth said he rode into Scim territories, seeking the captured human soldiers. Seeking Shula.

More than once, Madeline came across the knight in some dark hallway of the castle, standing in front of a full-length mirror and muttering to himself. He carried a hand mirror on his person at all times. For all the time he spent in front of the mirror, he seemed to care little for his appearance. He wore his dark hair long, usually tied into a ponytail, thick streaks of grey painting the sides. The dirt and mud from his long rides sometimes caked his gaunt, lined face for days at a time, as if he couldn't be bothered to wash with a hot rag. Yet he stared into the mirrors at all hours.

Madeline wanted to escape the mirrors. They followed her like flat silver eyes watching everywhere she went in the castle. Sometimes she would catch movement out of the corner of her eye and turn to find only another mirror, another image of herself staring back. Sometimes she thought she saw reproach on her own face . . . and she knew she must have been thinking about Night's Breath.

She asked Ruth if she could cover the mirror in her room with a sheet. It was a strange moment, watching the little girl with the blindfold standing in front of the mirror, a sheet in her hands. Her head was tilted to one side, as if listening intently to someone speaking in a far room. Then with one swift motion, she threw the sheet over the tall mirror. "He won't come into your solar," Ruth said.

"What?"

"Your solar. That's what a room like this is called. Here, on top of the tower, your own room."

"Oh, I've heard others say that. I meant, what do you mean, he won't come in here?"

"The knight," Ruth said. "But if he does, you must pull the sheet off the mirror."

"Why so many mirrors? He seems almost afraid to be without one."

For once, Ruth did not answer. She hesitated. "It is not my story to tell."

Ruth talked like someone who had been born in the Sunlit Lands, taking on the peculiar formality of the Elenil. It shouldn't be a surprise, with her having arrived here so young. Madeline had asked Ruth once what she had agreed to in coming here, and she'd said, "A year's service in exchange for being saved from a massacre in my town." Madeline had asked what happened at the end of the year. Why was she still here? Ruth had simply put her tiny hand on Madeline's and said nothing. The knight, she assumed, had taken Ruth in after that.

Madeline couldn't imagine electing to stay here when her year was up. It was an amazing place, yes, full of strange beauty and terrifying dangers. She missed her parents, though. She missed her parents, and Sofía, and Mr. García. She missed Darius, and now that she could breathe again, she wanted so badly to see him, to be with him. She hoped after she and Jason jumped the fence to go into the drainage pipe that Darius had decided to wait for her. It was only a year, after all. But he had no way to know what was happening here, and she had no way to tell him. She hoped he still felt the same . . . And of course, she had broken up with him, so there was no reason for him to wait. No reason other than maybe he loved her.

She yanked the sheet off her mirror. A flicker of movement caught her eye, but when she focused on it there was nothing there. Since coming to Westwind she had been allowed to wear whatever she liked. But it wasn't the T-shirt and jeans or her pale hair she noticed. The silver glint of her magic tattoo held her complete attention. In the last few weeks it had spread further. It grew from her wrist nearly to her elbow in a looping, tangled design like ivy. The tattoo snaked across her palm and curled around the base of her fingers. She wore gloves even when she was alone with other humans now. Jason didn't know, hadn't seen yet, what was happening. She had tried, ten days ago, to ask Hanali about it, but when she started to tug her glove off, he had averted his eyes and firmly pulled it tighter onto her hand. Her only thought now was to ask Gilenyia, but she didn't completely trust her, and she wasn't sure the Elenil woman would answer honestly if it was to her advantage to lie.

In the aftermath of Break Bones's escape, she and Jason had been more or less under house arrest. They could wander the hallways, the kitchen, the great hall, and the grounds of Westwind, but they couldn't leave the castle walls without permission. There were chores to be done, of course. Stone floors to wash. Tapestries and rugs to beat with a broom, trying to get the dust out. Laundry. Dishes. Stalls in the stable to be mucked (a task left most often to Jason because of his insistence on remaining with Dee). But when she had a free moment, what she loved to do was climb one of the towers and watch the city outside Westwind's walls.

Someone knocked on her door, loud and insistent. Madeline threw the sheet over the mirror and pulled on a jacket to cover the spread of the bracelet on her forearm. She kept her gloves in her pocket when she wasn't wearing them, now. She slipped them on before opening the door.

Jason stood outside, panting. "Let's go," he said.

"What is it? What's wrong?"

"The knight just came in through the eastern gate. He's headed this way. He sent a messenger bird ahead." Jason shouted this over his shoulder, already running down the winding tower staircase.

"What's happening?"

Jason stopped, gasping for breath. She was in much better shape than him—she had taken to running every morning along Westwind's walls, early, before everyone else got up—and he had just run up the stairs too. "Shula. He found Shula."

"What?" She ran past him, taking the stairs two at a time. Jason yelled for her to wait, but she couldn't, she just couldn't stop. She burst out the bottom door of the tower and raced through the great hall before speeding across the courtyard and toward Westwind's front gate. Although the knight had come in through the eastern gate of Far Seeing, there was only one gate into the castle compound, on the western side. So he would be riding around the entire property to get in.

Ruth was at the gate, a somber expression on her face. A ten-foot-tall mirror stood at the entrance. She held her palm up as Madeline came rushing forward. "You cannot leave Westwind."

"Is Shula okay?"

Ruth raised her face toward the sunlight. "I have seen a path for you, Madeline. It is narrow and treacherous, and on every side the possibility of injustice, pain, and heartache. Remember the advice given you by the lady in the garden."

How could Ruth possibly know about that? "I passed out as she said it. I didn't . . . I don't remember her exact words." It was something about changing the world. *Change the world, change the* . . . She couldn't quite remember.

"I walked in the garden beside Archon Thenody's palace today. The Garden Lady came to me through a grove of trees. I could smell the citrus on her skin. She asked me to remind you. She said, *To change the world, change first a heart.*"

Yes! That was it. To change the world, change first a heart. She had no idea what it meant, but she remembered it now. She wouldn't forget again.

The Knight of the Mirror appeared, galloping across the cobblestones, a blanket-wrapped form in his arms. He dismounted at the gate's threshold, placing Shula gently on the ground. Madeline dropped to her knees beside her old roommate. Shula's hair was tangled around her face. The scar on her face looked pale, and her cheeks sank under her black-rimmed eyes. A sizeable bruise bloomed beneath her left eye. She shivered as the blanket fell from her shoulder, and Madeline quickly covered it again. "Help me get her inside," she said.

"I fear she will need a healer," the knight said.

Madeline, confused, shouted, "Let's get her to a bed while we're waiting for the healer."

Ruth said softly, "The Knight of the Mirror does not allow magic within the walls of his castle, Madeline."

Jason arrived and flopped on the ground, gasping for breath. "Made it," he said.

"Jason, I need you to run for a healer," Madeline said.

"But—"

"*Look at her, Jason!*"

"Okay, okay," he said, climbing painfully to his feet. He stepped across the threshold of the gate, but the Knight of the Mirror blocked his path.

"Sir Knight, you have to let him go," Madeline said. "Unless—have you already sent word?"

"I cannot entrust you—either of you—to the streets of Far Seeing. There are too many Scim here as servants or even as reformed citizens. I do not know which can be trusted and which may wish you harm. You see what they have done to your friend."

"No offense," Madeline said, "but the only way you're going to stop us is if you harm us yourself."

"Gilenyia comes," Ruth called.

The Elenil woman swept up the street, resplendent in a red dress and white elbow-length gloves. Two Scim flanked her, looking a great deal like the strange one they had seen on the tower on the night of the Bidding.

A "civilized Scim," as Hanali called them. One carried a leather satchel, and the other two carried long sticks wrapped together with cloth.

The Knight of the Mirror did not greet Gilenyia. He stood before the gate mirror, speaking under his breath, his fingers running through his hair. He seemed unconcerned now for Shula or Madeline or Jason or anything at all.

Gilenyia surveyed the scene. "Ah. The burning girl has returned to us. Day Song, set up my work space. New Dawn, prepare yourself." She spared a glance at the knight. "Gone into some other world," she said. "Madeline, I require your assistance."

The Scim rolled the cloth out from between the two long sticks, forming a sort of wall. He looked behind himself, as if gauging the amount of room, and drew the cloth out further. He took a ninety-degree turn, then another, then another, and formed a sort of square out of the cloth, which seemed to keep coming no matter how far he pulled it. In a matter of moments he had made a ten-by-ten room, complete with a cloth roof and a folding door. Madeline followed Gilenyia inside. Two long, flat beds had somehow been set inside already. Day Song entered, carrying Shula. He set her down on one of the beds. New Dawn lay on the other and closed her eyes, breathing deeply.

Shula moaned. Her skin burned, and she flinched when Madeline touched her.

"You are not to live with me," Gilenyia said. "And yet I wish to teach you as much as I may about healing. You know how this process works, do you not?"

Jason had followed them in. "What is going on? Is this place sanitary? Did you people even wash your hands?" He was rubbing his hands, bouncing from foot to foot. She hadn't seen him so nervous before.

Madeline nodded. "I know how it works."

"Then remove your gloves," Gilenyia said, her voice even and calm. "It is time for you to try your own hand at healing."

Madeline hesitated, then looked at Jason. "Maybe you could wait outside."

"Ha," he said. "I've seen your naked hands about a million times. They might not understand it here in the Sunlit Lands, but you and I were *chemistry partners* back in the real world. That's a pretty tight bond, you know. Covalent, even."

Fine. There was nothing to be done about it then. At least she wouldn't have to hide it from him anymore. She pulled her right glove off, and then the left. Jason gasped when he saw the silver tracings curling up over her fingers.

"Whoa," Jason said. "How did you get—"

"Hush," Gilenyia said. "Let her concentrate. Sit in the corner."

Madeline put one hand on Shula's chest. Her heart beat distant but strong, and her body felt feverish but otherwise normal. She put her right hand on New Dawn, who convulsed lightly at the touch, then fell still. She almost asked if New Dawn was doing this willingly, but what difference would it make? For Shula, she would do this again, just like she'd done for Jason with Night's Breath on the battlefield. And, yes, she would allow Gilenyia to teach her how. In this strange world of Scim and Elenil and masked children and giant wolves, she needed to be able to protect herself and her friends without relying on knights or Elenil or anyone. The sight of Shula's broken body told her that much. She couldn't go along with the flow, trusting everything was going to be okay. She was going to take care of her own friends.

"Now," Gilenyia said, "reach out through your bracelet. Find Shula's bracelet and use that to guide you to where she is broken."

Her bracelet. It was more than that now, though, wasn't it? It was a sleeve. A glove. She felt power rush through her, like hot liquid into the veins of her tattoo. The magic reached into Shula but found only flesh. No magic, no connection. "It's not working."

"Take hold of her bracelet," Gilenyia said. "Perhaps that will make it easier."

She moved her hand to take Shula's wrist, and instantly, like water pouring from a bucket, felt her power move into a flow with Shula's magic. She felt the branching, slow growth of her magic join in with the sudden bonfire of Shula's. Shula's felt jagged, bright, terrifying, and dangerous, where Madeline's was slow, consistent, building to something.

Moving past the magic, a deeper connection eased into place. Madeline's face ached from Shula's bruises. She felt the fever, the cracked dryness of her lips and tongue, the skin of her face. She was badly dehydrated. Her legs hurt so much she could scarcely keep from crying out. Taking a single breath took a week's energy. It hurt to move her eyes.

Then, somehow, an even deeper well. Shula Bishara. She didn't know anymore if that was her name or someone else's. She remembered her baba and mama, her little sister, her big brother. She saw a building collapsed into rubble and people pulled from the wreckage, the color of dust and blood, some still breathing, others laid out in a careful line. A tank sat outside their home, firing shells at the other side of the city. She remembered the little Christian church her family attended, and how crowded it became as the refugees flooded from one side of the country to the other, and how even Muslims filled the pews, desperate for a bag of rice, a roll of toilet paper, a place to lay a sleeping bag. The soldier's knife which had cut her face flashed beneath the streetlight. Her neighbors in the fire leapt out of the flames, towels and scarves covering their faces.

"You've gone too deep," Gilenyia said softly. "Come back. Now take New Dawn's wrist."

Gilenyia's voice came from so far away, and untangling her own hands and arms and thoughts from Shula's took a moment. She reached her right hand over, taking New Dawn's wrist. The moment she touched the inky tattoo of the Scim, it sucked her in. A gravity pulled at her, taking her deeper into the Scim woman's world.

New Dawn's body pulsed with strength. It had been bridled, controlled, and channeled by the Elenil, but she had strength enough to tear a person into pieces. Nothing hurt. Nothing ached. Her heart beat steady, regular, in perfect time. That strength reached through Madeline, questing. It touched on Shula's pain, her aches, her broken places, and latched onto them, urging them to flow back through Madeline's body and into the Scim woman.

Madeline pinched the connection. She didn't want to do that, not yet.

She wondered if she could go deeper, like she had with Shula. It might be good to know the Scim better. She pushed on the link to New Dawn, but instead of a deeper connection she found a wall—long, thick, and impenetrable. Gilenyia was saying something to her in the world outside, but she could not make out the words, nor was she trying. A weak spot in the wall caught her attention. She couldn't break it, but she could squeeze into it, she thought.

Her name was not New Dawn. That was her "civilized" name. Her Elenil name, so they would know she bowed the knee to them. Nor was it Shatter Stone. That was her war-skin name. Her true name she would not share, not even here. It was not right that the human asked for this, too, when she was giving so much already. In time she would heal . . . faster than a human. Gilenyia would credit her, and she could help her family in the Wasted Lands. One more humiliation, one more burden to carry so the human children could frolic and live without consequence. So give her the pain. Did Madeline think she could not shoulder pain? Did she not know the Scim? This exploration, this hesitancy was more painful than the healing itself. She would not wait any longer.

The sucking gravity from New Dawn increased. It pushed through Madeline and felt for the pain. Felt for broken places and fear, touched on fever and aches. Madeline's own pain increased. The bruise under her eye, hot and swollen, pierced her with blinding pain, then slid to New Dawn. The fever crept through her. The aches and throbbing, the brokenness passed through their connection like swallowing glass, leaving behind only a bone-deep exhaustion.

New Dawn tried to take even that.

Let me keep at least the tiredness, Madeline thought. *Let me carry that one small piece.*

Another presence glided into their shared space. Cold and ancient as a shark, unblinking, and revealing nothing of itself. Madeline's connection to New Dawn broke in a terrified moment, as if a magnet which had been attracting another magnet had flipped and now pushed her away.

Madeline gasped, her eyes flying open, just as Shula sat up, also gasping. Gilenyia's bare hand covered Madeline's. New Dawn lay on her back, her face bruised, one eye swollen shut, glaring at Madeline with the other.

"Do not go so deep," Gilenyia said. "Not with your friends if you can help it, and never with a Scim." She leaned toward New Dawn. "Did she harm you?"

New Dawn closed her eyes. "She shouldn't have gone so deep, mistress."

"Indeed not. Are you well?"

"Of course, mistress."

Gilenyia gave Madeline an appraising look. "Well then, take your friends and run along to the knight."

Madeline stood halfway before her legs gave out. Jason rushed to her and helped her to her feet. "I can help," Shula said. She stood, obviously shaky herself, and pulled Madeline's other arm over her shoulder.

Gilenyia tapped her fingers to her lips, then pulled her gloves on. "New Dawn. Did you neglect to take the exhaustion from the girl? To heal someone is quite taxing, and this was her first time."

New Dawn's eyes flew open. "Mistress, she would not give it to me."

"Hmph. Very well. I will adjust your credits accordingly."

New Dawn glared at Madeline again, but she could scarcely keep her own eyes open. Jason pulled back the flap on the tent, and the three of them made their way out, a hodgepodge of legs and arms, like people in a three-legged race. The Knight of the Mirror stood at the gate, still looking at himself. He dragged his gaze away unwillingly, but when he saw Madeline's state, he came to them and scooped her into his arms like a drowsy kitten.

"One more thing," Gilenyia said. "I happened along here because I was sent by the archon. He desires to see you both again. He requests your presence tomorrow night at the palace. I trust you will be rested by then, Madeline. Next time, do not be so foolish as to shoulder a Scim's burden. They are able to carry more than a human."

Perhaps Gilenyia was right. The knight carried her through the castle grounds and the castle itself, and then up the long stone stairway to her solar, where he laid her on her bed. He noticed the sheet over the mirror, frowned, and pulled it off.

Shula, who had just returned from captivity and a hard desert journey, sat by Madeline's bed. Jason sat outside the door and could not be persuaded even to go to the stable, and Ruth fell asleep curled beside him on the stone floor.

"A human can carry quite a lot when they must," the knight said before leaving her room, as if correcting Gilenyia, or maybe praising Madeline. It was the last thing she heard before she slept.

In her dreams that night, Madeline shuddered at the memory of the cold-eyed presence of Gilenyia during the healing connection. She shuddered and pulled her covers close. She cried out, and only the gentle reminder of Shula sitting beside her bed calmed her. She slept again, and remembered it only as a vague unease when she woke.

19
MUD

If truth is not your companion,
death walks beside you.

A KAKRI PROVERB

✦

J ason was not an idiot. He'd watched Madeline perform the healing and seen the bruises go from Shula to Madeline to the Scim.
Which meant his own wounds, which Madeline had described
as near fatal, had been transferred to someone else. He suspected
the words Night's Breath were significant in this regard. His chest
had been caved in, that's what Madeline had said. Could a Scim survive
that? He knew they healed faster than humans. He suspected that Night's
Breath was a name. He wondered if there was a way to meet him, the Scim
who'd saved his life. The other possibility—that Night's Breath had died as
a result of Jason's wounds—filled him with unimaginable dread. Madeline
wouldn't do that to him.

"Pay attention," Ruth said.

He shook himself aware. Ruth Mbewe, the weird kid with the blindfold, held his arm with one tiny hand. He had stepped into a puddle on the road. Ruth, despite having her eyes covered, had stepped around it.

"It's amazing how not being able to see makes your other senses sharper," Jason said.

"Don't be ridiculous," Ruth snapped. "I have average smell, taste, and hearing. I just use them. Unlike you."

Jason closed his eyes and took a deep breath. He tried to sort through the smells of the Court of Far Seeing. He didn't smell anything disgusting, now that they had left Westwind behind. The toilets at Westwind were just holes in the floor that fell several stories into the moat, which smelled like something hairy had exercised vigorously before falling in and dying. It backed up Jason's First Rule of Magic: poop has to go somewhere. Those magic toilets in Mrs. Raymond's place weren't eradicating whatever went in them, they were transporting it. He didn't know how (that's what made it magic), but he suspected it wasn't going to the archon's palace.

The First Rule had a corollary as well: if it ain't here, it must be somewhere else.

He had been thinking about Delightful Glitter Lady. To magically make her huge required a stone or some other object to become small at the same time. He remembered this from physics class: conservation of matter. Mass and energy were constant in the universe. Or something. Maybe that was the Pythagorean theorem. Whatever. The point being there must be something, somewhere, that allowed Dee to get larger or smaller by taking on the opposite. So his magic dial wasn't an embiggenator so much as a transference device.

"Ow!"

Ruth had pinched him. "Pay attention, I said, and you immediately stopped in the street, closed your eyes, and let your brain wander."

"It's creepy how you talk like an adult. What are you, eight?"

Ruth frowned. "Meanwhile, you behave like a five-year-old."

Jason gasped. "How dare you? A six-year-old, at least!"

"Charming," Ruth said. "Walk us to the cloth merchant over there. The one to your right."

The knight didn't usually let him or Madeline wander the city unattended, but the archon had sent specific directions that Jason was not allowed to wear his multicolored tuxedo to the palace. He had been informed that the tuxedo clashed "with everything." So Jason had been sent into the city to buy new clothes. Ruth was his babysitter. She had a tiny leather pouch tied at her waist with the money, or whatever passed for money here in the Sunlit Lands. Being watched by an eight-year-old—a blindfolded one, at that—did not do much for his self-esteem. He didn't even get to hold the money. He stared at the heavy little coin purse. He could keep track of something like that if they gave him a chance.

A small, quick hand snatched Ruth's money satchel. Jason stepped away from Ruth and grabbed the little thief by the neck before he could escape. An unkempt Scim kid wriggled in his grasp. The kid screamed and thrashed, but Jason had a solid grip. "See? I was paying attention," he said to Ruth. Except she couldn't see, of course. Ugh. "I caught a pickpocket," he said.

"I hear him," Ruth said. "What is your name?" she asked the kid.

The ugly little thing scowled at her. He peeled his grey lips back, showing them his protruding yellow teeth. "Mud."

"Why are you stealing from me, Mud?"

"I'm hungry," he said. "We're going to buy some fruit."

Ruth took the leather satchel from Jason, slipped it open, and dropped a large metal coin in Mud's hand. His eyes widened, and he looked quickly at the blindfolded girl in a way that made it clear he suspected she didn't realize how much money she had dropped in his palm. "Thank you, mistress," he said, ducked his head, and ran across the street, where a small knot of Scim kids enveloped him. They disappeared into a nearby alley.

"That better not have been my top hat money," Jason said.

"Top hats have specifically been vetoed."

"Outrageous! Who does the archon think he is! This is a free country, and I can wear a top hat if I want!" He realized with a strange little shock that the Sunlit Lands were not the United States, and he was still fuzzy on the political setup. "Wait. *Is* this a free country?"

"It was Madeline who vetoed the hat," Ruth said. "She described your previous hat in great detail. All the girls in the castle were laughing. One girl nearly fainted."

"All the girls?" Jason asked. "Who's that besides you and Shula and Madeline?"

Ruth smirked. "That's who I was talking about."

"Philistines," he muttered under his breath. "Still. You shouldn't give little thieves like that money. You're just contributing to the problem."

Ruth's face went still. "You have never been poor, have you, Jason?"

"Who, me? No way. My parents worked hard. There's a reason I hardly ever saw them. But we had money."

"So what would you suggest that little ruffian do? How would he eat if I did not give him money?"

Jason sighed. "You could give him a job or something, I guess. Can we go buy my suit now, please?"

"You don't have any money," Ruth said. "How will you get a suit?"

"Why are you acting like this? Are you—?" Oh. Ruth had been poor. Maybe here, maybe back on Earth. But she had lived without money. Maybe she had stolen fruit to survive herself. Maybe she had been a pickpocket on the street. "I'm sorry," Jason said. "I am. But stealing is wrong."

"Of course it is," Ruth said, as if it was the most obvious thing in the world. "But can honesty fill a rumbling stomach?"

"I suppose not."

"No," Ruth said. "Now walk over to the fruit stand and steal a piece of fruit."

There was a fruit stand across the road from them, on the right-hand side. Jason could smell it from here, the rich, pungent smell of ripe citrus baking in the sun.

"Um," Jason said, "as your elder, I feel like I should set a good example by *not* stealing a piece of fruit." The stand had stacks of beautiful fruit carefully arranged. A human girl stood behind it. There were other stands too, selling other things—carpets, buttons, vegetables, and so on.

"You have never worked for your money," Ruth said, her head cocked to one side. It was more statement than question.

"I did chores at home."

"Chores." She rearranged the cloth covering her eyes. "I also did chores." She tapped her fingers against her lips. "That street thief has worked harder in the last month than you have in your entire life."

Jason laughed. "Okay, okay, I get it. Feed the street kids. That's fine."

"Bring me a piece of fruit," Ruth said. She faced forward, waiting for an answer.

She wasn't going to drop it. This whole thing was ridiculous. He took a quick look around and didn't see any of the city guards. A lot of them were humans, anyway, and he had met them when they all lived together at Mrs. Raymond's. Anyway, he lived with the Knight of the Mirror now. That should give him an out if he got caught. "What kind of fruit should I get?"

"Whatever kind you want," Ruth said.

"Fine, fine," Jason said. He left her standing on the other side of the street. He couldn't avoid the feeling she was watching him, even though he knew that wasn't possible.

The young woman running the stand said, "May the light shine upon you, sir. Can I help you?"

Jason surveyed the fruit. An amazing variety of beautiful fruits were perfectly arranged by color. Oranges. Apples. Pineapples. A few things he had never seen before. "What's that one?"

"Addleberries. They only grow here in the Sunlit Lands."

"Ohh, what's that?"

"Guanábana. From Costa Rica." Huh. That was interesting. They must have some sort of deal set up. Or trained birds that flew fruit back and forth. Or, well, who knew in this place? Maybe they had magic penguins who carried the fruit in little backpacks.

"Is that a durian?"

"Yes, it's an Asian fruit."

Jason knew durian. They were gigantic, almost basketball-sized fruits with hard spikes covering the outside. If a durian fell out of a tree and hit someone, it could absolutely kill them. If you broke one open you would be greeted by a pale, creamy fruit that smelled like a gas leak. It was the worst-smelling edible thing Jason had ever run across. Strangely, the taste was sweet, despite the horrific smell. Most public places in Asia (like the subway) had rules about transporting durian because everyone—even people who loved the fruit—agreed that it smelled like corpses.

Jason debated what to steal. He could take a grape. Technically that would fulfill Ruth's request. The star fruit and the kiwi looked pretty good.

On the other hand, walking across the street with a giant spiky monstrosity of a fruit made a lot of sense. Ruth should be able to smell that thing coming, and it would serve her right.

He picked up a durian, then "accidentally" knocked a few lemons over. When the girl bent to pick them up, he turned his back so she couldn't see the spiky baby he cradled to his body and crossed the street.

"Sir!" the girl called. "You forgot to pay!"

Jason shoved the durian into Ruth's arms, then turned around to look at the produce girl. He shrugged. "I didn't forget!" he shouted. "I stole it!"

The girl put her hands on her waist and shouted back, "Then I'll call the city guard."

"I think you should," Ruth called.

"Hey!" Jason said. "This whole thing was your idea!"

The girl let a small green bird loose from her shop, and it darted into the heart of the market.

"You should run," Ruth whispered, pressing the durian into Jason's hands.

Jason stared at the gigantic thorny fruit. "Doesn't that make it worse?"

A roar came from the crowd, and an Elenil guard riding a tiger appeared. "He's looking for you," Ruth said. "Don't you wish I had given you a coin to pay for it now?"

Um, the police had tigers? He had seen Rondelo's stag more than once, but tigers? That changed everything. Jason ran, hands over his head, the durian bobbing above him, a stinky reminder of his thievery. "Make way!" he shouted, weaving through the crowd. The cries of people startled by a fast-moving tiger grew closer and closer. He ducked into a perfume shop but was immediately ejected. They didn't allow durian.

Ahead of him he saw a familiar shape—Rondelo, the captain of the guard, standing beside his white stag, talking to another citizen. "Rondelo!" he shouted.

Then Jason rolled to the ground, wrapped in a snarling, heavily muscled tiger. When the nausea-inducing spinning ended, he was on his back, the tiger was on his chest, and the durian was still in his hands, extended over his head.

The Elenil guard loomed over him, hand on his sword hilt. "Hello, citizen. What is that in your hands?"

"Where were you when that Scim kid was trying to steal our money?"

The guard narrowed his eyes. "We will come back to that, sir. What is that in your hands?"

"It's not a weapon, if that's what you're asking. I see why you might think that."

"Sir. Did you steal that fruit?" He sniffed twice, taking in the odor wafting off the durian. "Also, why?"

"I did steal it," Jason said earnestly. "Your tiger won't eat me, right?"

The guard grinned. "Not unless I give her permission. She follows the law, do you understand? You would like her to follow the law, right?"

"Yes," Jason said.

At a signal from the city guard, the tiger moved off his chest. "Go back and apologize, and pay for what you've stolen. Do not do that again. You do not wear the white any longer, you should know what is expected of you."

"Yes, sir."

The guard smiled at him, his perfect white teeth gleaming. "Now. What is this about a Scim stealing from you?"

"Oh, we took care of it," Jason said. "Just some kid named Mud, but we worked it out."

The guard snorted. "Mud. He is well known to the guard. I will speak to him." The guard pulled Jason to his feet.

"Like I said, we worked it out."

The guard stared at him, as if he couldn't understand the words coming out of Jason's mouth, then wandered into the crowd with his tiger.

Jason let out a long breath of air. Whew. His hands were shaking. He had almost been mauled by a tiger for stealing a durian.

Rondelo clapped him on the back. "You have run afoul of the city guard. That is Sochar. He is a hundred years my senior, but with a mercurial temper. I keep a close eye on him. You met him in good spirits." He laughed. "He has a soft spot for humans. Be glad you weren't a Scim!"

Jason could smell the tiger still, even over the constant stench of the durian. "What's the worst that could have happened?" Jason asked, doing his best to sound brave, like the whole event had meant nothing to him. "He'd take me to jail?" A memory rose of Break Bones, chained to a dungeon wall. Jail here might be a different experience than on Earth.

"He could have taken your hand," Rondelo said. "Or killed you if he thought you a threat."

Jason's stomach dropped into the soles of his shoes. Ruth was going to get an earful. Well. At least he could introduce everyone back at Westwind to durian. Honestly, it tasted great. It would be funny to watch them gagging on the smell before they tasted it.

He found Ruth in the center of the market, haggling with a merchant over a pair of pants. She had already bought him a shirt, jacket, and gloves. She didn't need his sizes, she told him, because she already knew.

"Did you know I could have died for this durian?"

"Yes. It was foolish to steal it."

"Well, I learned my lesson. No more listening to Ruth Mbewe!"

Ruth gave the merchant some money and handed Jason the pants. "We have your clothes now, so let us return home."

Jason kicked the cobbled street. "I need to go apologize to the fruit-stand lady and pay for my fruit. The guard said I had to."

Ruth's eyebrows raised from behind her blindfold. "But where will you get the money, Wu Song?"

"I was hoping from you."

"Maybe I will offer you a job," she said, her voice grave.

"I get it, I get it," Jason said. "Now give." He held his hand out, and Ruth dropped a coin in his palm.

The girl at the fruit stand smiled when he apologized, and Ruth gave her a handsome tip on top of the cost of the durian.

On their way home, Jason noticed the little gang of Scim kids again. They were gathered at the mouth of an alley, eating oranges. There were peels discarded all around them. Some of them sat on the curb, juice running down their chins as they shoved pieces in their mouths, while others stood against the wall, peeling segments of orange away and popping them in their mouths. "Better keep a hand on your purse," Jason muttered.

Sochar came from the other direction, his tiger at his side. They had a lazy gait to their walk, as if they were out for an afternoon stroll. Jason knew that look. They were about to hassle the Scim kids. Sochar had his hand on the hilt of his sword when he walked up to the kids.

"Where did you get that fruit?" Sochar asked, nudging Mud with the toe of his boot.

Mud gave him a surly look and kept eating.

"It's okay," Jason said. "I already told you, we gave them money."

Sochar grunted. "You buy that fruit?"

Mud didn't answer, and the other kids didn't speak up, either.

"Answer me," Sochar said, nudging Mud harder.

"The lady gave me coin," Mud muttered.

Jason stepped between Mud and the guard. Mud jumped to his feet, and the guard pulled his sword with lightning speed. The other Scim kids disappeared in a frenzied explosion of motion, leaving behind only peels, pulp, and Mud.

"Stay calm," Jason said to Mud. "Stand still and speak respectfully."

Mud stood beside him, trembling. He leaned toward Jason, half hiding behind his leg.

"Did you steal that fruit, sir?" Sochar asked.

"No, sir," Mud said, his voice quavering.

Sochar shook his head. "Do not lie to me."

"There's no need for that sword," Jason said.

"Get on your knees and show me your hands," Sochar said.

Mud bent his knees, and for a moment it appeared he would do as he had been asked, but then he whipped an orange through the air at Sochar's face and dashed away for the alley. Without thinking, Jason grabbed Mud's arm, trying to get him to stand still, but Mud yanked his arm away. He ran.

The tiger pounced, tearing the boy's leg. Sochar, crushed orange on his face, came two steps behind and with one practiced lunge skewered Mud through the side.

Mud fell to the ground, eyes open. An orange rolled from his shirt, coming to rest in a filthy puddle. His eyes flickered toward Jason.

Jason stepped toward them, but the guard threw his hand up. "Stay back!" Sochar rifled through the child's pockets, throwing out pieces of crushed fruit and a short black knife. "A necrotic blade," he said. "Dangerous. Illegal. No doubt meant for you or someone like you, sir."

The black metal of the blade didn't reflect light correctly. Jason felt a small relief to the tidal wave of guilt threatening to engulf him. Perhaps the boy deserved this, if he was carrying that knife. Maybe he was an assassin, a spy, a troublemaker. *He shouldn't have run*, Jason thought. But then he stopped himself. He was committed to the truth, and while it made him feel better to think Mud deserved this . . . Sure, the kid was a pickpocket, but he hadn't gotten away with the money. Ruth had given it to him. He had bought those oranges. Jason had run when he saw that tiger too. And maybe Mud needed the knife to protect himself. Or maybe . . . Jason thought about this carefully. Maybe it wasn't his knife. Sochar's back had been to Jason when he'd pulled the knife from the boy's pocket. Could he be sure the city guard hadn't planted it? He could not.

The boy lay on the ground bleeding because of Jason. Yes, Mud had tried to steal something. Yes, Sochar had wielded the blade that had skewered the boy. But Jason had been the one to speak up, to say that Mud had tried to steal from them. He shouldn't have done that, but he hadn't known, hadn't suspected for a moment this would be the end result. He didn't care what happened—it wasn't worth the kid's life to stop him from stealing a handful of coins.

"Take him to Gilenyia," Sochar said to the tiger.

"Is he alive?" Jason asked, a flutter of relief coming to him at the mention of the Elenil healer.

Sochar ignored him. The tiger lifted Mud's body in her jaws.

Two members of Mud's gang appeared, shouting and mocking Sochar. One threw a piece of fruit, which spattered the tiger's face. She dropped Mud, growling. Sochar, furious, shouted at the tiger, and they split up, each chasing a different Scim.

Jason fell to his knees beside Mud. Was he breathing? Jason couldn't tell. The black tattoos on his arms were fading, turning grey.

Four more Scim children came sliding out of the shadows. "Get away from him," one of them, a girl, snarled.

Two of them lifted Mud, pulling his arms over their shoulders, and a third swiftly gathered up the spilled fruit. The girl stared at Jason, hands clenched. "Why did you hold his arm when he tried to run? He didn't take anything from you. He didn't do you no harm."

Jason opened his mouth to answer and realized he didn't know, not exactly. He thought Mud shouldn't run. He'd thought, on some level, that if they stood there and talked it out, everything would be fine. That may not have been true, because stabbing the kid wasn't a reasonable response, not at all. Maybe he had wanted to teach Mud, to help him do the right thing. He'd wanted to teach him what was right, and only now, mud and blood on his hands, did Jason stop to wonder if he really knew what was right in this moment. What he knew with a deep, burning certainty was this: the boy's life was worth more than a few oranges. More than a whole cart of them.

The children were gone now, all but one. "Well?" she demanded, and he realized he hadn't answered her.

"I'm sorry," he said.

She spit on the ground between them.

"Here," Jason said, holding out the durian. "Take this. If he—*when* Mud wakes up, give it to him."

The girl lifted the durian over her head. Jason covered his face, tried to shield Ruth. The girl hurled the durian to the cobblestones with all her strength, and it burst. The stench of it exploded into the air. The sweet white meat flew up, splashing all over him, covering his new clothes.

He wiped the juice from his eyes.

The girl was gone.

Only the crushed durian remained.

20
PREPARATIONS

I saw a woman who sang as she slopped the pigs, though she had no apron
to cover her dress. A scribe laughed to see his papers blown by the wind.
A man whistled a tune when he saw his wagon wheel had broken.

FROM "THE THREE GIFTS OF THE PEASANT KING," A SCIM LEGEND

✦

Big rhino, little rhino," Jason mumbled to himself.

He stood in the square courtyard near Westwind's stables. Delightful Glitter Lady snorted at him, her ear twitching as a fly landed on her head. She closed her eyes halfway, enjoying the sunshine. She was in battle mode, much larger than a typical rhino. Unicorn. Whatever.

Jason had the embiggenator in his hand. The dial was turned all the way to the right, to get her to full size. He had been studying how the magical debt was paid. It was helping to keep his mind off what had happened in the market. Sort of. Anyway, for Dee to get big, something else had to get small, right? He had figured it out soon after the big battle by switching Dee's size a few times while walking around the stable near where he had first met her. There was a row of large stones near the city wall. He had noticed that one of them shrank when Dee grew, and vice versa. Once he'd figured it out, he had dialed Dee up to giant size and pocketed the corresponding small stone.

He tossed the pebble in his hand. So far he had managed to remember to not slip it into his pocket and then switch her size. He scratched Dee under the chin, and her eyes shut. She made a low, rumbling, contented sound.

Madeline came jogging around the corner of the castle. With the Elenil modesty rules, she had to wear a long-sleeved shirt and thin gloves when she ran. She had a small backpack as well. She stopped by Jason, hands behind her head, and caught her breath.

"You're sweaty," Jason said.

"Well, hello to you, too." Madeline grinned at him.

"Are you having trouble breathing?" he asked, studying the way she gasped for air.

Her grin grew wider. "It's what happens when you exercise, Jason. You should try it."

He tapped his temple. "I'm exercising my *mind*, Mads." He pointed at her backpack. "For instance. My mind is saying, why is Madeline carrying a backpack while exercising?"

"Interesting. My mind is wondering why you're doing magic in the courtyard where the knight might see and kick you out."

Jason nodded. "Fair question. I've been studying how Elenil magic works. For Dee to get big, something else has to get small." He showed Madeline the pebble in his hand. He tossed it by the wall. "Watch." He dialed the embiggenator to the left, and the rock grew to the size of a mailbox and then a trunk.

Dee flicked her ears again, but now she came to Jason's knee. She looked up at him lazily, unconcerned. She prodded him in the leg with her horn. Okay, maybe slightly annoyed.

Madeline knelt down and scratched the little rhino behind the ears. "Can I try it?"

Jason shrugged and handed her the embiggenator. "Turn it to the right to make her bigger and to the left to make her smaller."

Madeline turned the dial to the left. "Like this?"

"No! She can't get any smaller—"

Except apparently she could. Dee trumpeted and rose up on her hind legs, barely the size of a kitten. "Aw!" Madeline said, scooping her up in her arms. Dee cuddled in against her, squeaking and making happy unicorn noises. The stone, meanwhile, had grown still larger, leaning against the castle walls.

"Huh," Jason said. "I didn't think she could go that small."

"You could probably sleep in the castle now," Madeline said. "Just sneak her in your pocket until you get to bed."

"She's a noisy sleeper, though. Now spill, Madeline—what are you doing with that backpack?"

"It's got my clothes in it for our meeting with the archon," Madeline said. "I want to take a hot bath before we go to the palace, so I'm going to sneak over to Mrs. Raymond's."

Jason took Dee from Madeline and set her down. "How are you going to get out?"

"I have my ways," she said. "You should take a bath too."

Jason snorted. "My suit smells like durian. It won't make a difference. I could tag along, though—there's something I want to do too."

"Get your clothes, then, and let's go."

"They're in the stable, hold on." Jason ambled toward the stable, Dee frolicking at his feet. He nearly tripped over her several times. "Okay, girl, in you go." He turned the embiggenator to "normal" and shoveled some grass into her stall. "Don't give me that look. If the knight sees you the size of a stuffed animal, I'm going to get in trouble." He scooped up his suit and headed to catch up with Madeline.

He found her near the front gate, where one of the knight's soldiers stood guard at the drawbridge. She was a human teenager too, and the guarding was largely ceremonial. No one could get into Far Seeing without passing plenty of guards. This guard was supposed to keep the knight informed of who came in and out.

Still, Jason's stomach clenched at the thought of being caught. "How do you get past the guard? We're not supposed to leave the castle unattended."

"Watch," Madeline said. "Hey, Thuy," she called to the guard. Jason had no idea how Madeline knew her name already. She must have been hanging out with the other humans in the castle. He remembered Ruth's comment that "all the girls" had made fun of his hat, and he blushed.

"Hey, Madeline," the guard said. "Sneaking out to get a bath again?"

"Yeah. I hate how there's no magic in the castle."

"Tell me about it. You know we're going to get busted if you get caught out there."

"Don't worry," Madeline said. "We'll be careful."

"We?" Thuy glanced at Jason. "You're not taking him, are you?"

"If it's okay with you," she said.

"I don't know. He's sort of . . . unpredictable."

Jason wasn't sure how he felt about that. He tried to think of something unpredictable that he could do in the moment, but nothing came to him. Maybe that was unpredictable?

"I'll bring you something from the market," Madeline said.

"Not the market," Thuy said. "I want a cinnamon roll from Mrs. Raymond's place. I love the knight, but the food at Mrs. Raymond's is so much better than here."

"Deal."

"Great," Jason said. "That's easy."

The guard glared at Jason. "And a pudding."

"A . . . uh . . . a what now?"

"I want one of your magic puddings. We all know you get them, and I haven't had pudding in a long, long time."

Jason crossed his arms. "That's because pudding is terrible. People only want it when they're in the hospital or think they can't have it."

"Well, I can't have it now, so I want one."

"Fine," Jason said. "I'll give you a magic hospital pudding. Can we go now?"

Thuy looked straight ahead. "I don't know what you're talking about."

Madeline walked over the drawbridge. "Come on," she said, looking back at him still standing next to Thuy. "That's her way of saying she can't see us. Now get moving."

Oh. That made sense. He trotted across the drawbridge, and they headed toward Mrs. Raymond's place. The path they took would pass directly through the market. He told Madeline the story of Mud and that he wanted to check in on him. He felt embarrassed telling Mads about it . . . because, in retrospect, he felt he should have known better and especially because it had ended with such unexpected violence. But Mads took it in stride and didn't seem to think less of him for it. It was a relief to talk with her about it and to have her support.

He didn't tell her about the dreams he had been having . . . weird dreams filled with strange people. People that reminded him of the Scim, but less scary, kinder, and strangely endearing. They had looked more human than Scim, when he thought back on them, but he had known in his dream they were Scim. And there was the house: an old dilapidated mansion with moss hanging from the roof that came into his dreams over and over. He stood in front of it in near complete darkness, and he could feel a small breath of air on his neck. An old Scim woman lived in the house, and he was there to visit her, to check in on her.

"Jason?"

Startled, Jason almost lost his footing. They stood near the fruit stand now, a full minute's walk from the castle, and he had been so deep in his own thoughts he hadn't noticed. He vaguely remembered that Madeline had been talking to him a moment before. "Sorry," he said.

"Are you okay?"

"Yeah. I just . . . I was thinking." He cracked his knuckles. "Okay. The Scim kids ran down that alley."

The alley stank. It wasn't dark . . . There weren't dark places in Far Seeing, but it shouldn't have smelled, either. Apparently magic toilets were not in use wherever the alley took them.

Madeline strode ahead of Jason, who felt unaccountably nervous. He had a deep, unsettled feeling that the little Scim boy had already died. The cobbled alley gave way in places to patches of dirt and mud, as if whatever magic kept the city in perfect repair did not work here.

They found the gang of Scim kids huddled together along the alley pathway, throwing colored stones in a circle. One of the kids looked up at them, grimaced, and looked away. They kept throwing stones.

"Excuse us," Madeline said. They ignored her.

"We're looking for Mud," Jason said.

One of the kids grinned at him and, without warning, slung a handful of mud in his face. "There you are," the kid said, and the rest of their little gang chortled and laughed and continued throwing their stones.

Jason wiped a streak of mud from his face with his fingers. "I just want to make sure he's okay."

One of the kids, a young girl, stood. Her dark hands were closed in fists, her tusklike teeth rubbing against the disgusted curl of her lips. "Is that so? You care what happens to little Scim children? Then why is this the first time we've seen you?" She scooped up her rocks. "Mud is gone."

"Gone like . . . gone? Or like . . . dead?"

But the girl walked down the alley without turning back.

"The human lady took her," one of the boys in the circle said.

Madeline crouched down beside them. "The human? Do you mean the Garden Lady?"

The children laughed. "You don't know nothin', do you?" said the boy. "The Garden Lady, she only appears in a garden, don't she? Not in Scim alleys, huh?"

The children gathered their stones, evidently tired of the obtrusive humans. "What's her name?" Jason asked.

One of the smaller boys lingered back. "What will you give me for it?"

"What do you want?"

The boy licked his lips, looking at Jason's feet. "Your shoes, I think. Or . . . what's in the bag?"

"Fine," Jason said. He couldn't give him the suit—Ruth would kill him. "The shoes for a name." He kicked them off. He could snag another pair from David and Kekoa's room easily enough, and they could just order more.

The boy snatched the shoes up, cackling to himself. He held them against his chest. "She has a tame name."

"Tame name?"

"Like she was Scim once, but instead of being named Darkness Boils or some such she has a tame name, a sunlight name. You know."

The kid started to back away, but Jason grabbed him by the arm. "Don't sneak away, buddy. You haven't given me her name yet."

Another clod of mud came sailing down the alley and again caught Jason in the face. He lost his grip on the kid, who skittered backward with the shoes. "I don't remember it quite," the boy said. "But something about sunbeams. Ray Man. Something like that." Then he scampered off with his friends.

Jason wiped the mud from his face again, then wiped his hand on his pants. "Ray Man. Well. That was worth it, I guess. Mud is alive, at least. Or was."

Madeline looked at him in consternation. "You didn't figure it out? He's talking about Mrs. Raymond. Ray Man—Raymond."

Jason gasped. "Uh. I did not catch that."

Madeline had already turned on her heel and was running for Mrs. Raymond's house. Jason pelted after her, barefoot and embarrassed. By the time they reached Mrs. Raymond's sprawling residence, Jason's feet ached.

Jasper, the kid in charge of the armory, was sitting on the front steps, enjoying the sunshine. "Is Mrs. Raymond here?" Madeline asked.

He shrugged. "Haven't seen her since breakfast." He squinted at Jason. "Hey. Where's that unicorn? You didn't check it out of the armory."

Check it out? Dee wasn't a library book, and besides, no one had told him he was supposed to do that. It wasn't his fault Dee loved him so much that she wanted to be with him at all times. "I can't even keep track of my shoes," he said. "How am I supposed to keep track of a unicorn?" He chased Madeline into the house, ignoring Jasper's shouted instructions.

Madeline held her hand out, slowing him. She looked up the long stairway with the plush carpet. "Should we see if she's in her room?"

"There's no way she brought some Scim kid into her house. The Elenil would go nuts. Even a lot of the human kids here hate the Scim."

"But we can wait for her there, if nothing else."

"Okay," Jason said. They walked up the stairs, and Jason sighed with relief at the feeling of the plush carpet on his bare feet. He didn't know where Mrs. Raymond's room was, but Madeline seemed to. She took them through a series of hallways, twists and turns, and came to a simple wooden door. Madeline knocked, but no one answered.

"I guess we'll wait," Madeline said, and leaned against the wall.

Jason leaned against the door beside her. It gave way, and he stumbled backward into the room. He straightened, taking a quick look to make sure Mrs. Raymond wasn't sitting in the room watching him. He pulled the door shut again.

"What are you doing?" Madeline asked.

"It was an accident!"

She pushed the door open. "No, I meant, why are you closing it again?"

"Bad idea," Jason said, but he followed her in and shut the door behind them.

The room was about twice as large as the one he had shared with Kekoa and David. There was a window directly in front of them and a closet door on the wall to their left. A modest bed sat in the corner, a comfortable-looking chair was placed near the window, and there was even a fireplace, which was so clean he wasn't sure it had ever been used. But Madeline walked with reverent wonder toward the unexpected feature against the far wall: a rustic bookshelf packed with books.

She ran her hand across the spines. "Look at all these. Tolkien, Lewis, L'Engle, MacDonald, Rowling." She pulled one from the shelf, turning it over in her hands. "They're all fantasy novels."

"That's weird," he said. "Seems like you'd just want to enjoy living in your own fantasyland, not dreaming about other ones."

Madeline gasped, shelved the book she had been holding, one by T. H. White, and crouched down to a lower shelf. "I can't believe it," she said. "It's the Tales of Meselia. All of them and all first editions. Jason, these are my favorite books of all time."

It was a little strange, seeing books again after all this time in the Sunlit Lands. Jason picked up one of the books. It was called *The Winter Rogue*. He flipped through the pages.

"That's the second one," Madeline said. "Then comes *The Gold Firethorns* and then *The Skull and the Rose*. Oh, you'd love that one, Jason."

Jason sighed and put his book back on the shelf. He was glad Madeline had found something to distract her for a moment, but he couldn't keep himself from wondering about Mud. Which reminded him of Night's Breath. Which, somehow, reminded him of his sister. He put his hand against the bookshelf to steady himself.

"Are you okay?" Madeline stood and put her hand on his shoulder.

He nodded, just as the closet door swung open and Mrs. Raymond came walking out, drying her hands on a towel and talking as she walked.

"—will be fine, but you can't keep bringing me these orphaned—ah. For instance, these two."

Hanali had been walking close behind her and crashed into her when she stopped. He glanced up, the perplexed expression on his face changing into a look that said, *Oh, of course this is Jason's fault.*

"I do not recall extending invitations or permission to enter my private room," Mrs. Raymond said.

Hanali frowned. "The boy has a way of weaseling into places uninvited."

"The door was open," Jason said, realizing how lame it sounded even as the words left his mouth.

Mrs. Raymond took the books from Madeline and put them back on the shelf. "Nor did I invite you to paw through my library."

"We didn't mean any harm," Madeline said. "It's just that—"

"Your hands are filthy," Mrs. Raymond said. She looked at Jason. "His entire . . . What happened to your face, Mr. Wu?"

Oh yeah. The mud. "Hygiene standards are surprisingly lax here," Jason said.

Hanali rolled his eyes. "This from the boy who took a bath while wearing his shoes." He looked at Jason's feet and then, with a weary sigh, looked back to his eyes. "Where are your shoes?"

"I sold them to a Scim kid."

Hanali scowled. "You should not be fraternizing with the Scim, Wu Song. It reflects poorly on me as your benefactor."

Something in Hanali's voice caught Jason's attention. He knew somehow that Hanali was hiding something. Hanali's eyes flickered, just for a moment, back toward the closet door. "You know," Jason said, "certain doors in this glorified youth hostel go places they shouldn't." He walked toward the closet.

"Keep your hand off that door," Hanali said.

"I have a way of weaseling into places uninvited," Jason said, and swung the door open.

Mud lay sleeping on a narrow bed in a stone room. Day Song, Gilenyia's Scim assistant, looked up from the boy, a washrag in his hand.

Mrs. Raymond pulled the door shut with a firm hand. "Stay away from the boy. You are covered in filth. He's in pain enough without an infection."

Jason locked eyes with Madeline, but she appeared to have as little idea of what was happening as he did. He looked a question to Hanali, who plucked at his sleeves with nonchalance.

"Mrs. Raymond has a way of picking up unfortunate strays," Hanali said. "And should you not be dressing for our audience with the archon?"

"Don't get me wrong," Jason said. "I'm glad Mud is getting medical help, but why do you have him here?"

"Hanali is well known in the Scim community as the Elenil to approach if there are needs," Mrs. Raymond said.

Madeline's eyes widened. "He's *what*?"

"Enough," Hanali said, steel in his voice. "We will talk no further of these things. The boy will be returned to his home when he is well. No one here will mention this again. Not to me, not to one another, and certainly not to the archon."

Mrs. Raymond's face set to stone. "Hanali, son of Vivi," she said. "Have you not shared your plans with these two children, even though they are a central piece of it?"

"Nor would I have shared them with you if you were not so persistent and infernally nosy," Hanali snapped.

"Hey," Jason said, offended. "I'm persistent and nosy too."

Hanali glared at him. "You. To the baths. We leave here in one half of an hour. Every particle of mud must be gone from your face." He turned to Madeline. "And you? Have you more to say? Intrusive questions? Infuriating requests?"

Madeline blushed. When she spoke, her voice was so low Jason almost couldn't hear it. "Mrs. Raymond? Could I maybe borrow some books?"

Mrs. Raymond put her fists on her hips and rounded on Hanali. "These are the children you've staked everything on, and you've not given them so much as a clue as to the deeper game you're playing?"

Hanali gave her a shocked look, his gloved hand on his chest. "Deeper game? My dear Mrs. Raymond, I only desire invitations to more prestigious parties."

She glowered at him a moment more before turning to Madeline and saying, "Of course, dear, so long as none of them leave the house—and don't show them to the Elenil. Since they can't read, they always think we're passing secret knowledge. If they catch you with a book, they'll make you read the entire thing aloud before they let you leave. Now run along and clean up."

Jason hadn't seen Madeline so giddily happy before. She went to hug Mrs. Raymond, who turned her aside with a huff. Still giddy, Madeline grabbed Jason's hand and pulled him into the hallway. "Mud is going to be fine!" Madeline said. "And there are *books*!"

"Yeah. And Hanali has a secret plot. Big surprise, I guess."

As if summoned, Hanali opened the door and stuck his head out. "Mr. Wu."

"Yes?"

"Use soap."

Hanali closed the door again, leaving Jason alone with the laughing Madeline. "Use soap," Jason grumbled. He picked up his bag with the suit in it and tossed Madeline her backpack. He started off down the hallway, then realized he had no idea where they were in the massive maze of Mrs. Raymond's house.

"Your room is the other way," Madeline said, passing him. "Don't be late."

Jason turned back, listened to Madeline's footsteps headed the other direction. When she was gone, he paused by Mrs. Raymond's room. He could hear dim, concerned voices on the other side. He leaned his head close to the door but couldn't hear what they were saying. It sounded like Mrs. Raymond was angry and Hanali was trying to mollify her.

He cracked the door slightly.

Mrs. Raymond was talking. "—too great a risk, letting them in. Not just to you but to all of—"

"We've already discussed this at length, Mary."

"*Mrs. Raymond*, Hanali. You don't get to call me Mary anymore."

Hanali sighed. "It is a risk. A terrible risk. But, my dear Mrs. Raymond, how could the situation become any worse?"

There was a pause, and when Mrs. Raymond spoke again, her voice sounded tired and sad. "There is always a way, Hanali."

"I suppose," he said. "But it is the choice I have made. Now. If you will excuse me, I feel an urgent need to check on Mr. Wu. If I leave him alone for even a few minutes, he makes the worst kinds of trouble."

Jason jumped away from the door and hugged his bag close to his chest. He half ran, half walked to the end of the hallway and turned right, then speed walked until he knew where he was.

If he hurried, he should have just enough time to clean up and get dressed. Hanali had asked how the situation could get any worse. Jason had a sinking feeling that he would be the one to figure that out.

21

THE PALACE
OF A THOUSAND YEARS

*The glory of a king comes from neither wealth nor finery
but from the well-being of his people.*

FROM "THE THREE GIFTS OF THE PEASANT KING," A SCIM LEGEND

✦

The archon's palace stood at the center of Far Seeing. A hill rose gracefully beneath it, pastel-colored houses and buildings lapping up along the sides like waves. Shops and markets splashed beneath those, filled with people from all over the Sunlit Lands seeking a trinket or a necessity from carts and stands festooned with bright flags and flowers.

"None but the Elenil are allowed beyond this point without a host," Hanali said to Madeline as they stepped down from the carriage. "Humans may neither ride a steed nor carry a weapon. Nor may the Scim, the Aluvoreans, emissaries from the Southern Court, the Zhanin . . . all the other races. They must pause here before entering the heart of the Elenil world and the seat of our magic." Hanali paused and stared at the pulsing crescent-shaped stone at the apex of the main tower.

Jason, freshly bathed, straightened his jacket. They had tried to get the durian smell out, but it lingered. Without magic it couldn't be easily cleaned, and Ruth had told him buying another would be a "luxury" and that he could find his own money rather than spend the knight's. Shula had not been invited to the palace. She had business elsewhere, she said, and had wanted to reconnect with some of the other soldiers. Jason had asked her about Baileya, a Kakri woman he mentioned from time to time but whom Madeline had not yet met. Shula knew her and said she would likely see her and asked if Jason had a message. "Tell her—" Jason said, looking like he was thinking carefully, "—tell her, uh . . . I said hi." Shula, grinning, had promised to do so.

For the seventieth time Hanali launched into how to be polite in the archon's presence. Curtsy or bow. Speak when spoken to . . . with the proper restraint. Do not release Scim prisoners to wreak havoc in the court or mention previous instances where one might have done so. Do not touch the archon. Are you listening, Jason, *do not touch the archon*. Not with a fist nor with a fingertip.

Madeline found it painful to hear again, especially since it seemed to be aimed at Jason. The wonders of Elenil architecture distracted her in any case. The main tower of the palace stood in the center: a delicate, slender white column with graceful lines. Nine slightly shorter towers stood at equidistant points around it, with white latticework like lace covering their lower halves. Wide marble stairs arched between the towers, leading to meticulous gardens overflowing with bright, gorgeous flowers. A stunning variety of people and creatures moved up and down those stairs, each of them accompanied by at least one Elenil guide. None of the guards here were human, unlike elsewhere in the city, but only Elenil in splendid royal-blue uniforms with gold trim.

"It's beautiful," Madeline said, almost whispering.

Hanali paused his lecture and stopped, one gloved hand on the elbow of each of his charges. "It is known as the Palace of a Thousand Years. It was built entirely by hand. No machines from your world, no shortcuts or tools other than what can be held in a person's hand. Each stair is a single piece, mined by the Maegrom. The Aluvoreans coaxed the gardens into being. Not a single blade of grass was planted—they encouraged local plants to arrive of their own free will. Even the Zhanin participated, in their way, by not interfering with the amount of magic drawn upon in that century. It would cause a war today to use so much power so quickly."

"That century?" Madeline asked. "Didn't you say it was the Palace of a Thousand Years?"

"Yes," Hanali said, guiding them to the stairs. "It would have taken a thousand years without magic. There is no comparable architecture in any world I've seen. My forefathers built it, I am told, in less than two centuries. A hundred and sixty years, more or less."

Jason asked a question, trying to sound nonchalant, but Madeline could tell he asked with purpose. "I've been studying Elenil magic. So for these buildings to go up more quickly, there must be other places where building happened more slowly?"

Hanali's face lit with delight. "Ah! At last young Jason takes an interest in the culture of the Elenil. Indeed. There are trade-offs. The speed and beauty of this construction means that, by necessity, there is a balance elsewhere. The magic here was carefully wrought, and it is geolocational. Which is to say, the spells made it easier and faster to craft the palace here, on this hill. There is another place elsewhere in the Sunlit Lands, linked to this hill, where it would be immensely difficult—if not impossible—to build. Magic would fight you every step of the way."

Jason wrinkled his nose in distaste. He'd probably caught a whiff of himself again. "Where is that place, Hanali?"

"Somewhere in the Wasted Lands, no doubt. We could ask a storyteller. They keep tales about such things hidden away for curious minds such as yours."

They paused at the top of the stairway to appreciate one of the gardens. It sank away to the left of them like an amphitheater and was filled to the brim with fruit trees, luscious grasses, and exotic animals. Peacocks wandered in the shade, shaking their fanned tails. Birds zipped between the branches, and large cats lounged, uncaring, in the dappled sunshine. Madeline gasped. A white mare, as brilliant as mother-of-pearl in the sunlight, stepped out of the trees. She had a long, silver horn protruding from her forehead.

Jason's hand clenched Hanali's forearm. "What is that?"

Hanali smiled gently. "A rare Earth animal. I believe it is called—what was it now?—ah, yes! A rhinoceros. I'm told they are extinct in old Earth."

Seeing the look of impotent rage on Jason's face gave Madeline the giggles. She tried to keep a straight face, but soon she was leaning against Hanali, wiping tears from her eyes. Jason's face softened, and soon he was laughing too. Hanali asked what was so funny, but they wouldn't answer. A foal emerged from the trees and cavorted at the mare's feet. They both stopped to feed on the sweet grass.

"We can speak to them later if you wish," Hanali said. "Though it is rude to laugh at such noble creatures."

"They can talk?" Madeline asked.

"Of course," Hanali said, as if it were a ridiculous question. "All rhinoceri can speak."

They entered the palace through a gateway arch which soared above their heads, several stories tall. There were no gates or doors because, Hanali explained, most of the defensive capabilities were magical. And if an enemy made it this deep into Far Seeing, the defense of the city had already fallen, and it was better to allow their enemies entrance to the palace than risk its destruction.

The rooms in the tower wound up along the inside of the wall, leaving the center free all the way to the top. Birds glided above them, delivering messages. A series of long ropes hung from different levels of the palace, allowing braver souls to swing across the vast space between the walls. Toward the top of the tower, suspended in a glass room, was a crescent-shaped crystal. Significantly smaller than the one affixed to the exterior of the main tower, it was, like that larger stone, black and glowing with a purple aura. It could be seen even from the bottom of the tower, as the ceiling was made of some sort of glass or transparent crystal.

"The Crescent Stone. Also called the Heart of the Scim," Hanali said, noticing Madeline staring. "At the heart of all our magic is that stone. It is displayed there at the top of the Palace of a Thousand Years in a glass room which can only be accessed through the archon's quarters. It is transparent so all can see if any approach it. I do not know of a person entering that room in a generation or more."

"Don't you mean the Heart of the Elenil?" Madeline asked.

Hanali, surprised, drew away from her, as if trying to get a better look. "Ha! Of course, that would make sense. Many centuries ago, the Elenil and the Scim exchanged stones. The Heart of the Elenil is with them, the Heart of the Scim with us. Some find it distasteful to call the stone after the Scim, and so they call it the Crescent Stone. In those days, though, we were friends, and the name was without controversy. Those were better days. I am told the Heart of the Elenil is a beautiful stone—so transparent one seems to see a delicate blue sky within it and a faint shine of sunlight in a corona around it. More beautiful, most say, than the stone we keep watch over here."

"Wait, wait, wait," Jason said. "If that's the Crescent Stone, what is that big crescent stone that's on top of the tower? The one we can see from outside? The gigantic one?"

"Ah," Hanali said. "Another insightful question. The Crescent Stone itself is smaller than you would think, though great magic flows through it. The stone affixed to the top of the tower is an amplifier, which allows the magic to flow freely into the rest of the Sunlit Lands."

Jason's brow furrowed with concentration. He was working hard to figure this out. "So the true Crescent Stone is not the one on the exterior of the tower."

"Indeed not. As I have just said."

"Got it," Jason said, and it sounded as if he had filed that information away for some reason.

"So where do we meet the archon?" Madeline asked.

Hanali pointed out a gaudy throne, three times the size of what a normal person would fit on. It was on the fourth through sixth floors and could be seen easily from anywhere in the building other than directly above it. "On feast days and during celebrations, the archon sits on the Festival Throne. Today he desires a more intimate setting, so you are to meet him in the Apex Throne Room, near the top of the tower."

Jason groaned. "That's a lot of stairs. Couldn't he meet us down here?"

"We won't climb the stairs," Hanali said. "Step upon these circles."

The circles painted on the floor were about the size of dinner plates and all different colors. Madeline stepped solidly into the outline of two dusky-orange ones and, following instructions from Hanali, imagined herself moving to the 114th floor. The circles lifted from the ground and began to move smoothly upward. No ropes or pulleys, no seat belts, and no nets, air bags, or pillows waiting below. She yelped. Jason screamed.

Jason fell off from about ten feet up, landing in a clutch of Elenil who had the misfortune to be walking below him. They helped him to his feet, clearly unhappy, and sent him floating upward again.

"Stand up straight!" Hanali yelled to Jason. "Stop flailing!" He floated past Madeline, confidently standing on only one of the flying plates, his other foot moving in graceful arcs, toes pointed.

They were about thirty stories up now, and Madeline couldn't bear to look down at Jason. An Elenil swung past her, headed from one side of the wall to the other, his golden hair streaming behind him. "Are you okay, Jason?" she called, still looking toward the top of the tower.

"Jason wants to take the stairs!" Jason yelled.

"Posture," Hanali shouted. "Good posture is paramount, Mr. Wu!"

The Heart of the Scim stood above them, its purple energy crackling with power. The light gleamed against the glass walls, revealing that it rested on a glass pedestal—it was not floating, as Madeline had believed. It was about the size of a manhole cover—there must be some sort of magnification effect that allowed it to be seen so clearly from the bottom. Above it she could see the gigantic crystal crescent that hung over the tower.

Hanali floated up and to the left, disembarking with a careless step onto a wide landing. Relieved to be at the end, Madeline held out her gloved hand as she rose to his level, and he took it, helping her to step more or less gracefully from the floating circles.

Jason came only a moment behind. He panicked, leaning toward the solid edges of the wall, and fell from his circles, his arms grabbing the landing, his legs kicking out into empty space. Hanali dragged him across the floor. "Stand still and stand straight. Are these instructions truly too difficult for you?"

"I don't like hover plates," Jason said.

"They are perfectly safe," Hanali replied. "Only a child would fall from them."

Jason snorted.

A civilized Scim stood nearby, his entire uniform, from boots to gloves, a stark white. Even his dark hair had been caught up in a white tie, and his collar extended even higher than the current style. He had no tusks and small, white, almost human teeth. He bowed gravely. "Sirs and miss, I am called Bright Prism. I will guide you to your audience with the archon."

Madeline helped Jason to his feet. "I'm Madeline, and this is Jason. You probably already know Hanali."

"Indeed," Bright Prism said, politely inclining his head. "Kindly follow me." He led them through an endless series of sumptuous rooms—ballrooms and dining halls, leisure rooms and rooms full of paintings. One room was an indoor garden cunningly made to look as if it were outside by painting on the ceiling and walls and, as near as Madeline could tell, not through the use of magic. They did not pass any kitchens or bathrooms or bedrooms or any evidence that people lived in this section of the tower, though Hanali had assured them these were, in fact, the archon's quarters. Of course there were no televisions or other technology, though there was a room with a variety of musical instruments. There was no library, a reality of the Sunlit Lands that still struck Madeline as strange. No books, no street signs, no grocery lists, no notes to loved ones. Magic allowed them to mimic high technology in some sense, but they were illiterate.

Nevertheless, the tour, she suspected, was intended to awe them. They wandered in and out of strange halls, through parties and balls and choral performances. Madeline found it impossible to believe all these things happened constantly and had not been set in motion merely to impress her, Jason, and Hanali. They arrived, at last, at two large golden doors which met at a point two stories above. Bright Prism stood with his back to the doors. "The Duru Paleis are the only doors in the palace. When one seeking entrance places a hand against this door, it can sense their intention. It grants or refuses access based on what is seen in that person's heart. Archon Thenody has instructed that each of you place your hand upon the handle to request entry."

Hanali nodded brusquely, stepped up to the door, and took hold of the long handle that ran down the middle. In a moment he stepped away. "I have been denied entrance," he said quietly.

Madeline narrowed her eyes. "We can't go in without Hanali," she said.

"You must," Hanali said. "It will be worse for me if you do not."

Madeline strode to the door. Could it be that Hanali had pretended to be denied access? There had been no flash of light, no obvious display of power. She took hold of the door's handle. At once the world around her grew dim. The doors alone held light. She noticed, now, carvings in the door's surface. People moving about, as if in the midst of their day, in a village. One of them, a poor man in ragged clothes, waved to her. She waved back, and a smile spread across his wooden face. He motioned for her to follow him, which she did not understand, but as she concentrated on the man, the scene on the door shifted so that he grew to life size.

"Who are you?" she asked.

He smiled, and she noticed a simple crown upon his forehead. "An ancient king, long since gone from the Sunlit Lands. I reigned before this palace or city came to be, and my throne was a bale of hay, my crown a twist of holly. They called me the Peasant King. In mockery at first and later with respect. More titles came, in time, but the Peasant King is one I have cherished."

"How did you come to be a . . . a door in this palace?"

"Hmm? Oh! I'm not a door. I saw the door open your mind, and I thought I would say hello. I am no longer in the Sunlit Lands, but I think of the people there as . . . well, the closest word for it would be children. They are my children, and I like to look in on them."

"Your children are quite strange."

The Peasant King laughed at that. "As are most children! Now, my friend, a word of advice. There are a great many people who want you to be a great many things to them. A savior or messiah or agent of world change."

Madeline sighed. "You're going to tell me to be true to myself or something like that."

The king's eyebrows raised. "Not at all. You are already a person committed to being true to yourself and your friends. I wanted to say only this: the myth of redemptive violence is just that, a myth. Violence solves a problem in the way gasoline solves a fire. There are other paths. They are, almost always, more difficult. Seek them out." He smiled at her. "The door's magic fades. Farewell."

The king receded into the door, leaving it smooth and untroubled. Madeline jolted back into the real world and found the door had budged under her hand. She pulled, and it swung open. "Come on," she said to Jason.

"He must also put his hand upon the door," Bright Prism said.

"He comes, or I don't. It doesn't matter what the door says." She gestured to Jason again. He stepped ahead, carefully making his way past Bright Prism and through the doorway. The door shut behind them. The last thing they heard was Hanali calling to them, "Be sure to bow or curtsy!" She couldn't keep track of when one was meant to curtsy or not. No doubt that was why Hanali kept reminding them.

The room housed a wide pond with trees growing along the outer edges. A white path wound around the pond to a cottage on the far shore. A fish jumped in the pond. Two moons rose over the cottage. It was, for the first time in many weeks, nighttime. The stars made no noticeable pattern. "We go to the cottage," Madeline said. Without discussing it, Madeline took the lead and folded Jason's hand in hers. Her heart was beating fast, thinking about the encounter with the Peasant King and the upcoming audience with Archon Thenody. She was glad Jason was with her.

"Do we knock?" Jason whispered. They heard nothing but night insects and a brief crashing in the undergrowth.

The door creaked open as if in answer.

Madeline stepped in.

They were in a formal throne room. Archon Thenody sat on a raised throne, several civilized Scim standing near him at attention, two of the blue-clad Elenil soldiers at the base of his dais. "I hate this place," Jason said. "Everything is the wrong size. The outdoors are indoors, the indoors are outdoors. It's terrible."

Archon Thenody, again wearing his strange golden sheet, raised a hand as if acknowledging them. Madeline curtsied. So did Jason, badly, beside her.

"Jason," she hissed.

"Hanali said we could bow or curtsy."

"He meant for you to bow and me to curtsy."

"That makes sense. Curtsying is hard."

She snickered. Did he do these things on purpose? No doubt he had offended Archon Thenody again.

"Leave us," the archon said. The Scim left with crisp, quick steps. "And you," the archon said, and the guards stepped out the door Madeline and Jason had entered. "Come closer."

Madeline walked to the bottom of the dais. The archon stood and flowed down the stairs to her.

Archon Thenody removed his golden sheet with a flourish, letting it slide to the floor. Underneath he wore white-and-gold brocade clothes that covered everything but his head. Golden crisscross lines of magical connections spread across his entire face. If she hadn't seen it so close, she knew his skin would appear golden. Even the whites of his eyes had branching golden tattoos, even the roots of his hair follicles. Every bit of him was traced with magical tattoos. At his neck he wore a choker with a facsimile of the Crescent Stone—a black sliver of rock that sparked with purple energy.

"I thought we should get to know one another, we three. No need to stand on ceremony," the archon said. "You made me look the fool on that tower," he said to Jason. "Fortunately, it was only my closest advisers there. If that had happened on a feast night—the Festival of the Turning is coming, for instance—I would have had to punish you both publicly. Along with that young fool Hanali."

"He had nothing to do with that," Madeline said quickly.

"He invited you to the Sunlit Lands, did he not? There are rules we follow." The archon gestured to the floor, and three chairs appeared. He took one and invited them to take the others, which they did. "When recruiting, we only take children. What you call teenagers or younger. Never adults. Never."

"Why?" Jason asked.

"They lack a certain flexibility," the archon said. He tugged absently on his glove, taking it off, revealing more skin colored gold by his network of magic. "Secondly, they must be in dire need. Perhaps they are victims of war or refugees. Perhaps their parents are cruel and abusive. Some have medical problems, like you, Miss Oliver. There is also the question of whether they can survive the journey. The road to the Sunlit Lands winds through deadly, dire landscapes. If a child cannot cross that road, they cannot come to us." He tugged off his second glove. "Do you meet this requirement, Mr. Wu?"

Jason didn't come back with a joke or a quip for once. He bit his lip, concentrating. "I believe I do, Mr. Archon," he said.

"You may call me Thenody here, in private," the archon said. "May I see your agreement again?"

Jason pulled off his glove and pushed his sleeve up, then leaned over so Thenody could see it. The archon studied Jason's bracelet for a long time, the golden pathways on his fingers pulsing lightly. At last, he said, "Your heart's desire is a dessert. You are a curious creature."

"Do I pass your 'hard life' test?"

"I suspect you do. It is hard to say, for your agreement is scarcely magical at all. The delivery of a single pudding cup every day takes less magic than that necessary to make these chairs appear for a few minutes. There is little to be gleaned from your markings. It does not, however, include a promise of fealty to the Elenil, a third requirement of those who come here. Hanali has broken that rule at the least."

"But Jason promised loyalty to me, and I've promised mine to the Elenil," Madeline said.

Thenody leaned back in his chair, studying her, one fingertip resting on his lower lip. He dropped his hand casually to the side and a goblet appeared. He sipped from it lazily. "You speak with such familiarity to me. If I did not know better, I would suspect you contradicted me in that last statement."

"I didn't mean to," Madeline said. Was he doing this on purpose? Telling them to call him by his name, then accusing them of being too familiar when they disagreed with him? He seemed to be purposely pushing them off balance.

"She completely meant to, you crazy golden psycho," Jason said, and then dropped his own hand, staring at it to see if a drink would appear in it. When none did, he turned back to the archon and said, "Honestly, it feels like you invited us to a private audience so you could make sure we'd treat you with the proper respect in public."

The archon flew from his seat so quickly he knocked his chair backward. A frigid wind blasted Madeline, and when she could open her eyes again, Thenody had Jason by the throat and had lifted him out of his chair. Jason's hands held the archon's forearms, pulling his body up to try to lessen the choking. Thenody stalked across the room as if Jason's weight meant nothing. Madeline scurried after them. The archon moved down a long hallway, pausing in the middle. He muttered something under his breath, and the room expanded. Doors appeared along the hallway.

Thenody kicked one of the doors open. Instead of revealing another room inside the palace, it led onto a mountainous cliff overlooking a raging sea. The archon stepped onto the cliff, holding Jason over the ocean. Madeline rushed at him from behind, but with his other arm the archon easily stopped her by grabbing her forearm and forcing her to the ground.

"I would like to make sure," Thenody said, "that you treat me with the proper respect." He shook Jason over the edge.

Jason tried to speak, choking out his words. "I . . . knew . . . it!"

Disgusted, Thenody threw him aside, leaving him on the ground between the cliff and the door. "You have no natural fear of your betters," he said. "It is a troubling quality."

"He only speaks truth," Madeline shouted. "It's not troubling, it's amazing. I wish I could do that."

Thenody's golden eyes drifted down his arm until he found her face. "But you are bound to the Elenil—to me—through your agreement." He tore off her glove, revealing the silver latticework of her tattoo. He turned her wrist. "This agreement can be canceled," he said slyly. "No more Sunlit Lands. No more Elenil. No more breathing."

"Leave her alone!" Jason shouted.

"Ah. I have your attention at last."

"You already showed us you could do that," Madeline said. "On the tower."

Golden fingers readjusted their grip. The archon touched Madeline's wrist with his index finger. "See there? That's where the gem on your bracelet used to be. It has spread now. Much faster than most. But pay attention." He pushed into her wrist, and a surge of piercing pain spread up her arm and nearly to her shoulder. She screamed. "If I break the gem, the agreement is broken. No breath for you, no oath of fealty to the Elenil." He dropped her arm. It ached like she had just done a thousand push-ups. "Remember that when next you think to insult me in public. Break the gem if you want to be free from our agreement, but do not think to violate it without dire consequences." A bell rang, somewhere back in the palace. "Ah. I believe our tea is ready."

The archon stood by the door like a hotel doorman. Jason got up, then helped Madeline to her feet. They leaned against each other for strength.

The edges of this place were blurry, like a video game where the designers hadn't managed to get all the scenery finished. "We have to get away from him," Madeline whispered to Jason.

They made their way back to Archon Thenody's receiving room. He motioned to their chairs. They sat, and he served them tea from an antique ceramic teapot with delicate flowers. "Sugar?" he asked, holding a lump of sugar in a pair of golden tongs. Madeline shook her head.

"Yeah," Jason said. "Oh, more than that. Yeah. Like, ten of those."

The archon smiled faintly, counting them out. "Eight . . . nine . . . ten."

"Make it eleven."

Thenody frowned, but gave him one more. "Eleven, then. I believe that is all of them."

"I hope you wanted some," Jason said.

Thenody sighed. "Perhaps I have been overly harsh."

"Ya think?"

The archon took a sip from his cup and said to Madeline, "Perhaps this would be smoother if we were alone."

Madeline shot Jason a warning look, terrified they would be separated. "He'll behave."

"Ah, lovely. I suppose he will thank me for the sugar, then."

Jason's face flushed. He clamped his lips tight. "It's okay," Madeline said.

"Thank you," Jason said.

"My pleasure," Thenody said brightly. "Now. I asked you both here because I am concerned about your safety. The Scim—those vile creatures—have expressed an interest in you. I fear it is more than you have heard. The Black Skulls themselves have made it clear that they will not rest until they find you, Madeline. I do not know why they desire you, but they are not so . . . gentle . . . as I am." His eyes rested on her bare hand.

Madeline covered it with her napkin. She had left her glove near the cliff. She couldn't bear to have the archon's eyes on her bare hand, though, not after he had hurt her arm like that. "We'll be safe with the Knight of the Mirror," Madeline said. "Ruth explained his magic to me. Once something is given to him, it can't be taken away again, not without his permission. The magic doesn't allow it."

"Yes." Thenody licked his lips. "It was a clever solution the magistrates came to. A solution they arrived at when I was in great pain and unable to participate in the discussion because of—" his eyes flicked to Jason— "an unfortunate prison break."

"Hey!" Jason said. "I bet the knight's magic means you can't throw me over any cliffs!"

"You would be wise not to test such boundaries," Thenody said.

"In any case," Madeline said, "we're safe."

The archon sipped from his teacup. "It is said you will bring justice to the Scim, Miss Oliver. If that is true and not some outlandish tale of Hanali's, then you are immensely valuable to me. But you should know there are limits to the knight's magic."

"Like what?"

"A clear boundary: should he choose to give you willingly to the Scim, his magic will be no protection to you."

"He wouldn't do that!"

Thenody barked a laugh. "How delightful, the innocence of the young. There are certain precious things the knight might value more than your life. That is only one possibility. Or you could be taken during the Festival of the Turning, when all magic that flows from the Crescent Stone ceases. Or his magic could be neutralized somehow. Countered. Evaded." He raised a hand. "No, I do not know how, only that my seers have said that when the time comes, his magic will not protect you."

"The same seers who said Mads is the one who is going to save the world?"

Thenody sniffed disdainfully. "They have said no such thing. They do not see any special qualities in you or the girl. The other treasures we have given the knight to steward over the decades are of more value. The Sword of Years, perhaps, or the Ascension Robe. Have you heard those names?"

"Never," Madeline said, sipping her own tea.

"The Memory Stone? The Mask of Passing? The Disenthraller? He has mentioned none of these things?"

"No."

Thenody rubbed his smooth jaw. He had not put his gloves back on, and Madeline wondered how such a dainty hand could have so painful a grip. "I am filled with wonder that he has not mentioned those artifacts, since it is only a month past that the Scim came looking for them. To mention them would be no risk, since nothing can be taken from his hand. But perhaps he has been too busy gazing into mirrors. Surely he has not betrayed the Elenil and turned those artifacts over to the Scim. Although— it is strange that they have ceased warring against us."

Jason slurped his tea, loud. "You're saying you think the knight gave them back their stuff in exchange for . . . something he wants. Whatever it might be."

"The opposite," the archon said.

"You're saying he took the artifacts away from the Scim, and in exchange they took something he wants?"

"No, fool, I am saying he would never betray us in such a way."

"Ookaaaay," Jason said slowly. "But we would have never thought that."

"You're trying to plant the idea in our heads," Madeline said.

Thenody spread his hands wide. "Not at all. But if he had traded those artifacts away . . . I would want to know. I would want you to tell me. It could mean that you, my children, are not safe."

Madeline set her teacup on its saucer and, no table being near her, set it at her feet. "I think I've had enough."

The archon's face twisted in rage. "You dare dismiss *me*?"

"Enough *tea*," Madeline said, making an effort to sound calm.

Thenody stood angrily. He clapped, and all three teacups disappeared. Madeline gasped.

"Hey, I wasn't done!" Jason said. "I was just getting to the sugar sludge at the bottom."

"*I* am done, however, and you wait upon my leisure," Archon Thenody said, walking away from them.

Bright Prism appeared again, bowing low, and escorted them from Thenody's quarters. The journey out was not as long as the journey in. They passed a few dank corridors and a blazing hot kitchen. The servants' passageways, probably.

"Those doors," Jason said. "I don't think we actually went anywhere. The magic here doesn't work like that. He'd need to have three people waiting to come through another door into the palace if the three of us wanted to come out of it."

"It was an illusion," Madeline said. "I don't know why, but he's trying to make us see things that aren't there."

Bright Prism led them back through the golden doors, and they stood on a wide landing. They could see the Heart of the Scim glowing in the glass room at the center of the tower, just one floor above them. They could just walk up to it if they wanted. Bright Prism bowed and said, "The master wanted you to have this, miss." He held out a box meticulously wrapped in golden paper, with ribbons spilling off it.

"It's probably socks," Jason said. "He's just the type to give out socks. White ones, probably. Those short athletic ones."

Madeline opened the gift. Inside was one glove. A left glove, like the one she had lost, as golden as the archon's magic-infused skin. It filled her with dread to touch it. Her skin crawled just looking at it.

Bright Prism said, "He asked me to say, 'To remind you of our talk overlooking the sea.'"

Madeline's stomach fell. A burning sensation started in her center and moved up into her face, a boiling, furious heat. "Tell him I hope to repay him one day," Madeline said. "A thousand times over. Tell him that."

The Scim bowed. His small black eyes darted left and right before he spoke. "Lady, you ought not say that."

"Say those exact words," Madeline said. "Now, which way is out?"

Bright Prism pointed a large hand toward a stairway which hugged the outer wall. "That way, lady."

Of course he would make them take the stairs. Hanali was gone, no doubt sent away the moment she and Jason had gone through the golden doors. She balled up the archon's glove and threw it over the side. She watched it float a few stories, crumple, then fall. She didn't see where it landed.

Jason said, "Do you think they have magic toilets here? Because I want to use one before we go back to Westwind."

"Yes," Madeline said. "I'm sure they do."

It was a long walk to the bottom of the tower. Madeline spent the entire time figuring out what to do. It seemed she had somehow made an enemy of the most powerful of the Elenil—the people she was sworn to serve. The Scim army had withdrawn, though it appeared they wanted to kill her.

She couldn't believe it, but today she sort of missed chemistry class.

22

THE KNIGHT'S SOLAR

*Where is the fountain which brought joy
to the city, clean and clear at its heart?*

FROM "THE DESERTED CITY," A KAKRI LAMENT

✦

Madeline felt thrown off her rhythm. The confrontation with the archon went against everything she had expected. She wouldn't be waiting around anymore, waiting to see what other people told her to do. It was time for action.

Her legs had nearly given out by the time they reached the bottom of the stairs. They found Hanali leaning against an elaborate marble handrail and watching the unicorns munching grass in the garden below.

They started to tell him what had happened, but he shushed them. He smiled broadly, chatting amiably all the way back to the knight's castle. When they crossed the threshold of Westwind, he whispered, "Do not speak negatively of him. Not in this city and certainly not where magic is in use. Do you think he cannot hear?"

He whisked them into the great hall and called for the knight. The two of them listened with furrowed brows as Madeline and Jason told their story. The end result was not, as Madeline had hoped, a promise to keep them away from the archon. Instead, the knight and their benefactor debated which activities were safe for them in the city.

"They are not to leave the city limits, that much is plain," the knight said.

Hanali sniffed. "They have been watched carefully since arriving, just like any of the new arrivals. The one exception was allowing them on the battlefield. Even then I watched Jason from the wall, and Gilenyia accompanied Madeline."

"You are not to leave this castle during the Festival of the Turning, with or without accompaniment," the knight said.

Madeline objected that she didn't know what or when that was, although she did remember the archon mentioning it. Jason objected that a festival sounded like a party, and it hardly seemed fair to be locked away in a castle. "Not a nice Disney castle, either," he said. "No offense."

Furious about the whole thing, Madeline stormed off to her solar. Which, being at the top of one of Westwind's towers, was a long hike, especially after descending hundreds of flights of stairs at the palace. She had run out of anger by the time she made it to her room. She collapsed on her bed.

A half hour later a sheepish knock woke her. She opened the door to find Jason, a goofy smile on his face, a loaf of slightly burned brown bread under his arm, and a cutting board covered with a thick, salty cheese. Shula stood beside him, holding an enormous bowl of a red, juicy citrus fruit called burst. Jason had named it, of course, and failed to remember the common name. When placed on the tongue the skin of the fruit nearly exploded, and the flavor was both tongue-numbingly tart and chocolatey sweet at the same time.

Madeline and Shula tucked their feet up on the bed, and Jason pulled a large chair over, and they descended on the food. Halfway through her second slice of brown bread, Madeline began to feel human again. Partway through her third, she lay back on her bed, one hand under her head, the other on her full belly.

"I'm beginning to wonder," she said, "if the Elenil are the bad guys here.

Something is seriously wrong with the archon, and it doesn't seem like a huge request by the Scim to have their artifacts returned to them."

Shula popped some cheese in her mouth. "Artifacts returned, and you and Jason turned over," she said.

Jason added, "Killed, I think. Not just handed over. Break Bones was very clear about Madeline's 'lifeless body.'"

"Whose fault is that?" Madeline asked, throwing a crust of bread at him.

"I said I was sorry!" Jason protested. "He asked me your name. He didn't say, 'I'm going to murder someone, let's brainstorm names.'"

"The Scim are monsters," Shula said. "The Elenil have their faults, yes, but who threatened to murder you? The Scim."

Jason, his mouth full of food, said, "Break Bones said he wanted to usher in centuries of darkness. I can't even remember how many he said. At least five."

"Maybe you shouldn't have let him go, then," Madeline said.

"Who kidnapped me?" Shula asked. "Who held me prisoner in the wastelands? They gave me rotten meat and filthy water. They left me in public so they could throw garbage at me when they walked by. They beat me trying to get answers about you two, and trying to get me to tell them where their artifacts are." She paused, the muscles in her jaw flexing. "I don't even know what happened to Diego."

That was the boy who could fly. He had escaped the Scim but hadn't returned to Far Seeing. The knight couldn't find him. Madeline put a hand on Shula's knee. "I'm sorry, Shula."

"I don't see how the Scim can be the good guys," Shula said.

"On the other hand," Jason said, "Break Bones wasn't in a day spa. He was chained in a dungeon. So the way the Elenil treat their prisoners isn't much different."

Madeline crossed to the small, arched window in her solar, which looked out toward the city wall. "The city is so beautiful, though. The singing fountains! The palace gardens! Even the marketplaces are colorful and well organized. The Elenil create such beautiful things. The palace! It's amazing."

"It is beautiful," Shula said. "It was the Scim who hurt me, and the Elenil who used their magic to heal me. You, too, Jason. The Elenil are bright, beautiful people. They don't live in squalor and make speeches about destroying the light."

At the mention of Jason's healing, Madeline stiffened and looked straight at him. He stared back, one eyebrow raised. He knew something was wrong but hadn't asked her directly. Not yet.

"The magic," Jason said, "works in an interesting way. If I want to use a sword, I have to take those skills from someone else who earned them. While I have those skills, someone else doesn't. Or Shula, when Madeline healed you, that Scim woman had to take your wounds. Which naturally brings up the question, if I was nearly dead when I was healed by the Elenil—"

"Wait," Madeline said, interrupting him. She wasn't ready for this conversation. She couldn't talk about it, not right now, and she couldn't bear the thought of what Jason would say when she told him that Night's Breath had died so he could live . . . and that neither Jason nor Night's Breath had any choice in the matter. "Shula, what is the Festival of the Turning like?"

"I've only been to it once," Shula said.

"Once more than us," Jason said. Then, his voice bitter, "The knight doesn't want us to go. He says it isn't safe."

"He's right," Shula said. "Did he tell you why?"

Madeline shook her head. "He's not the most talkative."

Shula scraped the scraps of cheese from the cutting board out the window, into the moat below. "For one day, all the magic of the Court of Far Seeing is reversed. It's an entire day without Elenil magic. The Crescent Stone must rest for a day, and all the magic that runs through it must cease. The people of the Sunlit Lands celebrate the day in different ways. They go to their own territories and tell the story of the coming of magic to the Sunlit Lands and how the Majestic One—a magician from centuries ago—made the place. Rich people wear rags, and the poor dress in fine clothing. It's a time of reversals, and people playact that they are something other than what they are. The highest society people take pride in appearing to be impoverished, because it announces their high status at other times."

"I don't see how it puts us in danger," Madeline said, making room for Shula to lean on the windowsill. "The Scim will be in their home territory. Who is going to harm us?"

"There will still be Scim here. If one of them hurt you, there would be no healing magic available. You never told me what your deal with the Elenil is, but you'll lose that for the day too. I won't be able to light myself on fire in battle."

Jason said, "Madeline can't breathe by herself. She's got a terminal illness. So she won't be able to breathe?"

"Jason!" Madeline shouted. It wasn't right for him to share that—it was hers to share or not. People looked at her differently when they knew. It had happened a hundred times with her friends. Her disease wasn't contagious, but people acted as if it were. They made suggestions about how she could take care of herself, even though she was healthier than most. Or they gave her pitying looks . . . as if they were healthy because they were better than her.

But Shula acted as if she had just learned Madeline had asked for a haircut. She didn't make a big deal out of it or look at Madeline with pity. She only rubbed the long scar on her face and said, "That's right. Once the ceremony starts, all magic starts to fail. We could go to the palace for the beginning, but once night falls, she won't be able to breathe."

"Night falls?"

"Of course. Once a year the Elenil experience true night and see the stars. It's their magic that keeps Far Seeing in perpetual day. When the sun sets, magic starts to fail . . . It takes a while, and some magic fails faster than others. But before the night is over, you won't be able to breathe. I won't be able to light on fire."

"I won't get pudding for breakfast," Jason said, but his jovial tone of voice rang hollow, and he looked nervous.

"That's the dumbest thing I've ever heard," Shula said. "Was that your deal? Pudding every morning?"

Jason acted offended. "Every morning for the *rest of my life*. Except festival days, apparently." He deflated a little. "What about you, Shula? You just got healed a few days ago. Will that be undone?"

"Yes," Shula said, "though my Scim counterpart will have healed some by then, so I'll only get a portion of that damage back, and only for the day."

Madeline beat Jason to his question. "What if someone was almost dead and healed?"

Shula shrugged. "It depends. If the counterpart died from the wounds, then the transfer is sealed and permanent. Someone like that would remain healthy. If the counterpart has been recovering, they would get the wounds back for the day."

Jason held Madeline's gaze. She could tell what he was thinking: on the Festival of the Turning, he would know what had happened to Night's Breath. Madeline wouldn't be able to avoid the conversation any longer. She tried to hold his gaze, but she couldn't. He must suspect, because why would she be avoiding the conversation if all was well? A pang struck like a knife in her ribs. The thought that Night's Breath was gone, dead, because of her had been keeping her awake, watching the light on the ceiling of her chambers. *That decision kept Jason alive*, she reminded herself. That ridiculous, overly truthful, loyal, infuriating guy who had gone from chemistry partner to good friend mostly on the strength of picking her up when she had fainted and driving her to the hospital. That had to count for something.

The archon's accusations against the knight lingered in her mind. What if he wanted to keep them in the castle so he could trade them away to the Scim? If he had already given the Scim the artifacts, maybe she and Jason were next. She didn't think the knight would do such a thing, but no one had seen the artifacts in some time, according to the archon.

"We have to search Westwind," she said. "We have to find the Scim artifacts. It might help us figure out what is going on."

"I don't even know what they are," Shula said. "It's not a topic the Elenil share about freely."

"The archon mentioned some of them to us. There was a sword called the Sword of Years, I think. A robe called—what was it, Jason? The Robe of Ascension?"

"Yeah," Jason said. "Plus something called the Socks of Silence. Lets you sneak around all sneaky like. I don't know. I clearly can't remember."

Madeline ignored him. "There was a mask, I think, too."

Jason jumped out of his seat. "Ahhh! That kid with the bark mask was so creepy!"

"Calm down. That was before we even got into the Sunlit Lands."

Shula paced the room. "Could we just ask the knight to show them to us?"

"No way," Jason said. "That's crazy. Let's tromp all over his home opening locked doors and hope he doesn't notice."

"If he's secretly working with the Scim, we don't want to tip him off that we know," Madeline said.

Shula, still looking out the window, said, "He left earlier, going toward the palace. He never tells us what his business is day to day, but he will be gone at least an hour or two. So. Where do we start?"

Madeline had been thinking about this ever since Thenody had suggested the knight might have done away with the artifacts. If the artifacts were well hidden, that might make them as impossible to find as if he had already given them to the Scim. The only way to prove his innocence was to find the actual artifacts, all of them. Not that she needed to prove his innocence, but she needed to know if she and Jason were safe. "Is there an armory?" she asked.

"Yes," Shula said thoughtfully. "I've been in there, though. Not much to see."

"Nothing in the stables," Jason said in a tone of voice that suggested he honestly believed this to be a helpful data point. "Or the kitchen."

"The knight's solar?" She still thought it strange that in a castle a private room was called a solar, but she wanted to use the correct terms.

"It would make sense for the artifacts to be somewhere near where the knight sleeps," Shula said. "If someone broke in, he would want to be nearby."

"We could ask Ruth," Jason said. "She knows an awful lot for a kid."

"She's loyal to the knight," Shula said. "He's like a father to her."

Did that mean that the three of them were disloyal? Madeline didn't like to think that. She wanted to think they were protecting themselves, doing what was best for them and the Elenil, checking in on the knight to make sure he was keeping those Scim artifacts safe. "We'll start at his solar," Madeline said. "We can work our way down the tower from there. If they're not in his tower, we'll regroup and try again."

Jason tucked the cutting board under his arm. "You know I'll tell the knight everything if he asks me."

Shula winced. "Jason also has a bad habit of volunteering information he doesn't need to."

"It's part of my charm," Jason said, batting his eyelashes at Shula.

"Well," said Shula slyly, "Madeline, why don't you and I go look in the solar to see if the knight is there. We can chat with him and ask if it would be okay for you to go to the Festival of the Turning if I go with you. We can take care of all this artifact business later."

Madeline frowned. "But he's—" It dawned on her what Shula was doing. "Riiiight. Jason could stand at the bottom of the stairs and shout up if he finds the knight. If the knight asks what we're doing up there—"

"We'll say we're looking for him."

"You already know he left for the day," Jason said. "This isn't a loophole that will work. I know you're lying to me right now."

"Are we?" Shula asked, and she poked him in the nose with her index finger. "Bring your cutting board and let's go."

A quick stop in the kitchen and then they cut across the great hall toward the knight's tower. A huge mirror was fastened to the wall at the entrance of the stone stairway. "Stay here," Madeline told Jason. "If someone comes, shout up to us."

"You mean if the knight comes," Jason said.

"Anyone who comes might know where he is, so go ahead and shout up the stairs," Shula said.

Jason slumped against the wall. "Uh-huh."

A thick wooden door with iron bands blocked the entrance, but it swung open at a light touch. On the other side Madeline noticed a beam of wood which could be placed in an iron bracket to brace the door from the inside. The door being open at all was a good argument the knight was gone. Unlike the stairs to Madeline's solar, there were no tapestries on the upward climb. There were small gaps in the stone, just wide enough to shoot an arrow from, which let in the pure light of the Sunlit Lands. Across from each gap, right where the sun would hit them full on, were mirrors.

"The Knight of the Mirror earned his name," Madeline said.

"Yeah." Shula paused to look out an arrow slit. "He's a careful man, Madeline. We should be cautious when we enter his room. There may be traps or alarms. Even magic."

"He doesn't allow magic," Madeline said.

"The artifacts are magic," Shula pointed out. "Nothing can be taken from his hand—that's magic too."

They passed a small room that projected out from the tower over the moat. A garderobe, complete with the wooden stool with a hole in it. "No magic toilet, though, as I'm sure Jason would say. I don't know about you, but if I were going to cheat on my no-magic rule, that's where I would do it."

"We should still be careful," Shula said.

A fair amount of shouting came from downstairs. Madeline couldn't understand what Jason was saying. She leaned down the stairs and shouted, "What?"

His words were garbled, but she heard "something in the mirror." Madeline asked Shula if she had caught more than that, but she shook her head.

"Probably making a joke," Shula said.

That could be. They studied the closest mirror, seeing only the backward versions of themselves. Madeline shrugged and started up the stairs again.

"Hmm," Shula said. "I thought I saw something move in the mirror."

"Maybe you saw me."

"Or a bird flying past the window, I guess. Nothing to worry about," Shula said.

They continued their climb. Jason shouted something else, and although they couldn't understand his words, his tone of voice seemed calm. They debated turning back, but at this point turning back didn't mean they wouldn't be caught—there was only one stairway in the tower—it only meant they wouldn't get a chance to check the solar.

The stairway rounded the final loop, and the knight's private room stood ten steps ahead of them. There was no door, which made sense since there was nothing in the tower other than this room, and the door at the bottom of the stairs could be locked. Shula crouched, climbing the last few steps on her hands and knees, peeking over the top of the landing. Madeline joined her, marveling again at how wonderful it was to be able to breathe. Her heart was pounding, adrenaline pumping, but she could take full, quiet breaths without coughing. She felt energized and alive.

The knight's room had open windows in the masonry. Sunlight streamed in. There were no curtains or anything to prevent his room from being essentially in the open other than the fact that it had a roof with a long overhang that would keep rain out. A bed sat more or less in the center of the room, the sheets twisted as if they had fought the knight to keep him from sleep. A sword leaned against the bed on one side. Between the windows stood full-length mirrors, and a simple table was pushed against the wall, empty.

Madeline entered and took in the whole room, turning in a circle. She saw a flash of white in one of the mirrors, maybe caused by the sunlight. She inspected the mirror more closely and saw something strange. "Shula, look at this."

The rumpled, unmade bed was not rumpled in the reflection. It was perfectly made, with tight corners. She looked at the table's reflection in the mirror. She put her hand against the glass. There, on the other side, lay the Scim artifacts.

23
THE KNIGHT'S SECRET

She weeps into the fountain. She lingers at her
window and sobs to hear the silent streets.

FROM "THE DESERTED CITY," A KAKRI LAMENT

✛

The sword caught Madeline's eye first. Nicked, rusted, and neglected, the sword could have been found in an archaeological dig or at the bottom of the ocean. Worn leather straps wrapped the pommel. A pristine black scabbard worked with gold sat beside it, though it was clear the sword hadn't been cleaned, sharpened, or put into the scabbard in a long time.

A silver mask lay next to the sword, almost as reflective as the mirrors. Thick red ribbons spooled from the sides of it, and its empty eyes stared at the ceiling.

A robe, carefully folded to show off the finery of its design, sat in the center of the table. It appeared to be handmade and hand dyed. It was blue with gold trim, and oxen, eagles, humans, and lions danced up the edges and around the collar.

There was a stone, white and smooth. And a thin key. Madeline tried to reach through the glass, but of course she couldn't.

"What are you doing?"

Startled, Madeline and Shula jumped. A woman stood in the mirror, her black hair swept out of her face, her olive skin flushed with anger. She wore a rose in her hair, and her white dress, long and beautiful, pressed against the glass where it billowed out from her waist. "You are not to be in this room of Westwind," she said. "Nor should you attempt to touch these instruments. They are not yours to handle."

Jason stumbled into the room. "There's someone in the mirror!" he shouted. "A woman!"

Madeline pointed to the woman with her eyes.

"Oh," Jason said. "I see you've met."

"Who are you?" Shula asked.

"You break into the knight's solar and demand my name? Who are *you*, thief?"

Madeline stepped forward. "I'm Madeline Oliver. We didn't mean any harm."

"We did know we shouldn't be in here, though," Jason added. Not helpful, but true. "I'm Wu Song."

"My name is Shula Bishara."

"All of them should have known better." The Knight of the Mirror stood in the doorway. His long black hair hung in thick curls to his shoulders, streaks of grey cascading through them. His nose, obviously broken many times before, drew one's attention more than the piercing brown eyes, or the white scars on his brown skin. His wide shoulders filled the doorframe.

"Who, me?" Jason asked.

"Silence," the knight said.

"You can't learn if you don't ask questions," Jason said reasonably.

The knight gave him a withering glare, and Jason fell silent. "I have invited you into my home. I have extended protection to you both, and you repay me by violating my privacy. I should send you back to Archon Thenody for this." Madeline gasped. Jason's hands tensed. They would have to run. They might be safe here in this castle, maybe, but she could not go back to the archon's palace. But where would they go? They might be able to return to Mrs. Raymond. Or they could petition to enter the Bidding again. Gilenyia had offered to take Madeline, more or less. Maybe she could be convinced to take Jason, too, if he could keep his mouth shut long enough for Madeline to ask.

The woman in the mirror must have seen the distress written on Madeline's face, because her own face softened and she said, "He speaks from anger. He would not do such a thing."

"Has your anger passed so swiftly?" The knight moved past them and put his palm on the mirror. The woman put her hand on his from the other side.

The woman's lips twitched into a gentle smile. "You of all people should know better."

"Ah," the knight said. "You use my words against me."

"That's not exactly what you said," Jason said, and Madeline elbowed him.

The knight turned to them. "This is Fernanda Isabela Flores de Castilla. She is the greatest lady in the Sunlit Lands or any other—compassionate, kind, and generous even to those who would burst into her chambers uninvited."

"Is she . . . your wife?" Madeline asked gently. The knight's lip turned up in a half snarl, then fell neutral again. His eyes narrowed, softened, then closed. One of his gloved hands rose to hide his face.

"It is not your place to ask such questions," the knight said. "That story is for those I trust and them alone. Today," he said, looking pointedly at each of them, "you have lost what trust you had previously earned."

"We'll go, Sir Knight," Shula said.

"Sir Knight?" Fernanda said softly. "Has he not told you even his name, then?"

The knight turned his face from hers. "They call me the Knight of the Mirror. It is name enough for one such as I."

Fernanda dropped her face toward the ground. "What I would not give to see you in your glory once again."

The knight said nothing.

Shula looked heartbroken. Although she didn't fight in the knight's company because she was a magic user, she often spoke of her respect for him. "It wasn't Shula's idea," Madeline said.

"Or mine," Jason chimed in.

Madeline continued, "Archon Thenody implied you might have given the Scim back their—well, whatever this stuff is—and that you were going to turn me and Jason over to them also. The easiest way to prove him wrong or right was to find these."

The knight pushed his hair back. He sighed heavily. "Come then, the three of you. Come close to the table." They moved over to the table, each of them on a side. Fernanda moved to the other side of the mirror, sitting down on the reflection of the bed. "Close your eyes," the knight said. Madeline obeyed. When he told them to open their eyes again, the reflected artifacts were now on the table in front of them.

"Whoa," Jason said.

Madeline felt almost light headed. It was such a strange thing to see. But then, why didn't he allow Fernanda out of the mirror if he could pull these tools out of it so easily?

The knight picked up the mask. "This is called the Mask of Passing. It is filled with Scim magic. He who wears the mask appears to be what others expect. You can see why the Elenil fear it."

"A Scim spy could wear it and walk into the city," Madeline said.

"He could walk into the palace," the knight said. "Into Archon Thenody's bedchamber, should he desire. No one would think twice, for the spy would appear to be whatever or whomever made sense." He handed the mask to Madeline. It was shiny on the front side, like a mirror, but dark as space on the other.

The knight took the mask from her and set it back on the table. "My lady cannot leave the mirror. Nothing can be taken from my hand, save her." A sadness washed over his face, and hers, too.

"You can pull swords out of mirrors," Jason said. "This is better than a Las Vegas magic show. Do you do card tricks?"

"Jason," Madeline said, annoyed. When he felt uncomfortable he made jokes. This was not, however, the time.

"Why is this sword in such disrepair?" Shula asked. "Do you want me to clean it?" It was such a clear request for forgiveness it made Madeline wince. Shula wanted to show him she could be a good soldier, to serve him in some way. He ignored her question, though, and instead told them about the Scim artifacts.

"Long ago, the Elenil defeated the Scim in a great battle. They had been long at war, and in response to an attack on Far Seeing, the Elenil rode down upon the homeland of the Scim with great fury. They killed three Scim for every Elenil who had fallen at Far Seeing. When the Scim begged for mercy, the Elenil gave it. The terms of peace included taking away any magical items the Scim might use in war. These are the most significant of them. In time the Elenil grew concerned the Scim might try to take them back. In fact, the Scim have told us more than once they intend to do so. I had been given a certain magical boon which grants me the ability to hold on to anything that is given me. None can take it from my hand unless I allow it. So long as magic reigns in Far Seeing, these things cannot be taken from this room without my permission." He paused. "This same magic protects you two."

"How did Shula get kidnapped?" Jason asked.

"She has not been given to me."

"She was one of your soldiers, though."

"Jason, hush," Madeline said.

"No! He's trying to make Shula feel bad for being a good friend and coming in here with you, and at the same time he doesn't take responsibility for her being kidnapped and gone for weeks while he did nothing about it."

"She was not my soldier—she was a magic user! You say I did nothing? Nothing but ride into Scim territories, seeking for sign of her. Who brought her home at last?" The knight's face flushed red.

"You shouldn't have lost her in the first place!" Jason shouted.

Shula put her hand on his arm. "Peace," she said. "What happens in a battle is not one man's fault."

"I almost died trying to keep the Scim from taking you, Shula," Jason said. He looked at Madeline. "Some people did die. Didn't they?"

Madeline's heart dropped, still beating, into her stomach, falling like a star through her body. Blood rushed to fill every square inch of her skin. She wasn't ready for this conversation, not now.

"No," the knight said. "He is not wrong. I did not realize the Scim were taking our magicked soldiers until too late. It was a bold move, and one that cost them dearly. If not for the Black Skulls, they would not have succeeded. They did, however, succeed. That must fall to me and me alone." He shook his head. "These Black Skulls. Wherever they have come from, may the Majestic One protect us. They fight like old hands but have the strength of youth."

"It's good there are only three," Shula said.

"You will find a way to defeat them," Fernanda said. "You always have."

"So far," the knight said.

Fernanda stood and moved toward the knight's reflection. "It is time to let your anger sink away," she said.

The knight closed his eyes. "As always, my lady, I do as you wish." He took Shula's hand. "Shula Bishara, you must not clean this sword. It, too, is magic. The Sword of Years it is called or the Sword of Tears by some. The Sword of Ten Thousand Sorrows." He lifted the sword. Rust covered the heavily nicked blade. "Some have called it Thirsty, for it thirsts for the blood of those who have wronged its master. It is an old blade and a deadly one. It must not be cleaned, nor must it be placed in its scabbard again, for on the day that happens, its magic will be renewed, and it will seek again to kill those who are on its list."

"So it's a blade of revenge," Shula said quietly.

"Yes. An old magic in response to ancient wrongs. Some who would feel this blade's bite would not know the origin of its fury." He placed it carefully on the table, beside the scabbard. "This is why I do not allow you to clean it, not because of any wrong you have done me."

"We did wrong you, though," Madeline said. "We didn't believe in you when Thenody made it sound like you might betray us."

Fernanda smiled at her, but it was the pitying smile of an adult knowing there is no way to explain to a child how little they understand. "The Elenil are ancient creatures, and they think in craftier paths than we humans. Their thoughts wander in labyrinths, and they rarely reveal their deepest hearts. No doubt the archon expected you to search here and expected the knight to learn of it."

"It may have been a warning," the knight said. "Or merely a reminder that he watches me."

"Or perhaps," said the lady, "it is because these instruments are safe not only from the Scim but from the Elenil, too. Should Archon Thenody ask for one of these tools, who knows what answer he might receive?"

"I know what answer," the knight said. "He would not take them from my hand."

"Thenody wasn't totally wrong, then." Jason said this while sitting on the floor, tying his shoes. "You're not completely loyal to him."

"I am as loyal as he has given cause for me to be," the knight said carefully. "Now. Peace, children. Leave my chamber. Do not come here again without permission."

They said their good-byes to the lady, who inclined her head to them. Madeline realized with a start that she did not wear gloves and that her dress was open around the neck. She did not dress like the Elenil.

The knight escorted them down the spiraling tower stairs. At the wide wooden door he paused.

"I fear you will not obey me regarding the Festival of the Turning," the knight said.

"We will!" Madeline said.

"I'm not making any promises," Jason said, and Shula pinched his arm.

"It is a great deal to ask of you to stay in the castle," the knight said. "Jason has made his frustrations plain."

"Just being honest," he said.

"I will make this agreement with you. You may go to the festival in the day. Walk among the people, hear the stories, eat the food. But when the time comes for the Fall of Dark, you must make all haste back here. Magic will be upended in those hours. Madeline, you will not be able to breathe. Jason, what wounds you had may return. Shula, yours, as well. When night has passed, we will see how you have all recovered. I may allow you to attend the Celebration of the Sun." He paused, looking at each of them in turn. "Do you understand?"

"Yes," Madeline said. "We understand. We can go to the festival, but we must be home before night falls."

"Shula," the knight said. "Bring them here if they disobey me in this."

"I will, Sir Knight."

"Keep a special eye upon the fool."

"Hey!"

With that the knight slammed the door shut. They heard the sound of the heavy wooden bar falling into place.

"That went better than expected," Jason said.

"Are you kidding?" Madeline asked. "We got caught."

Jason shrugged. "I thought we might get killed. Or thrown in a dungeon. Also, what is that delicious smell?"

Madeline sniffed the air. Golden pastry. Beef? Onions, for sure. Some sort of savory pie, maybe. Jason floated toward the kitchen like a fish on a line.

Shula put her hand on Madeline, stopping her. "You can't breathe without magic. It is a difficult situation." Shula hugged her. "We all take hard roads to come to the Sunlit Lands." She traced the scar on her own face. "If your every breath draws on your magic, though . . . that is more magic than any Elenil agreement I've ever heard."

Madeline didn't know what to say to that. "It's keeping me alive." The thought of losing her magic during the Festival of the Turning made her queasy.

Shula took both Madeline's hands in her own. "Your bracelet," she said. "How far has it spread?"

Madeline had been trying not to look at it, not to notice. It had helped to cover her mirror. Still, she could almost feel it, like a burning itch from an infection, spreading across her body. "All the way up my arm and onto my shoulder. It's branching out onto my shoulder blades. It will be on my neck soon, and it's spreading onto my back."

Shula's face fell, and a dark look of determination moved across it, like a cloud. "Your term of service, then, how long was it? A year?"

"Yes."

Shula dropped her hands. "We still have time, then," she said. Then, again, as if reassuring herself, "We have time."

24

THE FESTIVAL OF THE TURNING

When the world was young and foolish, the people burned the cities.
The oceans, enraged with violence, flooded villages and
carried away children. The ground shook, and the sky wept
blood. The people cried out day and night for help.

FROM "THE ORDERING OF THE WORLD," AN ELENIL STORY

✦

I don't need a babysitter," Jason said for the third time.

Baileya stopped in the festival throng and looked down at him with those glowing silver eyes, her brown hair in loose waves around her face. "I do not know this word."

"It's someone who cares for children," Madeline said, grinning. Madeline and Baileya had instantly hit it off, which made Jason nervous. Baileya and Shula were already friends too, from fighting together against the Scim. Jason had been following behind them through the crowd like some sort of fourth wheel. Wait. Third wheel? But there were four of them. Four wheels were good. Whatever. He was following behind them like the fourth, less happy, wheel.

"I do not understand," Baileya said. "There are no children with us. So you are telling us that you do not need someone to watch the children who are not here?" She looked at Madeline and Shula. "Is this a joke among your people?"

"It's a saying," Madeline said. "It means he doesn't think he needs anyone to watch over him. He can take care of himself."

Baileya put her gloved hands on Jason's shoulders. "You are a man who always speaks truth, Wu Song. Do you need someone to watch over you?"

Jason couldn't look into those silver eyes for long. He had a hard time concentrating on her question when her hands were on his shoulders. He tried to ignore the thrill of energy coursing through him and focus. Did he need someone to watch over him? So far he had escaped a weird mermaid thing on the way into the Sunlit Lands (okay, okay, with Madeline's help), made friends with some warriors, adopted a rhinoceros, and fought some nightmare monsters using magic. On the other hand, he had managed to make an enemy of the most powerful Elenil in the city, and he had accidentally told Break Bones about Madeline, then released Break Bones into the world. Those were pretty big mistakes. He cleared his throat. "On second thought, it might not be bad to have someone watch over me."

"I will be that person tonight," Baileya said. "The Knight of the Mirror has ordered this."

"Okay," he said. His knees felt weak.

"Madeline and Shula also will take care of you," she said, dropping her hands. "You will have only three 'babysitters.' Now come, we must get to the palace in time for the story."

Madeline looped her arm through Jason's. "Come on, buddy. I'll take care of you."

The crowd pressed in around them. There were people from all over the Sunlit Lands. You had to be careful not to step on the tiny grey-skinned folks called Maegrom—they were the size of toddlers. He hadn't seen any other Kakri, like Baileya. He wasn't sure there was another person like Baileya in the whole world anyway. A clutch of women with shadowy blue skin passed. "Aluvoreans," Madeline said, rubbing nervously at her wrist. There weren't, he noticed, any Scim. He asked Baileya about it.

She pulled them underneath the awning of a fruit stand and bought a small, hard, yellow fruit for each of them. "The Festival of the Turning is celebrated by many of the people of the Sunlit Lands. The Scim celebrate differently than the Elenil. Some have been given permission to return to their people for a time. Others are gathered in some quarter of the city, no doubt."

"Do you wish you were among your people?" Shula asked.

Baileya took a bite of her fruit. "The Kakri do not celebrate the Turning," she said. "We have a festival close to this time, when the third and fourth spheres meet. I do not think we will hear the music of the spheres' meeting here in Far Seeing. That I will miss. It is a festival where stories are given freely to one another among my people. It is a cherished night."

"If the Scim are all holed up in some other part of the city, we should be able to stay out as long as we like," Jason said.

Madeline stiffened. "I won't be able to breathe, though, Jason."

"Oh yeah."

Shula didn't say anything, but she would have wounds returning to her, too. And Jason . . . well, he'd either be half dead, or he'd be fine. The daylong reversing of magic was going to be a mess for all of them. Jason didn't know if he'd rather be in a hospital bed or completely well, because if he was well that meant Night's Breath, whoever he was, was dead. Dead, and it was Jason's fault. He had told himself he was going to look into it, but he never had. He wasn't sure if that counted as lying to himself.

"The first magic to Turn," Baileya said, "will be the light. Night will come upon Far Seeing. Other magics will begin to Turn soon after. It is unpredictable. But this much is certain . . . whether within a few minutes or many hours, all Elenil magic will Turn by night's end. We should make our way to Westwind during that first hour of darkness, so that you may each be settled safely into your beds."

"I sleep in the stable," Jason said absently.

"We will stay in the outer ring of the crowd, before the stairs leading to the gardens, so that we may leave the festivities early and return you to Westwind. Besides, we have no Elenil to accompany us to the inner courts."

The magistrates, all nine of them, stood upon a massive dais that had been constructed in front of the main entrance to the palace. Jason shivered at the thought of Archon Thenody catching sight of them. He didn't want to be in the same room with that guy ever again. "Where are the guards?" he asked. There were always people milling around with swords or pikes or some sort of weapon. Today he didn't see any.

"Everyone's celebrating," Shula said. "All wars and grievances are set aside for a day. Tonight it will be day in the Wasted Lands and night in Far Seeing. The wealthy will go about in rags, and the poor will feast. It has long been tradition among the Elenil and Scim and all the peoples of the Sunlit Lands that there can be no fighting or war on this day, the most holy of their celebrations."

"They've given everyone the day off," Jason said.

"Yes."

"That's crazy," Jason said. "They don't have any guards on duty?"

Shula shook her head. "A small group of guards remain on duty. But the thought that someone would attack during the Festival of the Turning is inconceivable to them, and all the gates are locked. If someone were to try to break into the city, they would have plenty of warning. They would have to fight, in any case, because the humans would not have any fighting skills. Besides," she said, "the Maegrom have an agreement with the Elenil. They use their earth magic to block the entrances to the city and guard the walls. No one can get into the city during this time."

Baileya said in a low voice, "It is foolish of the Elenil to be so careless. It was only 137 years ago that the Maegrom broke the Treaty of the Turning to attack my people with magic. Even now there is a city hidden among the dunes where some of my people live under their curse."

"Are you saying we're not safe?" Madeline asked.

"My people can celebrate without setting aside caution," Baileya said.

Jason snorted. "They must be fun at parties."

"Yes," Baileya said. "There is much dancing."

A thought occurred to him. "Are you carrying a weapon now?"

Baileya reached into the loose blue folds of her sleeves and pulled out two long wooden shafts with a metal connector on the end of one. "The blades are easily accessible." She nodded, as if confiding to a friend that of course she kept a roll of paper towels in the kitchen in case of spills.

"I only have my fists," he said.

Shula laughed. "I hope there's no trouble, then!"

Madeline laughed, too, but Baileya considered Jason carefully, sizing him up like a football coach weighing a freshman at tryouts. "Do not forget your feet," she said with level sincerity.

"Yeah, okay," Jason said, looking down at his feet. Baileya's taking everything he said with complete seriousness had confused him at first. Now, though . . . he was getting used to it. Baileya treated him like someone worth listening to. She treated him like an equal, even though she was better than him at everything. He looked up from his feet to see her smiling at him. He blushed, and her smile widened.

"They're about to say something," Madeline said. Grateful for the interruption, Jason turned toward the magistrates.

Archon Thenody stepped to the front of the dais. He wore a long robe that was emerald green and gold. The golden sheen of his skin matched the robe precisely. Madeline said, "Jason, look, he's not wearing that covering he usually wears. I wonder why?"

Jason shrugged. "My mom always says you have to wash your sheets once a week. Probably laundry day."

"It is to show the extent of his magic. It will be more dramatic when the magic fails," Baileya said. "Now listen."

The archon raised his arms, waiting for the crowd to quiet, and then he said, "May the light shine upon you." His voice reverberated through the city square, as if the stones of the buildings themselves were speakers. No doubt it was magic, but it made Jason feel like the archon was all around him, beneath his feet, dissolved into the wall beside him, watching and aware of anything Jason might do here, in his city.

The crowd answered in unison, "May it never dim or wane." Oh, that first part was what the woman at the fruit stand had said to him. It must be a traditional or old-fashioned greeting, because he didn't hear it often. Hanali, for instance, had never once used those words.

"The world is about to Turn," Thenody said, and the crowd cheered. "Many centuries ago, before we learned to harness magic, this was a chaotic, dangerous world. Our ancestors lived lives of considerable toil filled with pain and the constant fear of death. Different peoples have used magic in different ways. But we, the Elenil, have wisely made this great city. We have used our magics to bring light to the Sunlit Lands. We have grown beautiful buildings. We have extended our lives in more years and beauty than any people before us." He held his arms up at this, and the people cheered again.

The Crescent Stone, pulsing with purple magics, descended from the top of the palace, floating down toward the archon's hands. The stone was enormous, three or four times the size of the archon, and it floated with a slow but implacable motion. As it came closer to the people below, it began to shrink. It didn't happen all at once. Jason thought at first it was moving down and also away from him. By the time it reached Thenody, it was small enough for the archon to hold it up in two hands. "Our magic is made possible by this great gift: the Crescent Stone."

"I thought it was called the Heart of the Scim?" Jason looked to Baileya for confirmation. He also noticed that Thenody had used the stone from the top of the tower, not the stone in the glass room. It must be for show, he realized. It was more dramatic to have a gigantic crystal fly down from the apex of the tower than to walk a smaller stone down the stairs. And likewise, he must not want to put the real stone in harm's way. Interesting.

"Some do not care for the true name," Baileya said in a low voice. "You would be wise to be cautious when using it."

"Once a year," Thenody said, "we live as our ancestors lived: in a world without magic. In a moment I will silence the stone, and bit by bit magic will leave us. But fear not, my friends! This lesson in darkness will end in light. For tomorrow, our magic will return."

Jason watched the crowd. So many interesting people and creatures wandered through the crowd. Something like an ape, but with ten-foot-long arms and purple-streaked hair, made a whooping sound. A group of the little Maegrom stood on a stand they had constructed, bringing them more or less into Jason's sight line. There was a man dressed in what looked like seaweed leather and a woman in a green robe and a tall hat covered in flowers. Three human-looking people stood about halfway between him and the dais, their backs to him. They wore black clothing, and slung backward over their shoulders were what appeared to be white masks. He couldn't see the masks clearly because they were partially covered by hoods the three people had left hanging down over their backs.

"Do people dress up, like for Halloween?" Jason asked. "Is that a thing during the Turning?"

"No," Shula said.

"Look at those three," he said. As he watched, the middle one shifted, and an arrow's fletching poked up from under his robe. He readjusted, and it disappeared again. "Um. They have weapons. From here it looks like they're dressed like the Black Skulls."

Baileya, without a word, stalked into the crowd, shrugging her weapon from her sleeves and assembling it.

"There's Rondelo," Madeline said, pointing into the sea of people to their right. "Sitting on his white stag. We should tell him."

"It's probably nothing," Jason said, staring at the middle figure, who had moved his robe to put his hand on the hilt of a sword. "Wait, it might be something." Jason pushed his way forward toward Baileya, calling back to Madeline, "Get Rondelo!"

Baileya had her long staff with the blades on either side out now, and the crowd parted before her like water moving aside for a ship. She spun the staff twice, as if reassuring herself of its heft. Jason pushed into her wake and ran to catch up. He didn't have a sword or bow, but he might be able to grab something off one of the Black Skulls if Baileya managed to stop one of them.

Hanali appeared beside him, matching him step for step. "The Sunlit Lands," he said, "are full of things that are not what they appear to be."

"I've seen those Black Skulls in action," Jason said. "Also, nice outfit." Hanali was wearing a tuxedo that looked suspiciously like a toned-down version of the insane riot of clashing colors Jason had worn to the Bidding.

Hanali smiled, his teeth and eyes sparkling. "What color," he asked, "are those skulls again?"

Jason blinked. The Black Skulls were wearing black robes, but their skulls were white. The exact opposite of the Black Skulls he had seen on the battlefield. "Uh-oh," he said.

Baileya grabbed the shoulder of the middle stranger—the White Skull—and spun him around. His face shone with a strange iridescence, almost as if it were covered with small, fine scales. He had no hair—what had appeared to be hair from behind was only more, differently colored scales. His eyes had yellow irises with vertical slits in them, and sharp white teeth crowded his mouth.

Baileya didn't put away her staff, but she no longer held it in a threatening way either. When Jason and Hanali arrived beside her, she was already talking. "—understand why it appears to be a threat to the Elenil."

The first White Skull bowed low. "Now that you explain, Kakri woman, we understand."

A second White Skull spoke, his voice as harsh and unpleasant as the other's. "It is, among our people, considered a comedic statement."

"Your humor is notoriously difficult to understand," Baileya said.

"This is a joke?" Jason studied the three of them carefully. They looked like the Black Skulls, but as if someone had switched all the colors around.

The White Skulls laughed, and the center one said, "We see, and our hearts understand, Kakri woman. This human male does not perceive the joke, and his soul is not lightened with laughter." They ignored Hanali completely. He, for his part, did not seem bothered by this. He turned and waved Rondelo away. Madeline and Shula were making their way to them.

"They are from the Southern Court," Baileya said to Jason. "They thought it would be funny to pretend to be Scim at the Elenil celebration."

All three White Skulls laughed. "Our cousins have appeared as Elenil at the Scim celebration," one of them said. "It is a cause of great merriment, no doubt."

"I'm going to dress up like your worst enemy and come to the Southern Court next time," Jason said.

All three Skulls burst into uproarious laughter. "Yes, friend, do!" They all three clapped their left hand onto his left shoulder, then turned and wandered into the crowd.

Baileya gave him an affectionate look. "They liked you," she said.

Jason wasn't so sure. "I am likeable," he said tentatively.

"It is rare for them to invite someone to their land," Hanali said. "You showed respect by telling them you would come as their enemy, because that means you know there is no enemy who frightens them. It is a great compliment among their people."

"I was trying to insult them."

"They are a strange people. Shape-shifters and tricksters. The Elenil have an uneasy alliance with them. Now come, all of you," Hanali said.

"Thenody's long-winded speech will end soon, and I want you to meet my parents before night falls."

Hanali's parents, Vivi and Resca, looked precisely the same as Hanali. Vivi, his father, had the same ageless face and wore a silken brocade jacket that reminded Jason of what Hanali had worn the first day they met. Long curls of blond hair spilled out of a wide, floppy silk hat. Hanali's mother, Resca, wore a loose, flowing robe that covered her completely and a sheer veil through which could be seen yet another ageless face and a gentle smile.

Jason looked at each of the three of them, baffled that they all looked to be the same age. "You must have had Hanali very young," he said at last, and Hanali's parents burst into delighted laughter.

"We were young," Vivi said, looking lovingly into Resca's eyes. "We were—what? Three hundred years old? Infants!"

Resca put a hand on Hanali's arm. "No one else our age had a child. What a blessing you are, my son."

"Your parents are super nice," Jason said. "That's more nice stuff than I've heard from my dad in my whole life."

Resca smiled again. "It is lovely to meet the children Hanali has ferried into the Sunlit Lands. They are always so delightful and interesting and loyal."

Loyal? Jason glanced at Madeline. "Loyal to who?"

"To Hanali, of course," Vivi said with a delighted laugh.

"Enough, enough," Hanali said. "Unless I am much mistaken, our friend Thenody is finishing his speech."

Friend? Jason gave Hanali a sideways look. Was it just him, or did the Elenil reserve the word *friend* for people they disliked?

Vivi took the arms of Shula and Madeline and turned toward the dais, chatting amiably. Baileya stood nearby, collapsing her war staff. Resca took Jason's arm. "One day Hanali will stand on that dais," she said softly.

"Like . . . as a waiter or something?"

"You are delightful. Perhaps he will be a butler for a magistrate. I doubt a waiter." She smiled at Jason as if they shared a deep secret. He had no idea what she was talking about.

"Okaaaay," he said. "That will be nice."

"Yes," she said, patting Jason's gloved hand. "He is a good son."

Her hand gripped his arm tighter as the audience murmured, then fell silent. The archon held the Heart of the Scim over his head now, and the black color was leeching out of it, leaving only a brilliant white. Without the darkness inside of it, the stone looked like a gigantic diamond or maybe a piece of glass. "Now," the archon said, "darkness falls, and our magics leave us for a time, that we might remember the great sacrifices made by our ancestors who created the Court of Far Seeing, and remain thankful for the light!"

Then, for the first time since they had come to the Sunlit Lands, night fell.

25

A FLIGHT THROUGH DARKNESS

Another turning shall come.

FROM "THE DESERTED CITY," A KAKRI LAMENT

✦

A s the archon spoke, night fell on the Court of Far Seeing. Madeline gasped. Her hand tightened reflexively on Vivi's arm. She reached across him, reassuring herself that Shula was still there, and called out for Jason, who bumbled into her, asking if she was okay.

There were no stars. No moon, nothing. No torches or streetlamps, doubtless because the Court of Far Seeing almost never experienced true dark. The crowd, to Madeline's surprise, did not seem panicked. On the contrary, they cheered the darkness.

"Do not worry," Vivi said. "We allow complete darkness for but a moment. It is part of the story of Ele and Nala, when they stopped the sun in the sky and caused darkness to flee. In a moment there will be—ah, there they are—stars."

More stars than Madeline had ever seen. Enough to wash the whole city in pale, blue light. She had seen the Milky Way once on a camping trip with her parents, but this was more than one swath of white spilled across the sky. It looked like someone had scattered a chest of jewels across a dark floor. Yellow, blue, and red stars shone with a purity of color she had never seen on Earth, and they moved just fast enough that she could see their motion if she stared for even a minute.

"Why wouldn't the Elenil want to see this every night?" Madeline asked, but no one answered.

The archon, on the dais, lit a torch. In the new dark that torch was like a bonfire of glaring brightness. "We must not let the light fade," he said. "It is in the darkness that our light shines brightest, and tomorrow we will light the world again." He lit another person's torch near him, and that person lit yet another torch, and soon candles and torches were being passed into the crowd.

Shula leaned across Vivi. It was just bright enough to see her face clearly. "Madeline, we should make our way back to Westwind. Other magics will begin to fail over the next hour, and it's unpredictable which will go first."

Madeline nodded and then, realizing that it might be difficult to see, said, "Okay, Shula. I'll follow you."

They said their good-byes to Hanali and his parents, who tried to encourage them to stay for the festivities. "The feast begins in a few minutes," Vivi said. "The Elenil will eat dry crusts of bread. The Scim servants who remain in the city will come and feast, and the humans will be given food and drink as well."

"We should definitely stay," Jason said. Madeline wanted to remind him that when the magic left, she wouldn't be able to breathe, but she didn't want him to think about Night's Breath or to think about the fact that if he felt well when the magic faded, it was only because she had allowed the murder of a Scim to save him.

Baileya saved her the trouble, though, by looking down at him and saying sternly, "The Knight of the Mirror has ordered me to return you to Westwind, and that is what I will do."

"But the feast!"

"I will bring you a pastry," Baileya said, "if you behave."

Madeline laughed. This amazing, sculpted warrior woman bringing Jason a pastry . . . Something about the image struck her as funny.

Jason hung his head. "I should stick close to Madeline, anyway."

"Then it is settled," Baileya said. "Let us make our way to the castle."

"Should we wait for some torches?" Madeline asked.

Baileya shook her head. "All four of us come from lands where night and day trade places with regularity. We are not afraid of a small spell of darkness."

Jason said, "We do have lightbulbs where we come from, though, Baileya."

A dark shape skimmed the crowd, flapping its wings, and landed on the dais near the archon. "Did you see that? Was that a bird?"

It was a bird. In a few seconds another bird zipped in from the direction of the southern gate, and then another. Then a massive flock of birds, all different sizes, appeared over the crowd in a chaotic swarm of chirping, hooting, cawing messengers. They flew from all places in the city and lit beside different people in the crowd, relaying their messages before flying off on their next errand.

"No one told me about this part of the festival," Madeline said.

Baileya had already pulled her weapon out, swiftly assembling the two bladed ends. "This is not part of the festival," she said. "We must move quickly to Westwind."

Instead of putting her staff together, she held half out to Jason. He took it in his hand, looking uncertain what to do. She snatched it out of his hand and gave it to Shula. "We will flank you," she said. "You must go as quickly as you are able."

Madeline grabbed Jason's hand so they wouldn't lose each other in the dark, and they pushed through the crowd. She could feel a surge of energy in the crowd. She didn't know what message they had received, but it must be something dire, because the people were all moving with a panicked purpose now. Rondelo and Evernu leapt past them, headed south.

"Hurry," Shula said. "I've seen this sort of crowd before. We need to get out of it."

A horn sounded, harsh and discordant, from the square behind them. Madeline didn't stop to look but felt Jason hesitate. Then he ran ahead of her, yanking on her arm. The crowd around them started to run as well. Someone fell to her left, then disappeared beneath the thundering feet of the crowd. Madeline cried out, but Shula pushed the small of her back, urging her forward.

A voice boomed out over the crowd. "Release the girl to us, and you may live. Deny us, and face the consequences."

Panicked, confused cries rose from the crowd. "What girl?" "Who is he speaking about?" "What does he want?"

"The girl who cannot breathe," said the voice again. "Madeline Oliver is her name."

Madeline stopped, turning back to look. Jason yelled at her to move, yanking on her hand, but Shula had stopped too, Baileya's weapon at the ready.

A Black Skull stood on the far end of the crowd, a scythe in his hands. "Very well," he said. "The archon first." He raised his white-clothed arm, then dropped it again.

A volley of arrows flew from the edges of the crowd. The archon tried to run, but an arrow caught him in the calf, and as he fell, several more pierced him. Screams rose from the people, and the stampede began in earnest.

"This way," Baileya hissed and pulled them into the sheltering alcove of a merchant's shop. "Listen closely. Run if you can, hide if you must, fight if there is no other option. I will be with you in the crowd, sometimes ahead and sometimes behind. Shula, you must stay near them in case one gets past me. Do not hesitate, and do not stay your blade. Be it Scim or human or Elenil, let no one hinder our path."

"What if it's a Maegrom?" Jason asked. "Or a . . . a Kakri or something?"

"Pray it will not be a Kakri warrior," Baileya said grimly, "or you will be lost. Follow the path I direct, even if it seems to take us away from Westwind. The desert has no paths, but a city has many. If we cannot find one that leads where we wish to go, we will make our own."

An Elenil couple fell out of the crowd, pushing up against them in the alcove. "It's her," the woman said, her eyes wide. "They're killing Elenil out there. Elenil! We must give them this girl."

Baileya sliced the woman's arm with her blade. She cried out in surprise, covering her arm. "How dare you, desert vermin!"

Baileya's face twisted in disgust. "There is no magic and thus no healing until the festival ends. You had best run for safety, citizen. If you fall on my blade today, you will not rise again."

The woman said, "Our bird told us someone has allowed the Scim entry to the city. A traitor! The Scim bypassed our guards, they found the gates unlocked. No Elenil would do such a thing, and here we find a company of Kakri and humans." She sneered at them.

Baileya moved toward the couple, but Madeline put her hand on the Kakri woman's arm. "We had nothing to do with that," Madeline said. "But you should run. I can't hold her back for long."

The Elenil couple backed away, and the man said, "When the festival passes, we will speak again."

"Hope that I have no blades on that day," Baileya snarled, and the two of them, wide eyed, stepped back.

"Go," Madeline said. "Run! She's not joking."

The couple stepped into the crowd and disappeared.

The crowd swirled and crashed in on itself. Trying to find a stream of people moving in the right direction seemed overwhelming. Madeline wasn't sure the four of them could go the right way and stay together. "It's too crowded," Madeline said. "The roofs?"

Baileya studied the flat roofs on either side of the street. "You must stay low so the Scim do not see us." With one practiced kick she knocked in the merchant's door. "Swiftly now."

They stumbled through the dark shop. Madeline found a narrow stairway that led to the roof. Baileya forced the top door open. The small, flat roof held a few potted plants and a short wooden bench. The buildings huddled together, and the distance from one roof to the next was rarely more than a single step. They hunched down as they ran to keep from making silhouettes on the field of stars. "The torches are going out," Jason said.

It was true. Starting at the dais and rapidly spreading in a wave across the square, the torches were flickering and dying. Screams came from behind them, and guttural war cries. "Scim warriors," Shula said. "They're in the square."

"Why are they after me?" Madeline asked.

Baileya held still on the edge of a roof. "We should cross the street here," she said. "It's a long jump, but going down among that crowd seems foolish."

"No way," Jason said. "We could wait here for sunlight. No one will see us up here."

Baileya looked to Shula. "I know a thing or two about battles in a city," Shula said. "If they can't find you, they'll set a fire. They'll trust the fire to flush you out."

"We should jump," Madeline said. It was a narrow cobblestone street, but the jump was long enough to be intimidating. Baileya jumped first, soaring across with ease, landing on her feet on the other side. Then Jason went, landing clumsily but whole. Madeline would go next, and Shula last. Madeline's heart beat fast, and her breath came in shallow pants. She squeezed Shula's hand, then backed away from the edge. Jason and Baileya crouched low on the opposite side.

A searing pain shot through Madeline's left wrist, traveling in complicated whorls up her forearm and over her bicep, ending with a series of branching swirls on her shoulder. She gasped and stumbled. Shula hurried to her side.

"Are you okay?"

"I—" She stopped, struggling to breathe. Of course. The magic had just given out. Jason was staring at his own wrist. His eyes met Madeline's, cold and hard.

"We have to get you across," Shula said. She inhaled sharply, and Madeline watched bruises bloom on Shula's face. Her wounds had returned as well. "Should we go into the street or—"

"No. I'll . . . jump."

"You can't breathe!"

"I'll . . . hold . . . my breath." Racking coughs squeezed her chest. She lay on her back and gave herself to the count of ten. Then she reached her hand out, and Shula helped her to her feet. She took as deep a breath as she was able, then ran. Her feet hit the end of the roof, and she jumped, arms pinwheeling, toward the other side.

She hit the lip of the roof and bounced backward, but Baileya snatched her like a hawk grabbing a rabbit. Then Jason's hands were on her arms, and they dragged her onto the roof. Shula landed beside her a moment later.

All three of them lay on the roof, panting. Baileya let them rest for nearly a minute. "We need to move," she said. "We can rest inside Westwind."

They helped Madeline sit up, but she wasn't able to stand. The guilt over Night's Breath crippled her every time Jason looked her way. "Jason," she said. "Night's Breath—"

"Later," Jason said but not in an encouraging way. Baileya ran along the roof to make sure all was clear. Shula and Jason managed to get Madeline standing. Jason picked her up and started to move. He couldn't run, but at least they were headed in the right direction, Baileya scouting and Shula keeping a watch behind them.

Madeline tried to talk to Jason twice more, but each time he quietly rebuked her. The torches had gone out only two blocks behind them. Sweat poured down Jason's face.

Baileya came to them. "We must move faster," she whispered. "The Scim are nearly upon us." She looked Jason up and down. "Give her to me."

"I've got her," Jason said. Baileya wrapped her arms around Madeline, lifting her gently from him.

"Take my weapon," she said. Jason reached out to her waist and unlatched it from a small strap of leather. "Now we run."

Shula took the lead, and Jason came last. Westwind stood like a beacon in the distance, the walls and towers covered in torches.

A horrible croaking sound came from below. It was a laugh. A laugh Madeline recognized. "Wu Song," a voice called. "Wuuu Sooooong, do you remember me?"

"Run if you can," Baileya reminded him. "Keep moving."

"That's Break Bones," he whispered, as if she didn't understand, as if she didn't know.

"All the more . . . reason . . . to run," Madeline said.

They ran, Madeline jostling in Baileya's arms. They leapt over another small alleyway. Baileya didn't even slow. She catapulted herself across with Madeline.

Below them, a horse panicked in the street, pulling a cart of hay, running over people in the crowd. Madeline could see the Scim now, massive creatures making their way through the crowd, smashing people, hacking, cutting and crushing indiscriminately. Everyone ran. No one fought. The Scim caught anyone with a torch and stamped it out.

Jason paused at the edge of the roof, crouched low, watching the Scim.

Trying to find Break Bones, probably. One of the Scim on the ground across the street saw him. The Scim nocked an arrow to its bow, taking aim at her friend.

Without thinking she shouted, "JASON!"

Startled, he fell backward, and the arrow flew harmlessly past. He grinned at her. "Thanks."

They enjoyed a brief exchange of smiles. One of the Scim shouted, "They're on the roof!"

"Run," Baileya said. "By the time they find stairs, we could be ten buildings away."

Ugly horns sounded in the streets around them. Baileya ran, her long legs eating up the space. "They're not waiting for stairs," Jason shouted.

They scaled the walls, grey hands and granite arms hoisting them to the top, where they bared their yellow teeth and, shouting, joined the race. The Scim loped behind them with surprising speed.

"We might have reached 'hide if you must,'" Jason said, panting.

"It's too late for that," Break Bones said, climbing up from a narrow space between the buildings ahead of them. He licked his lips, then pulled a heavy stone ax from a strap on his back. More Scim followed. There were Scim ahead and behind. To each side was a sheer drop to the rioting crowds. "The girl first," Break Bones said. "Then you, Wu Song. Just as I promised."

Baileya set Madeline on her feet and held out her hands. Shula threw her half of Baileya's staff. "Jason," Baileya said, and he threw her the other half. She put the staff together and spun it. "Back to back," she said. "Fight until none remain standing."

"We skipped hiding," Jason said. "I was really looking forward to hiding."

Madeline tried to get a breath and couldn't. She grabbed Jason's sleeve, trying to keep on her feet. Then the Scim were upon them.

26

BATTLE AT WESTWIND

The knight at last his sword lays down,
His grimace gone, no more a frown,
His helm replaced with glorious crown,
A gift from the Majestic One!

FROM "THE GALLANT LIFE AND GLORIOUS DEATH
OF SIR SAMUEL GRYPHONHEART," AN ELENIL POEM

✠

he girl first." One of the Scim said it, his voice deep and full of
violent intention.

Jason shuddered. Shula and Baileya's backs were against his,
and he knew Baileya would slow the vicious Scim who advanced
on them. But Madeline, doubled over and coughing, would be
an easy target for Break Bones.

His stomach clenched at the thought of failure. His molars ground
into each other, and his jaw ached with the sudden pressure. He hadn't
left everything behind to come into this crazy place to fail. *I will protect
Madeline.* He would fight Death himself if it came to that. Thoughts of

Jenny came piling in. Not the good thoughts, not the memories of how they had cared for one another, the fun times, of making jiaozi with their mom or reading books together at night. Not the memories of how she always called him didi—the Chinese word for "little brother"—and he always called her jiejie. No, he saw her upside down and covered in blood, begging him for help. Because he hadn't spoken up. He hadn't spoken the truth. His lack of courage had led the way to that moment.

That cowardice a year ago had built his courage today. The pain and suffering his silence had caused were so much more than he could have ever imagined possible. He would never take the coward's path again, especially not when the life of a friend was in danger.

Baileya's spinning blades kept the Scim at bay, and Shula stepped away from them and lit on fire. Her magic must not have left her yet. She waded into the Scim with a grim determination, and they fell away in terror. One of the Scim dropped a sword, and Jason snatched it up. He could barely lift it, but he managed one awkward swing at the Scim in front of him. They fell back. But then, with laughs like monstrous frogs croaking, they advanced again. One of them knocked the sword from his hand with ease.

Jason yelped.

Madeline leaned against him, losing consciousness. She said his name just before her eyes rolled back into her head and she fell.

He scooped his arm around her, holding her up. He couldn't pick up a sword again, not that it would help, and the Scim had him backed against the edge of the roof. Baileya saw them and spun in their direction, but there were at least four Scim between them now, and Break Bones was engaging her complete attention. Shula was at the far end of the roof, clearing a path for them, lighting the Scim like torches.

Jason wrapped his arms around Madeline's waist, holding her in front of him, whispered a quick prayer, and leaned backward. The world tilted, and they fell. His body would cushion her fall, or at least he hoped so. The looks on the faces of the Scim on the roof, peering over the edge with wide black eyes and frog-like mouths agape, was almost worth it. If it was the last thing Jason saw, he would be satisfied with that. He hadn't seen another option. He couldn't make it to the stairs, and no way would he let Break Bones murder Madeline, not if falling to their deaths could prevent it.

The impact took his breath away.

He groaned. They were still moving.

They had landed in a hay cart pulled by a stampeding horse plowing through the crowd on the street. A quick glance at the Scim showed them even more startled. If they had been cartoons, their jaws would have hit the street.

He and Madeline were alive. "I'm alive!" he shouted up to the Scim, instantly regretting it. They disappeared from the edge, then reappeared, descending the wall feet first.

The cart bucked wildly, knocking Madeline off him. He shoved her deeper in the hay, hoping it would keep her in the cart. The cart hit a hole in the street, and he flew, for a moment, off of the pile of hay and into the air. He fell into the cart, biting his tongue in the process. An arrow zipped past his head, lodging in the wooden plank beside him.

He leapt onto the driver's seat and grabbed hold of the flailing reins. "Yah, mule!" he shouted, because that's what they always shouted in movies, even though this wasn't a mule.

Or a horse.

A closer look made it clear his rampaging "horse" was actually a gigantic, furious goat.

"Yah, goat!" he yelled, and the beast came under some semblance of control. Which is to say, it stopped careening side to side on the street and ran straight ahead, scattering the crowd as Jason yelled, "Runaway goat! Make way!"

Baileya was keeping pace, running along the top of the buildings to their right. Her long legs stretched to their maximum, she vaulted over Scim, dodged weapons, and cleared the spaces between roofs. She flew from a rooftop, her legs tucked beneath her, her bladed staff held under her left arm, her hair flying out behind her. She landed in the hay beside Madeline.

She slipped beside Jason, taking the reins. "A clever escape, Wu Song."

"It was an accident," he said, and she grinned at him.

"We should be able to get to Westwind quickly with this cart," Baileya said.

Shula came falling like a white-hot meteor toward them, also landing in the hay and lighting it immediately on fire.

"Come on!" Jason yelled. He scrambled into the back and dragged Madeline clear.

Shula's flames only grew brighter. "My magic is out of control!" she shouted.

"We have to stop the cart," Jason said to Baileya.

She shook her head. "We ride as long as we can. The Scim are faster on foot than we."

She was right. The Scim were loping in their wake, in the street and along the rooftops. If they abandoned the cart, they'd be in the same situation they had been in on the roof. The cart shuddered as Baileya steered the goat around a few runaway Scim children.

Shula was shoveling flaming bales of hay out the back, sending up jets of sparks behind them. They hit a corner hard, and a wheel on the cart wobbled, letting out a tremendous shriek. "We're losing a wheel!"

Baileya whipped the reins harder, shouting at the goat. Jason wasn't sure how going faster would help, and then he saw the arched rise of a narrow bridge ahead. There was no way the cart would fit. "Hold Madeline!" Baileya cried, furiously driving the goat toward the narrow passage.

Bracing his legs as well as he could against the footboard, Jason wrapped Madeline tightly in his arms and ducked his head, waiting for the impact. Just before they hit, the right-hand wheel came off, rolling alongside them as the cart crashed to the ground, sparks rising from the cobblestone streets. Shula barely managed to grab onto the cart's rail. The terrified goat lunged for the bridge, wedging the cart between stone columns rising on either side.

His head ringing, Jason dragged Madeline over the front of the cart, weaving his way past the angry goat. Baileya motioned him forward, already beyond the animal and facing the bridge. "I will hold the Scim here. Those who refuse the bridge will be slowed by the river. Make all haste for Westwind. Do not pause, do not linger!"

"No loitering? Your advice is no loitering?"

He hoisted Madeline onto his shoulder with Baileya's help and stumbled down the street. The crowds had thinned, whether because they were farther from the square or because the goat had flattened or blocked everything headed this way, Jason didn't know. Smoke curled through the city now, along with the distant cries of terrified people. The city was no longer dark, because it was on fire.

Jason was sweating before he got out of earshot of Baileya. The whistling sound of her staff was often followed by the impact of metal on leather armor. He felt Shula before he heard her, the blazing heat of her flames moving alongside him.

"My flames won't go out," she said. "I can't help you carry her."

"We're almost there." He could, in fact, see Westwind's gate. It wasn't open, though, and he wasn't sure how they would get through it. Five blocks to go, more or less.

"I'll run a full block ahead of you," Shula said. "Make sure it's clear."

"Right," he said, gasping.

Madeline stirred. "Jason?"

"It's okay," he said. "We're almost to Westwind."

"I can . . . walk," she said.

He set her down. Walking together might make them faster. He wasn't sure. She leaned on him, and they struggled onward. Shula stood at the intersection, her head turning both ways to take in the people on the street. "Quickly," she said.

Madeline was able to nearly trot, though her breathing came in fits. Her skin was clammy and alarmingly cold. "I can carry you," he said, but Madeline shook her head, a determined look on her face.

When they reached the intersection, Shula immediately ran to the next. At the next intersection she did the same. They were three blocks away now. Jason shouted at the top of his lungs for someone to open the gate. Ruth Mbewe's tiny blindfolded face appeared at the top of the wall. "We cannot open the gate," she called. "The Scim are too close!"

Jason craned his neck to look back toward the goat cart. He couldn't see the cart anymore, or hear the battle, but there were no Scim, either. "I don't see any," he said.

"Swim the moat, and we'll throw you a rope!"

Madeline's face set in a grim, determined frown. She would try. Jason didn't see how she would do it, though. And the Scim couldn't be that close, he hadn't seen any. Shula hadn't seen any.

Then, a block ahead of Shula, on the street that crossed in front of the gate, a figure loomed out of the deep shadows of the street. His massive arms had gashes, his clothes were burned, and he was dripping with water. No doubt he had swum the river rather than fight his way over the goat cart. Break Bones.

Shula picked up the pace, deliberately running at him, her flames burning ever hotter.

"Quickly," Madeline gasped, and Jason limped alongside her, moving toward the moat.

Shula danced around Break Bones. His superior strength was nothing compared to her speed. She scalded his arms badly every time he took a swing at her, and thus far he hadn't managed to connect. Jason got Madeline to the edge of the moat. It was still a three-foot drop into the foul water around the castle. He helped Madeline to a sitting position and got ready to help her slip in, then follow.

Ruth's face appeared again above. "The knight is opening the bridge!"

The knight? Jason squeezed Madeline's hand. Why was the knight inside instead of at the festival? Why didn't he open the gates as soon as he saw Madeline and Jason on their way? Wasn't his job to fight the Scim? Why was he hiding in the castle?

They made their way toward the descending bridge. When it was nearly to the ground, Jason boosted Madeline onto it, and she hobbled inside. The Knight of the Mirror flew over the bridge on his silver stallion, Rayo.

Shula's flame went out.

Break Bones laughed. "Your magic is extinguished for the night!" He backhanded her, sending her flying into the moat.

Then the knight was upon the Scim, barely missing him with his lance. Break Bones grabbed the knight by the waist, twisted hard, and smashed him onto the stone road. The Knight of the Mirror was no fool, and he rolled to the side just before the Scim's fists pounded the pavement. "Go to the lady of Westwind at once," the knight called to Jason.

Jason, flat on his belly beside the moat, was able to reach Shula's outstretched hand. Several people ran from inside the castle and helped him pull her out of the putrid water. "What about Baileya?" he asked. The knight fought the Scim using only his sword.

"She is Kakri," Shula said. "She won't stop fighting."

"Get Madeline to the knight's solar," Jason said to Ruth. Ruth stood close to Madeline, letting the breathless girl lean on her.

Jason had to get to the wall. He needed to get to higher ground, so he could find Baileya. If he could get his hands on a bow, maybe he could help her.

When he reached the top, he was breathless and exhausted. His heart sank as he looked over the lip of the wall. It wasn't just Break Bones out there. There were hundreds of Scim, all converging on the castle like a swarm of ants. He scanned the crowd—or what he could see of it in the darkness—and saw, to his dismay, the three white-robed Skulls moving toward the castle as well.

"Send out the girl," one of the Black Skulls demanded. "The one who cannot breathe. Madeline Oliver."

A few of the castle's residents were trying to hold the drawbridge long enough to keep it open so the knight could return. Rayo was nowhere to be seen. The knight was in the thick of battle and making a slow, tortured path back. One of the Black Skulls was moving toward the drawbridge now, and nothing stood in its way.

In the guardhouse, a small room built into the stone wall, Jason found a bow. He stood as he had been taught and put his fingers on the string, an arrow nocked between them. It felt strange without the magic to guide him. He sighted along the arrow, pointing at the heart of one of the Black Skulls. He pulled back carefully, then released the string. The arrow went sideways. The string snapped his forearm, and he dropped the bow, crying out in pain. The arrow fell awkwardly into the moat, followed by the bow.

A horn blew, a brighter, higher sound than the horns of the Scim. Rondelo bounded into the fray on Evernu, his white stag. Close behind him came some of the army of the Elenil, the men and women who were loyal to the Knight of the Mirror. Rondelo, whose battle prowess had never been a gift of magic but rather of hard-earned skill, cut through the Scim. David and Kekoa came behind him. They weren't wearing their war gear, but they had their weapons of choice. They moved slower and with less fluidity than they had with magic, but still, they were making a difference in the battle.

"Hold the bridge!" Rondelo cried, and his people spread out in a semicircle, pushing the Scim away from the entrance. The fighting grew vicious along that semicircle, but the Elenil army managed to hold it. There were more Elenil warriors in the crowd than Jason had ever seen. Near Rondelo an Elenil man in a shining silver helmet repaired every break in the line, running back and forth to the places in most need. He held two swords, and when he waded into the Scim, the swords flashed with reflected firelight.

Rayo came galloping back toward the castle now, Baileya on his back. "The bridge has fallen!" she shouted. "More Scim are on their way!"

The Knight of the Mirror turned to his side, and as Baileya thundered past, he grabbed her forearm and slung himself up behind her. "Close the drawbridge!" he cried, and immediately it began to ratchet upward. Westwind's defenders continued to fight as the drawbridge inclined. The knight's horse jumped onto it, and as soon as they hit the ground inside, the knight slung himself down and joined the people in closing the bridge, lending his strength to turning the wheel.

Rondelo and Evernu and the Elenil with the silver helmet leapt off the drawbridge, remaining outside the castle. They guarded the closing gate, keeping the Scim off, pushing them back. The three Black Skulls shoved their way to the front of the conflict. The silver-helmeted Elenil spun and danced as his twin blades easily deflected two of the three Skulls. Rondelo joined him, leaping from Evernu's back to engage the third Skull, allowing the stag to hold another hole in their line.

Break Bones slunk up behind Rondelo. Jason shouted a warning, and Rondelo spun, kicking Break Bones in the chest. During this momentary distraction, the third Black Skull turned his attention to the silver-helmeted Elenil and ran a sword through his heart. He fell like a puppet with cut strings. Rondelo screamed and skidded into the trio of Skulls, fighting them with a fierce passion.

Jason ran for the gate, shouting at them to hold it. The knight heard him and paused. "The silver Elenil has fallen," Jason said, and he ran up the bridge, which was so high now he could scarcely make it to the top. He hung over the lip, swung his body twice, and just managed to jump across, landing with a bone-jarring thump.

Rondelo kept all the Scim at bay himself, with only Evernu's help. Jason scooped up the body of the silver-helmeted Elenil. He felt lighter than he should, even though he was completely limp, as if Jason had picked up a bag that should be full of bricks but was stuffed instead with pillows. "Evernu," he shouted, and the stag fell back to his side. He put the body over the stag's back and, at Rondelo's instructions, climbed on himself.

The stag leapt to the top of the bridge, skidding inside the castle walls. The Knight of the Mirror shouted for them to close the bridge, just as Rondelo vaulted through the gap. Jason slipped from the stag, pulling the Elenil man down and laying him gingerly on his back. David and Kekoa appeared beside him, helping Jason get the man's arms and legs laid out gently.

He didn't appear to be breathing. Jason carefully removed the silver helmet. The still, quiet face looked familiar.

"Aw, no," Kekoa said. "It's Vivi."

Jason knew that name, but the terror of the last hour prevented him from remembering. But David filled in the blanks when he said, "Hanali's dad."

Rondelo fell to his knees beside Vivi's body. "Ah, brave soul." Tears sprang from Rondelo's eyes. "On this night of all nights he fought, when his body cannot be mended with the magic of the Sunlit Lands. He is lost to us." He closed his eyes, and his next words came slowly but surely, like a poem being quoted: "His bowl is spilt, his thread unspun. His life is past and just begun. He treads now in a clime of sun . . . in the land of the Majestic One."

"They're climbing the walls!"

Rondelo rose smoothly to his feet. "Come, friends. Let us avenge Vivi, son of Gelintel, father of Hanali."

"No," the Knight of the Mirror said. "These three young men must come with me to my solar. Rondelo, protect Vivi's body so the Scim will not take possession of him."

Rondelo lifted Vivi in his arms and set him gently on Evernu's back. "When the wall is breached, I will take him to Hanali."

The knight put his hand on Rondelo's shoulder. "Let us pray that our people can hold the walls long enough to accomplish one more task. Come, boys. Stop staring at the walls and follow me!"

27
PARTINGS

It is no shame to travel with crows.

A KAKRI PROVERB

✦

She missed Darius. It was a ridiculous thing to think as she labored, breathing heavily, to climb the tower stairs. Nevertheless, there it was. She had met him freshman year. He was charming, kind, and smart. Rare enough in a boy at all, nearly extinct among high school freshmen. One day in English, when they were right in the middle of studying Romeo and Juliet, he had shown up at class with three roses for her.

On the note he had written, "Madeline. 'That which we call a rose by any other name would smell as sweet.' I called these 'Madeline,' and they seemed sweeter. Yours, Darius."

It wasn't the most emotionally competent way of breaking the ice, but it could have been worse. Besides, they had been freshmen. He was an emotional genius compared to some of the other kids.

And when she had gotten sick, he had been amazing. But once she knew what was going on—not just her diagnosis, but once she really understood—she'd had to break up with him. She couldn't let him spend a year of his life watching hers slip away. She knew he would stick by her until the end, and she couldn't let him do that. She regretted it now. Maybe if she had stayed with him, he'd be with her on this staircase. One thing was certain—as much as she appreciated Ruth's help climbing the stairs, and as strong as Ruth was for an eight-year-old, Darius could have scooped her up in his arms and carried her. She worried she might not make it through the night, and even after they'd broken up, she'd still secretly imagined that Darius would be there when . . . well, when she breathed her last.

"Are you able to continue?" Ruth asked, her blindfolded face turned toward Madeline's.

The clash of weapons and the cries of warriors echoed through the courtyard and up the tower. Although they ascended as quickly as Madeline was able, she was afraid the battle would overtake them before she entered the knight's quarters. "Yes," she said, and they moved forward another eight hard-won steps before she doubled over, hands on her knees, taking breaths that rasped through her like knives.

"There is a window here," Ruth said, although how she knew it with her eyes covered Madeline couldn't say. Perhaps the cool night air touched her face.

Madeline put her hand on the narrow stone window. Waves of Scim had crested the walls. Human soldiers worked to push them back. Madeline suddenly understood why the Knight of the Mirror must require those who fought at his side to do so without magic. Was it all in anticipation of this night? He would be uniquely vulnerable during this time. In fact . . . his magical blessing that nothing could be taken from his hand would be broken tonight, wouldn't it? That meant the Scim artifacts he was meant to protect would be at risk. Not to mention her and Jason.

The sound of shattering glass came from further up the tower.

Before they could investigate, a bird, green and black with a plume of bright blue on its head, landed on the window.

"Do you bring a message for the Knight of the Mirror?" Ruth asked, her words tumbling out with intense concern.

"The gates are fallen," the bird said. "Malgwin, harbinger of chaos and suffering, swims the waters of the Sunlit Lands. The Scim have taken the Court of Far Seeing—"

"That we can see ourselves," Ruth snapped. "What more?"

"They enter the Palace of a Thousand Years, intent on reclaiming the Heart of the Scim. The palace guards hold them floor by floor. The archon is wounded and has retreated to his chambers with the stone. Tirius commands the knight come lest—"

"He could not even if he wished it. The knight is trapped here in his own castle."

"Then we are lost," the bird replied. "The Court of Far Seeing is burning. Three magistrates are dead, killed in the square by the Scim. More are wounded, and hours yet remain until daylight."

"Vivi, too, has left us," Ruth said. "I have heard the mourning cry of the Elenil from the courtyard."

"Woe! Woe! Woe to the Sunlit Lands!" the bird cried. "Is the Sword of Years safe? Or have the villains retaken their instruments of destruction?"

"For now they are safe," Ruth said. "Though the Scim beat upon our very door."

"This is one bright kindling of hope."

"Is there no other news, then?"

"None good. The Black Skulls roam our streets. The Scim are fierce and the Elenil all unprepared. It is said the Maegrom have joined their side and allowed the Scim entrance through their own clever tunnels. Even now the—awk! Awk awk awk!" The bird's head bobbled, as if choking on something in its long neck. It flapped its wings and flew away, high over Westwind, headed toward the center of the city.

"What . . . what happened?"

Ruth, her face set in a grim frown, said, "The magic has faded now even for the messenger birds. It will not be long until the last of the Elenil magic fails for the night."

They made their way farther up the stairs. One of the stairway mirrors was shattered, and the broken glass crunched beneath their feet. "Is . . . someone . . ." A series of coughs battered Madeline's chest.

Ruth lowered Madeline to the stone stairs, careful to avoid the broken mirror. "Perhaps there is help above. I will go. Patience."

Help above? The only person above was Fernanda, trapped in her mirrors. Maybe Ruth was getting one of the magical artifacts. But if the magic was failing, what help would they be? Even the magic mirrors were breaking. A terrible thought crept into her mind. What if someone else was in the tower? One of the Scim or the Black Skulls? That seemed impossible, but what if they had used some sort of magic and arrived before them? Madeline had allowed an eight-year-old to go alone up the stairs.

Madeline struggled to her feet and rested her hand against the wall. Her heart beat frantically, and she felt light headed. She waited for the black waves at the edges of her vision to recede. Then she made her way, step by painful step, upward.

A yelp of surprise came from above, and Ruth pushed herself under Madeline's arm. "I told you I would bring help. You should have waited."

She *had* brought help too. Rushing down the stairs, holding the hem of her dress so she could move more easily, came Fernanda Isabela Flores de Castilla, the lady of Westwind. She draped Madeline's other arm around her neck, and together the three of them made their way steadily toward the top.

"How—?"

"On this night the cursed enchantment is broken," Fernanda said. "Tonight alone in the year I walk among you not as a ghost but as a woman."

A sob caught in Madeline's throat. She was exhausted, she couldn't breathe, and she needed to keep climbing. This poor woman, though, had been trapped in the mirrors for the entire year, and now, tonight, she was using her few moments of precious freedom to help Madeline. It was too much to bear.

"Come, come," Fernanda said. "It is not so bad. Being trapped in a mirror saves me looking in them."

They had reached the knight's solar.

"On the bed there," Fernanda said, and together she and Ruth lowered Madeline onto the rumpled bed in the main chamber. The table with the Scim artifacts sat in full view, unprotected.

"Need . . . to hide . . . the artifacts," Madeline said.

Fernanda stroked her sweating forehead. "Do not worry, child, my beloved will be here soon. He has a plan, I know, to keep them safe."

Jason burst into the room, followed by Delightful Glitter Lady trotting along in her golden retriever size. "Madeline!"

Jason's friends David and Kekoa came in behind him. Kekoa carried a strange weapon with teeth. Then Shula came behind them, her face covered in dirt and gore, her hair loose and wild. She carried a canvas package, which she immediately unfolded in the center of the floor. It was full of weapons. Then Baileya entered, panting.

"The knight bars the tower door," she said. "He will be here in a moment. For now he asks that each of you arm yourselves, for the battle to leave here will be fierce."

Shula and Jason were at Madeline's side now, talking over each other, both concerned for her and trying to figure out how they could help. Of course there was nothing to be done.

The knight appeared a moment later, his sword in hand. His eyes lingered on the magically shrunken rhinoceros, and he frowned at Jason. "Make haste," he said. "Gather quickly."

Madeline got to her feet and met them at the table. Fernanda pressed in to the knight's side, and he took her under his arm, pausing only to kiss her once and say, in barely more than a whisper, "Ah, my lady, at last I hold you for a moment. Forgive me that I must make haste in giving instructions."

She kissed his cheek and said, "My brave knight, do as you must."

The Knight of the Mirror looked around the table. "We are nine," he said. "Before you lie five magical artifacts, weapons of the Scim. Should they retrieve these weapons, tonight's attack will be only the first course in a veritable banquet of destruction."

"Maybe we could skip to dessert," Jason said. The knight ignored him.

"My magical boon returns at first light, but even now the Scim are within the walls of Westwind. I fear what may come. I must ask a brave favor of you all."

"We'll do whatever you ask," Shula said.

"Within reason," Jason said.

The knight nodded. "Your honesty does you both credit. I fear my request is neither reasonable nor easily accomplished. I desire to fling these five artifacts to the other peoples of the Sunlit Lands so the Scim will not easily recover them."

Baileya said, "I can take them to the Kakri, Sir Knight, with little difficulty."

"I hoped you would say so." He picked up the silver mask. "This is the Mask of Passing. Entrust it, please, to your tribe. I would have Jason join you in your journey."

"Whoa," Jason said. "I should go with Madeline. I came here to protect her, not your drama mask."

Baileya folded her arms. "The desert is harsh, Sir Knight. I fear Wu Song may not be easily accepted among my people. If something were to happen to me before we reached the Kakri, he would surely be lost."

"Better the mask be lost than returned to the Scim." Then, to Jason, the knight said, "I do not have the people to send more than two together, and it is more important that each artifact have a warrior to help transport it than that you be near your friend. Your pledge to the Elenil binds you to take this order."

"Except I didn't make a pledge to the Elenil, I made a pledge to Madeline," Jason said. "I'm not leaving her."

"The knight's right," Madeline said. "I will need . . . protection . . . and someone to help . . . me move. At least until . . . morning."

"Besides," Shula said. "How would you protect her? Not with bow and arrow."

Jason blushed. "You saw that, huh?"

Baileya put her hand on Jason's arm. "I heard tell of it from the knight. It is no shame. You acquitted yourself bravely. To attempt the bow is better than to have run. Better a failure than a coward."

"Thanks, I guess?" Jason said, still blushing.

The knight handed a folded robe to Kekoa. "Ruth will accompany you to the Zhanin. She knows the way. Sail west, and wait for the song of welcome. If they do not welcome you, or seem hostile, wear the Robe of Ascension for one day . . . only long enough to explain yourself and our situation. Remind their holy ones of my service to them many years ago."

Kekoa took the robe. "Okay, kid," he said. "Let's go."

"Godspeed," said the knight. "Do not fight unless you must."

"We should go as well," Baileya said.

"I want to know where everyone is going in case something goes wrong. Something always goes wrong," Jason said.

The knight nodded. "Quickly, then. David, to you I give this key, called the Disenthraller. It can open any lock: gate or door, chest or drawer. Take it to the Aluvorean people."

David nodded once, quickly, and put the key in his pocket. "Anyone I should take with me?"

"You will move faster alone, I think," the knight said. "Leave the city by the western gate if you can, and head to the southwest. You will see the great trees rise up like mountains. Follow them to the heart of the wood and say these words: 'Beneath the shadows of the great trees I beg your mercy. Take me to your heart that I might grow.' If the people reject you, speak to the trees."

"Beneath the shadows of the great trees I beg your mercy. Take me to your heart that I might grow." David looked to the knight for confirmation. They exchanged nods. "Good luck to all of you," David said. He scooped up an extra knife from the canvas covering on the floor and trotted down the stairs.

"I will bar the door behind him," Fernanda said.

"O wise woman," the knight called after her. "Shula and Madeline, you must take this stone, the Memory Stone, to the Maegrom."

Madeline held up her hand. "A bird told us . . . the Maegrom . . . have allied with . . . the Scim."

The knight deflated. "That is grave news. I fear, then, that I must take the Memory Stone and try to hold it until dawn. May I be successful! I must ask you two, then, to take the Sword of Years to the Pastisians. They live in the far northeast, beyond the mountains, near the crystal horizon."

Jason's tiny rhino whined, and Jason said, "Wait, aren't those the necromancers? I heard about them."

"Indeed," the knight said. "It is a dark time that we have come to this."

Fernanda burst into the room. "The door is barred, but the Scim are outside the tower. In moments they will knock upon the door."

The knight placed the rusted sword in Madeline's hands and the scabbard in Shula's. "This sword must not be returned to the scabbard, or it will come out new and thirsty for blood. Once awakened it cannot be put to sleep save through bloodshed. It must not fall to the Scim. Guard it with your lives!" He pulled the canvas from the floor, dropping the other weapons with a great clattering of metal. He wrapped the sword and tied it with rope. "Upon the roof a great bird awaits. You are too weak to run, Madeline, but not, I hope, too weak to fly. Head northeast until you think the very world will end, and you will see the lights of their city by night or the smoke of their magics by day. They have great contempt for the magic of the Elenil and the Scim. Tell them they may destroy this sword if they wish and if they are able!"

"Will the bird's magic last so long?" Shula asked.

A crashing sound came from below. The knight thrust a short sword at Jason. "It is a risk, Shula, but one we must take. Fly low if you can. My lady Fernanda, take Shula and Madeline above. Baileya, Jason, with me to guard their retreat."

"I thought you wanted us to leave," Jason said, taking the sword gingerly.

"I fear only Baileya can help me hold the door now," the knight said. "We must hope we can then provide an exit for the two of you."

Jason hugged Madeline. "Once we deliver the mask, I'll find you."

"Hurry, boy!" the knight cried, running down the stairs. Baileya followed. Jason winked at Madeline and shot after them, Delightful Glitter Lady at his heels.

"This way," Fernanda said urgently, leading them to a corner of the room where a wooden ladder lay, a ladder that Madeline hadn't noticed before. With Shula's help Fernanda propped it in the corner. She climbed the rungs and pushed open a sort of hatch. The roof was sloped, but built onto the side was a wide wooden platform. An enormous bird perched there, a saddle on its back.

Shula climbed on first. Madeline passed her the sword, then mounted behind her, encircling her waist with her arms. Her breathing came shallow and fast. "Farewell," Shula said.

"Go with God," Fernanda replied. "Come home once your duty is done!" Then she whispered to the bird, "To Pastisia!"

The bird let out an ear-shattering call, crouched down, and shoved itself into the sky. Its wings spread wide, and it circled once, twice, around the tower, gaining height with each pass. Far below, the Scim fought their bloody battle with the Elenil. Fires blazed throughout the city. The bird turned northeast, gliding over the city walls. A Scim far below loosed an arrow at them, but it fell away long before reaching them.

The darkness was so deep, they couldn't see the ground once they left the firelit city. Despite the knight's warning, Shula kept the bird flying high, saying she was worried about trees or other obstructions in the dark. The stars burned above, but there was no moon. A dark ribbon glittered with starlight below, a river wending its way through the land. They flew with astonishing speed, the air cold and piercing. It seemed to help Madeline's breathing a little, though she shivered almost without ceasing. It was because of her shivering that she didn't feel the bird shaking at first.

"Oh no," Shula said.

"What . . . is it?"

"Hold on," Shula said. Then again, yelling, "Hold on!"

Madeline wrapped her arms tighter around Shula.

The bird was shrinking. It was still large, large enough to hold them both, but not large enough to stay airborne. It was struggling, flapping with all its might, but they were falling, falling toward the unseen ground below. The Sword of Years tumbled from Madeline's grip. She reached for it, gasping, and then she was falling, faster than the bird and Shula. She closed her eyes and braced herself.

She hit the water, hard, before she had a chance to take even half a breath.

28
THE FALL

✢

The door shuddered in its frame, but the heavy bar held. Splinters flew, and a thick stone blade split a hole. The knight stood three steps above the door, sword at the ready. Baileya stood two steps above him, her double-bladed staff as wide as the stairway. Jason stood six steps up from Baileya. The knight had taken Jason's short sword and given him a mace. It was, essentially, a weighted club with spikes on it.

"Always keep the upper ground," the knight said. "If I fall, do as Baileya says. The narrow stairs work to our advantage. Any creature that passes me and this warrior maid must be fierce indeed, but hopefully wounded."

Jason cleared his throat. "Then I whack it in the head with the pointy club."

"The mace," the knight said. "Indeed. Well said, young warrior."

There came another shuddering crash from the door and guttural shouts from the Scim on the other side. The knight clasped Baileya's forearm, and she his. "It has been an honor to fight alongside you, daughter of the desert."

"If we live," she said, "this shall be a story of great value among my people. The honor is mine, Sir Knight."

"Likewise," Jason said. "Honor to die with everyone, et cetera."

Baileya grinned at him, and her pale-silver eyes twinkled like starlight. "Even in the face of death you raise the spirits of your companions."

He managed not to blush this time, but her words warmed him right to the tips of his fingers. He shrugged, trying to look nonchalant, something he found challenging when holding a mace. "It might be my only contribution to this fight."

"Make ready," the knight said, as another fall of the ax tore a hole in the door. Great grey fingers reached through, trying to rip the boards apart, but the knight sliced at them. Howling erupted from the other side of the door.

For a bare second a black eye peered through the hole in the door, disappearing before the knight's sword could rise to meet it. "Beware, Scim, lest thou lose thine eyes at my door."

Jason laughed. "Nice one, King James."

"It is the ancient language of kings and knights," Baileya said.

"Behold! I doth know that so much already," Jason said, swinging his mace, which hit the stone wall and jarred his arms. "Ouch."

Delightful Glitter Lady leaned against him and let loose a high-pitched whine.

There was a momentary silence on the other side. A Scim shouted, "They have a unicorn upon the stairs!"

Jason patted Dee on the back. *That's right, you nutty people of the Sunlit Lands. Be afraid of my rhino. Call it a unicorn if you like.*

The door shattered inward. The first Scim to cross the threshold fell to the knight's sword. Three more Scim rushed upon him. He sidestepped the stroke of an ax, kicked a second Scim, and drove his elbow into the jaw of a third. Baileya darted forward and stabbed a Scim over the knight's shoulder.

Then, chaos.

The knight stacked the bodies of the wounded Scim before him to impede their comrades, but the Scim snagged feet and arms and dragged them away so that a fresh wave of attackers could advance. For a time, Baileya switched places with the knight so he could rest. The fighting seemed to go on for hours, and the smell of sweat and blood and the sound of metal on metal rang endlessly in Jason's ears. When Baileya and the knight switched places again, the Scim retreated and moved away from the doorway.

"What's happening?" Jason asked.

"They will try a new approach," Baileya said. "Perhaps they will scale the tower?"

The knight shook his head and said softly, "They do not know our numbers. Perhaps we have guards above with hot pitch or bow and arrow."

"Sir Knight," came a booming voice.

"I am here," the knight called.

"In time we will take this tower. Is this not true?"

"Aye," the knight said, "unless ye be a battalion of knaves and cowards."

"Thinkest thou that we are such?"

"I said not so, sir."

"Sir Knight, may I approach in peace that we may exchange a few words before the fight recommences?"

The knight whispered something to Baileya, then called, "Aye, but with empty hands, sir."

A Scim came into view, palms up. He looked up the stairs to see the knight, Baileya, and Jason standing there, each holding a weapon, and the rhinoceros lounging at Jason's side. The Scim laughed and leaned against the doorjamb, crossing his arms. "Wu Song. Truly, you are a thorn of great length and sharpness inserted deeply into my side."

Jason waved. "Hey, Break Bones. Good to see you."

"Why dost thou seek parley?" the knight asked.

"Oh, good Sir Knight, I thought it might be pleasant to converse before thy death."

The knight set his sword against the wall, point on the stairs. He massaged his sword arm with the other. "Speak then, sir. Night is burning away, and when the sun returneth so doth the magic of the Elenil."

Break Bones laughed, his great grey boulder of a head nodding in delight. "Ah, such a pleasure, Sir Knight, to speak with thee. Thou art as fierce in words as in battle. Yes, soon the magic of the Elenil shall return." His grin disappeared, and his wide hands clenched at his side. "Not so the army of the Scim. Thou and the Kakri child have killed or wounded a full two score."

"Speak and be done," Baileya said. "I grow weary of your stalling."

Break Bones stood straight. "Ah, the child has a tongue, and sharp enough. Surrender the artifacts of the Scim to us, and we shall take you captive until first light, then release you—you and all in the tower, save Wu Song and his friend Madeline. For I have sworn to kill her and then him."

"No deal," Jason said. The knight and Baileya said nothing, staring at the Scim. "Right, guys? No deal, right?"

The knight spoke. "Break Bones. Didst thou pause our battle to insult us? I am a knight and a man of honor. Thou must live according to thy vows, and I according to mine. The artifacts of the Scim are under my protection, and I cannot give them willingly into thy hands."

"I intended no insult. My offer was meant as a kindness. We will fight ye for the hours it takes to wound or tire ye, and then take what ye will not give. In a moment we shall return." He paused, then said, "Wu Song. You have always spoken truth to me, so I must do the same."

"Is it that you like my shirt?" Jason asked. "A lot of people have said that."

"No, child. It is said among the Scim that you have murdered Night's Breath. Is this so?"

Jason considered this. When the magic had snuffed out, Jason hadn't. Which meant Night's Breath had died. Died so he could live. Madeline had made that choice, not him, but it was true. Night's Breath had died because of Jason. He took a deep breath and started to answer. Stopped. Tried again. He couldn't bring himself to say the simple answer—yes. Instead he said, "Technically, I was unconscious. So . . . not really. It wasn't my decision."

Break Bones seemed to deflate a little. "Ah. I had hoped it to be but a rumor. He was used to heal your wounds and died of them? Is that the shape of it?"

"I didn't choose it," Jason said, "if that makes a difference. It wasn't me, exactly. I'm horrified by it."

"But you are the one who benefited," Break Bones said. "You did not kill him, but you inherited his life."

"It wasn't me," Jason repeated. "It's a horrible thing, but I'm not a murderer, if that's what you're saying."

"No, it was not you," Break Bones said. "It was your allies. Now a great prince of my people lies dead, and his life throbs in your veins. His life was taken in payment for yours, and you stand upon those stairs and say it is not your fault."

"It's *not* my fault!"

"Yet he is dead, and you still breathe."

"I can't change that," Jason said. He stopped, uncertain of the rules of the Sunlit Lands. He asked Baileya, "Wait, I can't change that, can I?"

She shook her head. "Death comes but once."

"Yeah, okay," Jason said. "I can't bring Night's Breath back to life. So you can't hold me responsible for his death."

"Tell that to his orphaned children," Break Bones said. "Who will care for them now? Their father is dead, and you will use his life for some other purpose than to care for them. You will not serve his people or walk his mother to meet the Peasant King. Are these not your choices? You did not murder him, perhaps, but his blood is on your hands."

"That's not fair," Jason said.

"So says his wife. So say his children and his mother and his neighbors. Yet here you stand. Alive."

"Why are we talking about this? Did you just want me to feel bad before you killed me?"

The Scim frowned, his eyes sad. "No, Wu Song. I told you this so you would understand: every Scim in this city has made a blood oath to return Night's Breath's life to his people."

"Um," Jason said. "Just to be clear . . . Are you saying that every Scim in the city has taken an oath to kill me?"

"Indeed, and to bear your body back to Night's Breath's widow."

Jason's knees felt weak. "Well. Thanks for letting me know."

Break Bones bowed. "Sir Knight. Lady. Wu Song. In a moment our battle will recommence, at your signal. Fare ye well."

The Scim disappeared.

"Are ye ready?" the knight asked, still using his archaic speech.

Baileya shook her staff. Jason just shook. He couldn't say anything. He had known theoretically the Scim were willing to kill him, but that was a bit different than all of them taking a vow to kill him. Overwhelmed by the whole thing, he shouted, "You know, I'm actually a pretty nice guy if you take the time to get to know me!"

Break Bones's voice came echoing to them as he addressed his soldiers. "Kill whomever you must to take the tower. What belongs to the Scim we return to our people. Whoever lays hands upon the Sword of Years and returns it to our people, be it Scim or Elenil, human or Kakri, I shall be in their debt for every day of my life. Are ye ready, my brethren? Are ye prepared, sistren?"

A roar came from the army of the Scim.

The knight brandished his sword and shouted, "Come then, Scim! Do your worst."

They did. Four Scim rushed in, two in front and two in back. While the knight fought the front two, the two in the back sliced at him. He made quick work of them, but as he knocked the fourth down the stairs, it revealed a fifth Scim kneeling at the bottom of the tower, a crossbow in his hands trained directly at the knight.

The knight turned fast enough to spare his heart, but the bolt sank into his sword shoulder. With a cry, Baileya leapt over him, darted out of the stairway, and killed the Scim. She snatched the crossbow and two bolts that had fallen to the ground before scrambling back to the relative safety of the stairway.

"Well done," the knight said, pale and bleeding on the stairs.

"Whatever Scim next ascends the stairs receives a bolt for their trouble," Baileya shouted.

"Help me ascend," the knight said to Jason.

They retreated ten steps up, so that they bent around the corner and could no longer see the entrance. Baileya removed the bolt from the knight's shoulder with a swift and practiced hand. She loaded the crossbow and waited a few steps below them.

The blood flowed rhythmically from the wound. With the knight's coaching, Jason ripped some cloth from the knight's tunic and pressed it against the wound. He hadn't seen so much blood since what had happened with his sister.

"Press harder," the knight said. "Good. Now tie it. Yes, like that. Well done, Wu Song."

Baileya loosed a bolt at the first Scim to show his head, and all fell quiet again.

"Next they will overwhelm us with numbers," the knight said. "No doubt they grow restless at the thought of dawn's approach."

The next wave of Scim came in a vicious, angry mob. Baileya dropped one with a bolt, and the knight stood behind her, trying as best as he was able to keep them from passing him on the stairs. Jason reached for his mace only to realize with some horror that he had left it farther down the stairwell, leaning against the wall. He hadn't really needed it so far and had forgotten to bring it in the excitement of the knight's wound.

One Scim made it past the knight, and Jason kicked it in the teeth as hard as he was able. Baileya didn't notice, but he made a note to tell her later that her "use your feet" advice had worked.

That's when he noticed Delightful Glitter Lady twitching. Or shaking— it was hard to say. "What's wrong, girl? Are you okay?" She seemed to be having some sort of attack. She crooned to him, distressed, then ran down the stairs. "Come back, Dee! It's not safe!"

Then he understood.

The magic had worn off. The magic that made her small.

She grew to a monstrous, full-size rhino just as she squeezed between the legs of a Scim. The newly gigantic rhino smashed the Scim into the ceiling and kept growing. She filled the whole stairway. The stones started to give at her sides. No one would be getting past her. She snorted and cried, pawing at the stairs, eager to burst through the wooden doorframe and fight.

"Quickly," the knight said. "Take me up."

Together Jason and Baileya managed to get him up the stairs. Dee was snorting and shuffling below, the stairway starting to give way. The Scim were shouting and yelling from the other side. It sounded like the sudden appearance of a unicorn had frightened them so badly they were terrified to approach her. Who knew if there were more on the other side?

They passed the shattered mirror, then the garderobe, and came at last into the knight's solar. Fernanda had stacked everything heavy in the room close to the door, ready to form a barricade. The knight looked out the open windows of the tower. "Too many hours still until sunrise," he said to himself. He took Fernanda's hands, pulling them away from studying the dressings on his wound. "My lady, I must ask you a hard favor." He placed the Memory Stone in her hand.

"No!" she said. "It is too cruel. I have hours of freedom still."

The knight took the Mask of Passing from Baileya. "It is cruel, lady. And yet . . . only you can enter the mirrors. Come daylight the stone and mask will reappear in the world, and none will be able to take them from my hand. It will be some small victory tonight."

"What?" Jason stared at him, completely mystified. "Why didn't you send all of the artifacts into the mirror in the first place, then? And I thought magic didn't work right now?"

"I do not know for certain what daylight will bring," the knight said. "Perhaps the Scim will rule Far Seeing. In which case, the farther away the artifacts, the better." He paused. "And the magic that lets her enter the mirrors is not of the Elenil . . . unlike the magic that has trapped her there."

Jason picked up the Mask of Passing. "We can still get out of here," he said.

"The bird is gone," the knight said. "It won't return. There is no rope long enough, no weapon powerful enough, to remove us from this tower now."

Jason listened, his finger on his chin. "True. But you know what I always say? Poop has to go somewhere."

Baileya understood first. "No," she said. "It is too long of a drop."

"Into water," he said.

Baileya shivered. "I would not call it water."

"They will hear the splash," the knight said.

"They will be waiting for you at the lip of the moat," Fernanda said.

A chorus of shouts came from below, as well as the trumpeting of an enraged rhinoceros. Sounded like she was winning.

"I don't think they'll hear us," Jason said. Celebratory battle cries, followed by surprised shrieks of terror, drifted up the stairs. "I don't think we have much time."

Fernanda picked up the stone. She kissed the knight. "Until next year, my beloved." She walked to a mirror. She looked over her shoulder once, then stepped into the mirror, the knight running up behind her and pressing his hands flat against the glass. She put her hands on the glass too.

"Quickly," the knight said to Jason. "Head for the garderobe."

"What will you do?"

"I? I will make the Scim believe there are a hundred of us fighting them."

In the garderobe, Jason moved the stool and sat with his legs in the hole. It was a long fall to the moat. "Hurry," Baileya said. "So the knight can retreat to his solar and block the doorway." Jason had to wiggle a bit to get himself moving through, and he didn't want to think what he might be touching or about to touch in the sewage of the moat. Then he wasn't thinking anything at all but how fast and far he was falling, and he hoped he survived so he could avoid being murdered by all the Scim.

The water closed over his head, surprisingly warm. He made the dire mistake of opening his eyes, but in that darkness and the cloudy moat water, he couldn't see much. He surfaced and headed for the side of the moat.

Baileya splashed down near him. They pulled themselves from the water, and they both crouched low. Scim were everywhere . . . fighting, shouting, pulling the city apart.

Baileya checked the mask. She still had it. "Come, Wu Song. Stick to the shadows, and we may yet escape."

"I forgot my weapon," Jason said lamely.

Baileya squeezed his shoulder. "You also made our escape from Westwind possible. Fear not. We will avoid the fighting if we can."

They darted into an alley. Baileya said, "If something happens to me, Wu Song, you must keep this mask out of the hands of the Scim. Go to my people, the Kakri. If they do not kill you, then you will be safe."

If they don't kill me, I'll be safe, Jason thought. What a laugh. That nicely summed up his entire time in the Sunlit Lands so far. *If they don't kill you, you will be safe.*

He ducked low and followed Baileya across a shadowed street, his sneakers squeaking with water. They ran for the eastern gates of Far Seeing.

29

CAPTURED

Thou Scim I banish to outer darkness,
a land as black as thy heart.

FROM "THE ORDERING OF THE WORLD," AN ELENIL STORY

✦

Madeline woke lying on her belly. She couldn't move. Leather straps held her tight against a saddle of some kind. The wind was in her face, and she wondered if she had imagined falling. Had Shula tied her onto the saddle to keep her safe as they flew to Pastisia? "Shula?" she asked, but her voice swept away, drowned out by the wind.

A harsh, guttural voice answered. "I didn't kill her. I left her stranded beside the river."

She tried to lift her head and couldn't. Her breath came in such limited doses. She tried to remember what had happened. She had fallen from their bird, fallen through darkness. The bird must have been making its way down already. She had fallen into water—the voice had mentioned a river. She couldn't breathe. She had a vague memory of someone taking hold of her . . . She thought hard. Her neck? Yes, her neck ached still where she had been grabbed. They had taken hold of her neck and pulled her from the river. Someone with gloves and big hands.

She forced her eyes open and managed to lift her head. She was strapped to a giant bird. Its rider's white robes snapped and flowed around him like a flag. The black antelope skull gleamed in the starlight. He turned his head slightly, and the horns of his mask looked sharp even in this darkness. "It will be dawn soon. You will breathe easier then."

No.

"How did you . . ." But she couldn't get enough breath for the question. She coughed.

"I saw you leave from the knight's castle. I followed. I couldn't see you in the darkness, but my owl saw you easily enough. When you fell from your bird, I fished you out of the river."

"What do . . . you want?"

The Black Skull patted a canvas-wrapped parcel strapped beside him. The Sword of Years. "You are needed in the Wasted Lands. I don't know which of the other artifacts may have been recovered."

Madeline's heart sank. If they'd captured her when she had escaped the city, what were the chances the others had made it out at all? No doubt the Scim had already collected all their artifacts and were returning to their homeland now. The knight was right to worry that the Court of Far Seeing might fall.

She couldn't move her upper arms, but her forearms could still pivot. She studied the saddle, trying to see if there was something she could reach. The Black Skull was too far away. The Sword of Years couldn't be reached, either. There was a small saddle pouch near her left arm. She stretched for it. With the tips of her fingers she managed to get it open. The Black Skull didn't look back at her, didn't seem to notice.

Inside, she found a knife. It was smaller than a butcher knife but big enough to do some damage. Sharp, with a wooden handle. She tested it on the leather band around her arms. It was an awkward angle for her arms, but the band fell away easily once she got her blade on it. There was another band over her back and shoulders and one over her thighs, a fourth on her lower legs. Apparently the Black Skull believed in strapping in before flight.

She couldn't reach the Skull, not yet. Then another thought came to her. She could see the edge of the bird's saddle. What if it had a strap?

She had seen the Black Skulls in battle and knew they shrugged off even mortal wounds. A simple gash from a knife would do nothing more than annoy him. If she could cut the saddle loose, though . . . At least it would slow their progress toward the Scim homeland and give her a chance to escape. The band holding the saddle to the owl was thick. It didn't immediately give way when she found it with her knife. Her breathing came in uneven gasps, slowing her progress. She was sweating profusely and trying to keep an eye on her captor.

She was halfway through the strap when he saw her.

"What are you doing? We'll fall." The grotesque voice of the thing sounded almost panicked. The owl descended immediately, headed for the desert floor. The sun was almost here. Madeline could see the ground. She cut faster. She was still held tight by multiple straps. The one over her thighs and the one on her shoulder she was able to cut with relative ease, but she couldn't reach where it crossed her ankles, not without sitting up or moving, something she was afraid to do while the owl was still so far above the ground.

When the owl touched down, Madeline sliced the last remaining fraction of the saddle band, then cut the strap holding her ankles. She slid off, out of control, landing on her back in the sand. The Black Skull jumped from the bird, landing on his feet and facing her.

"Give me the sword!" Madeline shouted, lungs aching, the knife held toward the Black Skull. Her hand shook with adrenaline.

He stood before her in his white robes, his black gloves held up in supplication, his horrible horned head facing her. "That can't hurt me."

"Come closer and . . . we'll find . . . out."

The Black Skull reached up and put his hands on his mask. "Madeline."

His voice sounded rough and deep, but something about the way he said her name was almost familiar.

The Black Skull pulled off his mask. It came away as a complete whole, more helmet than mask. He set it aside in the sand. She couldn't breathe. She struggled to keep upright in the sand, to keep the blade pointed at him, but she wasn't sure she could do it. Consciousness was shrinking down, pushed to a small pinpoint with blurred nothingness pressing in on the edges.

"Look at me," he said. "Maddie, look."

She knew that voice.

She focused, or tried to. He had stepped closer. She spat a warning at him, swinging the knife wildly. He said her name again, crouched down in front of her. Her vision cleared, and she saw him—saw the face of the man who wore the Black Skull.

"Darius?"

"Hey," he said with a gentle smile. She knew that smile. This was her boyfriend. He wasn't a hallucination or a shape-shifter. It wasn't magic. It was him—she knew it with an immediate certainty.

Her heart beat faster, her chest hurt, she took a deep breath, tried to speak, passed out.

She came back to consciousness with an enormous, gulping, chest-expanding breath of deep air. Oxygen flooded her body, making her light headed and giddy. Her left wrist felt like it had been burned, and the sensation spread like liquid flame up her arm, over her shoulder, down her back, onto the bicep of her right arm. It throbbed a few times, then lessened. She scrambled to her feet, stumbling away from Darius.

He sat on a small folding stool made of a wooden frame with a piece of canvas stretched over it. He gestured to a second one beside him. "Sunrise," he said. "Your magic just came back."

She put her hand on her chest and took two deep breaths, forcing air through her nostrils. The scent of cool water and the faint perfume of desert flowers permeated the air.

"We've had a misunderstanding," Darius said.

"You stole my sword!" she shouted.

"It's beside you. I returned it while you slept."

Slept? While she was unconscious, he meant. But there it was, still wrapped in canvas. She pulled the rope off and inspected the sword. "How did you get here? Why are you fighting for the Scim?"

He didn't move from his stool. He watched her carefully, as if she were a wild animal and he wasn't sure what she would do. "When you and Jason disappeared into that pipe, I went crazy. I had to find you. Your parents . . . Madeline, your parents went insane. They thought maybe I had done something to you. They said maybe . . . Well, they said they thought I might have helped you commit suicide."

"WHAT?"

He made calming gestures with his hands. "They were upset. You'd been missing for months, Mads."

"For months? What are you talking about?"

"Time . . . time works strangely in the Sunlit Lands. A day here might be a few months at home. Or a century here could be four weeks there."

Madeline let that sink in before she spoke. That meant . . . a human year could be a millennium in the Sunlit Lands. Or a few weeks. "That makes no sense—is time faster or slower here?"

"Neither. Both. It's magic, Maddie. It's the weirdest thing. I came here months after you. Six months after you."

"Six? Darius, I haven't even been here two months."

"Two months in the Sunlit Lands. Six back home. And get this, Mads. I arrived before you."

"What do you mean?"

"I mean, I left six months after you, and I've been in the Sunlit Lands for a year and a half looking for you."

Madeline took another deep breath, running that through her head. "Okay. It's magic, so it doesn't make complete sense. It's not like science."

He shook his head. "Different rules. Right."

"What did Jason's parents say when the police talked with them?"

Darius threw his hands up. "Weirdest thing. They said he wasn't missing. Said he was in China visiting relatives, that they had picked him up from the hospital and taken him straight to the airport."

"Did the police believe them?"

Darius shrugged. "They didn't arrest them or anything, so I guess so. His dad acted like I wasn't in the room the one time I saw him."

Wow. Jason had said his dad hated him, but that was really strange. "So . . . how did you get here?"

"You had been gone six months. I was reading fantasy novels, trying to figure out if there was some clue, some piece of reality between the lines. Every day I hung out by that pipe where you and Jason disappeared. I had gone through Lewis and L'Engle and was almost done rereading the Meselia books. I had just started *The Azure World*, and I kept coming back to those first three chapters—"

Madeline interrupted. "The part where Okuz gathers the adventurers from across space and time."

"Right. I kept wondering, what if one of these is real? Something about the story of Karu stuck with me."

Madeline smiled despite herself. Karu had always been one of Darius's favorite characters in the Meselia books. He only appeared in a few of the books, but he was a charming adventurer who always saw the positive side of things. "Karu notices an owl in the middle of the day, blinded by sunlight, and follows it into the deep woods," Madeline said.

"Right. And I remembered that hummingbird with you and Jason. That day I went back down to the pipe where you had disappeared, and I sat by the fence and read the book. It was Saturday, just about noon, and this possum came walking down the street. All the dogs in the neighborhood howled and barked. Possums aren't usually out during the day. It stopped when it saw me, then turned and walked back the way it had come. So I followed it."

"Did it take you into the pipe?"

"No. Into an empty lot behind the houses. There was this weird dome of—I don't know how to say it—a dome of darkness. About the size of a one-person tent. The possum went into it and didn't come out. I waited for about ten minutes, then I followed." He shifted in his chair and looked off to the side. She recognized that look . . . He wasn't telling her everything. "I ended up in the Wasted Lands with the Scim. I told them I was looking for you, that the Elenil had kidnapped you . . . and they agreed to help me rescue you."

"*Rescue* me?"

"From the Elenil. Right. I became a Black Skull. Using Scim magic, I can go into battle and never be harmed, so long as I keep my helmet on. I spearheaded the new campaign against those monsters."

She crossed over to him. "Darius, you don't understand. The Elenil aren't monsters . . . they *saved* me. Their magic is why I can breathe. You've been to Far Seeing. You've seen who they are. The city is beautiful . . . It's amazing."

"Yes," Darius said, his face still as a stone. "Meanwhile everything in the

Scim territories is broken, rotting, and falling apart. It's abject poverty and ruin. And while Far Seeing has sunlight all day, every day, the Wasted Lands have night. The brightness of their day is a weak twilight. Their brightness and Far Seeing's darkness are the same. Do you see?"

She grabbed his hands. She couldn't understand how he had gone so wrong, how he had been twisted so badly. "Darius, listen to me. The Scim are *evil*. They want to destroy the Elenil. I've heard them say it themselves—they want to bring a thousand years of darkness to Far Seeing, they want to break bones and murder people. You were there tonight, you saw it!" She fell back from him, sudden realization coming to her. "You were part of it. You were part of the attack on Far Seeing."

Darius stood, anger flashing across his face. "How did they get utopia, Mads? Who paid for it? The Scim, that's who. The center of their magic, what is it called? Do you know?"

"The Heart of the Scim."

"Yes. If they want sunlight, they take it . . . from the Scim. If they want to construct a building faster, that can be accomplished by magic . . . so long as a Scim building goes up slower. If they need rain for their crops, the Scim get drought. If they need to get rid of their waste, their garbage, their sewage, they just have to find a place to put it. Why not the Wasted Lands?"

"All their magic," Madeline said. "All their wealth, their power. What are you saying?"

"Stolen, Madeline. Stolen! Is that so hard to understand, so hard to believe?" He rubbed his hands over his eyes. "Maybe it is. You've been their prisoner so long, been hearing their propaganda, of course you believe it."

Madeline's own anger flared up. "I wasn't a prisoner!"

His face softened, and he reached up with his hands, as if to put them on her shoulders. "Madeline. Were you allowed to leave the city?"

"Yes, I—" She thought of the knight. Hadn't he specifically said they weren't to leave the city? "Not without a chaperone," she said.

"Chaperone? Or guard?" Madeline didn't answer, so Darius went on: "Did they want to make sure you heard their side of things? Did they have some sort of class or book you had to read or something like that? Something that told you all about how the Elenil are the chosen ones who are meant to rule the Sunlit Lands?"

She thought of the woman in the ivy. The storyteller. "Something like that," she said.

"Did they make you take an oath of loyalty? Threaten to take away the magic if you didn't obey them?"

Yes. They had done both those things, and she had scarcely noticed. She bit her lip, willing herself not to cry. She felt the world tipping. "Darius. They gave me back my breath. I'm *alive*."

Tears welled up in Darius's eyes, and he spread his arms wide. She melted into his hug. "I know," he said. "I'm so sorry. I know."

He held her for a long time.

A sudden thought occurred to her, and she pushed him away. "Are you the one who kidnapped Shula?"

"Yes," he said. "I would have done worse things if I thought it would get me to you."

"You almost *killed Jason*," she said.

"I never—" he said. "Wait. The kid in the white armor?"

The kid in the white armor. Her hands balled into fists, and she pounded on his chest. "You didn't know it was him? Is that what you're trying to say? How does that make it any better, that you thought you were killing a stranger?"

Darius stepped away from her, the hurt clear on his face. "Do you remember in—which one was it—*The Gold Firethorns*, I think. Do you remember when Lily betrayed the Eagle King?"

Yes, of course she remembered. Lily, deceived by Kotuluk, thought her friends could only survive the flames of the firethorns if she turned her back on the Eagle King. She couldn't tell them what she was doing, or the magical agreement keeping them safe would be violated. Terrible consequences came as a result, and Lily was banished from Meselia. But her friends were safe, and as she left Meselia for the last time, she said she had no regrets. "I remember," Madeline said.

"Everything I've done has been for your protection," Darius said. "Or to protect the Scim. If that means I'll be punished, so be it. But I did it all with good intentions, just like Lily."

She knew that. She knew it before he said it. It didn't make her happy about things, but she knew he had a good heart. She crossed her arms. "Okay. Explain it to me, Darius. Help me understand."

He held his hand out to her, but she didn't take it. He nodded, put his hand back at his side. "I'd like to show you something," he said at last. "You should know both sides of the story before you make a decision. I won't take the sword away from you. If you want to go back to the Elenil, I'll take you myself. You can return the sword, stay with them, do whatever you want."

She looked him in the eyes. He was telling the truth. "And you'll go with me?"

His face hardened. "I'll take you wherever you want to go." He didn't say he would go with her, though. She knew him well enough to know that he wasn't making that part of the promise.

"Okay," she said. "Show me."

He stowed the stools and the sword on the saddle. He had repaired it while she was unconscious. He mounted and she slipped on behind him. "I have to wear my helmet," he said. "So I can fly the owl."

"Okay."

He settled the helmet on his head, his horns sharp and silhouetted against the risen sun. She wrapped her arms around his body and turned her face to lay it against his back. He ordered the bird to fly, in the fearsome, guttural voice of the Black Skull. They lifted into the air and headed toward the dark night of the Wasted Lands.

30
THE STORM

The desert claims the land, and so we,
we must claim the desert.

FROM "THE DESERTED CITY," A KAKRI LAMENT

✦

Faster, Jason." It was a mantra Baileya repeated endlessly. His legs felt like bags filled with sand, which for all he knew they now were. All he could see in any direction was sand. Sand dunes ahead. Sand dunes to the left and right. Behind them, the other sand dunes they had passed and, sometimes, the sand clouds created by their Scim pursuers.

They had lost the Scim for almost nine hours in the Tolmin Pass. Baileya knew a shortcut that required confronting an eleven-foot-tall knight with glowing eyes and a scary sword made of flaming night. Apparently she had some sort of deal going with him, though, because she said she had already paid her toll, and he let them through. The monster knight wasn't so sure about Jason, but Baileya convinced him that Jason was part of the deal.

Jason didn't know if the Scim went around or through the scary toll road, but it didn't take them long to get on his and Baileya's trail again. He wondered aloud how the Scim were surviving. Baileya knew every trick. Certain plants hoarded water in the mornings. She poured it along the leaves and into their mouths. She had hollowed a gourd for a canteen and saved some water for the evening. She made a sweet mashed food out of a certain cactus. It had tubers that grew among the roots, which she smashed and mixed sparingly with water. It had the consistency of paste, but the taste had grown on him. He was still getting his daily delivery of pudding too. He shared it with Baileya, and she seemed genuinely impressed by his ability to find a new cup of "this food you call pudding" every morning.

She warned him of the various dangers of the deserts. Sandstorms, naturally. Most of the nasty desert animals you could think of from Earth. Plus something called a ghul that changed shapes to look like your friends and then ate you. And something that sounded like a hyena, sort of, except she said it was "as smart as a woman." He wasn't sure if that meant smarter than a man or not, but he knew not to ask. Either way, it was a hyena that was smarter than a hyena. He was glad to hear it didn't have opposable thumbs, but she said it would lay clever traps and had to be avoided.

The Kharobem, too, should be avoided—a strange, magical race of creatures who changed shapes ("a common power for desert folk," Baileya said) and were known for interceding in the business of the people of the Sunlit Lands. Massively powerful, with a magic more formidable than any other, they could settle a dispute between warring peoples in a few minutes. They rarely intervened, but when they did, it was the stuff of legend. The last time had been hundreds of years ago, when they had destroyed a Kakri city called Ezerbin.

"Why is their magic so powerful?" Jason asked.

"The Kakri trade in story," Baileya said. "It is the foundation of our economy. Do you understand? It is like money for us. The Kharobem are *made* of story."

Jason snorted. "Okay. Thanks for clearing that up."

"They are world shapers. They alter things in a way no other magic can. They tell the world the way it should be, and it is."

Jason's tongue felt thick. They hadn't stopped for a drink in hours. The sun squeezed the sweat out of him. "Still, that's not the same as being made of story. That's like, I don't know, word magic or something."

"Faster, Jason," Baileya said, and for a while he didn't speak at all. Keeping up with her exhausted him, and she was going slow for him. He would be embarrassed by how easily she outpaced him if not for the fact that he wasn't sure any person he knew would be able to keep up with her. She seemed to be on a casual holiday stroll while he was doing the most strenuous march of his life.

Sometimes she would stand beside him and mark out a certain land-mark. A thorny tree, maybe. She would tell him to walk to it as quickly as he could, and then, if she wasn't back, he could rest until she returned. She would disappear then, for spans of time as long as twenty minutes. He would stand beneath the thorn tree (or lie in the narrow shade of a boulder or rest at the bottom of a dune), sweat rolling from his face, his tongue thick and dry, waiting for her to return. When she did, she would say, "Quickly, Jason." They would set off again, sometimes in the same direc-tion, sometimes in another. She never explained why she made the choices she did, but he accepted them with mute appreciation.

This time she left him in the shade of a rock jutting up from the desert floor. It angled toward the horizon in a way that let him sit beneath the overhang in the relative coolness of the shade. Baileya disappeared, telling him to be silent and conserve his strength. She would return in time.

Drowsy from the heat and exhausted from walking, he fell asleep in the shade of the stone.

"—somewhere near here," a guttural voice said.

"Climb up on the rock there," another replied. Jason shook himself awake. Those were Scim voices.

"So the Kakri woman can fill me with arrows? Do it yourself."

The second Scim grunted. "The Kakri are fearsome, but the boy . . . How could he have killed Night's Breath? Did you see him with the bow upon the walls of Westwind?"

They both chortled.

Apparently everyone had seen Jason's spectacular failure. More concern-ing was that the Scim—at least two of them—stood on the opposite side of this rock. He wished he had somehow walked faster all those times Baileya had told him to do so. He had to hope these two wouldn't want a break in the shade. What should he do? Make a run for it? He didn't think he'd have much of a chance. Maybe he could bury himself in the sand if he did it slowly so it didn't make too much sound.

"This accursed sun," one of the voices said. "Oh, for the cool embrace of night."

"I can barely speak, my throat is so parched."

"Could we sit in the shade of this stone, even for a few moments?"

"But if one of the war chiefs finds out—"

"I will not speak of it."

"Nor I. But how far behind is the rest of the war party?"

There was a pause. No doubt they were looking back, trying to judge the distance. Jason began to carefully pile sand in his lap. He didn't think he would get himself buried in time, but he had to try something.

The Scim came around the stone, still speaking to one another, and stopped, still as statues, when they saw Jason sitting in the shade. He sat up straight, doing his best to look like he had known they were coming and had been waiting for them. "Hello," he said.

The great shambling soldiers looked at one another, uncertain what to do. One had his hand on the handle of his ax, the other stood with his mouth wide open.

Jason almost laughed. "When someone says hello, it's polite to say hello back."

"Ehhhhhhh," said one of the Scim. "Hello?"

Jason smiled broadly. "That's better. Now. If you don't mind being a little crowded, all three of us should be able to fit in the shade of this rock."

"We have captured him," one of the Scim said. Jason decided he would call him Fluffy, because his thick black hair was in a braid that had come loose, giving him a fluffy halo.

"Not true," Jason said.

The second Scim (Jaws, Jason decided, because of how far his jaw had fallen open upon finding Jason sitting serenely under the rock) said, "It is true. You have no weapon. We are heavily armed. We will be joined by our army in a few minutes' time."

"Then we might as well sit in the shade and wait," Jason said.

Fluffy gave him a sour frown. "We will not sit with the murderer of Night's Breath."

Jaws said, nearly in the same moment, "It is a trap."

"A trap?" Jason laughed. "How could an invitation to sit in the shade be a trap?"

"If we could see how it worked," Jaws said, "it would not be a trap, would it?"

Jason acknowledged his point, while racing through a plan to get himself out of this mess. He might be able to hold these two off, but he couldn't expect the whole Scim army to stand in the sunshine for fear of a non-existent trap.

"You are too clever for me," Jason admitted. He turned away from them, and when they could just barely see his face, he smirked.

"Wait," Fluffy cried. "I saw the look on your face!"

Jaws said, "Tell us, have we stumbled into your trap already?"

"There is no trap," Jason said truthfully.

Jaws pointed at him accusingly. "Precisely what someone would say if they had set a trap!"

Baileya descended on them from the top of the rock, twisting her body so that each of her feet connected with one of their jaws. They fell backward, and she snatched the ax from Fluffy's belt, flinging it toward Jason. "Catch!" she cried.

He barely avoided getting brained with the ax. He grabbed the handle and tried to lift it, but he could scarcely get it up to his shoulder. Baileya had her staff in two pieces, and she whirled like a desert wind, meeting Jaws's blade and keeping Fluffy at bay. Unable to do anything else constructive, Jason dug a hole and buried the ax.

Distracted by Jaws's sword, Baileya didn't see Fluffy reach for her hand, crushing it. She cried out and dropped half of her staff. She tried to wrench away from Fluffy, but he held her hand fast, making it nearly impossible for her to parry Jaws's blows. Jason scrambled to them, snatched up the fallen half of the staff, and drove the bladed end into Fluffy's knee.

Fluffy yowled and released Baileya, who brought the haft of her staff up into Jaws's face, hitting him hard enough to knock him, stunned, to the ground. She yanked the other half of her staff from Fluffy's knee and said, "Quickly, Jason!"

"Sorry about your knee, Fluffy!" Jason called as they scrambled over a dune.

"My name is not Fluffy!" the Scim warrior roared.

Baileya made him run for almost thirty minutes. Finally she let him collapse at the top of a dune, the sun burning his face. She crouched, facing the direction they had come. "They are craftier than I supposed. The larger part of their forces was closer than I knew, while they left another small group behind to kick up dust, so we would think them in the distance. That was a close moment, indeed."

"Thirsty," Jason said.

Baileya stood over him and shielded his face with the sleeve of her flowing shirt. "There is a small oasis near here. I will need to check it first for wylna." Those were the hyena things. Wylna. Jason thought he could fight off a pack of hyenas to get a drink of water. "First," Baileya said, "I need you to bind my hand. I fear it is broken."

Jason sat up immediately and gingerly took her wrist in his hand. A nasty bruise spread beneath her golden-tan skin. The fingers were swollen, the center of her hand like a balloon. With her good hand she unwrapped a long piece of cloth from around her waist. It held her loose garment close against her body. She tore a strip of it with the blade of her staff and handed it to Jason. "Bind it tight," she said.

He wound it around her hand.

"Tighter."

He yanked it, hard. He winced. Her face had gone pale. He didn't like to see her in pain, certainly didn't want to be the one causing her pain. But it had to be done.

"Still tighter," she said.

She gritted her teeth, and he pulled as hard as he could. Sweat beaded her face, and she gasped. "Good. Now we find water. Then we run."

He helped her to her feet. She stood, weak with pain for a moment. He gripped both her arms, keeping her steady. He carefully wiped the sweat from her face. Her eyes met his, and her lips parted, but before she could speak, Jason said, "I know, I know, 'Run faster, Jason.'"

She leaned on him while they walked down the dune, but by the time they climbed the next, she had transferred her staff into her wounded hand, flexing her hand and spinning the staff lightly. She sent him up one dune, the wind blowing so it obscured his footprints, and she went in another direction. The Scim were close enough, she said, that it was wise to give them a false trail. He objected, but she assured him her strength had returned. He didn't know how that was possible, but it was true that she looked better. He felt dehydrated, light headed, and exhausted, but she looked like she could run again. She slipped away to make the false trail.

After she rejoined Jason, she pointed out an oasis.

Oasis. The word made him think of a palm tree with coconuts next to a pure stream. This was a muddy puddle. An animal stood beside it, lapping water.

"Is that . . . a lion cub?"

"Perhaps." Baileya squinted her silver eyes. "Not all is what it seems in the desert."

Jason was reminded of her stories about the many creatures of the desert who could change their shapes.

The sand around the water hole quivered. "What's that?"

Baileya froze. So did the lion cub.

A dog-sized creature shook itself free of the sand, its jaws clamping onto the cub's rear leg. The cub cried out in panic, and two more of the creatures leapt out of the sand. They looked like wild dogs with thick, cracked lips and white patches in their sandy fur.

"Wylna," Baileya whispered. "We must go. Quickly, Jason."

"They're going to eat that cub," Jason said.

"Better than eating us."

"Give me your staff," Jason said.

"No," Baileya said. "We will not stop to fight three wylna with a battalion of Scim at our backs."

A faint sound came to them on the wind. "The Scim," he said. "They're nearby."

Baileya listened. The wylna had paused, their pointed ears pricked toward the Scim army. "They're following the fake trail," she said. "We must go now."

Jason had another idea.

He jumped to his feet and shouted as loud as he was able, "Hey, Break Bones, we're over here!"

He ran to the oasis. The wylna crouched down, watching him warily. He ran full speed toward the wylna with its maw latched onto the cub. He aimed a terrific kick at its head, but at the last moment the wylna let go, skittering away and growling at Jason.

The wylna triangulated Jason the moment he stopped moving. No matter how he turned, there was one he couldn't see. "I was a kickball champion in eighth grade," he said. "Get close enough, and I'm gonna send you sailing over the fences like a red rubber ball."

The lion cub slipped away, limping, the wylna distracted by this new, larger prey. Jason kicked toward his blind spot, hoping the third wylna wouldn't get a bite in. He turned in a circle, trying not to let any of them out of his sight for more than a second. "The Scim are gonna come over that hill soon," Jason said. "When they do, we're all going to want to run. But if you want to attack them, I won't complain."

The Scim were shouting some sort of battle march. They were close. The wylna listened, backing up slightly from Jason. The chanting grew louder, and the wylna trotted away, one of them watching Jason over its shoulder. "This way," Baileya hissed. She had crossed to the other side of the oasis. Jason fell to his chest and slurped up three quick gulps of water.

Baileya was already running.

The wind had whipped up. "I outsmarted those dog things!" Jason shouted.

Baileya's eyes flashed. "You are a fool."

That stung. She was one of the only people who had never called him a fool. "At least I'm consistent!" he shouted back. He had saved the lion cub, at least. That was something. The wind whipped past them, kicking up sand.

He heard his name and, looking back, could see the Scim loping behind them. They were much too close, and there were at least twenty of them. An arrow whistled past his ear.

"They are within bow shot," Baileya said. "Run twenty paces ahead, then turn to the left. Run until you find a garden of stone. Climb to the top of the stones and wait for me."

"But what if you don't—"

"Then I will be dead, and you will soon join me." She laughed at the look on his face. "But at least the lion cub lives!"

She spun back, staff in hand, and shouted a high-pitched, ululating war cry. Jason counted out the twenty steps, then turned left and ran full speed.

The sand stung his face. He lifted his hands, trying to shield his eyes. The wind howled, and in the distance he heard the wylna raise an answering howl. Cries and the sound of battle came from behind, and then he couldn't see more than a step or two ahead.

Baileya appeared beside him, took his hand, and corrected his course. The sand lifted for a moment, and he saw the Scim, not far behind. He saw the lion cub between them and the Scim. Or no, it wasn't the lion cub at all, it was a young girl, limping in front of the Scim, as if she could stop them herself. The girl glanced at Jason and smiled.

She held up her arms and shouted something, and a curtain of sand lowered over the Scim, eventually obscuring the girl as well.

In the cover provided by the howling sandstorm, Baileya pulled Jason up a series of solid stones jutting out of the sand. She found a cleft in the rock, pushed him in, and followed after. She loosened her belt—more of a sash, really—carefully unfolding it until it was almost the size of a bedsheet. She lifted it so it kept out the sand, tucking it into the clefts of the rock to form a makeshift tent. They settled side by side, panting, and listened to the static of sand on stone.

31
THE WASTED LANDS

Do not cry in the darkness, but follow the small bright star.

FROM A TRADITIONAL SCIM LULLABY

✦

They flew for a while in sunlight. Madeline loved the blue sky studded with white clouds. She even saw, off to the west, the sparkling expanse of the sea. The Ginian Sea, according to Darius, the home of the Zhanin, the shark people. As they continued southward, she saw an impossibly large forest, with trees as high as thin mountains. She asked Darius about it, but he pointed instead toward the southeast.

"The Wasted Lands," he said in his harsh Skull voice.

It rose up like an angry, dark cloud or a tidal wave. Somehow the sunlight didn't penetrate the column of darkness that towered over that place. Campfires and torches dotted the distant landscape. The owl descended in lazy, looping arcs as they fell toward the northern edge of the blackness. They landed in a strange twilight where bright daylight shone at their backs and full night stood before them.

Darius slid off the owl. He offered Madeline his gloved hand, a motion both familiar coming from Darius and foreign coming from a Black Skull. She took his hand and slipped down. "We will walk a short distance into the darkness," Darius said.

"Can you take that helmet off? I'd rather be with Darius than with a Black Skull."

The horned head tilted for a moment before Darius reached up and removed the helmet. "Of course," he said and took off his gloves, too. "You don't have to cover up now," Darius said. "Only the Elenil require no skin to show."

She pulled her gloves off. "Why did you cover up, then? For the sake of the Elenil?"

Darius grinned. "Scim magic might have protected me from wounds as a Black Skull, but I couldn't get over the idea that I would lose the magic and be standing around with bare arms and no gloves. I wanted protection."

"*Scim* magic?"

Darius nodded. "It's the same as Elenil magic, really. If I'm wounded in battle, a Scim takes the wound. A team of Scim stay back for each Black Skull, and healers work to try to save as many of them as they can. It's a new technique, and one of the few that has given us an upper hand against those monsters." He saw the look on her face, raised his hands, and said, "Against the *Elenil*."

"But why have humans be the Skulls? Why not other Scim? And how is that different than the way the Elenil are using the Scim?"

"It's different because the Scim are in control." He looked her in the eyes. "And it's humans because the Scim insisted I be the first Black Skull. Because the whole thing was my idea."

Madeline, stunned, started to ask him another question, but he shook his head. "We should start moving." He led her into the darkness. After a few minutes, he reached out and took her hand. It felt natural, but she couldn't stop herself from thinking about him being a Black Skull, kidnapping Shula, almost killing Jason. Or even just the fact that she had broken up with him. But she had broken up with him because of her breathing, a problem that had been solved by the Elenil. Or, at least, mostly solved. Despite all those things she still wanted to be with him. He was the only one who had stood by her after she got sick. That Darius and this one were somehow the same man.

The Wasted Lands smelled of garbage and sulfur. They walked along a sickly stream of foul water. Refuse stood in random piles. When Darius took them too close to one pile, a mangy rat bared its teeth and hissed.

Madeline found herself clutching Darius's arm with her free hand. Something about this place felt unsafe. She had felt this way before, in the "bad part of town," only here there was no town . . . just garbage and rats and the occasional stunted bush. Nothing healthy grew here. She shivered. After the temperate warmth of Far Seeing, the cold of the Wasted Lands took her by surprise. Darius noticed and, without asking, unfastened his cloak and spread it over her shoulders. They trudged on through the dark. When she had warmed herself a little, she took his hand again.

"We're here," Darius said gently.

He led her to a broken-down hut made of mud and discarded wood. It was shaped like a half-melted scoop of ice cream. The door stood crooked in the doorway. A window with no glass had been dug out of the space beside the door.

Drifting from the hovel was a woman's voice, singing. "Do not cry in the darkness," she sang, "but follow the small bright star." Madeline wanted to get closer, to see the woman in the hut. Her voice, so clear and bright, was the first beautiful thing in this wasted place. Madeline moved quietly to the window. The woman's silver hair was pulled back from a lined, pleasant face. Black tattoos curled around her wiry arms, and as she sang, she dipped a dirty rag in a bowl of grey water. The only light came from a candle—at least Madeline thought it was a candle—about the size of a softball. A tiny wick stood out of it, and a pungent odor came from it.

The woman dabbed water on a young girl's forehead. The girl, too, had black tattoos covering her arms, as well as her neck and face. She wore a pale-green nightshirt, soaked in sweat and stuck to her stick-thin body.

"Who are they?" Madeline whispered.

Darius leaned against her back, whispering in her ear. "Look at her nightshirt," he said. "Look carefully."

It was a thin material, maybe cotton. A V-neck. It was stained, as though someone had done their best to wash out mud or old, dried blood, or both.

The child broke into severe coughing—coughing so extreme Madeline's hand moved unconsciously to her own chest. The woman lifted the coughing girl's head and shoulders from the bed and held her. She didn't stop singing, even when the child's coughing drowned her out completely. Madeline recognized that sort of coughing. A pang of sympathy pierced her. Madeline knew what it was like to lie in bed perfectly aware there was nothing anyone could do for you.

Confusion washed over her. "Are these . . . Scim?" she asked.

"Yes," Darius said, but he didn't elaborate, didn't explain the answer to her question, which she was sure he must anticipate.

"Why aren't they . . . ?" She stopped herself from asking the question that burned in her mind. It seemed disrespectful. But the fact remained: they didn't have monstrous muscles or wide, frog-like mouths. Their hair was not in greasy knots, and they didn't have tusklike teeth. The best word she could think of to describe them was *graceful*. The mother's hair shone with a lustrous light, and although the daughter was not well, a vibrant aura radiated from her.

"Why aren't they ugly?" Darius asked, no hint of warmth in his voice.

Madeline's ears went hot. It was her question, yes, but the way he said it only reinforced how ugly the question itself was. "They don't look like any Scim I've ever seen."

"What you've seen," Darius said, "is their war skin. Before going to battle they transform themselves to intimidate, to cause fear, to make it clear they shouldn't be messed with. You've never seen a Scim before, not really. You've seen a people at war, not the people themselves."

Living in this terrible, corrupted place . . . Madeline was amazed these people could show any sign of weakness, ever. A moment of vulnerability, a minute of dropping their guard, could be the difference between life and death. She didn't know them, not at all. Yet she had signed away a year of her life to fight them . . . to destroy them. "I want to meet them," Madeline said.

"That's not a good idea," Darius said.

Madeline turned on him, whispering fiercely, "I thought your whole point was that I didn't know them. So let me learn."

Darius deflated. "At least let me put my helmet on."

Madeline crossed her arms. "Why?"

"So they know my position. So they know you're with me."

She didn't understand what that meant. "Fine."

Once the helmet settled on his head, they stood together in front of the broken wooden door. Darius rapped on it and called out in his altered voice, "Open!"

"Who is there?"

"A Black Skull and his honored guest."

The door flew open. A man stood before them, thin but strong. He glanced at the skull, following the long line of the horns with his eyes before bowing his head. "Sir," he said, "please sit and sup with us."

The Black Skull bowed his head so he could enter the low-ceilinged hovel. He sat at a short table near a makeshift hearth. A small kettle hung over the fire. The girl did not turn to look at them. She stared, her eyes half-lidded, at the dirt ceiling. The mother hurried to Madeline, guiding her to the table. She took Madeline's hand to seat her. Something startled the woman, and she gasped.

"What is it?" Madeline asked.

"N-n-nothing, miss." She poured a small portion of gruel from the pot and set it in front of Madeline. A second portion went to the Black Skull. A third to her husband.

"Sit and eat with us," Madeline said.

The woman blushed. "There are but three bowls."

Madeline said to Darius, "Do you have a bowl, or a cup, on the owl?"

The Black Skull stared at her, unmoving. The woman said not to bother themselves, and her husband's face turned red too. Darius, his voice rough, said, "This is all their food, Madeline. Do not embarrass them further."

Now Madeline blushed. She held the bowl up to the woman. "Please. I'm not hungry."

The woman's dark eyes widened as if she had never heard such a thing. Darius put his hand on hers. "Eat, Madeline."

His voice carried the unmistakable tone of someone correcting a child. She had been rude somehow. Maybe in this culture you couldn't refuse food. She lifted the bowl to her lips. She had been among the Elenil long enough that this seemed a strange intimacy, to eat with her hands uncovered. The simple gruel warmed her as she sipped from it. As she tipped the bowl away from her face she noticed that the network of tattoos had moved onto her right hand now. It seemed to be moving faster, like ivy covering a tree.

The girl coughed and called for her mother. The mother stayed near her guests, hovering beside them. "Go to your child," the Black Skull said. "We will call if we have needs."

The woman bowed her head in a curt, thankful nod and rushed to her daughter's side, scooping her up in her arms. Madeline watched, her heart breaking for the poor girl. "Can we help?" Madeline asked. "Does she need medicine?"

The Scim man looked to the Black Skull, seeming embarrassed. When the Black Skull didn't speak, he turned again to Madeline and said, "Medicine will not help her."

"What is her name?" Madeline asked.

"She is called Yenil. Her mother is Fera. I am Inrif."

"I'm Madeline."

"We know you, Madeline Oliver." Inrif looked down at his bowl. He had not taken even a sip. "You are our benefactor."

"Your benefactor?"

"Yes. We are honored to have you in our home."

What was he talking about? She looked more carefully around their hut. There were a few clean rags, like the kind the Elenil used instead of toilet paper. Some clothes were hung near a small window. There was only the one narrow bed. Inrif and Fera must sleep beside the fire, she decided.

Yenil coughed harder, hacking. Her mother cried out and bit her own knuckle. Madeline couldn't take it any longer. She swept across to the girl and propped her up. "Sometimes sitting up helps with the breathing," she said. "It lets the lungs expand."

Yenil said, "Thank . . . you . . . miss."

This close to her, Madeline could see the green nightshirt better on the small girl. In fact, it looked surprisingly like hospital scrubs. But how would they get those, here in the Sunlit Lands?

Or, she corrected herself, here in the Wasted Lands?

Unless.

No.

The scrubs were too large for Yenil.

No, no.

Madeline saw the swirling black tattoos on Yenil's left arm. She saw the way they branched up her arm and crept across her clavicle. They came out again on her right arm, nearly to her wrist. Oh no.

Madeline put her left arm alongside Yenil's. The patterns and whorls matched. Precisely. Every leaf, every branch.

Yenil's breathing grew faster, shallow and erratic. She coughed, trying to get a breath. A tendril of black tattoo crept up from her right hand, encircling her pinky. Madeline held up her own right hand. Her silver tattoo curled around her pinky too.

A rush of understanding coursed through her.

"No," she whispered.

The nightshirt . . . It was a pair of scrubs. Her scrubs. The ones she had thrown away once she made it to the Sunlit Lands. Somehow they had come here, to this family. The cough—that racking, awful cough—that was hers too. It all fell into place with a terrible, grinding finality. She could breathe. She could run and jump and sing and shout and dance, and all it cost was a year of service to the Elenil.

Or so she thought.

She knew—she knew!—that the magic of the Sunlit Lands worked by taking something from one person and giving it to another. Jason received the skills and abilities of a warrior by taking them from someone else. He took the skills of an archer from a true archer, and during that time the Elenil archer could no more fire an arrow than Jason had been able to from the top of Westwind.

Which meant her breath . . . Of course. She hadn't stopped to think about it, hadn't spent a single moment considering that maybe for her to breathe someone else would not be able to. Her heart clenched in her chest. She felt dizzy and nauseated. She had to get out of this place. The walls were too close, the fire too warm, the smoke in the air too thick. How could they keep Yenil in here? Wasn't it obvious it wasn't a good situation for her? A furious anger rose in her chest.

Tears burst from her eyes, and she ran from the hut. She didn't know where she was going, didn't look at the ground, she just ran and ran and felt the breath filling her lungs. A sob tore from her, and even that wasn't her own, it was borrowed from Yenil. Stolen from a child.

She fell on the ground, sobbing.

What would she do?

Deep, racking sobs shook her body.

"M-M-Madeline?"

A hand rested lightly on her shoulder. Madeline wiped at the tears on her face. It was Fera, the girl's mother.

"It is for the best," she said, "you being our benefactor."

Madeline stared at the pulsing silver tattoo on her arm. She wanted to rip it off. The bracelet if she could, her whole arm if she couldn't. "I'm going to destroy it," she said.

Fera gasped. "No!"

Madeline couldn't believe it. Why would Yenil's mother argue against getting her daughter back? "Your daughter can't breathe."

Fera turned her face away, as if ashamed. "The Elenil pay us. Every month. So that Yenil will continue to share her breath with you. We agreed to the terms so that we can feed her and ourselves."

"How could you do that?" Madeline said.

"They also send us the things you discard. We are . . ." Fera struggled for the right words. "Our neighbors are jealous."

Madeline snatched a rock and began to beat it against her wrist where the bracelet lay beneath her skin. Fera covered Madeline's arm with her own and cried, "No! Please, no!"

"She'll die," Madeline said.

Fera's face set into stone. "Without this we will have no food. Yenil will die anyway. Then I. Then her father."

"How can you do this?" Madeline asked. "She's your *daughter*. Don't you understand?"

"It is you who do not understand. Yenil has made her choice. It is I who lie beside her in the night and wipe the sweat from her face. I who bore her, who rubs her back as she sends her breath to the sunlit corners where you live." A fierce anger came into her eyes. "It is I who holds her while you run. While you jump or dance and Yenil's breath comes harder and harder. It is I who cradles her body and weeps while you sing with your friends."

Madeline burst into tears again. "I didn't know. I didn't know the cost."

Fera studied her. "You did not know because you did not think to ask. You did not wonder what the cost of this magic would be, to yourself or others. But such is the way of those who have never paid for much."

Fera stood and walked, her back straight, to the horrible dilapidated hovel she called home, leaving Madeline to weep in the darkness.

32

THE MEETING
OF THE SPHERES

✛

When the storm passed, Baileya climbed from the cleft of the rock and disappeared for over an hour, checking the surrounding area for the Scim army. "I can find no sign of them," she said. "I do not think they will find us again."

The sunset painted the desert. Baileya led Jason down from the stones they had hidden in. "It is the night of the third and fourth spheres' meeting," she said. "It is a festival among my people. I hoped we would make it in time. Turn and look."

The rocks they had hidden among were not stones at all but the remnants of an ancient city. Broken towers and fallen walls protruded from the shifting sands. A statue of a Kakri couple stood above them. The woman's right arm encircled the man, and her left arm was raised to the sky. Or Jason assumed that's what it would be doing—it had broken long ago. A series of fountains remained, all filled with sand rather than water.

"What is this place?" Jason asked.

"It was called Ezerbin. Once it was the greatest city in the world. The Court of Far Seeing is a pale shadow of Ezerbin's glory."

"In the middle of the desert?"

"It was no desert then. Canals crossed the city. Fountains, irrigated fields. There were cisterns, too, yes, but mostly the water was plenteous."

Jason could barely imagine. The place looked like dried bones stacked in the sun. "What happened?"

"The city grew vile. The people oppressed their neighbors. In time they became horrible, filled with lies. The Kharobem came. They encircled the city and pronounced there would be no more water. The rain stopped. The river dried up. The people of the city had to leave or die. It is said a crow came to my ancestor and taught her to live in this new land, the desert. Others in the city denied this offer, for it was too much to humble themselves to a bird. They could not learn from such a lowly creature. But my ancestor believed it was no shame to walk with crows. So were born the Kakri, the ones who left the city and embraced the desert as our home."

Jason's mouth fell open. He had assumed the Kakri were some sort of nomadic tribal people, and maybe they were. But Baileya was telling him that they had once built the greatest city in the Sunlit Lands. "Whoa," Jason said. "Are they planning to rebuild it one day?"

Baileya leaned on her staff. "In the desert there is no room for a lie, Jason. You must walk either with truth or with death. The truth tells us that we cannot rebuild unless the water returns. It is not the choice of the Kakri people whether to rebuild. We must allow the Kharobem to tell us if such a time returns. In the meantime, every year at the meeting of the third and fourth spheres, my people congregate here and sing about the fall of old Ezerbin and tell stories." They rested in the shade of the fallen wall, and Baileya showed him where the Kakri would gather, near the statue.

Night settled in. The stars, strangely, did not appear like at home, the brightest first, in the darkest parts of the sky. They climbed up from the eastern horizon, bright and multicolored, a blanket of galaxies being pulled over the world. From the north came a small, warm moon, faster and brighter than Earth's, racing ahead of the stars at an angle like a surfer before a wave.

Somehow, while Jason had been watching the stars rise, the Kakri had entered quiet as breath and gathered before the statue. Half stood beneath the oncoming stars, the other half beneath the moon. Jason's breathing quickened. These silent warriors terrified him.

"Do not fear," Baileya whispered. "On this night there is no violence among the Kakri. It is a night of mourning our lost city and celebrating our marriage to the desert."

When the stars and the moon met, a song began among the moonside Kakri. "Where is the fountain which brought joy to the city, clean and clear at its heart?" There were no instruments, just voices.

The starside Kakri answered, also in song, "It has been carried away, the water spilled to the sand, the water given to the sun." The song, beautiful and strange, reached out to Jason like the tendrils of a plant opening in the morning dew. He felt himself alive, transported, and filled with a deep, melancholy sadness.

When the song ended, a woman ran among the singers, dressed as an enormous crow. She invited them into the desert. She told them they could become a part of it, that she would teach them how to thrive. She would teach them, she said, how to become people again, and not the corrupted creatures which had come to live in this city. They must leave everything behind—their houses, their possessions, their friends or family members who would not embrace the desert and the wisdom to be found there.

As the crow said these words, those near her cheered and embraced. They threw off their dull capes and coverings, revealing beautiful, brightly colored outfits beneath. They turned to their neighbors and shouted the news, inviting them to the desert, and color rippled through the crowd. Baileya threw off her own cloak and grabbed Jason's hand. "Come! Now we dance!"

Musical instruments came out (Jason's favorite was a stringed instrument Baileya said was called a bitarr), and the Kakri danced in a whirling, leaping style. Those who jumped highest and whirled fastest moved toward the center of the crowd. Jason tried to imitate them but found himself on the outer limits of the dance with the smallest children and most infirm elders.

At times a Kakri man would appear, laughing, and try to teach him how to leap higher. A drink that tasted like honey and goat's milk was passed around, and a crowd gathered to watch Jason take his first sip. When he held the bowl to his lips, Baileya pushed it higher, and he took in several gulps of the drink, which burned and left him sputtering and gasping. The people cheered, applauding and laughing, and a trio of muscled women lifted him up on their shoulders and began to jump in place, tossing him higher each time. "Spin!" they called to him, and he did his best, trying to spin as they had in their dances. When he reached the ground again, there were many hands clapping his back and arms thrown over his shoulders.

Sweating and exhausted, he sat down between two old women who rested on the edge of the deserted fountain. They wore bright clothes, but a chill had set in without the sun, and their dun-colored cloaks were over their legs.

"Hello," Jason said to them, wiping the sweat from his forehead.

"Greetings, Wu Song, slayer of tigers," the old woman to his left said.

His heart immediately started pounding again. How did this old woman know the story of Wu Song? Back home only people with Chinese family knew the story. "Forgive me, but I don't know your name."

The old lady on his other side chuckled. "She is Mother Crow. Do you not see her feathers?"

He looked more closely at her cloak. It did have black feathers sewn into it. She must have been the one in the play who invited the people into the desert. Mother Crow smiled at him, her face wrinkled and aged as the desert itself. "Would you leave behind all to learn the wisdom of the desert?"

"Uhhhh." Jason's mouth twitched. "I don't think so. I have things to do. My friend Madeline . . . I have to protect her."

"Indeed," Mother Crow said. "I suspected you would say so."

The other old lady patted his hand. "You cannot protect another person," she said. "Not in truth. Death comes for all. Your friend Madeline, too."

"But there's value in keeping people safe until that time," Jason said. "You can't save people forever, but if you can do it today, you should. People are . . ." He paused. He wasn't sure how to say the next bit. "People are the most important thing in the world. Anything else can be replaced, but people . . . Each one is unique, and when a person dies, they never come again. They're gone forever. Other people might come but not that one. So we have to protect them while we can. And if it's someone you love . . . you should protect them no matter what."

Mother Crow smiled. "You see? He has some of the desert in him. I see why she likes you."

"Who, Madeline?"

Both the old women laughed, and one pointed at Baileya, who leapt and spun near the center of the crowd, her bright-blue smock flying around her like wind. She caught his eye as she twirled, and she smiled, looked away, and kept dancing. He noticed the gold armband she wore. She had rolled her loose sleeves up so you could see it, glittering on her muscular arm.

Mother Crow said, "Wu Song. May I see the mask?"

Baffled that she knew so much, Jason pulled the mask from his sack. Mother Crow held it up, studying the mirrored surface as it flared and shone in the starlight. "The Knight of the Mirror asks that you keep it safe from the Scim."

"The Scim made it," the other old lady said.

Mother Crow nodded and said, "They could make another if they chose. No, we will not hold this mask for you, Wu Song. It has too little of the truth in it. This mask is deception. To live in the desert one must embrace who one is. This mask does the opposite. It tells the world you are who they desire you to be. It is a small death to cover your face in such a way."

"So I came all this way for nothing."

The old woman's eyes widened in surprise. "You gained a story, did you not?"

"Now," Mother Crow said. "When the sun rises you must leave this place. So long as you hold that mask, you are not welcome among our people. If one day you desire to leave all and learn from the desert, come and seek what you may find among the sands."

Jason tucked the mask away, disappointed. How did they know all these things before he told them? What was he meant to do now that their entire mission had failed? And of course he had been the one to fail, not Baileya, who was good at everything. He paused. "Is there, perchance, a Father Crow I could speak to?"

The old women cackled with laughter. "Sweet child, go along now. How can you protect your Madeline when she is so far away?"

He wasn't sure what to do. He wandered out beyond the new firelight flickering up near the elders. He stood and looked at the moon, now completely enveloped in stars. The music and joyful cries of the people faded as he considered all that had happened since coming to the Sunlit Lands.

After a while, Baileya leaned up against his shoulder, handing him a chunk of roasted meat. "Hare," she said. He hadn't realized how hungry he was until she put it in his hands, and he ate it gladly.

He told her all that the old women had said. She listened carefully. When he was finished, she said, "I will go back with you to Far Seeing."

"You're not upset?"

"It is foolish to be upset about what is. Let us instead attempt to shape what will be." She shivered, as if suddenly cold, and pulled her dun cloak over her shirt. "Why have you tied yourself to Madeline?" she asked. "Why do you seek to protect her even from Death, should she come?"

Jason and Baileya sat down on the edge of a broken piece of statuary. It looked like it had been a group of people sitting at a long table. The table was flat and smooth and broken in such a way that they could lean up against it like a chair. "I haven't told anyone this story," Jason said.

Baileya jumped up. "Then why tell it to me? Such a story is priceless. An unknown, untold tale?"

He had forgotten how stories were money here among the Kakri. Huh. That meant that she had shared something valuable with him when she told him the story of the crow inviting the Kakri people into the desert. "You deserve to know. You're my friend," Jason said. She looked skeptical. "It would help me to tell someone."

Her face softened, and she sat down again, legs crossed, facing him. She put her hands on her knees and said, "I will listen attentively."

"I had a sister once. Her name was Jenny. She was three years older than me." Jason cleared his throat. He hadn't said her name in a while. His eyes burned. "You have to understand that my parents . . . They meant well, I think, but they did things differently. They weren't like the other American parents, you know, even though my mom came to the United States when she was young. My dad thought the best way to encourage someone to work hard was to never be satisfied with their work. If we got straight As, he would barely acknowledge it. He'd say things like, 'Grades in middle school do not count.' But if you got terrible grades, they suddenly counted quite a lot."

"I do not know what this means, grades and As."

"Right. Think of it like . . . lessons. If we did well at our lessons, he didn't say anything, but if we did poorly, he had a lot to say. So Jenny and me, we were like a team. When I got my grades, I'd go to her bedroom, and we'd close the door, and she would look at them and tell me what a good job I was doing. She'd show me her grades, and I'd tell her how proud I was. We talked about everything. It was us versus my parents in everything, and we always stuck together."

"It is not a good way to live as a family."

Jason laughed cynically. "I don't think it's what my parents intended, but it's what happened. Well, after a while Jenny started dating this guy named Marcus. He was Korean."

"What does 'dating' mean?"

Jason stopped, trying to think of the right way to say it. "More than friends, I guess?"

"Like you and Madeline. More like siblings than friends." She raised an eyebrow, as if asking whether she had understood his relationship to Madeline correctly.

Jason ran his hands through his hair. "No . . . like husband and wife, but they weren't married yet."

"They were betrothed?"

Jason debated whether to explain the entire process in modern-day America, but decided it would cause more questions and misunderstandings. She didn't need to get it perfectly, anyway. "No, they weren't engaged. They wanted to be engaged, though." That seemed close enough.

"Ah," Baileya said. "He had not yet told her his story. I understand now."

He wasn't sure she did, but he couldn't spend forever on this little detail. "Right. So Jenny and Marcus, they were . . . they were spending a lot of time together. My parents didn't like him, though. They kept saying he was irresponsible. They wanted Jenny to date a Chinese boy, not a Korean one."

"What does this mean?"

Huh. What *did* that mean? "He came from another . . . like, another tribe than us."

"Like you and me," Baileya said.

Close enough. "Right. Yeah. So . . . my dad had a big fight with Jenny, and he told her she couldn't see Marcus anymore."

Baileya leaned forward. "She did not obey him."

Jason shook his head. "Jenny would say she was going to a friend's house or that she was working on her lessons. One night she didn't come home. She had told my parents she was meeting someone at the library, but as the hours went by, my dad started to suspect she was with Marcus."

"Your mother killed the boy," Baileya said, as if it were the most obvious thing in the world.

"What? No! My dad started asking me where Jenny was. She told me everything, and Dad knew that. I knew Jenny and Marcus had driven to a mountain near our house to watch the sunset. She had texted me from there."

"Texted?"

"Sent me a message. My dad got more and more angry as the night went on. He shouted and screamed. My mom tried to get me to tell her what was going on. I kept sending messages to my sister telling her to get home quickly. At last my dad grabbed me by the shirt and dragged me to my sister's room. He threw me on the floor and told me he knew she was seeing Marcus. That it didn't matter now, that it was three in the morning and he needed to know where she was. I was so tired. I hadn't slept. My whole body hurt. I told him what I knew. He called the police, and then he and my mother and I went to the mountain in my father's car." Then he had to explain about police and cars.

"The . . . police . . . they found your sister?"

"No," Jason said. "At sunrise my mom noticed skid marks on the road. There were broken trees. My dad stopped the car in the middle of the road, grabbed me by the neck, and dragged me to the edge of the cliff. Marcus's car was down there. My father was yelling, and I didn't know what to do, so I climbed down. By the time I got to the car, I was bruised and covered in mud. My clothes were torn."

"Did your father follow you?"

Jason shook his head. "Jenny was . . . The car was upside down. Broken. Marcus was dead. Jenny, though. She looked at me. She tried to speak. I couldn't get the door open. She said . . ." Jason couldn't get the words to come out. His lips trembled, and his throat closed tight. His hands shook, and tears spilled from his eyes. "She said, 'Didi, I was waiting for you.'"

Baileya did not say anything, but she reached across and took his hand in hers.

Jason explained to her about doctors and ambulances. "When the ambulance came, they said that Marcus had been dead for six hours. Jenny had been there beside him that whole time. If they had been able to get to her even an hour sooner, they could have saved her." He hung his head. "If I had only told them the truth."

"You have not lied since that day?"

"One lie. I told my parents that Jenny had said she loved them, and she was sorry she disobeyed."

"What did your father say?"

Jason stared into the distance. "He said I had killed my sister. He hasn't spoken to me since the funeral."

Baileya sat still, her hand resting in his. "You did not kill her," Baileya said.

"I—" Jason could not handle Baileya saying that. Even Jenny had blamed him. *I was waiting for you*, she had said. And he hadn't come, not in time. He had never told anyone that part of the story, he had only turned it over and over in his own mind. Jenny had wished he had told the truth, that he had let his parents know where she was. If he had told them right away, or even if he had told them sooner, Jenny would still be alive. "I can't let someone else die," Jason said. "I have to protect Madeline. If she were to . . . to pass, and I could have stopped it . . . I can't live with that."

Baileya said, "I have heard your story, and I will consider it carefully. It is a good story, Wu Song." She pulled the gold armband from her arm and placed it on Jason's. "I will keep the story safe." She stood. "Come, the sun is rising. Bring the mask and we will return to Far Seeing." She took his hand and helped him to his feet. "I understand now why you must protect

Madeline, and I, too, will protect her. Wait for me at the fallen gate of the city, and we will begin our journey soon."

Jason wiped his eyes, thankful for the easy way Baileya had taken his story, and thankful, too, that she had not condemned him but seemed more serious than ever about joining him. She made her way over to the remnants of the dancers. She spoke to them. He couldn't hear their words, but there was a great ululating cry, and the dancing began again with more fervor. He turned the gold band on his arm. It felt like a declaration of friendship. It meant a lot to him that she had put it on his arm, that she would loan it to him for a short time.

Mother Crow stood at the broken gate. She pressed a small bag of food and a skin of water into his hands. "For the Kakri people, courtship is different than among your people."

"Dating advice, huh, Mother Crow? No offense, but how long has it been since you dated someone?"

She ignored him. "If you wish to marry Baileya, here is how it is done among our people. First, the man has a story he has kept secret his whole life. It must be a story he has never told anyone, ever. He pulls the woman aside and shares the story with her. This is a valuable story, a secret story." Jason felt a small flutter of panic in his stomach. Mother Crow continued, "When the story is done, the woman must decide whether to marry or not. If she wishes to become betrothed, she tells the man his story was a good one and that she will consider it carefully. She has one year to think on his story."

"So if she says it's a good story, they're *engaged*?"

Mother Crow smiled and shook her head. "First she must give him a token of her affection."

Uh-oh. "Not like a gold armband, though, right?"

"That would be a fine token," Mother Crow said. "Then she tells her family, and there is a celebration."

There would be a way to explain the misunderstanding, he was sure. Celebrations weren't bad, anyway. Right?

"For the next twelve cycles of the moon," Mother Crow said, "the family tries to kill the suitor, and the woman must prevent it through the strength of her arms and her prowess as a warrior."

Wait, what? "Say that again? The family tries to murder the suitor?"

"For one year. The betrothal celebration lasts one day, after which the family seeks the suitor to kill him. If they fail to kill him, then there is great rejoicing, and he becomes a member of her household."

"And if they succeed?"

She shrugged. "What does it matter?"

"What if the suitor backs out of the engagement?"

Mother Crow narrowed her eyes. "The family still attempts to kill him, but he is no longer under the protection of his betrothed."

Great. He would be married or dead within a year. Possibly both.

"Mother Crow," he said.

"Yes, Wu Song?"

"Good-bye." He ran into the desert, knowing that Baileya would catch up easily.

She did. She was beaming. Her skin seemed to glow. She smiled at him and took his hand.

Soon her family would follow them into the desert, bent on killing him as part of their strange marriage ritual. The Kakri would move faster than the Scim military, and they knew these desert wastes.

Baileya squeezed his hand. "Faster, Wu Song."

Wu Song ran.

33

THE ELENIL AT WAR

One of the Peasant King's followers, a knight in his service,
said to him, "My lord, where are you going?"
The Peasant King replied, "Why, to meet Death.
Would you go with me, Sir Knight?"

FROM "THE TRIUMPH OF THE PEASANT KING," A SCIM LEGEND

✠

Madeline's tears had stopped. Darius found her staring silently at refuse in the field. He had taken his helmet off. He smoothed his white robes and sat beside her. "The Elenil will come soon," he said. "After our attack on the city, they will respond. You can help Yenil's family, Madeline."

"How? By throwing away better garbage?"

"You can make sure they aren't harmed. You're a high-value human to the Elenil. They want to make sure your deal is kept. They'll want you happy. Tell them to leave her family alone, and they will."

The darkness here was so deep. There were no stars. It was as if a thick cloud layer hovered overhead. "The Elenil don't fight their own battles, Darius. They won't sweep in here and hurt anyone. If anything they'll send some human soldiers. How many Elenil even died in your attack?"

Darius rubbed his jaw. "I haven't spoken to the war council yet, but no more than a hundred. They are long lived, though, and not used to death. Not anymore. You don't know them, Madeline. They'll come, and when they do, it will be to punish our people. We crossed a line by attacking during their holiday. They will make it clear that such a thing cannot happen again."

Something stirred within her. It was wrong for the Scim to murder the Elenil. The Scim were in poverty, yes, but why did that make killing others okay? "Darius, you make it sound like the Elenil could come in and wipe out the Scim in a single day."

"They could. They've taken the Scim's weapons . . . their most powerful ones, anyway." He turned to look at his owl, which had closed its golden eyes, resting perched on a log sticking out of a garbage pile. "Except for the Sword of Years, which I have now. The Elenil have all but enslaved these people by building an economy based on taking from the Scim to empower and enrich the Elenil. The Elenil could crush the Scim in an afternoon if they truly wanted to do so."

"Then how are they at war?" It didn't make any sense.

"They can't destroy the Scim completely. Who would be the object of their magic then? Where would their sewage magically disappear to? Madeline . . . if there is a Scim woman with a beautiful voice, she sells it to the Elenil. If you have talent, or ability, or anything the Elenil want, you can get ahead. If you're a gifted musician, or athlete, or artist. For a while at least. If you don't have those things, you can get a meal, maybe, or a roof over your head for a few weeks by giving them some small piece of your life. Healing magic, maybe. You take the flu for a week so the Elenil can be healthy. In exchange, three days of food. Follow the money, Madeline. When you see this sort of injustice in the world, you always follow the money. Who benefits? Who loses? Then you know what kind of game is being played."

It still didn't make sense. It was a terrible deal, and she didn't understand how getting a few days of food would be worth being sick for a week. "Why would the Scim agree to this?"

Darius looked embarrassed. He stared into the night for a while. When his eyes met hers, there was a calculation being made, a decision being weighed out. "Okay," he said. "Okay. You know my cousin Malik?"

"Yeah. The one who went away to college last year. Your mom mentioned him."

"He's not in college, Madeline. Listen, it goes like this. We start with a private prison somewhere."

"A private—?"

"Contracted. They make a deal with the government, so the government doesn't have to run a prison. It works like this. They make a deal for a bunch of money. The government guarantees a quota . . . a certain number of inmates a year or the company won't make money, right?"

Madeline shook her head. "What does this have to do with Malik?"

"Just wait for it, Mads. So to meet the quota, a certain number of people have to be arrested. But there's not enough. The cops are working hard, but they're not getting enough convictions. So the legislators, they make tighter laws. Then the cops can arrest more people, the judges can put more away. They make mandatory minimum sentences for small crimes so they can fill prison beds."

"That's a cynical way of looking at things."

Darius squeezed her hand. His eyes held something like compassion, but it might have been pity. "It's experience, not cynicism." He took his hand back. "So Malik, he's trying to make ends meet. His mom's in the hospital, and his girlfriend is pregnant. He can't get ahead fast enough, even being careful with his money. His friends keep saying he could make good money fast if he's willing to sell drugs. He keeps pushing them off. His mom would be furious if she ever found out. His girlfriend would be furious too, and he has a kid on the way. He can't risk that. But he knows who to talk to if he decides he needs the money."

Madeline could scarcely believe what she was hearing. "Did Malik start selling drugs?"

"No," Darius said, obviously frustrated. "No, that's what I'm telling you . . . he decided not to. Then one day he's hanging out with some of our friends, they're sitting on the sidewalk, just catching up, and a police car comes flying out of nowhere, up onto the curb. Everyone scatters, and Malik runs too."

"Why did he run if he didn't do anything wrong?"

"That's exactly what the cops say. And the thing is, one of Malik's friends, he was holding. He ditched his drugs on the sidewalk. The cops ask Malik who they belong to, and he knows, but he won't tell them. So they take him in, and they sweat him at the station and try to get him to talk. But he won't give them a name, so they write up the report and they say that the drugs were Malik's."

"Wait. Are you saying they lied?"

"They wanted to bust a dealer, and my cousin was sitting there, right where the drugs were found. You know, in the scramble maybe they thought they were his. Maybe they think that's what really happened. I don't know. But the cops are adamant. The public defender doesn't put up much of a fight, and Malik goes to jail."

"Malik's in *jail*?"

"In jail it costs ten bucks a minute to make a phone call, because some company has a monopoly on outgoing calls. Plus he's doing prison labor. Growing produce for some fancy big-name grocery chain."

"Malik was hanging out with drug dealers? Darius, why didn't he just give them a name?"

"Malik gets paid this tiny bit of money for his work. A lot less than the phone company, the private prison, and the grocery chain are making off him. Meanwhile his kid is growing up without a daddy, his girlfriend has no money and has to figure out who can take care of the baby so she can work, his mama can't afford the hospital. Some white dude on the television is talking about how Malik needs to learn to take responsibility for his actions, but meanwhile Malik has nothing and never has. He was loyal to his friends, that's his crime. Meanwhile he's got no safety net, no one to bail him out on rent one month."

"Are you sure he was telling the truth?"

Darius snorted. "Why would he lie at this point? He's already serving the time. He's never lied to me before, even when he did stupid things. What makes you think he's lying? Because a couple cops have a different story? A couple cops you don't even know?"

"Okay," Madeline said. She could see it happening. "It's a really terrible story. I'm sorry about Malik. But what does this have to do with the Scim?"

"Okay, I'm almost to that. So Malik, when he gets out, he won't have any money. He'll be worse off than he was going in, and what's going to happen? He tries to join the military, but they won't take him because of his record. He doesn't have a car, so he can't leave the neighborhood very easily. He's taking the bus to work on the other side of town. He can't afford to live there, so he's taking the bus two hours each way to work, where he gets just enough money to stay in debt. His kid gets sick, so he takes out a payday loan. His mom dies, he can't pay for the funeral, but he has to get the cash somehow. It starts all over again. He's gotta make the decision—is he gonna work inside the system and suffer or gamble on breaking the law to get ahead? His kid, he's going to inherit the same thing."

"If he just works hard—"

Darius slapped the back of his hand into his palm. "No, Mads, no. He's working harder than your dad. Fifty-hour weeks plus twenty-eight hours of travel. I'm not saying he can't get out, people do. You asked why the Scim would agree to this deal. It's the wrong question. The question is, how are the Elenil keeping the deal in place? You start following the money, and you find the politicians, the prison owners, the lobbyists and corporations, they need more bodies. They need legal slavery. So they write the laws tight. They make sure it's a law that will catch young black men, because the young ones are cheaper to take care of in jail. Then they wait for you to slip up. One mistake, and they've got you. That's how it works in the real world, and that's how it works here."

Madeline felt raw. Like Darius was accusing her of something, like she had participated in some way in what was being described. She felt like they were on two boats that had been lashed together, but he was cutting the ropes. He was headed out to sea, watching her drift away.

Darius crossed to the owl and came back with the sword. He unwrapped it and put it in Madeline's hands. The worn pommel, the chipped and rusted blade—the only way it could look more pitiful would be if the blade was broken.

"The Sword of Years," she said.

"Five hundred years ago, there was a battle," Darius said. "The Scim and the Elenil were at war. All the men—in those days only the Scim men fought—had gone out to battle, dressed in their war skins. They had left behind a small city, called Septil. The Elenil had fought the Scim warriors and been forced to a draw. The Scim offered to make a peace treaty, and the Elenil also agreed. They met to discuss the treaty, but one of the Elenil captains snuck away with his soldiers and came upon the city."

"During the peace negotiations? The Elenil were scouting out the Scim land at the same time?"

"Yes," Darius said. "Septil was filled with women and children and elderly men. They saw the war party come to the gates. The Scim people debated whether the Elenil might be there with peaceful intentions. They had received messenger birds saying the peace talks had begun. Others were skeptical. They had few weapons in the city, but there was one sword, rusted and nicked and half useless. The old men put a blood spell on it: the sword would be harmless except against those who harmed the Scim. If the sword found people who had harmed the Scim or gained from their harm, it would not be sheathed until it had spilled their blood. All of it."

Madeline turned the sword over in her hands. It didn't seem magic, it seemed like an old broken piece of junk. "What happened?"

"They let the Elenil in. The Elenil began to slaughter the people . . . They thought they would leave a parting gift for the Scim warriors, who would return home from their peace talks to find their families butchered. But a child picked up the sword, and when he pulled it from the scabbard, it became sharp, shiny, and new. It drank the blood of the Elenil, and that one child defeated the entire war party. They retreated."

Five hundred years, he had said. This sword was older than the United States. How strange. The bitterness between the Scim and the Elenil ran deep and ancient. "The Knight of the Mirror said not to sheathe the sword. He said it was dangerous."

Darius laughed bitterly. "To the Elenil. The sword still fulfills its calling. It spills the blood of those who would oppress the Scim. It is patient and will wait centuries to exact its vengeance. That is why it's called the Sword of Years."

A horn blew, clear and cold as the moon. Darius scrambled to his feet.

"What is it?" Madeline's hand closed instinctively around the sword's handle.

"The Elenil," Darius said. He threw the canvas to her. "Cover the sword."

Fera and Inrif burst from their hovel just as Darius pulled his helmet on. "Are they near?" Fera cried.

"Madeline will protect you," the Black Skull said, climbing onto his owl. "I must warn the elders." Then, to Madeline: "I leave the sword to you, Mads. Do what you think is right."

To Madeline's astonishment, the couple didn't ask how she would protect them. They wished the Black Skull a safe journey and returned inside. She followed, carrying the wrapped sword under her arm.

Yenil moaned. She had fallen asleep. Her breathing came in short, raspy breaths.

Inrif bolted the door, and Fera lifted squares of wood over the windows, barricading them in. The tiny hut felt claustrophobic now, and the smoke from the fire burned Madeline's eyes.

Inrif and Fera tried to hide their curiosity about the package, but their eyes drifted toward it over and over. Madeline placed it on the table, trying to be quiet so as not to wake Yenil. She unwrapped the sword. Fera gasped. Inrif hissed through his teeth.

"The Sword of Years," Madeline said.

Inrif hurriedly threw the canvas over the sword and wrapped it tightly. "The Sword of Ten Thousand Sorrows," he said. "The Sword of Pain. Blood-Spiller. The Strife of Generations."

Fera placed a hand on Madeline's arm. "It has many names. We are simple people, miss. We do not go on blood feuds with Elenil lords."

"Take my advice," Inrif said. "Do not use this sword, nor give it to any who would."

"Why? This is one of the artifacts of the Scim, made with Scim magic." She pushed the wrapped sword across the tiny table. "You should have it."

Inrif held up his hands, as if to ward off a blow. "Do not offer that foul thing to me again. It is a curse, miss, a curse whether you meet its point or its hilt."

Fera didn't look at the bundle. "My husband speaks truth. Some Scim would have it returned to us, others would have it destroyed. If such a thing were possible."

Madeline didn't understand. "What should I do with it, then?"

"Throw it in the sea," Fera said.

"Return it to the Elenil," Inrif said bitterly. "Let them keep the cursed thing within their own walls. May the Peasant King take pity on them when it is unsheathed!"

A bright light blasted through the planks on the windows. Beams of summer sunlight lit the room. When the light hit them, Fera and Inrif both twisted away, letting their arms and legs swell and grow. Tusks jutted from their faces, and their lean bodies grew heavily muscled. War skin, that's what they called it. They looked like monsters. They looked like Break Bones. Madeline couldn't help but recoil.

Yenil neither woke nor changed.

Fera cried out in her new, guttural voice and held Yenil to her chest. "She does not put on her war skin, husband."

Madeline crossed to them. "What does that mean?"

"It means," Inrif said, walking to the door, "that our sweet child is nearing the end of her illness. Her war skin should protect her when the light threatens, even when she is not conscious. This is dire news indeed."

"Our sweet child," Fera wailed. "Only yesterday she laughed and sang. Only yesterday she ran about the neighborhood and played with the other children."

Yesterday. Because of the Festival of the Turning. Because Madeline had not been stealing her breath. Madeline's tattoo burned.

A knock on the door nearly shook it from its frame. Inrif opened the door carefully. Outside stood the Elenil. No humans. No Maegrom. Nothing and no one but the Elenil.

They were dressed for war. Silver helmets. An army of shields. Swords like polished moonlight.

"Wait," Madeline shouted. She ran to the door. "I am of the Elenil. These people are under my protection."

The first blade went through Inrif's chest. He fell forward, his heavy war-skin body knocking the Elenil soldier back.

Madeline stared in horror. Fera slammed the door, wincing against the light outside.

The immediate thumping against the door moved Madeline to action. She snatched up the Sword of Years, uncovering it.

"No," Fera hissed. "The back wall. Dig!"

"But with the sword—"

"And if you fail, they will only kill more Scim. They will say we fought against them."

Madeline fell beside the wall and dug with her hands. The dirt was packed and hard. She used the sword to break into it, and it crumbled beneath the blade. The door shivered, and the Elenil shouted for them to open it.

Fera leaned against the door, grunting each time the Elenil smashed into it. "Take Yenil," she whispered, her voice a passionate plea.

"Come with us," Madeline said.

"The hole is not large enough," Fera said, tears falling.

"I can dig faster."

As if in answer, the door buckled. Fera shouted and smashed it back. "Go!"

Madeline scooped up Yenil. She weighed almost nothing. Yenil stirred but did not wake. Madeline wiggled out through the hole first. The Elenil were on the other side of the hut, light hovering over them, coming from tiny, floating orbs of sunlight. They didn't see her. She reached inside and took hold of Yenil's hands, dragging her through the hole.

She hoisted the child in her arms and ran.

She ran until she could no longer see the light, letting the darkness fold over her, envelop her. Yenil's breathing came harder while Madeline ran. They fell together into the dirt. Noises of battle came from the direction of the hut.

Fera screamed, and there was the sound of metal on stone. Shouts, distant in the darkness. Then silence. No more screams. No sounds of battle.

Tears burst from Madeline's eyes.

Yenil leaned against her. Still asleep and struggling for breath, she said, "Mother . . . I am cold."

Madeline wrapped her arms around her.

They were in a sickly garden. Orderly rows of malnourished plants lay crushed between them. Madeline listened to the harsh, labored breathing of the girl in her arms. She could feel the pulsing connection of their tattoos. She sobbed and held the girl tighter.

"Oh, sweet lamb, don't you cry now." An old woman sat beside her, a floral hat on her head, her grey hair like the straws of a broom. "I'm not saying it isn't sad, dear. But this isn't the time for tears, not yet."

It was the Garden Lady, the one who had met her in her mother's garden a million years ago. "They killed Fera and Inrif," Madeline said.

The old lady nodded. "They will kill that sweet girl you're holding too, should they find her." She rearranged herself and smoothed her skirt. "You have three favors yet, dear. If I can help, only ask the question."

Madeline wiped her face. "Can you get us somewhere safe? Westwind?"

"Hmm. Not all the way to Westwind, dear. There's no garden there for us to enter. But close. Close enough. Do you agree this will be your first favor, leaving you with only two more?"

Lights were coming toward them. The sunlight bounced and shone across the garbage and refuse of the Wasted Lands. Elenil soldiers, resplendent in the reflected sunlight, made their way toward Madeline's hiding spot, like living mirrors.

"Yes," she said. "Yes, quickly."

"Close your eyes," the old lady said.

She did.

Sunlight hit her face, and for one panicked moment she thought the Elenil had found her. Birds sang around her. They were in a lush, green garden in the shadow of the archon's palace. An Elenil couple stood a few yards away, surprised by the sudden appearance of the human and the Scim girl.

Madeline said nothing. Being this close to the archon filled her with panic. She lifted Yenil and trotted away from the garden toward Westwind and, she hoped, safety.

34
AN END TO HOPE

During the storm, hope.
After the storm, peace.

A KAKRI PROVERB

✦

o then a Kakri warrior hidden in the sand dune comes flying out with a sword, and he's shouting this crazy oooolalalalalalalala, and I'm like uh-oh, and I don't know what to do, so I run straight toward this big rock, and I climb on top, and then Baileya comes and fights the guy until she knocks his sword out of his hand, and then she steals his ride, which is this huge bird like an ostrich—"

"It is called a brucok," Baileya said, smirking.

"—steals his brucok, and after that no one else could catch us. She had left me sitting there by myself as *bait*," Jason said. He glared at Baileya accusingly.

"Not bait," she said. "You were the tantalizing reward in the center of my trap."

"That's bait!"

Madeline grinned. She had shared her story about her time in the Wasted Lands. It had been painful, telling them about Darius and the Scim family and explaining young Yenil, who even now slept on Madeline's bed. Shula hugged Madeline again. She had been terrified when she lost Madeline to the Black Skull, thinking Madeline had been imprisoned . . . or worse.

It was a relief to hear Jason share about his journeys with such wide-eyed wonder, though Madeline could tell he was holding back part of the story. He looked at Baileya with a strange nervousness, and she smiled back with a certainty and warmth she hadn't shown before. What had happened out there in the desert?

"Anyway," Jason said, "we don't have time to go into it all, but there were also gigantic moving statues, a death blimp—"

"It was the Pastisians in one of their machines. It was not a 'death blimp.'"

"You said they were necromancers, and that thing was like a . . . I don't know, some sort of weird dirigible. So death blimp is good enough for me. We had to hide! Baileya buried me—"

"You don't know how to conceal yourself properly."

"And then! Then she made her giant bird—"

"Brucok."

"—she made her giant brucok *sit on top of me*."

Baileya shrugged. "You would not stay still beneath the sand. I needed to cover you."

Yenil stirred, her body racked with coughing. The network of silver tattoos that covered much of Madeline's body tingled. That evidence of Yenil's burden—of what should be Madeline's burden—reminded Madeline who had put that burden on her back. The Elenil had taken away Yenil's breath and given it to Madeline and done it without Madeline understanding what the bargain entailed.

Jason asked, "What do you want to do, Mads?"

His quiet voice startled her from her thoughts. Jason, with a look both open and determined, waited for her response. She had harmed him, too. She had made a bargain for his life, knowing full well the consequences and not allowing him a choice. Night's Breath's life for his. He was the beneficiary of that death through no fault of his own. The blood guilt for that one lay on her.

She knew what had to be done. "Did the Scim recapture the Crescent Stone?"

"No," Shula said. "The Elenil magic returned just in time to repel them."

"Then we have to destroy it," Madeline said.

"That is the source of all Elenil magic," Baileya said. "To destabilize it would be catastrophic."

"For who? It's catastrophic already for the Scim."

Jason shook his head. "You won't be able to breathe, Madeline. We'll be kicked back to our world. Right?"

Shula, wiping the sweat from Yenil's brow, said grimly, "I can't go back to Syria. I'll be killed."

"I can breathe, but she can't," Madeline said desperately. "I need your help if we're going to do this. We need to make a plan to get our hands on that stone."

An awkward silence fell in the room. Maybe they couldn't see. Maybe they didn't understand that every beautiful tower in Far Seeing was a broken-down hovel in the Wasted Lands. The fine clothing they were all wearing was the result of putrid rags among the Scim. Every good thing the Scim had, the Elenil stole it and threw it carelessly onto their hoarded piles of wealth. Madeline benefited from this with every wonderful, full-chested breath of air she took into her lungs. She couldn't live with that, couldn't stand by and do nothing. Madeline said, "I'll do it by myself if I have to."

"Some wrongs cannot be easily righted," Baileya said. "But that does not mean we should not try. I fear the magic of the Elenil is woven so centrally through their life and culture that you cannot destroy it without destroying them. Yet it is true that their gain is the Scim's loss, and their wealth, the Scim's poverty. I do not know if removing it completely is wise, but I will stand with you, if you think this the best course."

Shula put her hand on Madeline's shoulder. "We should at least think through the consequences for others. It won't be only the five of us who are affected."

Jason shrugged. "I guess I can live without my morning pudding."

Baileya seemed to be the one who would know best what the costs would be, as she was the only native to the Sunlit Lands in the room—other than Yenil, who, in addition to being a child, still slept. Madeline asked Baileya what she thought.

"There will be some good," she said, and Madeline bristled at the "some." "My own people have chosen not to use Elenil magic since it began. Nonetheless, there are good things that come from it." She raised her hand for silence when Madeline objected. "You asked for my thoughts, you will receive them."

"What good—"

Baileya cut her off immediately. "The Aluvoreans are protected from the Scim by the Elenil. With their magic gone, the Scim will plunder Aluvorea. The Elenil also keep the Pastisians at bay. The necromancers could sweep the land if the Elenil are weakened. Make no mistake, the Elenil as you know them will cease to exist. Their long lives, for one, will disappear, and they will become like flowers in the desert . . . beautiful, but for a few moments only."

Madeline felt her face flush. "Do they shorten the lives of the Scim to make themselves live longer?"

"No, it was a payment far more terrible," Baileya said. "However, now is not the time to tell stories but to live them. The death of Elenil magic may collapse buildings. It will definitely destroy certain families. The Scim will cease to receive payment for their 'donations' to the Elenil magical economy. Their poverty will go from crippling to absolute. It will take time for them to recover. Many will die. The Elenil will, largely, keep the wealth that remains to them and many of the advances they made on the backs of the Scim and others. Make no mistake—if you choose to destroy the stone, there will be suffering and pain and death."

"What about justice?" Madeline snapped.

Baileya inclined her head. "Perhaps justice, in some measure."

"The city is a mess already," Jason said. "Parts of the wall are down, and people are in mourning after the attack on the city. You're talking about taking a bomb to the center of their culture, basically."

"They shouldn't have built it around stealing from the Scim," Madeline said, and no one seemed to have a response to that. They sat quietly, as if waiting for instructions from her. Which maybe they were. They were loyal friends . . . willing to follow her into this mess.

Shula spoke first, her voice low. "I've always been on the side of the Elenil. You know this." As Madeline had explained everything to her, it was like multiple puzzle pieces fell into place for Shula. She understood now why the Scim acted in certain ways. But what seemed to change everything for her was Yenil. Seeing that child, orphaned and on the run, changed something for her. It reminded her, she said, of herself. "I have no love for the Scim, but we can't just walk into the tower and fight the Elenil. We need a plan."

"Actually," Jason said, "we sort of can walk into the tower. There aren't any doors. I could ride Delightful Glitter Lady straight up the steps."

"They will sever you from your magic," Baileya said. She grinned at him. "Your riding and archery skills will not be of much use, I think."

"I was sort of hoping you would go with me," Jason said, smiling.

"I can almost pass for an Elenil," Madeline said. "With the right dress and a little luck . . ."

Jason pulled a small sack from his side and opened it, revealing a mirrored mask. "We have this, too. Someone could wear it."

"I want to go," said a small, weak voice. Yenil leaned on her elbow, coughing. "I want to help."

Madeline hesitated, then took her hand. "Of course you can go."

"She can hardly walk," Jason pointed out.

"The Elenil killed her parents. She deserves to be there." Madeline couldn't bring herself to add that once she destroyed the stone, it was she who would not be able to breathe or walk or run or speak.

"Humans are not allowed in the tower without an Elenil escort," Shula said. "But it might work if they think Madeline is Elenil and I'm either one of the human guards or, using the mask, an Elenil. We could say Yenil is a prisoner . . . or that we're looking for a healer. We need to gather weapons and clothing. It could get us partway to the stone at least."

"I will gather weapons," Baileya said.

"I can find the clothes we'll need," Shula said. "How soon will we go?"

Yenil lay back on the bed, sweating. She struggled for breath. Madeline rearranged her, trying to make her comfortable. Yenil's eyes closed. She groaned and slipped into sleep. They couldn't wait long. Yenil wouldn't last. "As soon as we're ready," she said.

Baileya stood. "Jason, will you come with me, or do you have other business?"

"I want to talk to Madeline for a few minutes. Then I'll go get Dee."

Baileya nodded once, curtly, and she and Shula left together, Baileya already asking her what sorts of weapons she preferred. Jason turned his attention to Madeline. She knew what was coming and felt her heart clench and shrink into a tiny ball. She didn't want to have this conversation.

"I have these memories now," he said quietly. "Almost like dreams. I can't always remember them clearly, but sometimes they are so vivid they feel more real than the world around me. Especially this world."

Madeline breathed softly, her heart pounding. "Jason—"

"Night's Breath, that was just his war-skin name, you know. His family called him Geren. He had children and a wife. His mother is old . . . She lives on the edge of the Wasted Lands in the shell of what once was their family mansion, which has been handed down through the generations. It's collapsing. None of the walls are complete. Weeds grow in the dining room. Rain falls in the bedrooms, and mold grows across the walls."

"Jason, I didn't know any of—"

"Just—" Jason paused and pressed his palms against his temples. "Just listen. For a minute." He waited for Madeline to sit back, silent, listening to the blood thrumming through her head. When she was quiet, he said, "Once a year, Geren—Night's Breath—took his children through the wastes to visit their grandmother. The children would run through the darkened hallways, and their laughter always made Geren think, *This must have been what it was like once, when my family was powerful.* He had a scar. Did you see that?"

Madeline shook her head. "I don't remember it."

"Once, in the waste, he came across an Elenil traveling alone. She demanded he give her his steed and some supplies. She was on her way to the Court of Far Seeing, and he was headed there as well on some business. So he offered to let her ride with him, to mount up behind him, and together they would split his rations and arrive in a few days." Jason's fists tightened, and his face flushed. As if this had all happened to him and not

Night's Breath. "She told him it would bring shame on her to arrive with him, and she would be needing what she had originally demanded. She sliced him across the chest with her sword and took all his provisions, not just the few days' worth it would take her to arrive at the court."

"That's terrible," Madeline said.

"It gets worse. When he arrived at the Court of Far Seeing, delirious with hunger, his chest wound infected, he found that she had left word with the city guard that he had attacked her in the wilderness. They arrested him and put him in a dungeon for fourteen months. He had been a farmer. When he returned home, his crops were dead. His family lived with his mother, barely surviving. That is when he joined the Scim army and took the name Night's Breath."

Madeline sighed. "Then I killed him."

Jason didn't answer. He stared at the palms of his hands. "I don't know, Mads. His last memories are lost. It's like I only got the strongest ones. The ones he revisited over and over. There's this one story he loved, about this magician called the Peasant King."

"The Peasant King?" Madeline had met him, had seen him in the wood of the tower door.

"There's a story about the Peasant King, about how when he built the Sunlit Lands, he went to the wealthy and the powerful people in the world and offered to let them come in. He told them it was paradise, and that meant everyone would be equal. They would leave their power and their wealth at the door, and in the Sunlit Lands all their needs would be provided for—they would never be hungry or sick. They would be happy. But they didn't want to leave their wealth and their power. The Peasant King got angry, and he said those people could never come in, ever. He cast a spell so only the outcasts, the losers, the broken, the homeless, and the wounded could enter. He made the doors hard to find and in the worst places in the world."

Madeline found herself leaning forward, eager to hear the end of the story. "What happened? Why isn't that the situation now?"

"Mads, that's the thing. I think someone broke the Sunlit Lands. Night's Breath, he had this deep conflict going on inside of him because he saw the war against the Elenil as a betrayal of the Peasant King's original purpose.

You don't fight for a higher position in the Sunlit Lands. It's the beggars who are kings, right? The wealthy and powerful, they're the fools. But his family didn't have food to eat. So what was he supposed to do? And Mads, I get it. I know why you did what you did. I've been thinking about it, and I know—I know I would have done the same thing for you. Because I know you, and I didn't know Night's Breath." He sighed heavily and looked at the little girl on the bed. He whispered, "I know you, and I don't know Yenil. I'd be lying if I said there isn't a part of me that thinks we should leave all the magic alone until your breathing . . . until the magic is permanent."

Madeline gasped. "You mean until my disease kills her."

Jason looked away, ashamed. "Yes. Listen, Mads, we've all been following along at school while you've gotten sicker. We've had the updates and passed along the rumors and felt awkward when you showed up in class. I know there's not a cure, you've told us that. There's not any hope, Madeline. There's not any hope, and what I want to do more than anything is to make you well. I want to save you, and I don't know how. Except I could let that little girl go, just like you did with Night's Breath—"

Madeline grabbed his arms. "No. Jason, promise me. No! I couldn't live with that."

His eyes brimmed with tears, and it hit her all at once that she had done the same thing to him. He would have to live with it. He didn't get a choice. The poor Scim soldier was dead so Jason could live, and that had been Madeline's decision. It had been her call, and she had chosen her friend to live and the stranger to die. It couldn't be changed now.

She leaned her forehead against Jason's. "When you're sick," she said, "when you're really sick . . . you just want one more normal day. I hated walking into school. Hated the looks on people's faces. Hated the way everything stopped while I coughed and hacked, like everyone else was holding their breath. I hated the way people who had been mean to me the year before asked how I was doing and tried to be nice to me. I wanted to have a day where I showed up and someone called me a name. I wanted the boys to flirt with me and the teachers to lecture me for not turning in my homework. Or to walk through a room and have no one notice me, just once."

"In my defense," Jason said, "I was still a jerk to you sometimes."

She grinned at him. "True." She sat beside him and leaned her head against his shoulder, and they watched Yenil struggling to breathe. "That disease will be mine again soon," she said.

"Maybe since we were gone, the doctors have found a new treatment," Jason said.

She patted his arm. "I've spent a long time trying to have hope, Jason. There's a certain point when you realize that hope isn't what you need anymore. You can't hope forever. Sometimes people die. Terrible things happen. Evil wins, and farmers end up in jail while the wealthy get richer. Injustice rules the world. Your lungs get more and more scarred and there's nothing to be done."

"But maybe—"

"No, Jason, listen to me. Sometimes hope isn't what you need. This disease is going to kill me. I'm going to take it back, and I will die. Maybe not today or tomorrow. But I will. Sometimes you don't need hope anymore."

Tears streaked Jason's face. He rubbed at them with the back of his hand. "If we don't need hope, Mads, what do we need?"

"Courage," she said. "I don't need hope anymore, Jason. I know what's coming. I need courage to face it."

He took her hand. "We'll face it together."

35
THE CHOICE

To change the world, change first a heart.

THE GARDEN LADY

✛

Jason rode on Delightful Glitter Lady's back through the crowded streets of Far Seeing, like a king. "Are you sure you don't want to ride up here?" Jason asked Baileya.

"I do not wish to be so conspicuous," Baileya said, but Jason had already seen several people take note of her Kakri clothing and her double-bladed staff and give her a wide berth.

"It's not every day you get to ride a rhino," Jason said absently, watching the tower. "Unicorn, I mean." They were at the bottom of the stairs, quite a way from the massive garden at the base of the palace. They were supposed to wait until Madeline, Shula, and Yenil reached the main entrance. If they entered without any trouble, Jason and Baileya would follow a little way behind. If there was a problem, they'd make some noise and see if that helped them slip inside the tower.

An Elenil guard stopped them. He glanced at Baileya, who had hidden her staff in her sleeves. "You cannot bring weapons into the courtyard unless you are Elenil."

Jason flexed his biceps. "You talking about these guns?"

The guard clearly had no idea what Jason was talking about. Baileya gave him a quizzical look too. Whatever. That was comedy gold. Fine. He went back to the original plan. "I don't have any weapons, sir." That was true. Jason wasn't carrying a single weapon.

The guard gestured to Dee. "This unicorn is a war beast."

"Ha!" Jason shouted. "THIS IS A PEACETIME UNICORN."

"I do not know what that means."

"It means she is retired from military service and is now a civilian unicorn."

The guard's hand fell onto the hilt of his sword. "You cannot go farther unless you shrink your unicorn to its smallest size. And where is your Elenil guide?"

Jason pulled the magic dial off the saddle. "I've got the embiggenator right here. The only problem is, I also have this." He held up a small, smooth stone.

The guard looked at it dispassionately. "A stone? Why is that a problem?"

"Well, you know how magic works, right? If something gets small, something else has to get big. I accidentally brought along the stone that gets big when Delightful Glitter Lady gets small."

"I see," the guard said.

"There's Madeline," Baileya said.

She wore a tightly bound Elenil sheath dress. Another Elenil woman he didn't recognize stood beside her, a small Scim body in her arms. A guard had stopped her and was saying something, but they were too far away to be heard.

A flurry of birds flew into the square, squawking and calling out as they delivered messages to their various recipients.

The guard Madeline was talking to drew his sword. Jason didn't know why, but he knew what it meant. It was time to shout the secret phrase he had taught Baileya as their signal. It was time for them to make their loud, impressive, over-the-top distraction.

He cleared his throat and shouted at the top of his lungs, "It's morphin' time!"

✣

With her hair pinned up and the Elenil dress on, Madeline barely recognized herself.

"The eyes give you away," Shula said. "We should remove the neck."

The high neck of the dress could be unpinned. Fernanda stood in the mirror across from them, watching closely. They weren't in the knight's upper room, so she couldn't speak, only make motions to them. Another side effect of her curse. She made it clear, though, that she agreed with Shula.

With the neck removed, however, the silver tattoos that had been spreading across Madeline's body were visible. They coiled up from her collarbones, working their way up her neck and toward her chin in the front, the nape of her neck in the back. "No one ever shows their tattoos, though," Madeline said.

Shula pulled Madeline's hair back, pinning it up. "Only the Elenil have access to this much magic. It's rare to show it off, especially if someone other than Elenil are around. But it would be unthinkable for a human to have so much magic, and it will distract them from your eyes."

Fernanda nodded her approval from within the mirror.

Madeline studied her reflection in a different mirror. Her skin was not pale enough to be Elenil, and her hair had too much yellow in it. Most of the Elenil had blonde hair that leaned toward silver. Her eyes were definitely a distraction, the wrong blue. But she might pass if no one studied her too closely.

Shula opened her knapsack. "Now this," she said. She held up the shining, mirrored Scim artifact known as the Mask of Passing. She held it up to her face and tied the ribbons behind her head.

Her clothing—jeans and a long-sleeved shirt—flickered, then became a light-violet Elenil dress. Her face reappeared, only not dark any longer . . . It was similar to Madeline's own skin color. Her hair was golden blonde rather than black.

"You look . . . surprisingly like me."

The woman who was not Shula nodded. "The mask causes you to see someone like yourself. That's how it works. Anything that might make you think I'm 'the other' goes away, so you know I'm the same sort of person you are."

"You look human still, though."

"To you. To the Elenil I'll look like an Elenil. To the Scim, a Scim."

"We should test it on the way," Madeline said.

"That would be wise."

They stopped at a market stall a few hundred meters from the main tower. Shula hailed an Elenil soldier and told her to send a message to the wall, asking if there was any danger. The soldier sent a bird without hesitation.

Yenil had tried to walk, but it had been too much. Madeline carried Yenil, perched on her back. Shula would take over when they reached the tower, they decided, and carry her in her arms. They planned to say, if stopped, that they were looking for a healer.

They were stopped. Of course. It wasn't Yenil who was the problem, at least not at first.

"Is that a sword, miss?"

Madeline hesitated. The Sword of Years, wrapped in cloth and rope, hung from her shoulder like a purse. "Yes," she said. She did her best imitation of Gilenyia. "We Elenil are allowed to walk armed wherever we please."

"Of course," the guard said, his eyes lingering on her neck. "The archon has requested, though, that we catalog the weapons as they come through."

Would he recognize the Sword of Years? She didn't know. If he did, they wouldn't make it into the tower, let alone to the top. They wouldn't get the Heart of the Scim.

"This girl is in distress," Shula said smoothly. "We seek a healer and do not have time for pleasantries."

The guard frowned. "To call the archon's order a mere pleasantry is a grave insult." He glanced at Yenil. "Is that a Scim girl? She looks almost like . . . a human."

"She is gravely wounded," Shula said.

"Gilenyia herself has ordered us to bring her," Madeline said, taking a chance.

The guard looked over his shoulder. "Gilenyia is at the ceremony within," he said.

"As is any Elenil of consequence," Madeline snapped.

The guard stepped backward as if she had struck him. She could see the truth of her own words in the shocked look on his face. The guard started to step aside, but just at that moment a flurry of birds circled the tower. Hundreds of them flew past in a great swarm, knocking the Mask of Passing from Shula's face. It clattered to the ground. The guard unsheathed his sword despite the storm of birds.

"What trickery is this?" he shouted. His gaze met Madeline's eyes, and his own widened. "You're no Elenil."

A small yellow bird perched on his shoulder. "Lieutenant," it said, "the Scim have breached the walls again."

"It is full daylight!" the soldier cried.

"They pour through the walls like water. Pray they do not drown us. Break Bones rides at their head upon a grey wolf, and the Black Skulls ride beside him."

"May the Majestic One protect us!"

Shula bent for the mask, but the guard stopped her. "I do not know what game you play, but none of you three may enter."

"She will die!" Madeline shouted, pointing at Yenil.

"Scim die," the guard said. "Such is their fate."

The sudden bellowing cry of a runaway rhinoceros echoed across the square. Shula hoisted Yenil onto her back. Madeline grabbed Shula's hand, and they ran past the terrified guard and into the tower.

✛

Whatever message the cloud of birds had brought, the Elenil guards had taken a sudden interest in Jason and his rampaging unicorn. He burst past fifteen or so guards without any trouble. He pulled Dee up short when a row of Elenil appeared ahead, each on one knee with a spear shaft pushed into the ground, the points ready to pierce the rhino's chest. He couldn't see Baileya . . . She had slipped away into the crowd somewhere.

"Halt!" one of the guards shouted.

"We already halted," Jason said.

"Don't come any closer," another shouted.

"We're not moving."

Madeline and Shula had made it into the tower already. That was the main point of the distraction, but it would be better if he and Baileya could get into the tower too, to help them get to the top and retrieve the Heart of the Scim.

Another flurry of birds sped through the crowd.

One of the guards shouted, "The Scim have breached the outer walls!"

A howling sound came from the west, just before a monstrous wolf loped into view, Break Bones on his back. "Wu Song," he called, pulling his wolf to a stop. "The Elenil have invaded our territories and murdered our people for the last time. We have come to destroy them and retrieve the Heart of the Scim."

"I am pretty sure we called dibs," Jason said. "Only we're gonna do the opposite. We're here to destroy the Heart of the Scim and . . . retrieve the Elenil?"

The massive Scim dismounted from his wolf. "You must not destroy the Heart. It is ours! It is not yours to do with as you please!"

As he spoke, the Black Skulls arrived.

"Hey," Jason said. "Good to see you all. Before anyone kills anyone, I just want to remind you that I go to the same high school with at least one of you, and I think school spirit should count for something."

The antelope-headed Black Skull spoke, and despite the magically modulated voice, Jason could recognize Darius's voice beneath it now that he knew who he was. "Return the Scim artifacts and no one need die."

"Hi, Darius!" Jason said. "I feel like we're basically on the same team here."

Break Bones laughed. "Unfortunately for you, Wu Song, I have made a blood oath to murder you."

"Um. There's no time limit on that, though, right? I mean, you could wait until I'm 130 years old."

An arrow blossomed in Break Bones's shoulder. Baileya appeared from behind a column. She didn't say anything clever. She wasn't one for talking needlessly in battle. She did, however, unsling a massive bag from her shoulder and throw it to Jason. It fell open, revealing a huge collection of weapons. Jason felt intimidated by the fact she could throw it. He pulled out a sword, his magic flowing into it, and shouted a battle cry. The Elenil and Scim met like competing waves, with Jason and Dee between them.

✚

"These plates fly," Madeline said, placing her feet on the floating panels that had taken her to the top of the tower the last time she had been here.

"You dare to bring a Scim here? On this, of all days?" It was Rondelo, dressed in beautifully brocaded white clothing from head to toe. Evernu, the stag, stood beside him.

"She's ill," Madeline said.

Gilenyia peeled off from the crowd of elaborately costumed Elenil. "This is a funeral," she said firmly. "A rare occurrence for us Elenil. A certain solemnity is encouraged. Not only that, but it is the funeral for Vivi, the father of Hanali. You, of all humans, should respect his loss. I will attend to the Scim girl, if only to keep you from interrupting." Despite Madeline's protests, she tried to take Yenil from Shula's back. Shula stepped away from her, refusing to let her touch Yenil. Gilenyia studied the girl more closely, tracing the lines of the tattoos. Her eyes widened, and her face snapped back toward Madeline. "What is this? How did you come to find this girl?"

"How did the Elenil come to find her?" Madeline said fiercely.

Shula spoke in a quiet, calm voice. "Go back to your funeral and leave us be. We don't want to harm you."

Gilenyia looked at them more carefully. "Why, Madeline. You're dressed like an Elenil. Shula appears to be—ah, but what's that? The Mask of Passing?" It hung from Shula's hand. "What mischief are you two up to?"

Madeline's jaw clenched. She slung the package on her shoulder to the front and unwrapped it. Rondelo and Gilenyia watched in curious silence. When the cloth fell away, Rondelo gasped. Madeline took the rusted, nicked, dull blade and slid it into the scabbard. When she pulled it out again, the blade vibrated like a tuning fork. Bright, polished, and sharp, the Sword of Years sang for the blood of those who had benefited from the death of Scim people.

Rondelo's sword flashed, and the point fell toward Shula. "Madeline, do not try anything. That blade—"

Gilenyia had backed away from Yenil. "This is a magic blade, Rondelo. It is called Thirsty, among other names. If there is a healing spell to counteract that blade, I do not know it. Even at the height of my powers, if Madeline were to cut an Elenil with this blade, I would not have the powers to reverse it."

The sword hummed in Madeline's hand, the edge of the blade pulling her toward the Elenil. She felt its rage, felt its desire to drain them, to drain all of them. "Stand on the plates," she said to Shula. Shula edged away from Rondelo and toward the hover plates.

"You will have to take the stairs," Gilenyia said. "Archon Thenody is no fool. He'll not speed your way to assassinate him."

Assassination was not the plan, but Madeline felt the sword hum with glee at the thought. Still, it made sense that the archon's magic would not help them to the top.

"Let me help you," Gilenyia whispered. "There are those of us who would see the current archon replaced with someone . . . younger."

Shula stepped behind Madeline. "Perhaps as a hostage," she said quietly.

"Good idea," Madeline said. "Rondelo, give Shula your sword or I'll run Gilenyia through. That's right. Good. Now—Gilenyia. Up the stairs."

Gilenyia tipped her head slightly. "A pleasure."

The Sword of Years pulled in Madeline's hand. She hoped she had the strength to keep it from striking.

✠

Delightful Glitter Lady frolicked among the warring Scim and Elenil with joyous abandon, and Jason shouted and tried not to fall off. The Elenil fought with the terrifying certainty that no wound given them was permanent, and the Scim with a desperate anger. Baileya struck among them like lightning, wounding Elenil and Scim alike if they came too close to Jason.

The Elenil were confused about whose side Jason and Baileya were on. A Scim came up behind her as she nocked her bow, and Jason brained him with the hilt of his sword. The Scim went down hard, and Baileya gave Jason such a warm smile he almost lost his grip and fell from the rhinoceros.

Just as they fought their way through the tower entrance, a wind kicked in. It howled through the palace compound, blasting them with sand. Jason covered his face. If they had broken into the tower a moment later, he might well have been blinded by the sand, but as it was, the walls of the tower had protected them. "Sandstorm?" Jason called. "Baileya, what is going on?"

Everyone stopped fighting.

Floating like monstrous columns through the melee were fifteen-foot-tall creatures covered in wings. They did not turn, and they each had four faces, each one directly facing one of the cardinal directions on a compass. To the east, a face like a lion. To the west, an ox, and to the north, an eagle. The southern face was that of a human being. The wings sparkled. Or, on closer examination, they didn't sparkle—they blinked. The wings were covered in jeweled eyes, and as they blinked, the patterns on the wings moved like a school of fish.

"Kharobem," Baileya said, wonder in her voice. "They come to watch some story that is about to unfold. The last time they came in such numbers . . . it was the fall of Ezerbin."

Jason let out a war whoop. "That must mean we're about to win!"

"The people of Ezerbin did not win," Baileya said. "Even now their city is a haunt for jackals."

"Oh," Jason said. "Good point."

A barefoot girl in clothing that was little more than a sack limped into the center of the battle.

The Kharobem did not move or speak or make a sound, but Jason knew with a deep certainty that the Kharobem knew the girl. That they were, in fact, here because of the girl.

She stood at Dee's feet and looked up at Jason. "There was a cactus," she said, "born in a city. It lived in a pot upon a counter. It did not grow large. It did not flower. Until it returned to the desert. There it lived a long and happy life, and the desert and the cactus and the sun and the moon and the water and the sand lived happily together for many a year."

Jason shrugged. "Okay, thanks, I guess. And now we fight some more?"

There was silence from the assembled warriors. Jason slid off Dee's back and stood in front of the limping girl.

Break Bones stalked among the warriors, moving toward the tower entrance.

Baileya stepped toward him, her double-bladed spear at the ready.

"Wait," Jason said. "I have a better idea." He snatched the pebble out of his pocket and threw it into the tower doorway. He grabbed the embiggenator and turned Dee all the way to kitten sized. She let out a plaintive squeak as the tiny pebble became a door-blocking boulder.

Baileya squeezed his arm, just below the gold armband she had given him. "I would rather a clever warrior than a strong one," she said.

Jason blushed. In the middle of a battle. How embarrassing. He leaned toward her.

"They are working to move the stone already," she said.

She was right. The stone shuddered, and he could hear the shouting of the Scim outside, Break Bones's voice piercing through.

"Let's get up those stairs," he said, running ahead of Baileya.

She called his name, and he stopped to find her pointing at the ground. Delightful Glitter Lady struggled to get over the first stair, her tiny war cry lost in the cavernous room. But she squeaked again, scrambling for the next stair.

"Aw," Jason said. "So cute! C'mere, Dee." He scooped her up and settled her into his pocket. The sword and the bag of weapons Baileya had thrown to him were all discarded on the ground now. He sorted through it, searching for a lighter sword. He found one and tried to lift it over his head with one hand. He almost fell, and the sword went clattering to the ground. He dug through again until he found—well, he wasn't sure if it was a small sword or a long knife. He lifted it above his head and shouted, "TO WAR!"

Baileya followed him up the stairs. The strange limping girl followed too, silent and watchful.

✦

The Heart of the Scim.

They stood in the glass room at the top of the tower. The stone was on its pedestal. It was the true stone, not the ship-sized stone that hung outside.

Their journey had been easy—suspiciously easy. The Elenil had fallen out of Madeline's way when they saw the Sword of Years in her hand. Gilenyia had helped, shouting that there would be no healing for any who opposed the sword. No doubt it also helped having an Elenil funeral taking place at the base of the tower. Near immortals being reminded of their mortality turned out to be cowards in battle.

Madeline put her hands on the stone and lifted, but it wouldn't move. "Why can't I pick it up?"

"Only certain of the Elenil can remove it," Gilenyia said.

"You're one of them," Shula said. It wasn't a question.

"It would be an act of treason for me to put the Crescent Stone in your hand," Gilenyia said.

The black and purple energy moved inside the stone, almost like water trapped in crystal. Madeline strengthened her grip on the Sword of Ten Thousand Sorrows. She lifted the blade. "I don't need to hold it," she said.

"You don't understand," Gilenyia said, falling in front of Madeline, blocking the stone. "Killing the archon, that makes sense. Let someone else take his place. Perhaps someone more . . . understanding of the Scim. Perhaps that would be wise. But Madeline, if you destroy that stone, you destroy the Elenil. If you destroy the Elenil, my dear—believe me, this is true—you will destroy the Scim, the Aluvoreans, the Pastisians, the Maegrom, and all the people of the Sunlit Lands. I do not claim the Elenil to be without fault, but you must understand we are the foundation of this society. All else is built on top of our work, our city, our magic." Madeline's tattoo was pulsing now, linked to Yenil in a way she hadn't felt before. She could feel the magic guzzling, pulling at Yenil, siphoning her breath away and into Madeline. The Scim girl slid from Shula's back and stared at the source of all their trouble, her hair disheveled and half covering her face.

From where they stood, in the glass room at the apex of the tower, Madeline could see the chaos at the base. Fire had broken out somehow, and the strange creatures Gilenyia called the Kharobem hovered unmoving all around the tower floor, some of them on the stairs, a few floating in the center of the tower. She could see Jason and Baileya running up the stairs, Scim close behind them. They were almost to the top.

She hesitated, and lowered the sword.

A Scim came slowly across the glass bridge toward Madeline. It was one of the servants of the archon. She remembered meeting him but not his name. He was dressed like an Elenil. Madeline understood now that he was wearing his war skin, but it had been modified to make him look powerless, like less of a threat. He could have merely taken on his other form, like Yenil's. Instead they had kept him in his fierce battle skin and humiliated him. They had cut off his tusks. Even in war he would be unimpressive now. She did not remember his name because he was not someone to be remembered or to be seen. He was a decoration in the living quarters of the archon.

"Miss," he said, and his voice was raw. "My lady Gilenyia says all will be lost, but they have taken everything from us. What more is there to lose? They have even taken our language."

"Taken your language? What do you mean?"

"Does it not seem strange that we diverse people speak the same tongue? We are all speaking the Elenil language, through means of their magic. When you break that stone, those who have known their mother tongues will speak them again. But my children and grandchildren will know only Elenil. I speak it only through magic. We will not be able to speak to one another. You are not speaking your native tongue, either. Nor are your friends. When magic ceases, our language will be all but dead, with only the elders knowing it well."

Madeline, wide eyed, turned to Shula. "You're not speaking English?"

"I don't know English," she said. "Only Arabic and French."

Madeline turned back to the Scim. "Are you saying to destroy it or not?"

The Scim bowed his head. "Perhaps once all has burned, my grandchildren will rise from the ashes."

Madeline lifted the sword over her head. "Yenil?"

The girl nodded, a fierce look on her face.

"You don't understand," Gilenyia shouted again. "The magic of that sword cannot be sated. It will destroy the Heart of the Scim completely. Madeline, please, listen to reason!" Shula grabbed Gilenyia and pulled her from in front of the stone.

The sword came whistling down, and a fierce joy radiated from it. It smashed into the stone. The Heart of the Scim shattered into a hundred thousand shards, which flew like shrapnel through the glass room.

Nothing happened.

Nothing changed.

Madeline took a deep breath. Yenil struggled for oxygen.

"It was a fake," Shula said. Above them, the giant facsimile of the Crescent Stone still hung over the tower, crackling with power.

Madeline gripped the sword tighter. She knew, somehow, where the true stone must be. The archon. He would be carrying it on his person. She had a sudden memory of the first time she had seen him without his sheet. She remembered the choker he'd worn, with what she had thought to be a miniature facsimile of the Crescent Stone. Of course he would keep it on him. Now that she knew, it seemed so obvious. She spoke to the old Scim servant on the bridge. "Take me to him."

The Scim bowed his head and shuffled across the bridge into the quarters of the archon.

✛

Being shot with an arrow hurt. Not in a stubbing-a-toe sort of way, but in a screaming, burning, let-me-faint-now sort of way. The arrow came in through Jason's shoulder, from behind, at a high angle so it only caught flesh and muscle. One moment he was running up the stairs, the next an arrowhead appeared, sticking out of his shoulder. It was the worst pain he had felt in his life: a throbbing, burning, pulsing nightmare of excruciation.

"A lucky wound," Baileya said.

"Lucky?"

"Clean through, the arrowhead on the other side, no bones damaged, no major bleeding." She glanced back down the stairs. Some Elenil guards had engaged with the ascending Scim, giving them a moment.

Baileya steadied him and, without warning, broke the head of the arrow off, then yanked the shaft out. Jason's vision swam, and he put his hand against the wall. Baileya pulled out a handful of leaves, chewed them, then pasted them over the hole in his shoulder. "Bloodsop," she said. "To stop the bleeding."

It had a strong, almost minty smell. "You should probably carry more of that if we're going to be hanging out."

Baileya grinned. "Wait here," she said.

"Where are you going?"

"To throw any archers I can find off the stairs."

She slipped down into the battle.

Jason set Dee down, and she explored a few different stairs. Jason sat, putting pressure on the wound. It had been several minutes, he thought, but the blood had already stopped, and the chewed-up leaves had hardened. There must have been some sort of painkiller in the leaves too, because although his shoulder felt hot, the pain had lessened considerably. The limping girl stood below him, watching, but she did not speak or intervene in any way.

Across the tower, Jason noticed a single Scim sneaking up the opposite stairway. "Dee," he said. "Come here." The little rhino trotted to him, and he slipped her into his pocket. Jason had seen the Elenil swinging across the center of the tower to reach the opposite side. He found a rope tied alongside the edge of the stairs. He tucked his tiny sword into his belt.

"Okay, shoulder," he said, "don't kill us."

He swung. Shooting pain fired through his whole body, and he screamed as the rope spun him onto the stairs on the other side, landing a full flight up from the Scim. It was, of course, Break Bones.

Break Bones curled his lip in disgust, shifting his grip on the massive stone ax in his hand. "Thou hast no weapon, Wu Song."

"Break Bones. Hey. How's it going?" Jason pulled his tiny sword out. He regretted its size now. He wasn't sure it could even get through Break Bones's thick skin. Dee climbed out of his pocket and scampered off to the side, and Jason lost sight of her.

"Thou art in my way, human child."

Jason shrugged. The sudden pain in his shoulder made him regret it. "I get that a lot. Here's the thing, though. I feel like if I let you pass, you're going to murder my friend."

"The Heart of the Scim is ours. She must not be allowed to destroy it."

"Why do you want it so bad?"

Break Bones spit on the floor. "Fool! They have enslaved us with it for centuries. The balance is shifting. I would take it back so that we can enslave them. Without the Heart of the Scim we cannot use the Heart of the Elenil. We will reverse the flow of the magic. A few hundred years of justice should make things even. We shall live in towers of glass, they in mud hovels. Our children and grandchildren will rule over them. Your friend Madeline would break our chains and deny us our crown."

"Just to be clear," Jason said. "You're planning to kill her. Instead of talking things out?"

"The Scim have talked to the Elenil for decades, and what has changed?"

"Obviously I can't stop you," Jason said. "I only have this tiny little sword." As if on cue, Delightful Glitter Lady leapt down the stairs toward Break Bones, letting loose a full-throated kitten-unicorn war cry. She crashed into Break Bones's foot. "And a tiny unicorn."

Break Bones chuckled, ignoring Dee completely. "Then stand aside. Run if you can. When I have finished your friend, I will come back for you. Let no one say Break Bones breaks oaths."

"But first," Jason said, "Delightful Glitter Lady: ATTACK!" Dee trumpeted and hit Break Bones's foot, smashing into it over and over again.

Break Bones caught her easily and lifted her to his face. "Wu Song," he said. "Your perseverance is to be commended. But this little beast is no threat to me."

Jason pulled out the embiggenator. "Heh. That's what you think." He turned the knob all the way to the right, and Delightful Glitter Lady went from kitten size to the size of a Labrador, to the size of a rhinoceros, to the size of a juvenile Tyrannosaurus rex. Break Bones fell backward, pinned beneath her.

Delightful Glitter Lady scurried to her feet and trumpeted so loud Jason could feel the stones vibrating through the soles of his shoes.

Break Bones stumbled away, rushing down the stairs.

"Dee," Jason said. The rhino's enormous head swiveled toward him. "Fetch!"

Dee bellowed her delight and charged down the stairs after the retreating Scim warrior.

Jason raced up the stairs, laughing, his wound momentarily forgotten.

✛

They found the archon, at last, sitting in a three-acre garden built, somehow, on a balcony of the tower. He was sitting at a small metal table, sipping tea with Hanali. Both of them were dressed in the extravagant head-to-toe white mourning clothes of the Elenil. The archon raised his eyebrows when he saw Madeline and Shula, Yenil and Gilenyia, and the old servant. Madeline looked up. The crescent-shaped crystal at the top of the tower could be seen from here, glinting in the bright sunlight, still emanating the power of the Crescent Stone.

"So," Thenody said. "You are the ones causing the ruckus below and interrupting poor Vivi's funeral. Now you interrupt me while I have tea with his grieving son. What have you to say for yourselves?"

Madeline still held the sword. It shook in her hands, eager to decapitate the archon of the Elenil. She could feel its attraction, could see the generations of bloodshed and murder and pain that had given him so much power, so much wealth. Her breathing quickened, and as it did, Yenil swayed, her breath rattling in her lungs. "You would kill this little girl so I can breathe," Madeline said.

The archon rubbed his earlobe. The network of golden tattoos that covered his visible skin shimmered. The choker with the small crescent crystal crackled with power around his neck. "I believe your friend Hanali made that particular deal. I was not aware of it until this moment, though I cannot say I am surprised, nor that I disagree with his choice. How do you find these dirty little things, Hanali? Do you scout the Wasted Lands yourself?"

"Many of them come to me, my lord," Hanali said. "Indeed, this young girl's family needed food and offered her service for . . . well, for whatever we had need."

"How clever of you," the archon said. "Did they understand the terms?"

Hanali held Madeline's eyes for a moment, then looked back to Thenody. "The Scim did. Their child did. The human girl did not."

"She's dying," Madeline said.

The archon stood and walked lazily to them, apparently unconcerned about the magical sword in her hands. He looked carefully at the Scim girl. "Not for several weeks at least," he said. "Would you agree, Hanali?"

Hanali didn't move from his seat. He sipped at his tea. "Two weeks at least, sir. Beyond that it is hard to say."

An owl the size of a hang glider flew to the edge of the garden, and a Black Skull dropped to the ground. He carried a sword, and his white robes were covered in blood. "Stay back," Madeline said. Darius hesitated, then stopped.

"I see," the archon said, looking at Darius with interest. "You're going to save the world, is that it?" He tugged on the fingers of his left glove, letting it fall to the grass at his feet. "The Scim obey your orders now? Hmm. Curious." The network of golden tattoos on his hand glowed with a bright, almost blinding intensity.

Jason came running into the garden, a large knife in his hand. He stopped when he saw Thenody. A young girl dressed in rags limped in behind him. "Oh," Jason said. "You again."

The archon's lips turned up in amusement, but his eyes were hard and cold. "Indeed." He turned to Hanali. "Who are we waiting for? The Scim rabble-rouser, yes? What was his name? Break Stones?"

"Break Bones?" Jason asked.

"Ah yes. Charming. Break Bones. We can wait for him, I think."

Shula balled up her fists. "Why are we all standing around like we're at a tea party? Let's get him." She ran at the archon, letting loose a savage war cry.

The archon gestured toward her, palm up, and she fell to the ground, frozen in midstep. She skidded across the ground and came to a halt near his feet. "But you *are* at a tea party, my dear. Children like yourself should sit quietly."

Baileya slipped in beside Jason, breathing heavily. She had her double-bladed staff in hand. Then Break Bones came loping across the garden, a sinister look in his eye.

"Hey, where's Dee?" Jason asked.

Break Bones sneered. "She could not fit through the doorway. She is not pleased I escaped."

"Oh dear," the archon said. "It has become much too crowded. The garden looks positively cluttered." He spoke to Break Bones. "I have soldiers in your village. I have but to touch a certain mark on my left wrist and they will receive the orders to kill. So be silent. Or at least polite."

Break Bones did not speak in response to this but tightened his grip on his ax. Madeline could see Shula breathing, so she knew she was okay. Yenil leaned against Madeline, breathing hard. Still . . . they had Baileya and Darius. She thought Hanali would help them. Break Bones would at least work to get the stone, even if he wanted to do something different with it. She thought that, even with his magic, together they might be able to take Thenody down.

Hanali said, "I would advise all of you to remain still. The archon is powerful, and if he sees you coming, he will easily stop you with his magic."

"True," the archon said. He seemed unconcerned that Hanali was warning them to bide their time. "The question you are all asking yourselves, however, is whether I have the Heart of the Scim. Of course, I do." He put his hand to the choker at his neck. He unfastened it and held up a small stone . . . shining black, oblong, with a great chip in one side. "It is not so dramatic as my decoy. Amazing, is it not, that all our magic flows through such a little thing? The great crystal above the palace, your bracelets, all of Elenil magic—powered by this bit of stone. But that is the way of magic, I suppose."

Hanali looked down at his feet. "Forgive me, Archon Thenody, but I have always understood none but the Elenil should know they have seen the true Heart of the Scim."

Gilenyia said, "Why have a decoy at all if you are going to tell such a large assembly the truth?"

Thenody laughed. "Not one of them will leave this balcony alive, so what does it matter?" He turned the little stone in his fingers, holding it up to the light. He glanced at Hanali. "I see the hunger in your eyes, Hanali."

Hanali said nothing, but for a brief second his eyes flickered toward Gilenyia.

"Yes, I know about her, too," the archon said. "Though I am surprised she allied with you given her understandable hatred of the Scim." He must have noticed the surprise on Madeline's face, because he laughed and said, "Do you mean to say you have not told your human pets? How wonderful. You brought them to this place with no knowledge. I underestimated you, I think, Hanali, son of no one."

"Son of Vivi," Hanali said.

"Yes, but Vivi died when you and the Maegrom let the Scim into the city, didn't he? It is quite a price to pay."

"Whoa, hey what?" Jason said. "When Hanali did what now?" Birds had begun to settle in all the trees and bushes around them. Large and small, brightly colored and drab. All silently perching. A few flew overhead, watching.

Thenody inclined his head toward the birds, as if greeting more guests. "I have invited the messenger birds to come see what will happen next. I would like everyone in the Sunlit Lands to see and hear what happens in this little garden."

"I don't understand," Madeline said quietly.

"It is simple enough, my dear. Hanali has always been . . . unorthodox. It has been ascribed to his youth. His recruiting of humans has become more and more . . . eccentric. A violent girl from Syria I can understand. Those two boys Jason fought alongside, perhaps. But then he chose you. A rich girl with power and privilege who would require a great deal of unjust magic simply to walk among us. A girl who would be horrified to know the price she paid, if she could be made to see it. The kind of girl who would be used to power and privilege enough to believe that she could change things. Who would have hope and confidence, not shrink away and accept her lot in life. Someone who would speak up."

Jason nodded. "It all makes sense. Then Hanali needed someone who really loved pudding. Someone who wasn't afraid to eat it every day. For breakfast most days, but maybe he would be willing to eat it for lunch sometimes. Or even for dinner, even though that would mean saving it all day and that the next meal would also be pudding."

Hanali smiled, his eyes never moving from the stone in Thenody's hand. "I needed Madeline," he said, in an almost dreamlike voice, as if he was remembering something. "An activist." His eyes moved to Jason. "I did not think I needed you at first. I do not know who put you in my path. I realize now I needed a truth teller. A prophet. To help her see, and to stand beside her."

"It is not the first time you have tried," the archon said.

"Some have shied away from the truth. Others have despaired rather than taking action," Hanali said. "This time . . . some unseen hand aided me in my choice of champions."

"All this so you could be archon in my place."

"Perhaps," Hanali said. "Though only to undo our centuries of injustice. I did give the Scim entry the night of the Turning. They were meant to take the tower, not raze the city. And not to kidnap Madeline or try to take the Scim artifacts, which I would have returned to them when I took power."

The archon laughed at that. "Oh, you are young, Hanali. How delightful. I suppose they were not meant to murder your father, either."

Break Bones lunged for the archon. Thenody gestured, a look of disgust on his face, and Break Bones crumpled to the ground, groaning in agony. The archon twisted curled fingers toward him, and Break Bones tried to stand but couldn't. Thenody released him, and Break Bones got to his knees, panting, but could rise no farther.

"Do not approach me without permission," Thenody said, his face returning to the placid calm of a moment before. "Is that the Sword of Years you carry, Madeline? Yes? How lovely."

"It is magic," Madeline said, tears burning her eyes. This wasn't how it was supposed to go. She couldn't get near him, couldn't strike at the stone or Thenody.

"Indeed. I know it well. It could shatter the Heart of the Scim, destroying the Elenil connection to those filthy creatures. It would undo centuries of progress and beauty. You know this, of course. Your world is no different. I am no scholar, but I understand your own injustices have brought progress."

"I don't know what you're talking about."

Jason cleared his throat. "He's saying that the White House was built using slave labor. Or that computers and cars and planes and . . . and rockets were made better, made possible because of World War II. That if it weren't for the Holocaust, we would never have made it to the moon. That America would never have had a black president unless we had slavery first."

Thenody sipped his tea with his left hand, the right still holding the Heart of the Scim on display, mocking them. "The gears of an empire grind without respect for individuals. One does not throw away progress because a few people die along the way."

Madeline struggled to get her words out. "But . . . but that's such a narrow, strange way to say it. It's not worth killing Jewish people so we could get, I don't know, so we could get iPhones. Some people got rich off of slavery, but that's not an argument for it, that's a sign of the sickness."

"Nonsense," the archon said. "This city—this beautiful city—would be impossible without sacrifice. The Scim entered into our agreements willingly. Who are you to say you know better? Who are you to end an agreement made by our two sovereign nations?"

"I am Madeline Oliver," she said. "I hold the Sword of Years, a magical weapon created by the Scim people. It has fallen to me to choose how to use it, and I will do the right thing. The prophecy said I would bring justice to the Scim, and that is what I am going to do."

"Who am I to stand in the way of prophecy?" Thenody said, turning to smile at the messenger birds. "Step forward then, girl, and I will give you a choice."

Madeline stepped toward him warily.

"Look back at the tower," he said.

Madeline did. It rose above them, shining in the sun. Despite everything, that white tower framed against the cloudless blue sky, the giant crystal crescent glowing with power, was strikingly beautiful.

"My archers are in the tower. I do not need them, of course, but they have trained their weapons upon your heart and the hearts of each person on this balcony."

"Including you?" Jason asked.

Thenody ignored him. "Hanali has wagered everything on you humans. He thinks you will make a decision to upend our entire society, to create chaos, to bring suffering to all the people of the Sunlit Lands, all for your simplistic notions of justice."

"And what do you say?" Madeline asked.

"Not that we care," Jason said.

"I say that you are selfish little things and that you will leave it all in place." He set his tea on the table. "I will let you choose. You may have three options. One, you may raise your sword and kill me, allowing Hanali to take my place."

"Tempting," Jason said.

"Two, you may destroy the Heart of the Scim, eradicating all Elenil magic. The Scim will be released of their bargains, as will you and the other humans." Thenody smiled. "I believe your own self-interest will prevent this choice."

"I do like pudding," Jason said, and Madeline saw that he had been edging closer to the archon.

"Or three, I will allow all of you to leave. Alive."

"We could kill you *and* leave alive," Jason pointed out.

"Ah yes," the archon said. "I should have explained that more clearly. If you choose to kill me or destroy the stone, my archers have been instructed to kill all of you save Hanali and Gilenyia, as I do no harm to the Elenil people."

"How many archers?" Madeline asked her friends.

"I count twenty," Shula said.

"Five more in the garden itself," Baileya said. "Twenty-five."

Thenody wasn't bluffing, then. At least, she didn't think so.

She examined her three options. Kill the archon and let Hanali be in charge . . . although Madeline was unclear if it were even certain that he would be the next archon. Or destroy the stone and free them all from the Elenil magic. She looked to Darius, trying to read what was in his eyes, but he only gave her a firm, supportive nod.

Break Bones said, "Kill him."

"No," Madeline said. She was not going to kill anyone. She had decided that, at least.

"To destroy the stone will kill thousands," Break Bones said. "It will be a catastrophic failure of magical systems across the Sunlit Lands. And it will deny us the power we deserve! It will destroy injustice but deny us justice!"

"It's the right thing to do," Madeline said.

"It is the right thing to do," Hanali said. "You are correct. But is it for you to do? Or should the Elenil and the Scim figure it out together? Is it your place to choose for us?"

She looked to Jason, but he only said, "I'll back your play, Mads."

"Me, too," Darius said.

She raised the sword. She could almost feel the archers taking aim, preparing to loose their arrows when she made her choice.

She couldn't kill the archon. She knew that for certain. Night's Breath was dead because of her. She had failed to save Inrif and Fera. That was already three deaths too many on her conscience. She couldn't add the archon's. Not even if it was just. What had the Peasant King told her? Stopping injustice with violence was like throwing gasoline on a fire.

So it had to be destroying the stone. It seemed right and good to destroy it, but at what cost? Would it really mean the death of thousands to so suddenly alter the magical landscape? Could she live with that, even though she wasn't the one who had built the unjust system? And was that any different, really, than killing Night's Breath?

Yenil was gasping for breath. She sank to her knees.

Madeline couldn't accept that. Maybe she couldn't destroy the whole system, but she couldn't participate in it anymore. She wouldn't. She wouldn't let Yenil pay the price, not if she could help it. The Garden Lady's advice rose in her mind. *To change the world, change first a heart.*

She was about to force the Elenil to change their system, but would it matter if they hadn't changed their hearts? Wouldn't they just find a way to rebuild it, to replace it? Was it possible to change both? She knew this much: she was still benefiting from this unjust system. She was forcing everyone else to change when she hadn't changed herself. It was *her* heart that needed to change, her heart that could change the world.

She dropped to her knees and put her left arm on the ground.

"What are you doing?" Thenody said.

She raised the sword high.

"That was not one of the choices," he said, reaching toward her.

"There are more choices than those," Madeline said.

She brought the blade down with all her strength, smashing it into the center of her bracelet. An intense flash of light burst from her arm, and her tattoo burned so brightly she could see it even with her eyes closed. Crippling pain shot through her body. She fell backward into the grass, her arm smoking. She felt the magic draining from her tattoos like molten lava coursing through causeways in her body.

She couldn't breathe. Her back arched, and she inhaled with all her might and only got a half a breath, a quarter of a breath. Darius was by her side, his arms beneath her, trying to cradle her, to comfort her.

The archon was laughing. "Hanali, how delightful! She surprised me after all. What strange and creative creatures they are. It won't change much in the scheme—"

Yenil leapt to her feet with a feral scream. Madeline turned to look at her, wanting to tell her it was going to be okay now, that she would be able to breathe and live a normal life, but she couldn't say a word, could only gasp for air and watch in horror as Yenil snatched up the Sword of Sorrows.

Jason lunged for her and missed. Baileya shouted but was too far away. Gilenyia did not move, and a smile twitched to life on Break Bones's face.

The archon turned from Hanali, startled to find the Scim girl directly before him, already swinging the Sword of Sorrows. The blade met flesh, and the archon's left forearm flew from his body, bright golden light seeping from it and from the stump of his arm.

He fell beside Madeline, his face white with shock.

Gilenyia stooped over the archon, shouting instructions to people Madeline couldn't see. The garden they were in wilted immediately, turning brown. Trees cracked and fell. Flowers dropped to the ground, dead. The garden must have been powered by the archon's magic. The balcony began to crumble. A screeching noise came from the tower, and the massive Crescent Stone above listed to one side, then shattered, great chunks of it smashing into the garden and taking pieces of the tower with them as they careened to the square below. There were screams and shouts.

Madeline felt Darius lift her in his arms, heard him whisper, "To the ends of the earth." A hummingbird zipped through the garden, its high-pitched chirp standing out, somehow, from all the panicked sounds around her.

Then it all went still.

It was dark. Black and silent as night. She could no longer see the garden, the people running, the tower. She lay on her back, staring up into darkness.

The Garden Lady stood over her, a gentle smile on her face. "Hello, dear. What a day. What a day."

"Can't . . . breathe . . ." Madeline said.

"No, child, I expect you can't. Do you want me to change that? Your friend Jason, he might pay the price if you asked. He's loyal, that one. And brave."

"No," Madeline said firmly.

"You have two more favors to ask," the old woman said.

Madeline thought of her parents. She was so tired. She didn't want to die here, in the Sunlit Lands. She wanted to go home, and she couldn't do anything else here, could she? She couldn't even breathe. She knew she wouldn't be well again. She was past hope. She had come to acceptance. She needed only courage. "Take me home," she said. "Please."

"That I can do. And one thing more. For a few minutes. Just a few. I will let you speak to your friends before you go. And I'll give you the breath for it."

She was standing in front of Darius. He wasn't in his Black Skull outfit, just his regular clothes. "I'm going home," she said.

He wrapped her in his arms. "I'll come with you," he said.

She leaned her head against his shoulder. "Darius. When Lily said, in the books, there must be something better, she knew it in her heart, do you remember?"

"Of course."

"You're different here, in the Sunlit Lands. Back home you always pretended everything was okay, but here . . . you're changing things. You're trying to make that better place." It was true. The passion with which he protected the Scim, the way he helped her understand what had happened . . . he had opened her eyes. Without him she wouldn't have figured it all out, would have just lived out her year serving the Elenil, completely unaware of the injustice she was participating in. She would have had her breath, but Yenil would be dead. "You have to stay and help them."

"I won't leave you, Mads. I can't."

She took a deep breath. "Darius, when I broke up with you, it was because . . . How do I say this?" She tried to think of another way to say it, to make him understand, but she couldn't. How could she tell him how hard this all was for her? How could she make him understand that her heart was breaking to leave him, but not just him . . . everyone and everything she loved in the whole world? "Having you by my side every day, it's making it harder for me to leave. Harder to say good-bye."

"I would follow you to the ends of the earth," Darius said, his voice catching. He grabbed both of her hands in his.

Her lips quivered, and tears welled up in her eyes. "I'm going past the ends of the earth," she said. "You can't walk this path with me. It's impossible."

He leaned his forehead against hers. "The only impossible thing is that I would leave you," Darius said, quoting the book again.

She almost smiled. *Impossible* had never been a word that held much meaning for him. "When you're with me . . . it's making it harder, Darius. Harder to walk these last few steps."

She could see that he understood now. The most loving thing he could do was to say good-bye, to let her go. Darius said, "These last months without you, Mads . . . I've been so lonely."

Tears fell down her cheeks. "Darius, even when we're apart, we're together, because you're in my heart. And if we're together . . . if we're together I won't be afraid." She was quoting from *The Gryphon under the Stairs*, so she knew what he would say next.

He took both of her hands in his own. "Then let's see what beautiful things await." His face hardened, and he wiped the tears from her cheeks. "I'm going to fix things, Mads. I'm going to save the Scim, fix the broken system here."

Darius was starting to disappear. She could see through his hands. She didn't want him to go, didn't want this to be the end. "If I go—if you come home, and I'm gone—know that I have always loved you."

"I love you," he said. "How can I go on without you?"

He faded away before she could answer.

Break Bones stood before her. "What trickery is this?" He grunted. "The old woman in the garden. Is this her doing?"

Madeline wiped the tears from her eyes. "She said I could say good-bye to my friends. I'm not sure why you're here."

He frowned, his wide face contorted in displeasure. "I made a vow to my people that whoever returned the Sword of Years to the Scim, I would be in their life debt. You gave the sword to the girl, Yenil. I am at your service."

Madeline grinned in spite of her sadness. "What does that mean?"

"I am at your service," he repeated through gritted teeth.

"Take care of Wu Song," she said. "Help him. Don't kill him. Be a friend to him." And the Scim faded away.

Jason appeared. "The Garden Lady said you're going home. Shula and Yenil, they're going with you."

"They are?" She was shocked but pleased. It was right for Yenil to come. She didn't have any parents now, and that was because of Madeline. She could have a home and a family. It should be Madeline's. And it was good for Shula to come too. Yenil would need another familiar face if—when—Madeline wasn't around anymore.

"I'm, uh . . ." Jason blushed. "I'm engaged. To Baileya. By accident."

Madeline laughed and hugged him. "That's amazing. She's wonderful."

"She's . . . she's terrifying, mostly." He gripped her forearms. "Madeline, I made a promise to stick with you. To protect you. It's because . . . well, it's a long story. I lost my sister, and I don't want to lose you. But I've come to realize that I can't protect you. I can't save you. That's not in my power."

She squeezed his arms. "That's true."

He looked down. "I need to let what happened to my sister go. It wasn't my fault."

She didn't know what had happened, not exactly, although there had been rumors around the school. "That's true." She put her hand on his cheek. "You need to let me go too. There are things for you to do here, in the Sunlit Lands. Right?"

He nodded. "Something keeps pulling at me. The stories here. I'm not done. I think . . . I think you did the right thing, not destroying the stone. It was too violent. It would *force* people to do the right thing. We need to teach them to *want* the right thing. I see this story, or a thread of a story. I think if I pull on it, see where it goes . . . I think I might be able to find the right words. Do you understand what I mean?"

She did, somehow. She saw a flash, a vision, of Jason standing in the middle of a city, weather beaten and worn. He was telling a story, and people were weeping all around him. "The Peasant King," she said. "Is it his story?"

He looked at her, startled. "Yes. I keep seeing it in Night's Breath's memories. I need to find the rest of the story, and . . . and I need to go and see his family. I need to tell them what happened."

She held him for a long time. "Wu Song," she said. "If I die before you come home—"

"I'll see you before you die," he said, with a strange firmness in his voice. "You know I never tell a lie."

Tears crowded into her eyes. She wanted to believe him, wanted to think they would see each other again. He looked so certain, so sure. And it was true, she had never known him to tell a lie. "I know you don't," she said, smiling as the tears rolled down both of their faces.

Then Wu Song was gone, and she struggled for another breath, and she felt the branches of the hedge slapping against her face, and Shula's strong arm holding her up, and Yenil on her other side, and they appeared in her backyard. It was nighttime. She couldn't breathe. She fell to the grass, sobbing. A light came on, and Sofía came running across the grass. Shouts came from the house.

She was home.

36
A NEW JOURNEY

After the rain, the desert blooms.

A KAKRI PROVERB

✢

ven from outside the city, Jason could see the corrupted palace and the way it listed to one side, its holes black against the white stone. In the chaos of the collapsing tower, they had managed to make it out with almost no fighting. The shattering of the tower's stone and the subsequent departure of the Kharobem had distracted most of the people in the city. Many of the citizens, upon hearing that another Scim attack was happening, had barred themselves into their homes. The Knight of the Mirror had ridden out with Jason and Baileya through the southern gate, following Hanali's orders. "It will take some time to put it all back together," the knight said. "The archon's magic is struggling."

"Where were you, anyway?" Jason asked. "During the big fight?" He was riding the giant bird, the brucok, his arms around Baileya's waist. It might have made him blush on another day, but honestly, too much energy was going into making sure he didn't fall off. Delightful Glitter Lady let loose a high-pitched squeak, her tiny head peeking from his pocket. He scratched behind her ears.

The knight didn't answer. He had met them halfway down the tower, as if summoned, and escorted them quickly through the ranks of Elenil. The messenger birds had begun to spread throughout the city by then, passing along the story of the girl who had destroyed the magic that kept her alive. A debate had ignited, the Elenil arguing over whether such a thing was noble or foolish.

It wasn't safe in the city for Jason, though, that much was clear. Passions ran too high. Some Scim kids had thrown stones at him for not destroying the Heart of the Scim. An Elenil woman had given him a bouquet for the same reason.

Break Bones had met them outside the city. Baileya had advanced on him with her weapon, but he had thrown his own down and explained that he owed a life debt to Jason now. Wanting to make sure he wasn't lying, Jason had commanded him to dance and sing a silly song. When Break Bones assured him he didn't know such a song, Jason had taught him "I'm a Little Teapot," complete with actions, and Break Bones had performed it admirably, despite his scowl.

Darius had flown ahead to tell the Scim elders that Jason and Baileya were coming. Break Bones had given Darius the Sword of Years and told him to return it to the elders. Jason didn't know what sort of welcome would be waiting in the Wasted Lands, but he knew it should be the first step. Of course Baileya's family was still trying to kill him, and he hadn't told her yet that their engagement was accidental. He wasn't sure he wanted to. He wasn't sure he wanted out of it, either.

Hanali had disappeared after the events in the garden, but before he went, he had assured Jason he would be fine. He felt certain Thenody wouldn't make a public move against him. "The politics of the Elenil are subtler than that," he had said. Gilenyia had stayed at the archon's side, working her magic, bringing him back to health as best she could. The wound from the Sword of Years, she said, would not heal easily or well. Jason couldn't help but think that reattaching the archon's severed arm would mean some Scim somewhere without a hand. He didn't understand why she would try to heal Thenody when she had been part of the plot to overthrow him. He had asked Hanali before he left. "We are a loyal people," the Elenil said. "Thenody is still the archon and thus should be cared for and obeyed." Jason didn't get it, but whatever.

"When you return," the knight said, "enter through the eastern gate. Undetected if you can. You will be safe in Westwind. Send a bird ahead so I can warn you if it is unsafe." He paused and looked toward the west. A messenger bird was flying toward them. The knight held his arm up, and it landed on his wrist.

"What word bring you?" the knight asked.

"Word from the realm of the Zhanin," the bird said. "From a young man named Kekoa and a girl called Ruth."

Jason almost fell off the brucok. "What? What did they say?"

The bird turned its green head to see Jason more clearly. "They are in danger," the bird said. "They request your help. They warn that the Zhanin mean to kill the one called Jason and the woman Madeline." Jason groaned. Of course there were more people wanting to kill him. He hoped David had made it safely to Aluvorea.

"Why? We don't even know them."

"They assassinate those who threaten the balance of magic in the world," the knight said. "They must see your recent actions as a threat."

Baileya looked west. "We will be careful. To see more Zhanin in this part of the world would be strange indeed."

Jason slapped his forehead. "Is there anyone *not* trying to kill me?"

"Not I," Baileya said, and she gave Jason a look so loaded with affection that he felt a flush that ran from his face all the way to his toes.

"Nor I," said the knight.

Break Bones didn't say anything, but he was cranky like that. Delightful Glitter Lady honked her approval.

"Four," Jason said. "Well, that's a start."

They turned the brucok southward, and the knight wished them safe journey.

When both Break Bones and the knight were out of earshot, Baileya patted Jason's hand gently where it encircled her waist. "Your sister would be proud," she said to him. "You are a man who shares his stories generously. You are honest and kind. Such men are always threatened with death."

"You honestly scare me so much," Jason said.

Baileya turned so her silver eyes were all he could see. "She would be proud," she repeated. She turned away again and kicked the bird. As it began to run, she said, "As I am proud."

Jason held her tighter and let the wind push the water from his eyes. He promised himself that he would be worthy of Baileya's pride, no matter the cost. He did not speak until night fell.

EPILOGUE

To see another is the birth of Compassion.

FROM "RENALDO THE WISE," A SCIM LEGEND

✦

At night, Yenil liked to play in the garden.

Tonight there was a full moon, and the blue light washed over the flowers. It reminded Madeline of the Wasted Lands. Not what it was, but what it could be. She sat wrapped in a blanket, in a wheelchair on the crushed-seashell path. She held the book Darius had given her, the first edition of *The Gryphon under the Stairs*, in her lap. She didn't like to be apart from it—it reminded her of him.

Shula sat beside her. Without the magic of the Sunlit Lands, they spoke to one another in French or, increasingly often, in Shula's hesitant English. It had been two months. Yenil's English came quickly, and Shula was not far behind her.

Madeline's parents had been astonished, grateful, and disbelieving when they saw her that first night. She had been gone ten months, they said, and they had begun to believe the worst. They had taken Shula and Yenil in with surprising good grace, though Madeline could see the strain on them. She wasn't able to answer their questions in a way they could grasp. She couldn't explain her absence, or her sudden reappearance, or her silver scars, the ones that precisely matched the ones on the little girl who showed up with her.

Yenil—unless someone looked very closely—appeared human when not in her war skin. Honestly, Shula—a Middle Eastern girl who didn't speak English—had been a harder sell than Yenil for her parents. "Does she have a green card?" her mother kept asking in a hushed whisper. When Madeline explained about the Sunlit Lands, a confused look would cross her parents' faces, and they would stop pushing. She heard them whispering sometimes, sharing their strange theories of where she had been. But eventually the gravity of "putting on their happy faces" took over. Her mom went back to managing appearances, and her dad went back to work, and things were, more or less, normal again. Soon they stopped asking questions, whether because they didn't want to or couldn't understand the answers, Madeline didn't know.

Yenil was amazed by the house. She kept saying she lived in an Elenil mansion now. Madeline had tried to correct her at first but had given up. She wasn't wrong, Madeline had realized.

She couldn't breathe freely anymore. But she saw now that her family, her upbringing . . . She was more like the Elenil than the Scim. Which wasn't bad. It wasn't wrong. But she was looking at her life now, her privileges and power and wealth, in a new way. She was looking for those places where she could breathe only because others were holding their breath. And she planned to take a sword to each and every place she discovered.

Yenil bounded up through the moonlight, delighted at some treasure she had found. She placed it in Madeline's hand. "What is it called?"

"A bottle cap," Madeline said.

"Bottle cap," Yenil repeated and giggled. "Bottle cap!" she shouted. "Bottle cap, bottle cap!"

She danced into the garden, laughing and shouting. "Chase, Shula, chase!"

Shula jumped up, running after her into the garden. "Here I come!"

Madeline loved to see Yenil playing. Some nights Yenil woke from nightmares. Some nights she couldn't sleep for weeping. Shula slept with her and sang to her. Madeline's own mother went in to comfort Yenil some nights, a strange motherly action Madeline couldn't remember her mom ever doing for her.

"She's a dear girl and knows the value of a good bottle cap." The Garden Lady stood beside Madeline, her broom-like hair bursting out from her floral fringed hat.

Madeline smiled and moved her fingers in a tiny wave. She didn't use the energy to speak. She heard Shula and Yenil on the other side of the flowers, singing a Scim lullaby, which Yenil often hummed to herself. She had taught it to Madeline and Shula. *Do not cry in the darkness, but follow the small bright star.*

The old woman grunted and rearranged her hat. "I owe you a favor yet, dear. I'm not the kind who leaves a favor unfulfilled. What would you like? Silver and gold? Your breath back again? Anything in my power, child. Ask and I'll give it."

Madeline shook her head. She knew the cost now. She couldn't ask for magic that came at another's expense. "Sit . . . beside me," Madeline said. "Tell me . . . about . . . the Sunlit Lands. Tell me . . . about my . . . friends. Tell me . . . a story . . . about them."

"That I can do, my dear, that I can do."

The Garden Lady tucked Madeline's blanket in around her shoulders and sat in Shula's chair. She sat there long into the night, while Yenil played in the garden, and told her everything her friends had been doing in the Sunlit Lands.

And Madeline closed her eyes and was happy.

THE END

APPENDIX

*Stories, Songs, Proverbs, and
Poems of the Sunlit Lands*

THE THREE GIFTS OF THE PEASANT KING

A Scim Legend

A great while ago, when the world was full of wonders, there lived a wealthy king. He ate from golden plates upon a golden table. The floor of his throne room was polished silver, and his throne was studded with rare jewels. He often threw lavish banquets for his friends. Entire feasts' worth of food would go to the dogs, for the guests could not eat it all. He was called King Franklin, and he was deeply unhappy, for although he was rich, his subjects looked on him with disdain.

It came to pass that King Franklin began to hear tales of a strange king in a far country, a man beloved by all his subjects. This Peasant King, as he was called, had neither gold nor crown. But King Franklin decided he must see this strange man who was praised by so many tongues. So Franklin disguised himself as a servant and traveled through the deep forest, over the snowy mountains, and across the wide sea. And he brought with him three gifts for the Peasant King: a fine silk cape, a diamond the size of a man's fist, and a great disk of gold to fashion a royal table.

When at last King Franklin found the Peasant King, he was surprised to find him in a humble barn, where he sat upon a throne made of hay. Upon his brow he wore a circlet of holly, and his scepter was a piece of polished oak.

Franklin, in his disguise as a royal servant, presented the gifts he had brought to the Peasant King, explaining they were from his master, good King Franklin. Then he said, "I have traveled far to ask the secret of your great glory. But I stand before you now and see that a farmer in my master's land is wealthier than you."

The Peasant King stroked his beard and thought for some time. At last he said, "Tell me, O servant, did you see many of my subjects in your travels? Did they seem more fortunate than those in your own land?"

King Franklin replied, "No more fortunate than those of other lands, though happier in their misfortune. I saw a woman who sang as she slopped the pigs, though she had no apron to cover her dress. A scribe laughed to see his papers blown by the wind. A man whistled a tune when he saw his wagon wheel had broken."

The Peasant King laughed to hear this fine report and called for the woman, the scribe, and the wagoner. When they arrived, he greeted them each with a kiss upon the cheek. To the woman he said, "Good King Franklin has sent you this apron from across the wide sea," and he gave her the fine silk cape. Then he gave the scribe the diamond the size of a man's fist and said, "Good King Franklin has sent you this paperweight from over the snowy mountains." Lastly he rolled the golden tabletop to the wagoner and said, "Through the deep forest, good King Franklin has sent you this sturdy wagon wheel."

All three went away glad, thanking the Peasant King and praising the kindness and foresight of good King Franklin.

The Peasant King said, "The glory of a king comes from neither wealth nor finery but from the well-being of his people. Now I shall send you away with three gifts: a flask of local wine, a loaf of thick brown bread, and a letter for King Franklin which holds the secret to the great glory of the Peasant King."

Then the Peasant King sent King Franklin on his way. So King Franklin traveled across the wide sea, over the snowy mountains, and through the deep forest. When he had bathed and dressed again in his royal robes and returned to his grand throne room, King Franklin set out the wine and bread and opened the letter from the Peasant King. It contained only these words: "A true king must not pretend to be a servant, but rather become one."

So, too, this story bears three gifts: one for the storyteller, one for the hearer, and one for the heart which understands.

THE ORDERING OF THE WORLD

An Elenil Story

When the world was young and foolish, the people burned the cities. The oceans, enraged with violence, flooded villages and carried away children. The ground shook, and the sky wept blood. The people cried out day and night for help. And so it came to pass that a magician—the most powerful of his age or any other—set out to repair the world. He had many names, but the Elenil call him the Majestic One.

The Majestic One spoke, and his word was law.

"Order!" he called, and all the world stopped to listen. "Stop this foolish violence. Cease this chaos and come to me, for I shall remake the world."

But of all the people, only two came to him. The rest fought and tore at one another and screamed their defiance. The names of the two who came to him were Ele and Nala. He blessed them and said, in the ancient speech of wizards and knights:

> *I declare ye, Ele and Nala, lords of light*
> *and guardians of the wide world.*
> *All shall be under your dominion: water and wood,*
> *stone and fire, desert and ocean, light and darkness.*
> *And your descendants shall be called the Elenil.*

And he placed a tower in the center of the Sunlit Lands and called it Far Seeing.

Together with Ele and Nala and their children, the Elenil, the Majestic One tamed the peoples who warred with one another. The conflict turned bitter more than once, but none could stand for long against the might of the Majestic One or his servants, the Elenil.

When the war was ended and all had pledged fealty to the Majestic One, he gathered the people, and divided them into seven groups to receive their rewards and punishments and to give each people their own lands and homes so there would be no more war forever. When he spoke, each person heard his voice in their own mind, as if he spoke to them and them alone. First he spoke to the raiders who had harassed and harried the Elenil camps:

Kakri, desert dweller, eyes touched by the moon!
Thou shalt be silenced by sand in thy throat.
Thou shalt flee to the east, and walk dunes alone
     in sunshine and shadow, eater of carrion.
Thy sister shall be the crow, thy brother the hyena.

And so the Majestic One sent away the Kakri, and they live in the desert to the east, beyond the Tolmin Pass. They build no houses and plant no crops.

To the children of Grom, the Majestic One said:

How often hast thou dug beneath the walls of my fortress?
Short of stature, surly and clever, O child of Grom.
Thy home shall be beneath the ground.
Thou shalt hoard silver and gold, jewels and precious metals.
None shall be as skilled with hammer and tong,
     and none more obstinate than the Maegrom.

So the children of Grom went away to the world beneath the world, and there they remain until this very day. The Majestic One watched them leave, and when they had gone, he turned to those who had fought him in the great southern forests, who had attacked from the trees as archers and bandits. To them he said:

In Aluvorea grow the mighty trees
  so tall they touch the sun!
In their shadow thou shalt dwell
  and breathe the breath of leaves.
Be thou quiet and harmless.

Thus the Aluvoreans left in peace to populate the woods of the world. They are a gentle race, though some say they have come to love their trees more than people, a great misfortune.

To those who had been pirates upon the sea, the Majestic One declared:

Live, thou Zhanin, among waves and currents,
  wind and weather and the deep!
Forever a wanderer, without a home,
  thou shalt be melancholy,
Changeable, strange, and lonely as the sea.

So the Zhanin were swept away like driftwood. They cannot live long when separated from the water. It is a great marvel to see one at the market of Far Seeing. But occasionally such traders do appear, with strange stories and stranger wares.

Those who had used magic in their battle against the Majestic One he called human, to remind them they were neither gods nor beings of power but only mortals.

Humans! Ye shall live upon another earth,
  a people of science and dust.
Bereft of magic, short lived and passionate,
  there shall still be beauty and wonder among you.
In great need may ye return to the Sunlit Lands,
  for ye are our cousins and neighbors.

At last all who remained before the Majestic One were the Elenil, his servants of old, and the most rebellious of the people, who would come to be called the Scim. They were evil things, their hearts filled with wickedness and foul deeds. They trembled before the Majestic One, for his face shone like glowing metal. Indeed, his face shone with a righteous anger, and they feared he would destroy them completely.

Thou Scim I banish to outer darkness,
    a land as black as thy heart.
Thou shalt live by eating thy brethren's scraps.
Servant of darkness and night, in blackness
    shalt thou dwell, and in that eternal midnight
      may thine outer appearance match thy corrupted nature!

The Scim wailed and begged for mercy, but the Majestic One stood unmoved. He commanded his Elenil to remove the Scim from his presence, and they drove the creatures south and east to the Wasted Lands, where shadows cling and sunlight dares not go.

So it is that we say:

Zhanin on the western waters,
    Aluvoreans in forests dispersed.
To the east, the Kakri wanders,
    the Scim in deep darkness accursed.
Humans from magic are fleeing,
    Maegrom in dark earth beneath.
Elenil rule from Far Seeing,
    in lands by our master bequeathed.
The Majestic One keeps all in his sight,
    Elenil first in the warmth of his light.

RENALDO THE WISE

A Scim Legend

A great while ago, when the summers of this land could still be counted by those with long memories, a man named Renaldo walked the paths of the world. Hated and despised by all he met, Renaldo returned the hatred of his neighbors with vigor.

Now in those days, the Peasant King ruled. The Peasant King sent out a decree into all the land, telling his subjects that he wished to increase the happiness of all his people, and so he would give each subject a boon of their choosing. Magic or money, fortune or fame, long life or lilies, no request either small or large would be turned away, so long as it be not evil.

Renaldo thought for eight days and seven nights of what might bring him happiness, but the only boons he imagined would give him pleasure were misfortunes for his neighbors. He knew the Peasant King would not grant him his wish if he said, "Make old Mrs. Gaither's goats give sour milk" or "Tear the thatch off Mr. Havill's hut" or even "Take away the tongue of that calamitous child down the lane."

The day came for his audience with the Peasant King, and Renaldo dressed in his finest clothes and walked to the woods, where the king sat upon a stone, a sprig of holly wrapped about his forehead. He was playing a merry tune on a simple flute. "This," said the Peasant King, "is the Flute of Joy. Blow into it and such joy shall fill your heart that you will be at peace with all people and with the world. I have made it, dear Renaldo, for you. For often I have passed by your home and seen you scowling in your chair." The Peasant King held out the lovely gift, but Renaldo would have none of it.

"Such a gift is too fine for me," said Renaldo. "Now, Highness, you said you would grant any boon so long as it is not evil. Have I heard it right? For I would not speak and have you deny me."

"I will not curse a person or animal, nor take away their free will, to please you."

"Not even to make a goat's milk sour?" Renaldo asked hopefully, for the bleating and stench of Mrs. Gaither's goats truly vexed him.

The Peasant King laughed and said, "Truly not!" and played upon his Flute of Joy. The whole wood filled with dancing and laughter. The birds sang, the rabbits danced, the foxes stopped their hunting and smiled. Renaldo only frowned.

"My wish, then," said Renaldo, "is to see the coming death of every person in the land." For he thought to himself, *To know the death of a person is to have great power over them.* Besides, it might please him to see his neighbors and enemies and be able to say to himself, *But six months more and that one shall be gone. But a few years for that one. Ha! She shall be no bother after next Thursday.*

The Peasant King stopped his playing, and the whole wood fell silent. "It is not an evil gift," said the king, "though it is requested with evil intent."

"You have given your word," Renaldo reminded him.

"Indeed," said the Peasant King. "I shall grant your wish and something more: not only the time of death shall you see but also the cause."

Elated, Renaldo bowed low to the king and walked backward from his presence. The joyful playing did not start again until Renaldo set foot upon the road, which was a great relief. He hurried home to try his new skill.

He came first to Mrs. Gaither's thatched hut. The stench of her goats grew ever greater. Just last week he had convinced her to move her flock to the east side of her property, for on the west side their stench lived always in his nostrils. She complained that the east side was craggy and dangerous, but every day he wheedled and complained until she at last relented.

The old woman came out of her hut, and the moment he saw her, Renaldo knew her death. In two years' time she would take her goats out in the rain and slip upon the craggy rocks of her eastern property and break her hip. She would die within six weeks, weakened and alone.

"Serves her right," Renaldo said to himself, "for keeping such filthy animals."

He continued on to Mr. Havill's hut and knocked upon his door. For many years he and Mr. Havill had feuded about their property line. The great stones separating their property would move in the night, sometimes because Mr. Havill moved them and sometimes because Renaldo moved them. Neither could remember the true property lines any longer. Renaldo saw his end too: just one year hence he would catch a sickness during a storm. His poorly thatched roof (which Renaldo often called an eyesore) would not keep out the rain, and he would die feverish and alone.

"Serves him right," Renaldo said to himself, "for taking such poor care of his home."

He continued on to find the loudmouthed child who shouted and screamed day and night, sometimes in joy, sometimes in anger. The boy shouted whether happy or sad and could neither keep his opinions to himself nor his voice low.

Renaldo gasped.

The boy, a child of only seven summers, would die in one week's time.

And he would die trying to save Renaldo from drowning in the pond.

Renaldo liked to swim on crisp summer mornings, and next week he would sink from a leg cramp. The boy would charge into the water to save him and would succeed, but at the cost of his own life.

No more would Renaldo hear the boy's booming voice as he chased the geese. No more his disappointed cries when his mother called him to dinner. Never again the echoing crow of the boy emulating the morning rooster. All this because the boy would try to save his melancholy neighbor, the one who barely said hello and often complained that the boy was too loud.

Renaldo's heart broke as if struck by a great hammer.

Renaldo hurried to the pond and stared at the cool, placid water, and it was there that he saw his own death—sitting in a chair upon his porch many years hence, bitter, angry, and alone.

He hurried back to the Peasant King and begged for another audience.

He fell on his knees in the great king's presence and cried, "O Majesty, take away this curse! Give me instead a new boon!"

"What boon is that?" the king asked.

"Majesty, I ask only this: let the boy live a long and happy life. He does not deserve to end his life in such a way."

The king gave him a look of great pity and said, in the archaic way of knights and kings, "Stay thou out of the water, Renaldo."

Renaldo thanked the king and hurried home, determined not to swim in the pond that week. But was this enough to change the boy's future? He saw the boy and was relieved to see him living until the age of twenty-three, when he would die in battle. There was time to work on that, but for now he hurried to Mr. Havill's house and, in a flurry of activity and without a single complaint, rethatched his roof.

Then he was off to Mrs. Gaither's house, where he told her to live a long life and move her goats back between their houses, which she did.

That night he sat upon his porch, smoking his pipe, when the Peasant King came along, playing his flute softly in the moonlight. The Peasant King sat on the porch with crossed legs and did not use a chair, for the Peasant King would not sit on a chair fashioned by the hands of a living being.

"Has your boon brought you happiness?" the Peasant King asked.

Renaldo thought on this for a time, puffing upon his pipe. "We have more in common than we have differences," Renaldo said at last. "In the face of death these grievances with my neighbors seem petty."

"A wise observation," the Peasant King said. "You and your neighbors shall all be better for it. Now, I think, this flute is yours . . . for it requires a loving heart to play it."

Renaldo accepted it gladly, and in the years to come he became known as Renaldo the Wise, for he seemed to know the greatest needs of his neighbors, and all who knew him lived long and healthy lives. Many were the nights when Renaldo sat upon his porch and played his flute, and the people of the village shed their cares and kicked up their heels.

When he was very old, the whole village came to his bedside. His final words, we are told, were these: "To see another is the birth of Compassion.

Compassion is a seed of Love. Love comes hand in hand with Joy. So, little children, love one another, that your joy may be complete."

So, too, this story brings three boons: one for the storyteller, one for the hearer, and one for the heart which understands.

AN EXCERPT FROM
"THE GALLANT LIFE AND GLORIOUS DEATH
OF SIR SAMUEL GRYPHONHEART"

An Elenil Poem

O'er silent tower no banner flies,
Shouted laments from soldiers rise.
Upon the battlefield he lies—
Sir Samuel Gryphonheart!
The dragon slain, the battle won.
Alone he stood, the rest had run.
Strong armed he fought, the deed was done,
And now he must depart.

Behold! Now gentle hands take hold
The corpse of our defender bold.
To save our lives, his own he sold—
Sir Samuel Gryphonheart!
'Twas he who fought the minotaur,
'Twas he who slayed the Bolgomor,
'Twas he who saved Vald's sycamores.
Now dead upon yon cart!

His broken blade, his bloodied shirt,
Our lord is dead and we unhurt.
We cannot e'er proclaim his worth—
Sir Samuel Gryphonheart.

O minstrels, sing a glorious ode
To the chief knight who ever strode
This earth. He made the sun shine gold—
Sir Samuel Gryphonheart.

'Tis true he's left these shadowed lands,
All toil and trouble and demands.
Walks he now on gold-flecked sands,
To range sans map or chart.
And now upon that rival shore
All woes be gone, and sob no more.
No death, no tears, no pain, no war
For Samuel Gryphonheart!

Now draws near the Majestic One
To celebrate a life well done.
Homecoming his adopted son—
Sir Samuel Gryphonheart!
His bowl is spilt, his thread unspun.
His life is past and just begun.
He treads now in a clime of sun
In the land of the Majestic One.

Majestic One, all wounds he heals,
All righteous traits in hearts anneals.
Samuel's life like a bell it peals
To greet the Majestic One.
Watch them walking arm in arm
In golden fields beyond all harm.
Their laughter rings with friendship warm—
The joy of the Majestic One!

The knight at last his sword lays down,
His grimace gone, no more a frown,
His helm replaced with glorious crown,

A gift from the Majestic One!
The squire has let his horse run free.
The Sunlit Lands now mourn and weep.
Our friend is gone, no more we'll see
Till we see the Majestic One.

He stands before a riotous throng,
Those who've left all woe and wrong,
They greet him with a welcome song,
"You'll nevermore depart!"
With cries of joy they welcome him.
The night is past, the day begins.
He smiles, then laughs —they dance, they spin!
Deep joy has filled his heart.

Our greatest knight, our dearest friend,
Our defender bold has met his end.
With him our love and thanks we send,
Sir Samuel Gryphonheart!

A SAMPLING
OF KAKRI PROVERBS

IN THE DESERT, THERE ARE NO PATHS.
IN THE DESERT, THE WAY IS MADE BY WALKING.

✦

IT IS NO SHAME
TO TRAVEL WITH CROWS.

✦

WHAT IS STILL MAY NOT SLEEP.
WHAT SLEEPS MAY NOT LIE STILL.

✦

IF TRUTH IS NOT YOUR COMPANION,
DEATH WALKS BESIDE YOU.

✦

THE DATEEN TREE BEARS ONLY DATEEN
FRUIT AND THAT ONLY IN ITS SEASON.

AFTER THE RAIN, THE DESERT BLOOMS.

+

THREE THINGS WE CANNOT LIVE WITHOUT:
CLEAR WATER, DEEP STORIES,
A HEART THAT IS LOVED.

+

DURING THE STORM,
HOPE.
AFTER THE STORM,
PEACE.

THE DESERTED CITY

A Kakri Lament (to be sung to the tune of "The Water Bearer's Daughter," on the night of the third and fourth spheres' meeting, with a divided choir)

MOONSIDE CHOIR: Where is the fountain which brought joy to the city, clean and clear at its heart?

STARSIDE CHOIR: It has been carried away, the water spilled to the sand, the water given to the sun.

MOONSIDE CHOIR: Where is the young man who played his bitarr beneath the lady's window when the hot wind blew from the east?

STARSIDE CHOIR: His eyes are open, unseeing, his bitarr shattered in his hands, his lady . . . But we do not know where his lady has gone!

MOONSIDE CHOIR: Has she not gone to the west, to the city of the shortsighted?

STARSIDE CHOIR: She weeps into the fountain. She lingers at her window and sobs to hear the silent streets.

MOONSIDE CHOIR: Look at the walls, so bright and fair, each stone placed by a master builder.

STARSIDE CHOIR: They are drunken stones . . . They cannot stand, they cannot support one another.

MOONSIDE CHOIR: What has become of the wide avenues, the shaded alleys beneath the golden trees?

STARSIDE CHOIR: Weeds grow upon the streets, dead thorns and fruitless stunted trees line them.

MOONSIDE CHOIR: What of the birds? The wrens and sparrows? The magpies and swallows?

STARSIDE CHOIR: There are only empty nests. Even the birds, yes the birds, have fallen.

MOONSIDE CHOIR: We must rebuild these walls.

STARSIDE CHOIR: No, Sisters, set your face toward the wasteland.

MOONSIDE CHOIR: We must repair these towers.

STARSIDE CHOIR: No, Brothers, entrust yourself to the sands.

There is no one path through the desert,
the way is made by walking.
Let us turn our faces from this place,
let us seek solace in the desert.
The sheep pens are empty,
the gates broken, the king dead.
What use the sheep pen in the desert?
What need for gates in the waste?
He who sleeps upon the roof dies upon the roof,
she who sleeps in the house receives no burial.
The desert claims the land, and so we,
we must claim the desert.

MOONSIDE CHOIR: But one day the King of Stories will return—

TOGETHER:

> The Story King will tell a new tale,
>   the vineyards shall bear grapes.
> The orchards heavy with fruit,
>   the high plain will bear the mašgurum tree.
> Another turning shall come,
>   the city rebuilt, the gates rehung.
> The people will again be many.
>
> O Keeper of Stories!
> O your house!
> O your city!
> O your people!

A FRAGMENT OF
"THE TRIUMPH OF THE PEASANT KING"

A Scim Legend

. . . saw the Peasant King going against the tide of those who would evacuate the city. The Shadow had fallen, and destruction followed behind. The walls were breached, and the enemy swarmed down the tree-lined avenues.

One of the Peasant King's followers, a knight in his service, said to him, "My lord, where are you going?"

The Peasant King replied, "Why, to meet Death. Would you go with me, Sir Knight?" But the knight had promised to protect a caravan headed south, so he begged his leave. The king said, "Go in peace."

Another of his followers, a wealthy merchant, saw the Peasant King walking toward the city. Leaning down from his horse, he said, "Where are you going, my lord?"

The Peasant King replied, "Why, to meet Death. Would you go with me, sir?" But the merchant had a household to protect, and he begged his leave. The king said, "Go in peace."

Finally, in the rubble of the walls outside the city, the king's gardener saw him. She was an old woman, and her whole life she had been cared for by the Peasant King. The king's gardener spoke the secret language of all growing things. She knew the songs of the morning flowers and spoke the poems of the weeds. She spent long afternoons in conversation with the trees.

"Where are you going, my lord?" she asked.

"To meet Death," he replied, and she fell at his feet, weeping.

"Not so, my lord!" she cried. "But let me go in your place, for I am a simple gardener and you a majestic king. Let me go to my rest, and you go in peace."

The king raised her to her feet. "The knight offered me no sword, the merchant no steed. You have offered your life for mine." He kissed her upon both cheeks and again upon her forehead. He said, "Winter and summer, sunshine and darkness, planting and harvest. So long as these fill the Sunlit Lands, you will live. The story of what you have done will be told wherever my name is honored, and you shall ever walk among the people. To those who are pure of heart you may grant three boons with the magic I bestow you."

"But my lord, if you refuse the offer, 'tis but a small thing," she protested.

"It is the small things of the world which are most important," the Peasant King said. He continued on his way, but the gardener would not leave his side. She stayed with him through the Enemy's lines, past the looters, past the rioters, past the soldiers. They came at last to the great Enemy, who stood taller than a hill. He had no flesh but was only darkness in the shape of a giant. He wore a pale crown set with seven shining stars and carried an iron sword which wept blood. The Peasant King told the gardener she must now say farewell, for he must battle his foe.

"You have no sword," she said.

"Our great Enemy will give me a sword, and I shall give him my heart for a sheath."

"You have no steed," she said.

"I will ride Death's chariot ere morning," the king said.

"Your people have all deserted you," she said. "Throw down your holly crown. Toss away your oaken rod. If you are not king, you need not fight this evil."

The Peasant King laughed, and it was a clear bell in the clamor of war and darkness. "They have deserted me, but I have not deserted them."

She took his hands in hers and, weeping, bid him farewell. The Peasant King blessed her again and turned to face the great darkness. The sun shone upon his face as he stepped forward . . . [*Here the fragment ends.*]

THE PARTING

A Traditional Zhanin Song of Farewell for Honored Visitors

Your arrival—how like the sunrise!
When the cool eastern light shimmers
    upon the morning waves.

In the midday the birds sang,
    fish jumped, their scales aflame,
    water sparkled in our cupped hands!

We have paddled alongside you,
    but here our journeys part.
We are an island, you an ocean stream.

When the sun departs,
    she is most beautiful.
O western waters, shine!
Peace to you, come again,
    our blessed guest, beloved friend,
    charming one, farewell.

Until once more
    the cool eastern light shimmers
    upon the morning waves.

ACKNOWLEDGMENTS

Many thanks to the following people, all of whom helped make the Sunlit Lands a better place: Leilani Paiaina Andrus, Adam Lausche, Jermayne Chapman, Kat McAllister, Mark Charles, Sydney Wu, Leah Cypress, Mark Lane, Julie Chen, Gabrielle Chen, Koko Toyama, and Kiel Russell. Special thanks to my friends on the Codex writers' forum (quite possibly the kindest corner of the Internet).

Kristi Gravemann, thank you for your commitment to getting the word out about this book (and the books to come!). I am thankful for your creativity and hard work.

Wes Yoder, you are the source of magic in every project we pitch. Thank you for your unwavering belief in my books, for your advice, and for your friendship.

Thanks to Linda Howard, without whom this book could not exist. I asked, "What kind of book would you like?" and she said a book like this one. Here it is, Linda. Thank you!

Jesse Doogan lets me pitch thirty new projects a month and claims we will make them all. Jesse is a True Fan, and she can defeat all comers in Sunlit Lands–related trivia battles. Hufflechefs unite!

Matt Griffin (www.mattgriffin.online) provided the amazing art, and Dean Renninger turned it into the beautiful cover we all know and love. AND! Matt also drew the map, and Dean did the interior design. Thanks, Dean and Matt!

Sarah Rubio, you brought the music to the text, and asked the questions that deepened the relationships between the characters. Your influence is on every page, and I am grateful.

JR. Forasteros has been a source of encouragement, insight, and wisdom. Thank you (as always). And, of course, all of the StoryMen (Clay Morgan, Aaron Kretzmann, and Elliott Dodge), as well as Amanda and Jen!

Shasta Kramer, it's so strange not to hear your thoughts on this book. I'm thankful for all the times you checked in on me along the way while I was writing, and for celebrating with me when I finished. I look forward to talking about the book with you one day.

Thank you, Mom and Dad, for introducing me to Middle-earth and Narnia and for all your support and encouragement. And thank you, Janet and Terry, for being great in-laws!

To my dear wife, Krista, thank you for making room in our lives for me to go exploring fantasy worlds and for exploring fantastic places in the real world too.

Myca, you make me happy. I love reading with you and spending time with you.

Allie and Zoey, you were the first fans of the Sunlit Lands, and it was so fun sending you the chapters as they were written and talking through the story with you. I am thankful for your questions and your help in writing *The Crescent Stone*.

There are many more people at Tyndale House Publishers who have contributed to this book in big ways and small. I am thankful for your passion for this book and for the kindness you show to me in letting me be part of the Tyndale family.

Lastly, I am thankful for you, dear reader. Thank you for joining me, Jason, and Madeline on this adventure. I hope you'll join us for the next one.

ABOUT THE AUTHOR

MATT MIKALATOS entered Middle-earth in third grade and quickly went from there to Narnia, kindling a lifelong love of fantasy novels that are rich in adventure and explore deep questions about life and the world we live in. He believes in the hopeful vision of those two fantasy worlds in particular: the Stone Table will always be broken; the King will always return; love and friendship empower us and change the world.

For the last two decades Matt has worked in a nonprofit organization committed to creating a safer, more loving world by teaching people how to love one another, accept love themselves, and live good lives. He has lived in East Asia and served all over the world.

Matt's science fiction and fantasy short stories have been published in a variety of places, including *Nature Futures*, *Daily Science Fiction*, and the *Unidentified Funny Objects* anthologies. His nonfiction work has appeared on Time.com, on the *Today* show website, and in *Relevant* magazine, among others. He also cohosts the *StoryMen* podcast at Storymen.us.

Matt lives in the Portland, Oregon, area with his wife and three daughters. You can connect with him on Twitter (@MattMikalatos), Facebook (facebook.com/mikalatosbooks), or via his website (www.thesunlitlands.com).

THE ADVENTURE CONTINUES IN

THE
HEARTWOOD
CROWN

COMING SUMMER 2019

FOR MORE INFORMATION, CHECK OUT
WWW.THESUNLITLANDS.COM

**TURN THE PAGE
FOR A SNEAK PEAK AT
THE FIRST CHAPTER!**

1
HUNTERS

Where fear is planted, hate will grow.

AN ALUVOREAN SAYING

✦

J ason Wu had wedged himself into what he suspected might be a closet. It had never occurred to him that people who lived in a fantasy world would need a place to store their clothes, but of course they did. This particular closet was narrow and located in a dilapidated three-story house that had once been a mansion. There were holes in the roof, mold on the walls, missing stairs on the long winding stairways. He had managed to find this closet, though, with its door still intact, so he could slip inside and pull it quietly shut, certain his pursuers would not find him here, not given the size of this house.

Delightful Glitter Lady, Jason's kitten-sized rhinoceros, scrabbled impatiently on the floor beside him. Jason scooped her up and held her against his chest, trying to keep her quiet. He could hear the thundering footsteps of his pursuers outside. Dee let out a low whine, and the footsteps paused. "Dee," Jason whispered, doing his best to make it clear she needed to be silent.

"I heard him," a voice called. By now he recognized the distinctive sound of a Scim. He could tell by the guttural voice that the Scim had put on his war skin, a defensive magic all Scim had that allowed them to have thicker skin, heavier muscles, and a terrifying appearance.

Dee whined again. Jason pulled her tighter against him.

Outside the closet, all sound ceased.

Jason held his breath.

"In here?" another voice asked.

"I think so. I heard the unicorn." The people of the Sunlit Lands thought Dee was a unicorn. They were a little sketchy on zoological categories. Unfortunately for Jason, their tracking skills were fully developed.

A third voice asked, "Have you checked the closet?"

"Hold," said another voice, one Jason knew well. It was deeper, more resonant, than the others. Jason could practically feel it vibrating the house. It was the voice of Break Bones, the Scim warrior who had sworn to murder Jason more than once. "I must be allowed to kill him. But each of you may say first what you wish to do with him when the door is opened."

"I will stab him in the liver," said the first voice, and cackles of laughter came from the others.

"I will break his arms," said another.

Jason shivered.

"I will crush him with my hammer," said the third.

Jason pushed as far back against the wall as he could, feeling with one hand for a crack, a hole, a way out. But there was nothing. He was trapped.

The door flew open, and three Scim shoved and pushed, all of them trying to get in the door at once. Dee let out a delighted squeak and struggled to get out of Jason's arms.

The Scim piled on top of him, laughing and cheering as they pinned him to the floor and tickled him mercilessly. Jason begged for them to stop, and after thirty seconds or so, Break Bones called the Scim children off. They bounced out of the closet, Delightful Glitter Lady gamboling at their feet.

"Six minutes," Break Bones said. "It is the best you have done so far."

"Is Baileya back yet?" Jason asked. Baileya was a Kakri woman, a powerful warrior from a desert tribe to the north. She also happened to be Jason's fiancée, ever since he had accidentally proposed to her nearly six weeks before. The last several weeks, since they had made this broken-down mansion their base of operations, Baileya had taken to going on long patrols of the area.

Break Bones held out a wide hand and helped Jason to his feet. "She is safe, Wu Song. No one is trying to kill her."

"She'd be safe even if people *were* trying to kill her." You shouldn't mess with Baileya.

"Everyone's trying to kill *you*, Wu Song," one of the children said.

"Not you, I hope," Jason said, wrapping an arm around the nearest kid's neck and wrestling him to the ground. Soon all three kids were grappling with him. These little monsters had been his almost constant companions since he, Baileya, and Break Bones had moved in here. Nightfall was the oldest, maybe ten or so, and he was delighted by Jason's refusal to ever tell a lie. He liked to ask Jason's opinion on awkward subjects in front of the adult Scim. Then came Eclipse, an eight-year-old girl who most often won these games of Hunter and Prey. Shadow, the youngest, was a boy of around six, with a nasty habit of biting.

"Enough," Break Bones said. Jason and the kids stopped wrestling. "What did Wu Song do wrong?" Break Bones asked the Scim children.

"He got found!" Shadow shouted.

"He hid somewhere obvious," Eclipse said.

"He made every person in the Sunlit Lands want to murder him." Nightfall grinned.

"Hey!" Jason said, but it was true. The Elenil wanted to kill him for his role in crippling their leader, the archon (not to mention the extensive damage that Jason and his friends had caused to the archon's palace, the literal pinnacle of Elenil architecture). The Scim wanted to kill him because one of their nobles had died so he could live. The Kakri were trying to kill him as part of his engagement process to Baileya. It was a long story, but her whole family had a year to try to kill him before they got married. There was even some group of people he had never met, called the Zhanin, who were upset because Jason had supposedly messed up the balance of magic or something. Still, it's not like *everyone* was trying to kill him. Those necromancers in the north didn't even know who he was. And the creepy shape-shifters in the south had invited him to come to their land anytime. And the . . . well, he couldn't remember all the different people in the Sunlit Lands, but so far as he knew, only four groups were trying to kill him.

"Eclipse is correct," Break Bones said. "In a closet or under a bed—this is the first place most people will look. If you are being hunted, such places are to be shunned." He looked at Jason with pity. "For the Scim, at least. Humans are not known for their cunning in battle or survival."

"Hey!" Jason said again.

"Shadow," Break Bones said. "You are the prey now."

Shadow leapt to his feet and looked around shiftily.

"Run," Break Bones said, and the boy sped from the room. Break Bones gathered the two remaining Scim children and Jason in the center of the room. "This time you will hunt as individuals, not in a pack. Eclipse, you will take the ground floor. Nightfall, the second. Wu Song, the third floor and above."

"Why are we doing this again?" Jason asked.

"To help you survive," Break Bones said.

Oh. Fine. But it's not like Jason would be hunting anyone. If anything, he would be the one hiding, just like he was hiding now in this old house. It had belonged, once, to the family of Night's Breath, the Scim prince who had died so Jason could be healed of a mortal wound. Jason had come here hoping to make peace with that—and with Night's Breath's family. But as soon as he had arrived, Night's Breath's wife and children had left. The Scim prince's elderly mother still lived here, but she had made it clear she remained only to guard the house . . . from him. The children who remained were Night's Breath's nephews and niece. The kids had taken to Jason immediately, but the old woman showed no interest in him. Jason had to admit it hurt his feelings in a weird way. He was here, far from his own family, and when he tried to connect to this woman, she shut him out. She would turn her head away any time he entered a room. Not that it surprised him. He was terrible at family stuff. His own parents hated him and wanted nothing to do with him, so why should a family that wasn't even human be any different?

Meanwhile, Jason and Baileya had friends in danger, but Baileya wouldn't agree to travel to help them. Their friend Kekoa had sent multiple messenger birds asking for assistance, but Baileya said, "It is too dangerous at this time. One of my brothers is seeking our trail. Twice I have led him away. He is cunning and swift, and should he find us, I do not doubt he would succeed in killing you, Wu Song." His name was Bezaed, and Baileya spoke of him with reverence. He had killed one of their sister's suitors, and that was a Kakri man. He would make short work of Jason. At this point in the conversation, Jason had almost tried to explain to her about their accidental engagement. He had told her a personal story, not realizing that how the Kakri got engaged was by sharing a personal story one had never told anyone else. They were a month and a half into their yearlong engagement now, and Jason didn't want to break up with her. But he didn't want their engagement to be based on a misunderstanding, either. Plus, it was weird to be seventeen and engaged to be married to a terrifying warrior maiden from a fantasy world. She wasn't even human—at least her golden skin and shining silver eyes argued for something not quite human.

"Wu Song," Break Bones said.

"Hmm?"

"It is time to hunt," the Scim said to him, shaking his shoulder gently. "The other children have already begun."

Jason glared at him. "The *other* children?"

Break Bones grinned, his yellow, tusklike teeth protruding from his mouth. "Prove me wrong. Be the first to find Shadow."

"I will," Jason said forcefully. He strode out of the room and immediately had no idea what to do next. Finding a little half-pint Scim in a dilapidated mess like this place would be a challenge.

Delightful Glitter Lady romped down the hallway. Jason followed her into what must have once been a ballroom. Or maybe something else, because Jason thought a ballroom would be on the ground floor, but this room was large, and there were many gigantic pieces of furniture covered with moldering cloths.

Dee sniffed twice, then sneezed, almost knocking herself over. He had been keeping her at kitten size because he didn't trust the floors in this place. He worried she could fall through a rotten board if he let her be even a tiny bit larger.

"I know you're in here, Shadow," Jason said. He could hear the uncertainty in his own voice. He shivered. Anything could be under these sheets. He yanked one off, letting it fall to the ground. It revealed a sort of low sofa with no arms. He pulled another sheet to discover a pair of chairs. He would have to uncover them all, he knew, because Shadow was exactly the kind of kid to hide under a moldy sheet if he thought it would give him even a minute's advantage in a game like this. There were at least thirty sheets. Jason sighed and got to work.

About ten sheets in, Dee made a high-pitched whine. "What is it, girl?"

She snorted and shuffled toward the back of the room. Jason smiled. She smelled Shadow. He bent down low and whispered, "Where's Shadow, girl? Do you smell him?"

Dee made a quiet, distressed honking, looking at another large sheet-covered item near the wall.

"In there?" Jason walked to the sheet. It had to be a cabinet or something like that. It was taller than Jason by several feet and nearly square in shape. He yanked on the sheet, and a cloud of moldy dust rained onto him. He sneezed, grumbling to himself, and tried to shake it off. He studied the wardrobe that had been revealed. It was made of some dark wood and looked ancient. A star had been carved into the front of it and painted silver. A slight shuffle came from inside. Shadow was exactly the kind of kid who would hide in a closet immediately after being told not to hide in closets.

Dee turned in a tiny circle, whining.

"What's the problem, girl?" Jason put his hand on the door. The kids liked to say all the terrible things they would do when they found him, delighting in making it sound as terrifyingly gory as possible. Since Jason didn't tell lies, his threats sounded lame in comparison. "When I find Shadow, I am going to gloat about how I found him so fast and say that I'm better at Hunter and Prey!"

Jason flung the door open.

Shadow was inside.

A golden arm was thrown across the little Scim's neck. A young man with flashing silver eyes and loose, flowing clothes stood behind him. A knife point pressed against Shadow's cheek. Shadow struggled, and the man constricted his arms, pinning the Scim child.

"Be very quiet, Wu Song," the man said. "I have no desire to hurt this child. But if you call for help, I will." Jason opened his mouth, but the stranger's knife point pressed in, and a bead of blood appeared on Shadow's cheek. "I will take his eye if you scream."

"That is what a real threat should sound like, Wu Song," Shadow said. He had that defiant, almost nonchalant look he got in his eyes right before he would bite one of his siblings. Showing fear was not encouraged among the Scim.

"Well," Jason said, very quietly, "I did find you pretty fast. I am better at Hunter and Prey. Obviously."

The man's eyes flicked toward the room's entrance and then back to Jason. "There is room in here for one more," he said.

"Um," Jason said. "Maybe if we were closer friends."

The man pushed on the knife again, and Shadow's eyes widened. Jason's hands clenched. He wasn't a warrior. He was terrible at Hunter and Prey. He needed to be protected, and he was useless with any weapon. But he wasn't about to let someone threaten a child and get away with it. He opened the second door of the wardrobe and stepped into it.

"Close the doors," the man said.

When the doors were closed, the stranger's silver eyes shone out with a powerful light. When the man spoke, his voice came steady and low. "My name is Bezaed. My mother is called Willow, and my grandmother Abronia. I am here, brother, to kill you before you can marry my sister Baileya."